betrayal

WHISKEY PROMISES
BOOK TWO

A. R. THOMAS

Copyright © 2020 A. R. Thomas
All Rights Reserved.
No part of this book may be reproduced or transmitted in any form or by any means, electronic or mechanical, including photocopying, recording, or by any other information storage and retrieval system without written permission of the author, except in the case of brief quotations embodied in critical articles and reviews.
This novel is entirely a work of fiction, all names, characters, places, and events are the products of the author's imagination, or are used fictitiously. Any resemblance to actual persons, living or dead, events or locations is entirely coincidental.
All rights reserved. Except as permitted under the UK Copyright, Designs and Patents Act 1988.
A.R Thomas asserts the moral rights to be indentified as the author of this work.
A.R Thomas has no responsibility for the persistence or accuracy of URLs for external or third party Internet Websites referred to in this publication and does not guarantee that any content on such websites is, or will remain, accurate or appropriate.
Designations used by companies to distinguish their products are often claimed as trademarks. All brand names and product names used in this book and on its cover are trade names, services marks, trademarks and registered trademarks of their respective owners. The publishers and the book are not associated with any product or vendor mentioned in this book. None of the companies referenced within the book have endorsed the book.
First Edition.
Editing: Claire Allmendinger at BNW Editing
Cover Design: Abigail Davies at Pink Elephant Designs
Formatting: Abigail Davies at Pink Elephant Designs

Thank you to my Mother Bear for reminding me that dreams aren't only for when you're sleeping.

Chapter One

I'm not sure which is worse, my hangover, or the ache in my chest. I feel terrible about last night. I've had too many hours to play it all over, and now that my mind isn't as distorted by alcohol, I'm not sure I made the right decision. I know I didn't.

If there is one thing I have learned about myself in the past few weeks, it's that I react the second I feel emotionally threatened. A by-product of Adam's actions, no doubt, and Jace Bennett just so happens to make me feel like I'm on the cusp of the most thrilling and terrifying moment of my life.

Jace's behaviour was far from okay, but if that is his worst, I'm getting off scot-free compared to my last relationship. I've chalked it up as one of those make or break moments. It nearly broke us. I just hope we can fix us.

I knew deep down there was more to him, just like there is with me. I laugh out loud into the quiet room. Hell, name me a person that hasn't got a few issues. I cover my face with my hands and rub at my tired eyes—they're gritty and sore.

"You're a mess, Lil," I grumble and roll over, staring at the window. It's not yet light outside, and the faint blush of the moon is pressing its way into the edges of my blind, and I roll back and blink in a huff. I've barely slept because my head is too consumed by yesterday's events. Not to mention the crushing fact that Jace hasn't contacted me. His words come back to me: *One mistake, and we're done.* The second I felt overwhelmed, I did the one thing he asked me not to do. Run.

Always running. I'm cross at myself for hightailing it out of there and for leaving him feeling as dejected and bewildered as I am. I doubt he will be having anyone over for dinner now that his bedroom looks like the hulk took a swing at it. That's going to cost him a small fortune. Maybe I should contact him and offer to pay for it? Maybe I should get my head checked, and I most definitely need to stop drinking!

I groan once more, unsure how to move forward with this mess. I pick up my phone and consider calling Cass, but I know I need to deal with this alone. Besides, she will be mad at me and accuse me of overthinking, over-reacting.

Which I am now, analysing every word and second of yesterday until my brain is ready to evacuate and find a more suitable host. It's not yet five a.m., and my weak heart aches for Jace. I want him to cuddle me and tell me it is all going to be okay, but it's not. We're both on the edge of a cliff with a foot each in mid-air, free-falling into a relationship we have yet to understand because the stark truth is that we don't know each other. We've both been holding back, too consumed by lust. I open up his messages, tap the empty text box, and stop. I can no longer deny that with Jace, I feel like I'm on the periphery of something incredible.

Betrayal

What do I say? What if he doesn't want me back?

He probably thinks I'm an emotional loser.

I do too. I'm embarrassed at myself. I did a Cass: zero to psycho.

I try to tally the pros and cons of Jace Bennett. I'm not naïve enough to believe everything will be rose-tinted here on out, nor can I forgive his actions from last night, but I want to believe he is it for me. I've never, never in my life ever met a man like him, a man so all-encompassing, so consumed by another person that he is oblivious to the world and the silent riot he is causing around him—so consumed by me. He wants me, and not just with the partial indifference that I have witnessed in other relationships—he wants *me*.

Wants to know, learn, and love me.

How can anyone possibly say no to that?

One night is enough for me to know that I can't say no.

I won't. I refuse to let my fears crush what small amount of happiness I have felt in a long time.

―――

I begin typing: 'Hey', then delete it because it sounds lame. "Hey, sorry I turned into a crazy lady." I say out loud and then snort before I drop my head back—what a mess.

Maybe I could start with something more direct. I chew my lip 'I didn't deal well with last night. I'm sorry I didn't give us a chance to work it out.' I delete that too. Fuck!

Three dots appear. He's typing! I suck in a breath, and hot tears well up. Is he as cut up about this as I am?

Can't sleep? J x

This is it, my moment to bridge that gap. I know after one night of pain that I can't be without him. I miss The Hub. I miss hurtling. A vision of the splintered glass window shakes my resolve. It's his anger and his lack of control, not to mention his emotional abandonment in a moment that should have meant something—it's those things that have made me three-sixty into a massive ball of nerves.

I push my concern aside and mull over a response. I don't want to seem too keen because that would make me a pushover, and that's exactly what got me into a mess with Adam, but if I don't start fighting to gain control of my fears, I never will overcome them.

No. Too much going through my head. How's your hand . . . and the window? x

I chew my lip and sit up, rearranging my pillows while I wait for his reply. It takes him a little while, and when I do receive it, I smile sadly.

Hand is fine, heart, and lamp not doing too good. I miss you, beautiful x

I miss you too. I missed the man I knew, not so much, the one I met yesterday.

Last night is not something I want to go through again. I need to know why you did it? I'm sorry I left x

His reply is instant.

Betrayal

Lily, I can't stand myself for what happened. I hate what I have done. I don't want this to break us. Can I see you? We need to talk properly.
Forgive me x

Has it broken us? I don't think so. Truly, deep down, I believe that we both are at fault. Somewhere between morning and night, we both made more than one wrong move. He went one way, and I went another, and we missed being able to reconnect in the middle. I'm staring at my phone when another message comes through.

Forgive me and come to dinner later. I miss hurtling with you x

I don't want to be the old Lily, the one that ran. Not any more. I contemplate my answer once more. I know yesterday I set a precedent for the day. I reduced our relationship to nothing more than sex when it is so much more than that. I pushed him further when I refused to meet him in the middle, then I went out and wore something inappropriate to provoke him further. Am I surprised he felt loopy with anger? I shouldn't be. With a sigh, I pull my knees up and stare back at his last few messages, scrolling through with a sad smile. This is the Jace I know.

I've really tried to separate my feelings and figure out what it was about last night that hurt me so much.

In fact, drunk me is a pain in the arse.

I know it wasn't the sex. That was incredible.

It was his emotional withdrawal. He was confused and angry and possibly more hurt than I realised, and he held all that in until he could no longer voice it. Instead, he acted on it, and it hit something deep within me. I felt used, nothing more than an object. I suspect many a woman has been subjected to that side of Jace, and I refuse to be that woman.

However, I refuse to give up on us. We have a connection, and I want to keep it. I'm not finished with my whiskey-eyed man and his two a.m. lovemaking. I want to hurtle too.

Can I think about it? x

It's a pointless reply. I know I will go. I will do anything to mend this between us, but until it is fixed, I don't much fancy pretending everything is okay to his friends.

Sure, can I see you today? Maybe we can grab a coffee? x

Light is peaking through the clouds when I finally push free of my bed, taking my phone with me. I head to the kitchen gingerly, my hangover is out in full force, and I feel terrible. I put the kettle on—coffee sounds great, now and later. I smile as my thumb runs over the letters quickly.

I can meet at around 2? x

I'm smirking as I wait for his response. I want to tell him I can meet him every hour on the hour. I really do miss him that much. Last night feels like an age ago.

Our favourite time sounds perfect. J x

Meet at Bobo's? x

Betrayal

It's neutral ground. It's either that or the deli, and after the mix up with Travis, I think this is the more suitable option. Jace agrees immediately, and I'm grateful to have managed to make a few baby steps between us. Feeling a little better than I have all night, I begin to get ready for work and make it to the office just before it opens.

Harriet swans in a few minutes late, but with two steaming coffee cups at the ready.

"Sorry, the queue this morning was horrendous," she calls. I grab my head, wincing at her high tone, and she pulls back when she sees me. "Good night?" She smirks.

"Cass is the worst influence. Do you have any painkillers?"

Harriet dives into her bag and pulls out a pack of tablets.

"I'm going to go and grab you some breakfast."

"Oh, you don't need to." I smile delicately, conscious not to make any sudden movements, but both my head and my stomach disagree.

"It might help soak the alcohol up." She screws up her face.

"Oh god, do I smell?" I smell my clothes and look at her in horror.

"Just a little of booze." She laughs. I drop my head in my hands on a deep groan. "So, breakfast?" she reiterates.

"Yes, please," I grumble.

"Great! I won't be long." She places my coffee down and takes hers with her to pick our breakfast up. As she heads out, I move to the front desk, praying that no one comes in because I must look a state and smell bad for Harriet to point it out. God, how unprofessional—I'm acting like a teenager!

I jump when the phone blares, clutching my head as the shrill ring fractures my skull. I clear my throat before I answer, "The Loft, Lily speaking, how can I help?"

No one replies, but the line stays open. I frown and press my ear into the receiver, trying to hear for anything on the other end. It's definitely connected.

"Hello?" I say it a bit louder. A scuff and the obvious sound of someone breathing come down the line. "Hello, can I help?"

The repetitive hum is too deep to be female.

"Jace?" I say softly, wondering if he has called me by mistake. The line goes dead, and I sit back, looking at the phone in my hand, willing it to tell me who it was. I decide to call back, but the automated voice tells me the caller withheld their number. Well, fat lot of use that is to me!

I figure if it is important, they will call back, but soon forget when Harriet returns with two breakfast rolls. They smell amazing. We wrap up, sitting out in the courtyard with the door wide open to keep an ear out for the bell.

"You are a lifesaver," I state, taking a seat.

"I know." She laughs, biting heartily into her roll. "So, you and Cass have a good night then?"

I grin and roll my eyes before I ask her if she knows Nexo. The club we went to last night.

"I've never heard of it." She shakes her head, tucking a stray strand before it gets caught in her food. "Any good?"

"If you have heaps of cash, sure," I snort. For some

reason, I tell her about meeting Cass's friend and the free bottle we received.

"Ah, that's to blame for your hangover then?"

"Would seem so." I munch between answers and gulp the last bit of my coffee down. I already feel better, and with the painkillers working their way through my system, I'm ready to start my day. I stand and tell Hat I'm going to grab myself some water from the fridge, taking her rubbish with me.

"We're pretty quiet today. I need to do a post office run—we're running low on envelopes, and I forgot to order some," she tells me, taking a bottle I hand her. "Thanks," she adds.

"Can you grab me some highlighters?" I say as I remember I have that adapter I promised her. I hand it over, and she pops it into her own bag.

"Thanks."

"Okay, highlighters." She points at me, and she slips out, pulling her coat on as she goes. I watch her walk up the street briskly, a typical feminine grin on her face. Oh, she has got it bad for Simon!

My calls go from one to another, then another. Harriet returns while I'm still glued to the phone, chatting with the owner of Ebony Art.

"I will get it wrapped up and contact the courier this afternoon. If I schedule it for collection tomorrow, I can have it to you by Monday?" I suggest.

"Great, thanks, Lily."

"I'll email you the tracking number as soon as I've booked it in," I tell Stanley, checking the time. I'm ravenous.

"You're an angel!" he declares and briefly tells me about an exhibition he is having soon. Harriet walks in just as I'm putting the phone down, a pad and pen in her hand, a pen she is repetitively tapping against her notepad.

"The shadow piece is ready to be wrapped. Was he okay with the delivery times?" she asks, her methodical tapping never wavering. I don't believe she is aware she even does it.

"Fine." I shrug. "I don't think he was expecting us to move so quickly, so he's happy to have it as early as Monday," I confirm. I push my glasses up my nose and flit my eyes back to my screen to press send.

"Oh, good." She takes a seat opposite my desk. "I grabbed us some lunch, noticed you didn't have anything in the fridge."

"Harriet, I could cry. What the hell am I going to do without you next week?" I bury my head in my hands and moan softly, my hangover feeling more like a constant bruise.

She laughs and stands, and I lift my head and watch as she exits my office and returns with crusty baguettes and fruit pots.

"Make sure you give me your receipts," I tell her. I hold my hand out, and she drops a wrapped sandwich in my hand.

She sits with an amused look at the other side of my wide desk—a desk that not too long ago I was bent over, and my blush feels like a burn on my skin. I clear my throat to distract myself from my wandering thoughts.

"You're the best, Hat!" She really is.

Chapter Two

I arrive at Bobo's just before two o'clock. Jace isn't here yet, so I find a table near the back and pick up the menu. They have an array of drinks, each equally suitable to the décor in here. There are enough plants around to mistake this place as a registered forest. It smells like rain and foliage and gives the illusion of being outdoors. Each drink has some unusual organic ingredient that I haven't ever heard of, but luckily they sell coffee.

I sorely need coffee and lots of it, as my hangover is yet to leave me.

I'm rubbing at my temples when the chair opposite me gets dragged out softly. My eyes snap up, and there he is. His eyes are pinched tight, and his lips are pulled into a short smile. He looks to have run his fingers through his hair, leaving it in a ruffled mess on his gorgeous head. Even guilt-stricken and mussed, he is hot. Hot enough that his presence has caught a few women's eyes.

"Hey." He grips the chair but decides at the last minute to walk round to me.

"Hey," I whisper as he stops at my side. He cups my face, leans in, and places the most delicate of kisses on my cheek. Our eyes remain open, mine because I've missed this man, and I don't want to miss a second of his face. I just hope it's the same reason for him.

"You look nice." His voice is husky and accompanied by blazing eyes, and he holds my gaze as he walks back to take his seat.

"Thanks." I tuck my hair behind my ear and flick a look to the menu again.

"Harriet is leaving early, so I can't be too long," I say apologetically. He looks good, real good in his open-neck shirt and suit trousers. His sleeves are pushed back, and his face is coated with light stubble. He looks pretty damn fuckable. Damn this hot man and my weak flaming hormones. I force my gaze away and frown—why can't I be even marginally indifferent with him? I'm like a lovesick puppy. It's embarrassing.

"Okay, she's going away, isn't she?" His manner is relaxed, but I notice the set of his shoulders and the unease in his eyes.

"She leaves first thing. She's kept me fed all day. I drank too much last night and—" My eyes lift back to his. We stare at one another, and I let out a light sigh. I'm an emotional wreck. "I'm sorry I walked out," I confess quietly. I fight the compulsion to look around the room for people listening, but seeing the deep shine in his whiskey eyes keeps me rooted to his face.

"I'm sorry for what happened, Lily." His voice roughens. His face reddens. "It will never happen again. You have my word. I feel shit about last night."

"Me too." I chew my lip, and he reaches over and runs a thumb across my mouth.

He sighs roughly, and his hand clenches on the table

as his eyes cast away before they come back, looking full of guilt and hope.

"Yesterday, I wasn't myself. Neve wasn't in a good place. I was worried about her, and you seemed hell-bent on . . . " his voice trails off. "This isn't just sex for me, Lily. Trust me, if it were, it would feel like last night every time." He holds my eyes, conveying how sincere he is. "You're holding back, but I'm not going anywhere. I want to be with you."

"I'm sorry. I was difficult." I was. There's no way to deny it.

"I just wanted to come home to you after all this shit with Neve," he confesses quietly. He drops back into the chair and rubs at his forehead, "I was angry: at you, Travis, and myself, and I took it out on you. I'm sorry." Big, apologetic eyes burn across the table. "It will *never* happen again. You have my word," he breathes out, reaching for me and holding my hand tight in his. I nod. I believe him.

"Please come to dinner later, beautiful?" He lets his hand fall away when the waiter approaches.

"Hi, good afternoon. Are you both ready to order?" The waiter's smile is warm, his pen poised.

"Two coffees, please," Jace replies absently. His eyes are still focused on me. The waiter puts his pen down, having no need for it, and steps away.

"What about your window?" I ask and fiddle with the menu, bending the corner nervously. I realise what I'm doing and quickly smooth the paper back out.

"It's being fixed as we speak. I won't even know they were there by the time I get back." Of course he won't. I imagine before me, his life was as smooth and calm as his big, glass, house.

Our drinks arrive, and Jace finally seems to relax in his chair.

"Can we forget yesterday happened?" He frowns. "I'm not excusing my behaviour, or yours," he says lightly, "but that's not what we're about. I'm trying really hard, Lily. I'm not used to feeling like this, and it fucked with my head." His admission is one I had already figured out, but it's nice to hear all the same.

"I'd like that. I'm sorry too." I just want him back. "Need me to bring anything?" My lips tug when his eyes spark, and his big shoulders drop, revealing the level of tension he is carrying. When he runs a hand through his hair, I reach to take the other one, holding it tight. He grins at me.

"Just yourself. Minus the attitude." His eyes bang with fire, and my jaw drops. The cheeky sod!

"You can't help yourself, can you?" I laugh. He shakes his head, and I catch the table of women behind, snatching glances at him.

"Missed you, witch."

"Brute," I counter, sipping my coffee to hide my smirk. He lifts my hand and kisses my palm.

"Crazy about you." His whisper is low, sweet, and at complete odds with the man I was faced with yesterday. His earlier comment is still swirling around my head like toxic smoke.

"You said if it was just sex," – I rub at my throat, not liking the images his comment triggered, – "you said it would always be like that. You've really never been in a relationship, have you?"

Jace leans forward and takes my hand.

"No." He shrugs and looks about the café. "Never wanted one. Then you came along, and I have no idea how to be in one. I just know I want to be with you all the time," he confesses on a little wink.

"So, you've always been like that with other women?" I hate the question. I want to swallow it back up, pay someone to infiltrate my mind, stamp on it, and set it on fire. Jace's eyes sadden.

"Don't do this to yourself. I can't deny I've been with other women before you." Remorseful eyes plead with me to drop this.

I really don't want to get into any of this, so I hold my hand up, halting him from saying any more. "I know, I never thought . . . I don't really want details, Jace, but —" What do I want? I feel shocked by his statement. I feel sorry for those women, I do. "You were just so vacant—there, but not," I whisper.

"Lily, please, if I could re-do yesterday, I would in a heartbeat. Vacant Jace is who I was before you. My head was going crazy. I felt sick with jealousy, and it was easier to just shut everything off. Forgive me?"

Finally, some truth. I nod over at him, my hands still caught up in his.

"At least we know how not to be with each other," I say softly as my eyes flick up to his, and he gives me a slow and uneasy smile.

"No more yesterdays," he affirms, lifting my hand to kiss my wrist.

"Does that mean you won't go out searching for me on a night out?" I ask sceptically. Who goes searching for their partner? Surely he can see how messed up that is?

"We weren't on good terms, and it was driving me mad. I needed to find you and put it to rest," he confesses shakily. His eyes drop from mine to where my hand is held in his—his ambers are so sad. "The house was pretty lonely last night." He pouts, running his fingers in lazy circles over my hand.

"It won't be later. Carl will be strutting around, I'm sure." I laugh. I wonder if he has said anything to his PA?

"He's looking forward to seeing you," Jace replies. So Carl doesn't know. Good. I'd hate to think they'd all been talking about us.

"It will be nice," I say, checking my watch. "I need to leave in a minute. Can we ask for the bill?"

"Sure, I'll drop you back at The Loft."

Harriet leaves around four, a little earlier than I initially agreed, but I'm happy for the solitude. I whip home and sort an overnight bag, just in case. I stopped off at the shop on my way and picked up some wine and a few things to make a tomato and mozzarella salad. I've changed out of my work clothes and swapped them up for some cut-off chinos, and an oversized off-the-shoulder jumper—the colours make my skin tone look a shade darker, thankfully. I sorely need some sun. I look pale and shattered. I pin my hair up and swipe some gloss over my lips before trying to conceal the bags under my eyes. I look cute and comfy, and with it only being Jace, Carl, and his husband, I don't feel I need to put too much effort into getting dressed up.

There is no part of me that regrets my decision to get back with Jace. Let's face it; we hardly split up. One night doesn't count, surely? I just wish I could learn to rationalise my feelings and emotions like I am doing now, rather than just reacting. It has done neither of us any good. One thing I know for sure is I am still getting to know myself again after Adam, and Jace and I are still trying to get to know one another. We are bound to have a few bumps in the road.

I'll admit Jace's confession has stuck with me all afternoon. I can't get over his previous behaviour with other women. It's evident he was only interested in sating his own needs—he was so emotionless and cut off. He really was a playboy, chasing tail for his own satisfaction and not at all concerned who he might hurt in the process. I'm surprised I haven't had to deal with a string of emotionally dissatisfied and horny women. The thought makes me smile, but then I frown. I don't condone his behaviour but a small part of me, deep down, likes to think only I have been given the privilege of his true self. It's a nice thought, even if unrealistic.

I only know his date of birth from my online search. We still haven't discussed our pasts or family. He knows it's just me, but we've never delved below the surface of why that is, and I am still to ask him about his own family. These things will take time and evolve when they need to. For the time being, I'm going to be happy knowing that he is as crazy about me as I am about him.

Chapter Three

I have felt the pinch of Jace's distance all afternoon. We haven't spoken since lunch, and he gave me the barest of kisses when he walked me back to The Loft. I continually brush it aside on the journey to his, but as soon as I turn into his drive, my tummy does a little flip, and not of excitement. I feel nervous. I mentally scold myself, but it only picks up as I get out of my car, so much so that my hands shake a little, and my skin pimples with unease. He looks up through the window, and instead of the usually sexy smirk, he looks more serious now, his strong features more harsh and striking.

I collect up the wine and food, leaving my bags for later. Seeing my hands full, Jace meets me at the door, slanting it open so I can slip through. I eye him cautiously, trying to gauge his mood, and my anxious swallow doesn't go unmissed.

His amber eyes drop to the huge platter of salad.

"I told you not to bring anything," he scolds. When they lift to mine, I give him an awkward smile.

"Annoying habit. I like to do the opposite of everything you say." I blush around the truth of that statement because I'm constantly, unintentionally testing him, trying to gauge whether he is in this for real or just hurtling me along for the ride.

He cups my neck, his thumb running along my jawline.

"Isn't that the bloody truth?" His eyes dance with humour, and his mouth quirks in that sexy way. I inwardly sag and smile genuinely for the first time all day, unable to fight the tension pushing and pulling between us he drops his mouth and kisses me. I'm unable to do anything other than allow him to nip and lick at my mouth on sexy little groans and bites, as my arms begin to ache with the constant weight of the wine and plate grasped in them. But I don't complain, not when his mouth is adoring me.

"You look gorgeous," – he pulls back and takes me in, his nostrils flaring, – "and you smell like we should have sex," he states on a soft hum. I laugh, grateful when he takes the food out of my hands and quickly places it on the side before pulling me flush to him. He is hard, and my soft, accommodating body melts into him. Without the restriction of the food and wine, he cups my arse and bends to take my mouth once again.

His mouth is divine.

"Oh," I hum as he sweeps his tongue with a long silky brush against mine.

He drags his mouth away and drops a soft kiss to my bare shoulder. I contemplate reaffirming my apology because I still feel like there is an undercurrent of tension, but he beats me to it as he lifts my chin and stares down at me.

"It's done, okay?" I nod, twisting away when a ball of emotion threatens to break my stoic expression. "Hey," he kisses my worry away, "you're my girl, Lily. Don't doubt this. We're bound to have a few hiccups."

"That felt more like indigestion," I complain.

"A stroke," he grumbles. I flash 'sorry' eyes to him, but he winks. "Come on, give me a hand." He threads his fingers with mine, and he lifts my salad off of the side. I collect up my wine again as we move into the house properly.

"Something smells amazing," I tell him. The air is laced with garlic and other delicious herbs.

"Other than yourself, you mean?" he jokes. As soon as our hands are free, I move into him, and anticipating my need for him, he opens his arms. I drop my nose into his chest, inhaling that heady smell.

"I'll make it right later," he tells me. I very belatedly realise it is always him making it right for me, second-guessing my feelings or my next move, always anticipating my needs. And I let him. I begrudgingly admit I've become selfish, and if yesterday has taught me anything, it's that Jace isn't the nonchalant man I thought he was. Below his confident, polished exterior, he is very complex.

I nod against his hard chest, biting at the taut flesh beneath his polo shirt and causing his wide flank to vibrate with a deep laugh.

"How was work?" He lifts me, placing me on the only spare surface. "I thought you wanted my help?" I raise a brow at him, but he shrugs.

"This is helping," he replies, as he lifts the lid on my dish and nods his approval. "I'm impressed."

"Don't hold your breath," I mutter. I have long since accepted I'm a terrible cook, and although something can look delicious to the eye, it can taste like utter dirt.

"I wasn't." He throws me a grin over his shoulder, laughing at my gaping mouth. There he goes again, the cheeky shit. I smile anyway, dipping my head before answering him.

"Work was long," I admit. "Harriet flies out tomorrow, so I have the run of the gallery all to myself," I slip in. His eyes move from his furious chopping and meet mine with a naughty twinkle.

"Good to know." He winks.

"Yes, I thought you'd appreciate the information." I drop my gaze and smile softly. This is what I love: the playful nature mixed in with Jace's strong sex drive and intensity. It's an addictive combination.

A little while later, I watch him over my glass of wine as he moves around the kitchen, pulling on his beer and throwing things together as he drops a peck or two on my mouth. James Bay is crooning softly in the background, and I sing quietly along to the tune and nibble at a bit of salad to my right. I feel the weight of his eyes on me and hold back a smile. Slipping off the side, I cast a look over my shoulder and find him watching me.

"Kiss me, Lily." The cutlery is placed on the side slowly, and he takes his time walking to where I stand.

"Your guests will be here soon," I tell him breathlessly. He shrugs and hooks his arm around my lower back, pulling me to him. I know where this is headed, and I need to stop it.

I peck his cheek and pull away, but he tightens his grip and slants his mouth over mine.

"Don't refuse me, Lily!" he growls and bites my cheek gently. I laugh, pulling free, but it only makes him nip me more: my nose, mouth, and chin. "You taste like watermelon," he groans.

"Get off," I pant, pushing his laughing chest away. He lets me go but slaps my arse as I pass, making me yelp. "Thug," I mutter, casting a glance over my shoulder at him. He shrugs and moves quickly, grabbing my jumper and tugging me back to him.

"What the fuck is that smell?" he moans into my neck, inhaling my body lotion. Laughing, I try to sidestep and duck underneath him. His eyes flash into mine, and I make a sudden dash away. "Get here!".

I cry out in laughter when he barrels after me.

"Shit!" I squeak as Jace pounces around my waist, sending me flying onto the sofa with him, I'm shrieking as I go down, but the sound of his deep laughter softens the high note of my pathetic scream. Thick knees straddle my back as he pushes my arms up and my jumper high. In the seclusion of the house, he presses into my back and licks my shoulder blade.

"Delicious," he purrs.

I squirm, trying to waft a hand out for help.

"No," he chuckles, "when everyone has gone, I'm going to fuck you on the table under the stars." My breath leaves me in a gigantic rush of aroused air. "Do you want that, Lily?" He grinds into my arse, and every nerve ending springs to life to greet him.

I close my eyes, mentally already at the table—a torrent of explicit images running through my mind.

"Yes," I whisper.

"Good, next time you wear that perfume, make sure you're naked." He jumps up and lifts me with him.

"It's lotion," I tell him breathlessly. This pleases him somehow. His lips quirk, and he tilts his head, and I'm not left wondering the cause of his satisfaction very long.

"I think a massage is on the cards." He grins.

I fling my arms around him and kiss him hard on the mouth.

"You're too good to me," I tell him. We're going to be okay. I just know it.

"You're worth it." His lips touch my nose before he steps away. "I've got to finish up." I watch him walk away and take the opportunity to nosey at his bookshelf, mainly lined with architecture books, along with unique ornaments and the odd photo. I'd never really paid much attention to it before, as he usually occupied my focus. There are only a handful of pictures: Jace on a building site, I'm assuming it's one of his builds. He looks younger, maybe early twenties, and one of him on a bike, looking even younger still.

None of him with any family.

The last picture is of his shoulders and head as he looks out over a shimmering sea. I don't want to know who took that picture, and asking may rattle the shaky foundation we're walking on, so I take myself back to the kitchen island and pull out a stool.

"Cavalry has arrived," Jace says. I lift my head to find Carl and Rupert pulling into the drive in a four-by-four. Carl is already waving at me through the windscreen. I lift my hand as Jace dries his hands quickly on a towel, then wanders to let them in. Carl swans right to me and kisses my cheek, scooping up the bottle of wine by my side.

"You look lovely," he says in passing, his attention solely fixed on pouring himself a large glass. He walks around Jace's kitchen with familiarity.

When he looks back at me, taking in my outfit, I shrug my shoulder.

"This jumper is actually really old." I laugh. I've had it since my teens, but it's been faithful, and I love it.

Rupert joins us with Jace on his heel, and he's carrying a bottle of wine too. I smile at him and feel myself flush with embarrassment. The last time I met him, I was very drunk, not to mention I was whisked off to the loo for hot sex by Jace Bennett.

"Lily." He nods, far more reserved than his flamboyant husband.

"Hello, Rupert, how are you?" I feel my skin heat under his appraisal. Jace sees my fleeting look of embarrassment and hooks an arm around my neck, slapping a very showy kiss on me. He then gives me a wicked grin, and I drop my head against his chest. "You quite finished?" I smirk.

"Never, woman." I eye roll at him and lean back into the counter as he steps away, knocking my chin in that endearing way.

Rupert is regarding me with both amusement and delight, and in reply to my question, he smirks, "Far less flustered than you are."

I grimace, dropping my head, but he surprises me by giving me a gentle cuddle.

"Don't be shy. You've done what every other woman has failed to do." He winks at me, and I slip a startled look at him, then to Carl, who is leaning over the counter, chin in his hand, earwigging. He wiggles his brow, mimics a whip movement, and nods at Jace.

"I can't whip up eggs, let alone a man into shape." I'm over-dramatic, sighing helplessly, and Rupert barks out a laugh.

Jace looks to the couple on his right.

"There is nothing wrong with my shape." He throws a wink at me.

"Well," I let the word drag, gaining his full attention. "Your head has got unforgivably big." I wince.

Jace moves quickly and snatches my arm, tugging me

to him with a wide smile. His hand takes my neck and holds me so he can drop his lips to my ear.

"By the way I get you screaming, Miss Spencer, I think you rather like my big head." There is laughter in his whisper-soft words, and he nips my earlobe, making me jolt.

My eyes fly across the room, but Carl and his husband are caught up in their own conversation, so, knowing I'm safe from prying ears, I turn back, happy that we seem to finally be back to our normal, less argumentative selves, and whisper, "I think you need to remind me just how much I like it."

My eyes glitter into his, and when he smirks, slowly and widely, I rise swiftly and drop a kiss on his lower lip. He groans and adjusts himself, and I can't help the flutter of laughter in my throat.

"Let me cook," he grumbles.

"Be my guest."

He regards me softly, his big chest rising slowly, then he shakes his head and sends us all outside. The garden heater is pumping out steady warmth, and we have been lucky to get some sun most of the day. I grab a blanket anyway and slip outside with my wine and the guys, settling myself onto a wide bench seat.

The door is open, and the music carries out to us. Carl hums along, and I sip my drink, enjoying the purr of heat over my face.

Rupert sighs heavily.

"Thanks for the heads up," he says to Carl and jerks his head at the front of the house where Neve is hopping out of her oversized car. My eyes flash inside to see Jace is walking leisurely to the front door.

"I didn't know," Carl scoffs and pats my shoulder. "Brace yourself," he hums. It's the complete clarity I

Betrayal

need to affirm that my suspicions about this woman aren't misplaced.

I lift my glass.

"Have we got anything stronger?" To my surprise, it is Rupert who stands.

"I'll grab some whiskey."

"Shot of cyanide?" I quip. His laugh makes me smile, and Carl is trying his hardest not to laugh.

"Oh, you are bad," he drawls.

"That was really harsh and horrible, but she is such a bitch to me," I admit. Carl looks at me long and hard. We say nothing but the mutually unspoken dislike for this woman meets between us.

"Watch yourself, Lily," he warns. I follow his gaze to find Neve lifting on her tiny-heeled toes and wrapping her arms around Jace's neck as she kisses his cheek, then rather than drop back, she keeps her hands hooked and laughs up into his face. I'm grateful his hands are on her waist, holding her at arm's length, and when his eyes slowly find me, his mouth is pinched in unease. I hold his stricken gaze for a minute too long.

I can't bear to see her sliding all over him, so I drop my gaze as I feel my stomach hollow out. When I drag them back up, Neve is wiping at her eyes and folding into him, resting her cheek over his peck. He rubs her back, and I remind myself she is going through a difficult time and that they are just friends. I want to believe I can trust him—she has known him a long time and having me around has fractured her place in his life. I try to see it from her side; that perhaps she is trying to find where that place is now and not much liking how the dynamics have changed.

We are all waiting, and despite her bolshie attitude, she seems reluctant to join us. Jace nods her through, but she flicks sad eyes at him, and to Rupert's obvious delight, she moves back toward the door with the intent to leave, but Jace captures her hand and pulls her through the house.

"Hey," Jace breathes. He quickly meets my eyes, but I drop them to my drink. "Neve is joining us." Rupert has his face fixed on his phone, but Carl manages a smile.

"Grab a drink," he says by way of hello. She pulls at Jace's arm, trying to get him to stay outside with her.

"Hi, Neve." I muster up the strength to speak to her. Jace winks at me, but I don't return it with my usual grin. Instead, my eyes find Carl and Jace leaves to fix up the last food bits.

"Still hungover?" She smirks and leans into the door-frame—not so sad after all?

"No, I feel fine. How are you?" I try to be polite and take her feelings into consideration, but she apparently doesn't care for mine.

"Oh, it's just you look ready for bed; are those your pyjamas?" she scoffs. "I have some concealer too, if you need any?" She makes to go for her purse, and I can't help but grind my teeth together.

"I think she looks stunning," Carl slips in, and I mentally thank him for having my back.

"You would," she huffs, her eyes running over my attire as mine do her. I don't want to care or compare, but she looks amazing. Tight jeans, strappy sandals that are in no way appropriate for this weather, and a tiny cami tucked in. She's cold, because well, her ample assets tell me so. Smirking, she flicks a look over her shoulder.

"Jacey, can I borrow a top. It's colder than I thought." Her eyes find mine, desperate for my reaction. I snort out a laugh and lift my drink, absolutely adamant that I won't play her childish games. I could go down the same route and throw myself at Jace, but since her arrival, I feel well and truly put out, and I hate that she pulls that emotion from me.

"Rupert, how is business? I never got to ask much about it the last time we spoke." I give him my full attention, trying to ignore the catty bitch glaring at me.

"Well, I wonder why that was?" he muses, locking his phone and laying it on the table. I open my mouth to respond and slam it shut as he sniggers and winks at me. "You filthy buggers," he titters. Neve rolls her eyes and wanders off into Jace's bedroom and returns a few minutes later, sheathed in one of his jumpers. When he joins us, his eyes soften.

"You may as well keep that; you always bloody wear it." He laughs at her around his beer, and she snuggles further into the heavy wool jumper as her eyes blaze into his, just like how mine do, and I feel every ounce of my body fighting against Jace's admission that they are just friends. I always follow my gut, and I can't help the deep, aching burn, telling me that he is lying about their relationship.

I know my hurt is starting to show on my face, but I try everything to keep smiling.

"Top up!" Carl sings, and I jump up with him, happy to busy myself elsewhere. I'm tempted to text Cass and get her to feign an emergency so I can hotfoot it out of here. Carl takes my hand and pulls me through the door, but Jace snags it into his own and holds me at his chest. His eyes search mine, and I smile at him.

"I can start to bring things out if you like?" My ability to act indifferent surprises even myself.

Jace says nothing but holds my hand in his and wraps his free arm around my neck, his bottle dangling down my back.

"Kiss me first." His deep, gravelly voice brings my eyes back to his. He knows I'm struggling with this. He releases my hand, but only so he can raise it to cup my chin and angle my mouth for his. His mouth moves past mine and rests on my cheek. "It means a lot that you're trying with her." I nod, a ripple of emotion drowning me because I don't want to try with her, but I know if I want to be with Jace, I have no choice but to accept she is in his life. He must sense my inner dilemma because he sighs. "She is like family, Lily," he says with deep regard for her.

"I know," I whisper. He's trying. That has to count for something. I want to confess my feelings for him, but I know my unease at her presence is the root of that need. It's not the right reason to admit I'm falling deeply in love with him.

Chapter Four

The past few hours have been as pleasant as having teeth pulled, so when my phone dings, it's the perfect distraction and seeing Cass's name is a godsend. I excuse myself and slip away, aware Jace has eyes on me.

"Everything okay?" I nod over my shoulder and leave him to Neve. When I get inside, I call Cass and wait impatiently for her to pick up.

"Hey, things all okay?" She's referring to last night. She must have been tied up all day with work if we're only just touching base now. I give her a quick rundown of the evening. I don't want to seem melodramatic, but I can't stand Neve. And I'm astute enough to know the feeling is mutual.

"Need a getaway?" she hums sympathetically. *Yes*!

I want nothing more than to leave, but I've had too many to drive, and Neve is sinking them like an alcoholic at a beer festival. I don't trust her. I rest my elbows on the counter and look out of the window facing the drive.

"Can't," I mumble. I pick at some salad on the side and pop a thin slice of cucumber in my mouth.

"Oh, hun, don't let her get to you. She wants to drive you away." Cass reinforces her words with meaning as a timer goes off in the background and makes me jump a little. She swears and clangs about on the other end of the phone.

"I know. It doesn't make it any easier to watch, though." My eyes drift outside. "She can't keep her hands off him," I mutter, "how can he sit there and allow it when he practically lamped a man for swinging his arm around me?" I vent quietly.

"If I knew that answer, I would have a penis," she chortles, and I bite my lip because I am struggling to find anything funny at this particular moment. Footsteps bring my head over my shoulder, and I twist away as Jace saunters in. His eyes seek me out with concern when he makes his way over.

"Got to go," I say in a rush, trying not to show my hurt, "love ya."

"Oh, okay, ring me if you're stuck!" She cuts the call, and I twist to find Jace leaning against the counter. I snap a bright smile on my face,

"Tell me we're okay?" He drops his head and looks up through his lashes, a bottle dangling from thick fingers, his cheeks stained. I would usually take some satisfaction after yesterday's argument, but Neve's snake ways are very unsettling.

I nod, enforcing my smile.

"We are." I shrug, and he inclines his head that bit further, questioning my reply.

"Okay, let me rephrase, are you okay?" His bottle lifts in my direction. He's pressing further because I am doing a piss-poor job at hiding my dislike for his friend.

"Yes, of course, why wouldn't I be?" I tilt my head, copying him. I wait patiently for him to openly acknowledge that Neve is a little too tactile, but he is picking at the label on his beer thoughtfully.

"You seem quiet." That's bullshit. Carl and Rupert aren't talking either—we haven't been given the chance! And when the occasion does arise, no one has anything to say in response to all Neve's childhood tales of her and Jace or his escapades. I'd rather spend an evening with Adam or go and hang out with my dad and his wife than hear about his sexual conquests.

"I'm good," I assure. I head back towards the door as Neve strides in, heading towards the bathroom. I lift to drop a kiss on his cheek as I go. I don't want to make this awkward for him, and I will if I play into Neve's hands.

It's selfish of me to want him all to myself, but it's the only feeling I experience when she is about. He holds me to him and frowns.

"It doesn't feel like you're okay." His syrupy eyes search mine, and I let them, but I know he won't find anything, not when he is so blind to Neve's deception.

He dips and pecks my nose.

"I want that smile back." I flash one—it's false, and I feel the strain of its lie right up in my scalp. He knows that me having to watch her fawn over him is no different from having Travis sling his arm around me. I really don't want to get into an argument, but I hate her touching him, and for the first time, I understand his hurt and jealousy regarding Travis. I imagine if Neve has always been tactile with him, it would seem odd for him to start telling her to stop. She will blame me, and he doesn't want any animosity between us.

Jamiroquai's *'You Give Me Something'* comes on, and Jace begins to move his hips in sexy little rolls.

"What are you doing?" I laugh nervously, seeing the glint of purpose in his gaze. Jace winks and mouths the words to me as he moves to the beat. He goes all Patrick Swayze on me and bites his lip—I swoon.

"*We*," he emphasises, "are dancing." He spins me out, captures my wrist, and yanks me to his chest on a twirl. "To our song." His nostrils flare when my lotion wafts between us, and he licks his lips, causing me to go breathless and wide-eyed. He holds my hips flush to his and grinds them on a roll, and the first scrape of unease in me begins to flake away. "This reminds me of you," he says and spins me out. I go, laughing, and come back into his arms in a sharp tug. "Oooh," he laughs, encouraging me to roll my own hips along with his, our smiles chasing my worries away.

He sings on a soft husk into my ear, his hips rolling and swaying as he dances us outside. I brush my hands up his chest and thread them around his neck as he holds my hips, moving us together. I'm spun back out and pulled in so that my arse gets lodged in his groin. He grunts softly, and I laugh, my head lolling back. He pecks my cheek, anchoring me with thick arms, and when his hand slides down and bunches in at my hip, I twist around.

My face is flushed as happiness radiates off me, and his deep whiskey-gaze is sultry and honey soft.

"Ooh," he mimics the artist, biting his bottom lip and sending my illicit thoughts running wild. When I rise to capture his sinful mouth, he hauls me up, and my legs go willingly around his waist—the hot press of his thicker body between my thighs a delicious comfort. He groans into the kiss, grinning when Carl makes a retching sound.

"Piss off," he laughs, his face stuck on mine. I sigh in contentment, soul-deep happiness. This feeling. Right here. I need to keep that. This is what we have.

Betrayal

Something deep. Real. I may not have a past with him, but I have a present. Neve can't compete with that. Jace runs his thumb along my lower lip, his hips swaying so gently it's hardly noticeable. His eyes follow the path of his fingers and lift to my grey eyes, no doubt full of dazzling emotion. He swallows, and his hand shakes a little against my mouth. "Don't look at me like that, Lily." His gruff tone is low enough for only our ears, and my grin is slow. I quickly cover the distance and kiss him again. He tastes like beer, and I hum happily.

"I'd kill for that smile," he tells me. I hold him tight, just a quick squeeze, but enough to reiterate to myself that it's me he is with, and her underhand play is not on his radar.

"I need a refill," I say, very much aware that all conversation has stopped, and the attention is on us. I'm wrapped around Jace like a vine—our chests flush, our groins finely cupped together. All too happy to keep the close proximity of us; he sits us together. Neve's eyes are downcast, and her nearly empty drink is being swirled in her dainty fingers. Despite all my efforts this evening to pull her into conversation or take an interest in what she finds worthy of Jace's attention, her eyes hold mine with nothing but cold regard.

"Get a room," Carl snorts.

"I have one," Jace grumbles before nipping at my neck with a loud groan. "You're in it." He lifts a brow to his assistant, who pouts and turns his face away on a slow lift of his chin, flapping a hand as though Jace's little revelation had just given him an unwanted visual.

Rupert bursts out laughing.

"Tink, you've gone all red!" Carl shakes his head dramatically, and a chorus of laughter fills the quiet.

"Tink?" I question, and Carl sends his husband a look that could kill.

"Yeah, as in Tinkerbell," Jace explains. "Neve, pass me that blanket." He holds out his hand for her to pass it. She is clearly reluctant and barely looks at him, her face pinched in tight annoyance. I don't allow myself to wonder about her any longer because Carl is bitching quietly to his husband.

"So why the nickname?" I ask. Carl rolls his eyes and brings his drink to his lips, taking a long, loud gulp.

"I used to get called a fairy at school." He shakes his head in amusement, and though his perfect quaff barely moves, his preened brows are accentuated when he raises them in some semblance of boredom. "Original," he muses.

I squeeze his knee, and he nudges my shoulder in a grateful gesture.

It's short-lived when I say, "Personally, I think you resemble a gazelle," while taking a swig of my wine.

"Oh, you cheeky blighter!" he slurs, scowling at me. Jace is silently laughing, and Rupert leans in.

"You actually do, the way you prance about and stick your snooty nose in the air." I lift my glass high in agreement.

"I hate you all!" Carl pouts. He doesn't at all. His eyes are glassy but full of laughter, and his lips soon spread into a wide smile. "I like the food, hate the company." He is sullen and laying on the theatrics for our benefit.

"Present company or my company: Bennett and Klein?" Jace chuckles, drawing another wave of laughs out—even Neve has lost her sour face and has joined in.

"No, I love BK." He acts offended—his mouth is in a

practised pout, and his cheeks look even more gorgeous slanted just so.

"Just us then," I poke.

"Oh, piss off. You're all horrible." I dip for a hug, and he pecks my cheek. I lean back on a yawn, my head rolls, and rests on Jace's shoulder, and he takes the opportunity to rest his chin on the shelf my shoulder provides.

Curious hands knead my waist and slip under my jumper.

"Sleepy?" Hope fills his tone, and I don't suppress my grin.

I nod.

"Mmmm." He stiffens beneath me, and the long, delectable length of his impressive cock springs to life and nudges my arse.

"Mmm indeed." He's nuzzling my hair, and with our bodies sheathed by a blanket, his hand takes a leisurely journey up my thigh. I tense and feel him grin against my cheek, and it doesn't prevent him from reaching his target, as he cups me fully and applies just enough pressure to start a series of dull sparks in my sex.

I gasp lightly, and he shifts.

"Dammit, Lily," he grinds in my ear. I'm already chuckling at his frustrated state.

"What's going on?" Carl huffs, his pert nose heads up in the air as he tries to focus on us through drunk, thick-rimmed eyes.

"You lot need to go home—that's what's going on," Jace states and gives Carl a pointed look, as his PA screws his face up and grabs a full bottle of wine.

"I'm taking this!" He sniffs and winks at me. Rupert is the first to stand, but both Carl and Neve follow.

"Well, you certainly know when you have outstayed

your welcome." Carl's voice rises, and he staggers across the decking and slams into the window, eliciting a resounding thud. "Oh, shit!" He laughs.

"Bloody hell!" Rupert scoffs. "You're a damn liability." He mouths a sorry to Jace, who is laughing quietly.

"And that's an expensive bottle, think yourself lucky!" Jace calls as his PA is led through the house.

"Thanks for the invite, Jace," Neve murmurs. She looks forlorn and sour. I offer her a smile, but it isn't reciprocated.

"No worries, see you Monday." She stays for a second longer, hoping for something—what that something is, I do not know—but when Jace makes no move to give her his attention, she forces her lips into a tight line and scowls at him. I feel him sigh, rather than hear, but don't question him. She will only become a problem if I make her one.

A loud crash rings through to us, and both Jace and I swing to find Carl's intoxicated frame clinging on to the kitchen unit at a funny angle, his legs spread like a newborn foal. My burst of laughter causes him to curse profusely, and when he finally gets back to his feet, he begins dancing out of Rupert's way every time he tries to take his elbow to steer him to the car.

"Fuck's sake, Carl, just get in the car!" Rupert snaps, trying to steer his husband out of the house.

"So bossy. Are you going to smack my arse?" Carl wiggles his brows, and Jace groans, rubbing his hand over his face.

"I did not wish to hear that," he chuckles to me. I'm giggling my head off. Neve wanders off through the house, her head down, posture sad.

I grab Jace's top.

Betrayal

"You promised me starry sex." My cheeks heat, my thighs tighten, and when I lick my lip, Jace grins slowly.

His voice rumbles out in a deep, lusty purr.

"Yes, I did." He picks me up in a swift movement. I watch the car head away from his home into the dark and sigh, glad to finally be alone. The pale glow of the heater fans us as he walks us to the other end of the table which is free of plates. I kick my shoes off as we go, hearing them drop to the ground with a thud.

"A little eager?" Jace muses, and my only form of answer comes in the removal of his top. He perches me on the table edge and lifts his arms up to help ease the material off. Both hands come up to cup my face, his thumbs positioning my chin just so. "God, you're fucking beautiful." His amber eyes gaze over my face.

"I like you too," I admit on a breathy laugh, staring at his muscled shoulders.

"Good!" My chinos are yanked down, and his glittering stare lands on my skimpy thong as he murmurs, "Perfect."

"That's the drink talking." I grin, running my hands up his taut stomach. He unbuttons his fly so I can just see the top of his groin and the thick muscle straining to get out. His breathing is shallow, and I watch him roll his lower lip in his mouth as he pushes his jeans lower, freeing himself fully.

I lay back and stare up as deft fingertips hook into my knickers and begin edging them down. The blanket of darkness above is scattered with the tiniest specs of lights. Each one blinks down at me as Jace begins to rain kisses along the inside of my thigh. I can't think of a better place to be with this man.

I wake with a start. Jace is already awake and resting on his elbow, looking down at me.

"Morning." His voice has that early morning husk, as though day hasn't broken it in yet: sexy and gruff.

I bite my lip, taking in his honey gaze and darkened jaw.

"Morning." My hand stretches beneath the quilt and connects with toned flesh. "Can I stay here this weekend?" I ask, running fingers over his chest, focusing on his dark nipples. I'm taken by surprise when he rolls us quickly, and I find myself confronted by a gloriously fucked male with a beaming smile and sexy amber eyes staring back at me.

Last night was everything and more. Jace had made love to me and knocked every other moment out of the water.

"I've never had this kind of chemistry with someone else before," I admit, as I finger a stray curl of hair hanging over his tan forehead.

"I don't much fancy hearing about your previous conquests," he muses playfully as his hips jolt into me. I want to point out I was forced to endure that last night, but he is grinning openly at me, and I don't want to kill the moment. "In fact, I should have driven all thoughts of other men out your head."

My slim fingers run over the toned curve of his arse, and as he raises his brow, I direct them up his back and cup his face, bringing his mouth down to mine.

"You have."

Jace smirks, dropping to look at my mouth before eyeing me through heavy eyes.

"Good, because you're mine, Lily." His kiss is sweet and slow, and I'm so blissfully unaware of anything other than him. I blink in shock when I realise it's Saturday, and I have work!

"Oh, god, what's the time?" I try to push him off, but he stiffens, then drops on top of me, applying all of his weight. I grunt out a huff. "Jace, get off," I laugh, and he shakes his head.

"This is my happy place," he murmurs.

"I have work. I can't be late. Harriet isn't here." He grumbles and nips at my neck.

"I'm having words with your assistant when she's back. Does she not know she needs to work around my needs too?" He pouts up at me, and I laugh.

"No, I don't believe she got that memo."

"How selfish," he scoffs and leans to grab his phone. "Only eight forty." He frowns when his cock starts to stir to life.

"No!" I laugh. I need to get ready. He rolls us on a laugh and thrusts up, kissing me roughly. "Jace," I pant, "I have to get ready," I whine, sorely disappointed that I can't stay in bed with him. He drags himself away, and the constant tension in my womb objects as he rolls onto his side, biting my breast and groaning like any man would with his mouth full of nipple.

"You can stay this weekend," he tells me, dropping his chin to my wet skin.

―――

Jace makes it to The Loft in record time. He parks against the curb and watches me to the door, moaning idly about my skin-tight trousers. I catch a look at his profile. He looks hot in his designer jumper and jeans, he's styled his hair, and sunglasses veil his unique eyes from the early morning glare.

Smirking at my open appraisal, he pulls his shades away, subconsciously knowing the effect they have on me.

"I'm taking you dancing," he says.

I stall at the door.

"Later?" I beam.

"Later." He winks. "I'll pick you up, and we can go collect some bits from yours."

"Okay." I can barely contain my excitement. His mouth stretches wide.

"Have a good day, baby." He replaces his shades, and I watch him fly off down the street.

I step back to get the door when I catch sight of a dark Audi parked up the road, and my heart clenches with fear. A figure sits with a hooded jacket and sunglasses on, and although I can't see his eyes, instinctively, I know he is looking straight at me. Anxiety unfurls like a dark liquid through my stomach, and I rush inside. My gut tells me it's Adam, but I have no proof, nothing other than the growing sense of fear. I head straight to the back, pulling my phone free as I watch the door in palpable fear. My breathing is erratic, and my heart sinks further when I remember I didn't lock the door behind me. I move to lock it but stop, needing the seclusion and comfort my office gives me. After an age, the car slowly rolls past, too slow to be anyone other than Adam. Tears form, but I refuse to let them fall. I stare at the figure looking through two panes of glass, and it's like he is here in the room with me. Vomit threatens to leave my body. *Go away!* I mentally scream at him.

The car moves on, and I sag in my seat, my body letting go of the air trapped in my throat. I need to contact the police this week. I have seen Adam on too many occasions for it to be a coincidence, plus he sought me out at Finnegan's and came to my work. That's a clear violation of his order.

After my minor incident this morning, my day goes quickly, and I even start to believe I overreacted to the Audi being outside The Loft. Harriet has emailed and updated me on Paco's progress, along with a few images of where she is staying.

Looks stunning—have a blast! x

I send the reply and eat some leftovers from the fridge, working straight through my lunch when I make two sales. I'm finalising all the details with the gentleman when the door pings and Travis walks in. Seeing I'm busy, he wanders around. I manage to hide my surprise, mentally debating whether to admit his visit to Jace. We hit a milestone yesterday. I don't want to take us back a few steps.

"If you come by on Monday, it will be all ready for you, Mr Charleston."

"Wonderful. I'll leave you to crack on." His look wanders to the lean back of the man casually wandering around the gallery.

"Thank you. Have a lovely afternoon." I close the door behind him, and hearing the ping, Travis turns.

"Hi, Lily." His hands slip into his jean pockets.

"Hi, you."

He laughs at that, and his eyes do a quick sweep of me.

"Everything okay?"

"Yes."

He nods, taking that information in.

"Good." His hand moves to his hair. "I just wanted to check." He looks to the street, almost expecting Jace to come barrelling in. "I'd hate to think I'd caused a problem."

Oh, he has no idea of all the shit Jace and I are tackling. There is a shit storm swirling between us.

"No, Jace and are I good. He's just a little protective," I admit shyly.

"Rightly so," he counters. I smile at his compliment. Travis looks around the place, clearly impressed, and he points to an abstract piece that I love. "I like this." He squints, trying to make head or tail of it. I press my lips together, trying not to laugh. "This structure." The word comes out slowly, unsure.

I snort.

"It depicts pain," I tell him, my own head tilting to find a commotion of colours all slanting to one point and being knotted together in an angsty ball. His head pulls back in disagreement.

"Oh!" He tries not to laugh. "I mean, I can see that." He clears his throat.

"You're a terrible liar," I tell him.

"I actually don't like it at all," he confesses sheepishly, as he pulls a regretful face at me.

I shrug on a smile.

"It isn't everyone's cup of tea."

"I'm definitely more of a Stella man myself." He puffs out his chest, and I laugh on a groan. Travis has this young, happy-go-lucky persona about him; one that I figure involves a lot of Stella.

"Well, I appreciate you popping in." I try to move things along, very much aware that the more time he is here, the more annoyed Jace will be.

His resigned sigh has me bracing myself.

"Look, Lil—" He casts a nervous look at me, and I

mentally plead for him to just let it go. "You're obviously very beautiful—"

"Travis—" I wince, not happy to walk this road with him.

He laughs, holding his hand to his heart.

"Hear me out, okay?" I nod, and taking that as consent, he walks to me and stops at my feet. "But you being in love with someone else is a massive turn off." He holds his hands up and laughs at my expression. I instantly feel more relaxed. "Plus," he adds further, "you actually remind me of my sister." He visibly shudders.

"Oh god," I groan.

"Which," – he blows out a long breath, – "again, is a massive turn off."

"What exactly are you trying to say?" I try to help him out because he is stumbling his way through this, and it's painful to watch. I raise a curious brow at him, trying to lighten his tension.

"That if you need me, as a friend," he emphasises the last bit, and I smile at his cute offer, "I'm here, okay? If you need milk or a moan, or whatever—" He gestures with his hand.

"You don't need to do that," I tell him,

"I feel like I do. You're a nice person," he replies, "take my friendship." I study his sincere face and consider how silly it would be of me to decline.

"Okay." I breathe out slowly.

"That wasn't so hard, was it?" Laughing eyes meet mine.

"No."

He hands me a piece of paper with his number scrawled on it.

"Don't be a stranger." He dips to kiss my cheek, and I stiffen, purely because I feel I am betraying Jace.

"I won't." I finger the small slip of paper, conscious that he has already written it, and cares enough to turn up here and check on me.

"See you around, socks," he grins, his honeycomb eyes full of humour.

"Oh, bugger off!" He pulls a prancy pose that has us both laughing, and then he is gone, sending a small wave through the window at me. I take the paper and drop it in my desk drawer. Other than Cass, I don't really have any other friends, probably something I should begin to rectify.

Chapter Five

I relay my little interaction with Travis to Jace as we head away from The Loft, and he takes it better than expected, but I conclude that is because of the hell I had to endure yesterday by her royal vileness. He skims right over Travis, taking my word for it, although I omitted to tell him that he gave me his number.

"So you made a few sales?" His eyes are fixed ahead on the road.

"Yes." I lean back into the seat, more relaxed now that I have dealt with the Travis issue. "Two of my main pieces," I add.

"That's great, baby. Have you spoken to Harriet?" He flicks a look at me, then back to the congested road.

"Yes, she's enjoying herself in the sun." I sound envious. Jace knows and picks up my hand; the contrast of his tan skin to my paler complexion is embarrassing.

"Let me take you on holiday," he murmurs, lifting my hand and running his lips back and forth over the soft skin. My heart picks up. I can think of nothing better than sunning myself with Jace on some tropical island.

"Okay, yes!" I grin, excitement dancing in our eyes. "Abroad?" I confirm. He laughs and nods.

"I want to see you in a bikini." He wiggles his brows.

I don't want him to think I expect him to fund it—I'm definitely due a holiday.

"We can book it together," I state, conveying my meaning. "I have some savings."

"Let me take care of it." The notion doesn't sit well with me, and as though sensing my withdrawal at the idea, Jace bites my wrist. "Talk to me."

"Holidays aren't cheap," I murmur, shooting him an uneasy look. "I don't want you thinking I'm—"

"I don't," he cuts me off, refusing to even let me voice my inner debate. "That's why I'd like to treat you." We stop at traffic lights, and Jace takes the opportunity to lean and kiss me. "Let me treat you."

"I don't know—"

He checks the road and grabs my face. I hate the thought of not contributing to our first holiday; he squeezes another kiss in before we begin moving forward.

"A weekend, four days max," he negotiates. I search his eyes, sensing he really wants to do this. I sigh loudly, relenting slowly, and he grins knowingly.

"Okay," I nod, mentally talking myself into it.

"Think of all the starry beach sex we can have," he chuckles. I slap his thigh and realise I'm sitting up in the seat, full of excitement. His eyes roam over my loose blouse. "You better have a ton of bikinis, Lily."

"Ah, there's the real reason," I muse, "you have a bikini fetish you haven't told me about?"

"No, I have a Lily Spencer fetish."

I smile over at him. I very much have a Jace Bennett addiction too.

Betrayal

Jace pulls up outside my apartment block. He turns and raises a brow.

"You ready to get all sweaty and dirty with me?"

"At least buy a girl a drink first, jeez." I push free of the car and look back to find him now watching me over the roof.

"Won't a holiday do?" He pouts.

———

We both fly around the place, collecting things up for my stay this weekend.

"Would it be easier to stay here tonight?" I call to him from the living room. He is rifling through my clothes for a dress to wear later. I have stayed in the living room, hiding my amusement at his constant whining or disapproval at my wardrobe contents.

"What the fuck is that?" The clink of another hanger being forcefully replaced floats through to me, and I bite my lip. "Definitely not," he laughs shortly to himself, "too short, too hooker." His groan hits my sex. "Jesus, Lily, you got a secret past you want to tell me about?" I roll my eyes but walk to the door leading into my bedroom. Jace flings a red dress onto a pile of discarded dresses before he pulls out a strappy, silver slip dress and smiles to himself. His eyes lift, a hard sheen in them. "We're staying at mine," he tells me matter-of-factly. "Wear this."

"That shows my side boob."

"You don't have side boob," he spits, as though the possibility is ridiculous.

"No, I just meant, you can see the side of my boob," I warn him. His eyes darken and run over my body, already imagining me in the little dress. He lifts it, inspecting the material, and looks at my frame again, not entirely convinced by my admission.

"You'll wear it," he repeats softly, his tone light.

I scoff.

"I did warn you!" I tell him flippantly. I cross my arms. The material is deceptive and makes the dress look bigger than it is. The dress clings to my hips and tits, but falls away everywhere else, dropping low, either side of my ribs, giving a very ample view of my pert breasts. He will hate it.

He backs down a little.

"Try it on for me," he suggests.

"Oh no, Bennett." I laugh. "This is happening." I back away and leave him to ponder the shit he has just got himself into, and when I flick a look over my shoulder, he is advancing fast, a devious grin on his face, the material hanging limply in his grasp. I can see where this is going, and I wouldn't put it past him to pin me down and force it on. "We'll be late for dinner," I say breathlessly.

He laughs loudly.

"Dinner can be rearranged." He moves quickly, startling me, and I spin on a laugh and race off. I try to outmove him, but he vaults the sofa and grabs me up. "Gotcha!"

I squeal out a laugh and wrap myself around him.

"I could make you change your mind," he teases. "When you're all compliant and shaking," he groans, "I'll make you put it on."

"No, you won't." I dare to challenge him, lifting my chin, and my grey eyes clash with his own sparkling ambers, making him smirk.

"How so?"

Betrayal

He presses a very large erection to my groin and raises a brow.

"Because, when you see me in that dress later," – he knocks his cock into me again, and I swallow, trying to keep myself in check – "you'll thank me." I brush at his hair and peck his lips.

"Or kill you," he mutters. Oh, that too. He will love the dress but hate seeing me in it in public. He leans into me, so we slowly topple over the back of the sofa in a tangle of laughing arms and legs.

"I want a taste now." He sucks at my neck and grasps my breast roughly.

"No," I breathe. "No touching, not until later."

"Refusing me won't do you any favours in the long run. In fact, I vow not to hold back when I finally get in your damn knickers later." He growls and thrusts in warning.

"Oh, sounds like a challenge. Do you have something in mind?" I whisper. He is far more adventurous than any other lover I have had, more intense, playful, rough, and unforgiving.

"I don't have enough time to prepare." He sits back, looking away and mentally mulling it over.

"I swear, if I get back and find the place covered in clear sheets, torture devices, and a video camera, I will haunt you forever."

Jace barks out a laugh and slams his mouth to mine.

"Shut up." He nudges my nose with his. "But I do promise to make you scream," he admits. My breath leaves me on a shudder. I trust him with my body, but I also feel nervous because he has far more experience and control than I do.

"Better make sure you feed me first," I say pointedly.

Jace smiles and stares down at me and takes his time

stringing it out, making me feel vulnerable and cherished all at once before he gives his head a disbelieving shake.

"I'm crazy about you, Lily Spencer."

"I'm crazy about you too." I lift my mouth and kiss him softly. "Now take me dancing." I'm rewarded with a disarming smile.

I managed to get Jace to agree to dinner at his. I opted for something light, as my dress isn't very forgiving, and I wouldn't be able to disguise the food baby. He has already changed and looks sharp since he has had a shave and styled his hair. I can still smell his aftershave in the bathroom as I apply my makeup. I keep checking the entryway, conscious there is no door. I want to surprise him.

I have curled my hair, gone all out with smokey eye makeup, making sure to really emphasise the silver to match my dress. This style always makes my eyes pop, so I keep my lips neutral and gloss them, staining my cheeks with a little highlighter. My lashes are dark and sultry against my fair skin, and staring at myself all dolled up, I smile. He is going to die on the spot. I have lost a little weight since I last wore this dress, and it skims over my curves, looking better than I remember. I have paired it with some strappy black high heels. I give myself a slow twirl and stop when I see Jace in my peripheral, staring at me.

"Ready?" I ask nonchalantly, trying hard to hide my smirk when his mouth drops open, and he drags unbelieving eyes down my frame.

"Ah, fuck, Lily," he pleads. His hand finds the back of his neck, and he massages it while he contemplates

Betrayal

the mistake he made earlier.

"Something wrong?" I muse, leaning to apply more gloss in the long mirror, as I smack my lips together.

"You witch." I hear the smile in his tone and try not to let my own slip free. I keep my face as serious as I can and dust myself with my favourite perfume. I know Jace is getting a generous view of my side and breast as I flick my hair, checking my reflection. I feel the most confident I have in a long time, and it's partly down to the drooling man to my left.

"That's going to come away when we are dancing," he stutters. He walks to me and picks at the material. It doesn't budge, and I grin up at him.

"Titty tape," I purr. His anxiety lightens a little, but I can tell he doesn't want me to wear it. He moves back to the bedroom and rifles through my bag.

"Did you bring another dress?" he asks, pulling a pencil dress free and offering it up.

"That's for work. I'm wearing this," I tell him and walk past.

"Let's stay in." His voice sounds fretful. I can't help my shoulders shaking from suppressing a laugh.

"You're being ridiculous. I'm not changing."

He stops me, lightly running his hands down my side, they glide back up, and his thumbs brush my bare breasts. My big, enigmatic man is getting his knickers all in a twist over some little dress. It's priceless. Seeing my gleeful look, he grunts and rubs at his temples.

"I don't want you to wear that," he confesses, sullenly. I don't fully believe he wants me to change, but his little dramatics are making my confidence skip and glide ahead.

"And I don't want you thinking you can plan my wardrobe." I hold his stare, and his face hardens. I sense an argument coming on, and I almost relish it, knowing that is when he is at his most unforgiving, and when his stance widens and his flank rises with irritation, I drop a look beneath my lashes.

"You promised to take me dancing; stop stalling."

He tries the strappy material again, ensuring it won't slide off and offer anyone a free show of my nipple.

I wink and slip past, picking up my clutch and waiting impatiently by the door. He tips his head back and gives an over the top sigh.

"Please, Lord, make me patient, and do not let me punch anyone in the face for drooling over my girl." I bark out a laugh, loving his cheeky grin as I pull open the door and stare at his glittery gaze.

I am so in love with this man that my skin feels alive with electricity around him.

The club is in the city and high up above the rest of the bustling streets. We arrive late, and the place is full of energy. Jace laces his fingers with mine, and we walk to the bar.

"What do you want to drink, Lily?"

"A cocktail, please." I place myself beside him. This place is similar to Nexo, and it looks expensive in here. I'm so used to rocking up with Cass, club-hopping, and looking all sweaty and flushed that I feel out of sorts around such polished and glamorous people. I gawp at some celeb sitting in the VIP area and nudge Jace, who kisses my cheek with a laugh. I'm utterly terrible with names, but I know I have seen them on a reality TV show. He is gaining a lot of attention, women all pandering to his needs and laughing at something I'm sure isn't funny.

"Brent James, the guy is a prick," Jace enlightens me.

"Jealous, baby?" I pout. "Prancing on screen, yacht parties, and groupies not your thing?" He hooks an arm around my shoulders and pulls me in under his weight.

"No," he grumbles. "I like sassy photographers, and big, big—" His hand slips close to my boob. I raise my brow.

"—Buildings." He laughs. I scoff and look away from Mr James and his entourage.

"That bar I was in the other night, someone said you designed it," I drop in casually.

"Oh, Nexo, yeah, maybe don't go there again," he tells me. The bartender comes over, and Jace rolls off our order.

"Why?"

"The guy that owns it, he's dodgy." Jace is momentarily distracted when the bartender hands him his change.

"Who, Callan?" I say. This gets his attention, and he tilts his head.

"You've met him?" His face is tight with subdued dismay.

"He was there, with Zara Reid, the model." Jace's eyes widen, and Neve's words come back from the other night—she had suggested that Jace had dated a model.

"Is she the model?" I stutter.

Jace actually laughs.

"God, no, never met her in my life." I nod, and he pulls me to him. "It was some stupid, young fling that went to my head." He takes my chin and pecks my lips. "Honestly, I had forgotten about it until Neve mentioned it."

"How is Neve?" I steal myself for his reply. I know he has seen her because her car was gone when we got back earlier. He eyes me suspiciously.

"Do you really care?"

I refuse to lie, but I'm not heartless enough to ignore the grief she is battling.

"Not really, no, but you do, and that matters to me." I don't hide my dislike for her, but I'm not about to make his life awkward either. He smiles gently.

"She's okay." His fingers find the end of my hair. Our drinks get placed down, and Jace suggests we sit down in one of the booths. He has stuck to a soft drink because he is driving.

"If we had stayed at mine, we could have both had a drink," I tell him, sipping on my fruity beverage.

"I don't mind." He pecks my lips and twists to face me. "So, did you speak to Callan?" he questions further. I shake my head around my straw.

"He was all over Zara. Cass knows her somehow," I tell him. "He did give us a complimentary bottle of champagne though." I grin, and Jace grumbles. He lifts his glass.

"That explains why you were so wasted!" He smirks as he takes a sip.

"It was like liquid gold," I say. "I wasn't that bad." He sends me a pointed look and turns my hand over, revealing a series of grazes from mine and Cass's tumble.

"Need I say more?" His tone is soft but smug. I roll my eyes and lift my drink, ignoring his gloating grin.

———

Within an hour of us being there, things begin to pick up, and more people congregate on the dance floor. Jace has plied me with cocktails, and I'm eager to dance with him.

"I love this song." I grin, a little tipsy. He smirks, cupping my face, and kisses me sweetly.

"No slut dropping," he warns with a playful twist of his full mouth. I scrunch my nose up.

"I'm not a teen," I laugh, edging out of my seat and watching him stand to his full height. He hunkers down to cup my arse and kisses me.

"Thank fuck. I could be looking at a hefty lawsuit." He starts laughing, and my jaw drops. His hands fall away, and he holds his taut stomach until he gets himself under control, evidently finding it far funnier than I do. Eventually, it's his reaction that makes my mouth twist into a reluctant smile.

"Gross." I flap his hand away, but he anticipates it and snatches it midair, tugging me to him. When he drops his mouth to my neck, I sigh and run my hands to wrap them around his neck.

Latch by Disclosure is belting out, and I shimmy my hips to the beat.

"Show these stiffs how to move." He winks, encouraging me on to the open floor. I go on a strut and hear him chuckle behind me. His hand gropes my arse before I spin to face him, and he is there, rocking his own body to the beat. I wind my hips, and his eyes flash with a thousand filthy memories.

"Behave," he warns. I raise my arms, and he groans loudly, unaffected by the heavy crowd as he openly adjusts himself. "Lily, please?" I smirk and twist away, enjoying teasing him too much until I see the flash of unease he is feeling at my attire, and I dance into Jace and hold him to me.

"Keeping it PG," I coax him. He laughs over my shoulder, grinding into me.

"Good girl," – he kisses my hair – "we'll keep the slut drops for bedtime."

"Is that what you have planned?" I question over the music.

"I have many plans for us, Lily, many plans," he admits, sincere eyes meeting my more glassy ones. He lowers his head with a smile and kisses me thoroughly.

We dance through multiple songs, stopping only briefly for a drink now and then. My feet are achy, and my hair is sticking to the back of my neck. I'm more than tipsy, slurring, and I keep grinning—a sure sign I'm well and truly drunk. I fling my arms around his neck and plant a wet kiss over his mouth.

"Want to try that again?" he teases. I groan, vaguely aware I look a drunken mess while the rest of the women in here still look like a flock of exotic birds: prim and perfect. I head to the table and collect my clutch, using it to waft me, looking less and less lady-like by the second. It's another world. They all look as glossy as they did when they arrived; their makeup perfect—not a speck out of place. I do not have that level of dedication.

"Want to get a dirty kebab?" Jace whispers in my ear, and my head tilts on a husky laugh.

"You do say the most romantic things." I twist into him, latching on for support, as he leans back to look down at me. I'm blurry-eyed and sweaty from our dancing.

"Move in with me, Lily."

I snap my head back, squinting one eye to focus on him. He bursts out laughing, and I slap his chest.

"I'm drunk," I whine, "take me home." Rolling my forehead against his chest, I try to fight the ridiculous swirl of panic at his words. Plus, my dry mouth is pestering me for water, and each nervous swallow feels like I have sandpaper coating my throat.

"Is that a yes then?" He angles my head and keeps it in his view.

"That's . . . I'm drunk—ask me when I'm sober," I murmur, yawning. Deep in my subconscious, I'm screaming. He just asked me to move in with him, and my heart, gripping in fear, tells me I'm not ready to make such a big leap. If nothing else, the last few days have proved that I have a lot to learn about this man yet.

A lot, before I make such a huge step forwards.

I slip my hand into Jace's and wrap my other around his forearm as he heads us back to his car parked on the roadside. He puts the heating on full when I shudder in the large seat.

"Thanks." He drags a jacket from the back and hands it to me. I pull it on quickly and buckle myself in.

"I had the best night," I confess sleepily, pulling at the belt as I lean until I reach him and peck his cheek. "Thank you."

"You're welcome, beautiful." His fingers thread with mine so he can kiss my hand. "Hungry?"

"Very." A dirty kebab sounds perfect!

Chapter Six

"Baby, put your arm around my neck." I groan and lift my hand through closed eyes. I must have fallen asleep, and I want to stay in my slumber.

"I'm tired," I whisper.

"You're dribbling," he states. My eyes flash open and snap shut on a snort when I realise he is joking.

"Don't be mean." I pout at being pulled from the warmth of the car and thrust into the chilly night air. Jace swings me into his arms and kicks the door shut and lowers me, only so he can unlock the door. He pushes us into the warmth, and it's then that I see the place lit up with dozens of candles dotted all over the floor, petals decorate the large tiles, and his chin hits my shoulder ever so gently.

"Surprise."

I'm in shock. How did he?

"When did you? How?" I stutter.

"Carl," he admits, and I smile on a wobble.

"I don't know what to say." I don't. He is full of surprises, and other than the minor issue of Neve and his

61

little meltdown over Travis, he treats me like a queen. I take in the flicker of tiny lights through watery eyes. I'm too drunk to fully appreciate this. Plus, the petal path is narrow; I can't walk in a straight line, let alone follow a petal-strewn path.

"Say I'm not the only one feeling this crazy connection." He swallows. I blink up at him. His nostrils are flared, and he's regarding me intensely, pleading as though he can't quite bear to hear anything other than what he is asking.

"I feel it." My confession brings swirling ambers to my parted lips, and his mouth tightens momentarily. Instinctively, I know I haven't quite said what he wants to hear. Is he digging for a confession of love?

"Jace I—" I swallow the words back, scared to utter them, and in turn, make myself vulnerable. "Kiss me," I breathe out, but instead, he pinches the rim of my dress in his fingers and begins lifting it slowly up my body. It resists at my breasts, and I bite my lip under the slip of material obscuring my view of him. "Tit tape," I remind him. "Not so sexy." I giggle, wishing I could see his face.

"Where is it?" he mutters, clearly frustrated by the minor obstacle. I can't move my arms because they are skyward, so I try to drag the dress away with my chin. "Urgh, just rip it off, it will come away with the—" Jace yanks it up, and I yelp falsely.

"Oh, shit!" He flings my dress away, and I find worried eyes inspecting my breast. I gurgle out a deep laugh.

"Got you!" I'm barely able to speak through my laughter. Jace grabs my face and kisses me hard. "That deserves being put across my knee." Our eyes are locked, as are our lips.

"Is that what you had in mind when I asked earlier?"

Betrayal

I give my brows a little wiggle and tug at his belt. He clasps my hands and moves them away. Holding them still, he drops a kiss on my collarbone, down to my breasts, and sucks my nipple into his mouth. I moan and hold his head still, but he moves closer so that he is kneeling in front of me. His mouth and tongue petting my skin.

"You have the softest skin." He nips at my hip and pulls me so I'm perched on his widely stretched knees. Slowly, he lowers me back until I'm crushing the petals. Jace takes handfuls and sprinkles them over my body. The floor is warm, and I sigh when he slips a petal into my knickers.

"Jace, please—" My eyes flutter shut.

"Tell me what you want," he coaxes.

"You." I grin.

"Where?" Fingertips dance along the seam of my knickers.

"Everywhere." My own hands run to ease one ache, and I grope my breast, arching at the release of discomfort I offer myself.

"Fucking hell, Lily." He drags my hands back to my side and covers my breasts once more with both my hair and the rose petals; their smell is pungent and sweet, floral and fresh. With their waxy incense and Jace's male scent, I'm in ecstasy. I moan again, and he chuckles.

"It's painful, isn't it? That need. Imagine how hard it was for me when you kept running," he mutters. "I sat here, thinking about you constantly, imagining you naked in my bed." He is kneeling between my legs, looking all over my blushing skin. "God," he groans, lost in that thought. "I was so fucking desperate to taste you, Lily." My sex clenches, and his eyes flash when I squirm beneath him. "You kept running, and I fucking wanted to punish you for it." His hands tighten on my knees.

"Touch me," I purr.

"Don't move." He stands quickly and pulls his phone free. Swiping at his screen, he positions it so it's pointed at me.

"No, I am not displaying that in my gallery." I smirk.

"I'm going to get it printed on a canvas and place it over my bed." Oh, god, I hope not!

"Ha ha," I drawl.

"Come here." He leans down and lifts me to my heeled feet, the petals flutter away, and turning me, he covers my eyes and walks us through the house. He stops for a second, and I wonder what he is doing. I'm about to ask when the seductive sound of a raspy male voice floats through the speakers around the house. I'm pushed along further until Jace decides to stop. He pulls his hand away, revealing the wide bed, coated in petals and more candles glowing like mini beacons over the floor, but what really catches my eye is the blindfold resting on the pillow. I raise my gaze to his, burning over my shoulder. "Miss Spencer," he muses. I bite my lip and thread my fingers with his.

"Yes?" I fight off a nervous giggle.

"Get on the bed." He pushes me forward, and I go until his fingers drop away from mine. I crawl on to the low bed and feel it dip under his weight, and his lips drag over my arse.

"You're in a very playful mood tonight, and something tells me you wanted rough, but I can't give you rough tonight." He sounds remorseful. I'm not. I don't want rough, not when this is on offer. It's every girl's dream. I lie back on the bed, running my fingers into the plush petals.

"I can live with that." My lip disappears in between my teeth.

Jace is everything but rough. He is tender and patient; every thought, kiss, and thrust designed with me in mind. He makes love to me long into the night, exhausting us both. Saying everything we so desperately want to admit to each other but without uttering a single word.

I'm floating in euphoria when I get to work. I rush about my usual morning routine and make myself a coffee. The door chimes, and I stop stirring the dark liquid and call out Harriet's name. When she doesn't reply, I abandon my spoon and step out into the small hall leading to my office.

"Hat?" Thick hands grip my neck, turning my words into a gurgle, and lift me off the ground. I gasp and kick, desperate for air, my fingers scratching helplessly at the rope's tight clutch on my failing throat. Adam's furious eyes fill my terrified gaze, and I cry through the obstruction around my windpipe, thrashing at the restraint. Somehow, through sheer desperation, I manage to scream for help, and the sound rips from my lips, burning my throat and lungs in a high pitched horrifying scream.

"Lily!" The sharp shout splinters through my terrified mind. I jump up and blink through the fog, choking my subconscious. Fear has her dark claws in me, and it takes me a few seconds to fight the nightmare off.

I'm whimpering and shaking, my hands cupping my neck. I see Jace looking at me in panic, and it's an icy awakening to my fragile form.

I'm not at work—I'm here, in his bed, dreaming of my ex and his wicked hands.

"Oh god," I croak, as my arms push and kick at the quilt. I still feel restrained, choking on a fear nestled so deep into my psyche that I sob.

Warm hands drag me across the bed, but I push at him, desperate to get away.

"Get off," I beg. "Don't." I choke. His whole face is robbed of composure, and he looks horrified.

"Lil." His tone is softer, reassuring.

"Please. Just don't." I can't bring myself to look at him. "Just a minute." I stumble out of the bed and stagger to the bathroom, dragging in a lungful of air. "I need a minute," I tell him, beg him.

I feel sick with fear, embarrassment, and revulsion at Adam being so present in my mind. I remind myself it's just a nightmare, but it plagues me as I splash water in my face trying to chase it away. I'm slick with sweat. My legs are weak as I lean against the counter, allowing it to take my weight. I'm still a little drunk.

"Lily, talk to me," he coaxes.

I shake my head and cup more icy water, dowsing my face in it. Where the fuck did that nightmare come from? Why now?

"You're so pale. Please sit down." I can't meet his eyes in the mirror, but I expect his touch. His hands are gentle. He lifts me up and pulls me on his lap.

"Feel better?" I sag into his chest and nod. I know a million questions are going to come my way, so I force a laugh out, but it sounds fake to my own ears. Sighing, I look up at him, hoping that I have chased the look of dread out of my eyes.

"I don't know what that was," I huff on a short laugh. Jace is eyeing me with suspicion, and I don't blame him. I wouldn't believe the crap coming out of my mouth either. Cupping his face, I press my lips to his. I realise I'm shaking, but I hold my mouth against his. His tongue is gentle and soft, so at odds with his usually more aggressive manner.

"I'm cold," I say in the hope that he will take me back to bed. My voice is raspy and sore.

"Want to talk about it?" he presses. I shake my head and tuck myself into the crook of his neck, averting my face. Do I want to talk about it?

No. Not now. Not ever.

"Just a scary dream," I mumble, pulling at the ends of my hair. I force my shudder away. Jace stands with me in his arms, and I scrunch my eyes shut, dispelling the horrid dream away.

"Your heart is going like a piston." His observation gets ignored. The second my back hits the mattress, I burrow into the pillow and close my eyes, levelling out my erratic, shallow breathing. I can feel his eyes on me, and that alone has mine kept tightly shut.

Jace sighs.

"Night, beautiful." His fingers drift over my hair and rub my side gently.

I clear my throat.

"Night." His lips find my brow, and I stutter out a sigh and pray I can return to sleep.

I wake before Jace. His usually edgy self is face down and saturated in calm. I think I like him better asleep—I muse inwardly—when his eyes are not furiously watching everything I do. His body is relaxed, and my mind isn't pulverised into mush by his toxic eyes and sexy words.

Slipping free, I head to the toilet and wash before pulling some tight jeans and a hoody from my bag. I grab my underwear and converse before moving quietly through to the kitchen and getting dressed. My camera is out on the coffee table, so I scoop it up, find some paper, and write Jace a quick note before I slip out into the cool morning air.

The early morning sun is breaking through the dense tree line, making the branches look like widely spread fingers reaching to grasp for something that isn't there. I carefully make my way through the man-made path. I veer right and trudge my way down the bramble-lined decline. I'm going to regret all the scratches tearing up my ankles, but now, with the clean, fresh air filling my lungs and the glow of early morning touching my face, I don't care. It's too beautiful out here.

I need the crisp, clear air to rid my mind of last night's nightmare. I need the peace and distraction of photography, and I allow myself to soak into the silence. My tense body is relaxing in the comfort of my own company.

I walk for more than ten minutes, across an open field and towards more trees. Another lake sits nestled on the far side, and I am desperate to capture it first thing. Dew is seeping through my canvas shoes and soaking my toes, but I power on, my camera in my palm, and as soon as I round the wide trees, I lift the lens and begin snapping away, picturing the wild meadow in an eerie black and white landscape, just how it was last night. I cross along another path and kneel to get some of the water and tree reflection. When I stand and turn everything is set out before me, a vast craggy landscape. I focus on the scenery, adjusting my shutter speed, and getting the perfect image.

Betrayal

I spend an age taking photographs, sitting on my butt in damp grass, and flicking through the images. It is the perfect interruption after last night. I'd lain awake for ages after my nightmare, silently reliving it, over and over again, dissecting it and doubting myself. When Jace finally fell asleep, I let the hot tears fall. I haven't dreamt about Adam in a while, so I put it down to the numerous sightings of him and the undiluted fear I felt yesterday when I suspected it was him outside The Loft.

I hate that I'm slipping back into old ways and angry that I'm thinking about him again. I begin taking more photos until my stomach grumbles and forces me to head back up the track. I don't know how long I have been—time melts away when I'm taking pictures, and I become as immersed in the camera as I am Jace.

The only difference is, with my camera, I'm in control. That's what I need; a sliver of control because last night, I had none, and that petrifies me—even if it was just a twisted memory.

The sun is up, and so is Jace. I'm panting as I get to the top of the track and find him sitting in one of the deep chairs. My heart starts, and the familiar prickle graces my skin as I feast my eyes on wide shoulders encased in a heavy knit sweater and long, lean legs thrust into jeans. He hasn't shaved, and the darkness to his jaw adds another depth to him. He looks so sexy that I swallow a whimper. I'm so thankful he is in my life.

"Exploring, she says—" His husky voice is the sweetest sound to fill the air. I grin, oblivious to my state, and walk as quickly as I can until I'm in front of him. I flick an achy leg over his and straddle him, wrapping needy arms around his neck. My camera acts as a barrier, but our lips still manage to find one another. Large hands run up my back and cup the back of my head. "I missed you this morning," he manages to murmur between our lazy kiss.

"What time is it?"

"Just after ten. What time did you go out?" He frowns, wiping dirt from my cheek. I shrug. I hadn't bothered checking the time, but I knew it was first thing. His eyes hold mine, and I know he is speculating about my meltdown.

"You're freezing." His hands rub therapeutically over my body, and his eyes come back up to mine, soft and worried. "Are you okay? That dream really shook you up." I cast my eyes away and nod reassuringly.

"I got some amazing shots." He sits back, and I begin thumbing through them on my camera. His sigh is so soft that I barely make it out. He isn't satisfied with me changing the subject or my decision to keep him at arm's length.

"You pout when you're concentrating." His thumb brushes across his pout, and I nip his finger and lift my camera to show him some of my favourites.

"That reflection is incredible." Unhooking the strap, he takes my camera and flicks forward. "I love this." I climbed up a branch to get that one. It's a snap of the lake, the craggy trees hooked over and pouring into the water like dehydrated men. It's eerie and stark in its beauty.

"Me too." He thumbs through more, stopping at one of a startled rabbit.

"You scared him." He smirks. I nod and point at the image.

"He has such sleek lines, look at his leg." I run my

finger along the part I'm talking about. "He's so defined." My stomach gurgles again, and Jace frowns.

"You didn't eat him, did you?" His tone is laced with laughter, and I nudge him playfully.

"No, but I am starving," I admit.

"I already put the coffee on. I'll make us breakfast." He pecks my mouth and stands me on my feet.

"Great, I need a shower." I tug at my sodden knees.

"That can be arranged." He cups my neck and leads me to the kitchen. "Humour me and eat first." I don't argue. I'm enjoying his attention too much.

Jace leaves me to start the shower as I respond to a text from Carl. I let him know I'm fine after our night in with Neve, and we arrange to meet on Tuesday evening.

Can't wait, plus that will help me tons as my car is in the garage x

Sure thing, I'll be at The Loft for 6! Cocktails here we come! C x

After breakfast, Jace rushes me to get dressed. The weather, although bright, is still cold. I make sure to wrap up, and he bundles me in the car, tight-lipped and with a mischievous glint in his eye.

"So you're really not going to tell me where it is you're taking me?" I ask after an hour in the car. This is the third time I have asked. I don't do well with surprises.

He laughs and squeezes my knee.

"Just a few more minutes." As promised, a few minutes later, we pull up at a large lake on the outskirts of London. "Viktor used to bring me here," he tells me. It's a small snippet of information about him, and I feel a glimmer of hope that he just might divulge more.

I follow him out of the car.

"I thought we could hire a boat, and I could row us around the lake." He holds his hand out for me to take, and I slip mine in his as he lowers his lips to my ear. "Then, when we are freezing cold, I have an excuse to get you in the bath." I laugh and keep pace as we head inside to arrange the hire.

The water is serene but dark, and all the greenery has lost its fresh summer colour and is musty and brown, each branch now visible without the shelter of leaves. The steady swoosh of the oars sweeping through the water fills the quiet. I'm tucked up in my life jacket, and Jace looks like he is ready to burst out of his. It was quite comical watching him struggle into it.

"Stop," he smirks. "I've filled out since I last came here."

"You look like the action man I pestered my mother for because Ken just wasn't man enough for Barbie," I tell him with a soft laugh.

"Barbie? I can't imagine you with a doll?" He frowns through a smile, nudging my shoe with his large boot.

"It was a momentary slip-up. I usually was covered in mud in the garden or painting something," I admit, thinking back to a time when I was wild and doused in love.

"It's one of the things I like most about you," he remarks, his muscles rolling as he rows with a rhythmic flow. "You don't mind getting dirty."

"Your mind is filth," I tell him, enjoying his wide smile.

"Or yours is. I genuinely did mean that you're not

Betrayal

afraid to get your hands dirty." I blush at my wayward thoughts. "And the fact that you look delicate and feminine while doing it . . . well—" He grins. "It's a huge turn on."

"You're looking pretty good yourself. If we gave you a man bun, you'd look Viking ready." I wink.

"Man bun!" He visibly shudders. "Not even if you paid me!" My feet are placed neatly between his widely spread knees. His, tucked into dark leather boots and faded jeans. He has a thick jumper and his parka jacket on again, the fur compliments the fading lighter tips, and his hair is getting darker now the sun has fled. He looks gorgeous. I'm going to miss those tips—they really bring out his eyes.

"What are you thinking?" he murmurs.

"Just how good looking you are." I smile. He grins back and lifts his chin, giving me a view of his full profile. "Shame that you're arrogant with it," I muse.

"You love my arrogance," he states, "but I probably should have made you bring your camera." He pulls at the oars, grunting as he powers us over the lake at a faster pace.

"No, it's fine. I love that it's just us." I stare out over the water. It's really peaceful.

"You do?" His head tilts, and those damn eyes flash with satisfaction.

"Yes." I breathe with a genuine smile. It's another pinpoint of solitude on the map, and I love it here, love the connection he has with it, and that he is sharing it with me.

"But you don't want to move in?" The softly spoken comment has me tensing up. I'm sitting on a boat in the middle of a lake with nowhere to flee. I realise my schoolgirl error and remind myself just how determined a man Jace is.

We're having this conversation. He's made sure of it.

It's somewhat calculated, but I can't help but admire his determination and creativity when it comes to getting what he wants.

"I never said that," I murmur, not quite meeting his eyes.

"You didn't say yes either—" He does that leg-nudge thing again, and I chew the inside of my cheek, feeling under a microscope all of a sudden.

"I know." I look away and stare at the blanket of water below us. "The idea of it is everything I want," I tell him softly, seeing the murky outline of his reflection in the dark water. He is leaning forward, elbows resting on wide knees, face set in a well-mastered look of calmness. He's not, though. I can feel the slight jitter of his knee bobbing continuously.

"So, what's the problem?" His voice is light, casual.

"Me," I admit, "the rational and sensible side of me is trying to keep me grounded." I huff out a nervous laugh.

"Well, can you tell her to piss off?" He laughs softly. I give him a look under my lashes and hold my smirk back.

"I just need a little more time. It's only been a month or so. Do you not feel it's too quick?" I dare to counteract.

He has stopped rowing, and we are bobbing away on the lake, the water lapping gently at the sides.

"No, I won't change my mind about you, so why lengthen the inevitable?"

"Just give me a few weeks. I need to look into the flat

Betrayal

and where I stand with that," I reply, tucking my hair behind my ear.

It's not what he wants to hear, but it's a step in his direction.

"Sure." I relax a little and keep my face averted. "But," – my head pulls back his way quickly, – "I want you in before Christmas," he declares, "and I'm not taking no for an answer."

"And you think Cass is bossy—" I muse lightly.

"She is," he scoffs.

We spend a good hour on the lake, then walk around the surrounding path. Jace tells me about his latest project and what ideas he already has for another.

"Another wild card?"

"Yes, do you want to photograph it?" he slips in casually. I suspect he feels inclined to after the last shoot.

"Last time was a fluke. I won't be offended if you bring someone else on board." His fingers tighten in mine. The wind has picked up, so I have wrapped my scarf tightly around my neck. "You said Viktor used to bring you here?" I twist to look up at him, squinting my eyes against the dazzling sun.

"Yeah," he smiles, nostalgically. "He'd bring me here in the summer, just to get us out of the city to unwind. Marie would make us a picnic, and we'd hire a boat and fish—he would fish—I was never any good. When I bought the lakes, he was over the moon, not so much when I filled the top one partially in and built on it." He chuckles.

"Oh, does he fish on the back lakes?"

"Previously, but since he retired, he and Marie tend to holiday a lot. They never did that when he was working. He spent six days a week at the office, but Sundays were for Marie." He smiles to himself.

"And you?" I say quietly, not quite understanding their relationship. Their bond is deep—I see that much.

"Sometimes. They'd invite me over, or we'd come here, even took me to the zoo once." He clears his throat.

"Did you like it?" I used to love the zoo, mainly the elephants, but I keep this to myself in the hope that he keeps talking about himself.

"From what I remember, I was more bothered that I had time with them." He grabs a branch, pulling a stray leaf free and flicking it away. "They were my escape." His fingers knot tighter with mine.

"From what?"

"Life," he murmurs.

"What about your parents?" I ask. If he finds the question intrusive, he doesn't show it.

"Nothing to tell. It's just me." He means just him and Neve. Like me and my family drama, he doesn't wish to share, and I don't pry, even though I want to ask him. He quickly changes the subject and begins talking about possible holiday locations, and my mind is soon lost on the idea of sandy, half-naked Jace-filled beaches before we drive back and bathe together.

Chapter Seven

I find Jace bent over the bath, checking the temperature. He swirls his fingers in the bubbles, flicks the excess water off, and when he is happy with the heat, he takes his t-shirt and rips it off in the sexy way men do, one sleek tug over his head.

"Lily!" he shouts, and I laugh. He twists on a smirk and beckons me over with a jolt of his chin, his fingers working the buttons on his jeans.

"You're keen?" I raise my brow and begin shimming out of my jeans. I kick them aside and pull my top over my head so I'm left in my underwear.

"You judge me for wanting to have you all slippery and wet?"

"Never." I grin and walk to him. He is gloriously naked. His chest firm and toned, and his cock bobs as I near, causing me to bite my lip. "That for me?"

"All yours." He is fighting a smirk back, and as soon as I'm within arm's length, he tugs me to him and drops his mouth to take my own. He nibbles along my lower lip and groans lightly. "You ready to bubble up, Miss Spencer?"

"Sure am." He gives me a single deep kiss and then drops one to my shoulder as he undoes my bra. It falls away, and he takes a pew on the bath edge. I step between his legs, and his big hands run up my sides, his thumbs caressing my breasts.

"These damn breasts," he groans, leaning to pull a nipple into his mouth. I buckle and hold on tight for his onslaught. He is dragging my knickers down my legs as he moves to the other breast.

He nips, and I hiss, "Oh, god." I hold his head still and whimper when he sucks deeply, pulling my breast into his mouth. His hands are roaming, his fingers gently caressing my skin, over my back, and my thighs. His mouth keeps working, and then his hand is there, at the apex of my thighs. One stroke tells him all he needs to know. He kisses my sternum, then lifts me to straddle him. I grin at him, and then he is sliding us back with a splash!

Water careens over the sides and drenches the floor.

"Jace!" There is nothing elegant about our fall. We look like a pair of massacred mannequins, limbs all tangled and distorted. His big chest vibrates as he laughs deeply. "Mood killer." I pout.

"You're always in the mood, you nymphomaniac," he scoffs, tweaking my nipple.

"Ouch, and I am not! You are. You've always got a boner."

"Boner!" He throws his head back with a loud laugh.

"What?" I gawp. "What's so funny?"

"Oh, come on, Lil. You can do better than that." I scrunch my face up. Do better how? What does he mean? Jace is sprawled in his big bath, watching me intently. He bites his lip, and I feel the atmosphere shift. I squirm in his lap, and his eyes twinkle mischievously. "Talk dirty to me," he whispers. I watch him and see the way his eyes bloom at the thought. He chews his lip and runs a thumb over my cheek when it stains red. "Tell me what kind of things go through that mind of yours—what do you want me to do to you?"

Oh, god. I've never vocalised my desires to anyone, let alone someone who would more than happily bring them to life. My breathing shallows and I flick shy eyes up to him. He smiles softly.

"Tell me, Lily, what does your beautiful body need from me?"

"Touch me," I murmur.

"Where?" He moves me so I'm straddling him; his neck is relaxed over the edge, and I'm sitting with the cool air dancing over my bare skin.

I trail my finger down my chest, over my breast, and my lips press together, but he is still waiting. He wants words.

"Here," I tell him. His hand lifts, and he rolls his thumb over and over the hard nub. "Yes." I shift on his lap, but he keeps me still.

"Where else?" My eyes blink up to his, which are rich like fresh dark honey. My shaky finger moves down, right down to my sex. I'm panting.

"Here, I need you to touch me here," I tell him quietly. His stomach clenches, and he moves to accommodate my needs.

His fingers stop exactly where mine were. "Here?" He's still not right there. I want him there—inside me.

"Lower." I shift my stance, giving him more access.

"You've got to show me. Where do you want me?"

My eyes flash. He wants me to touch myself. I swallow. I can do this—of course I can. I love this man. I trust him.

I move my fingers back and skim them over his. He lifts his head as my fingers slip over my sex. I bite my lip and watch him, watching me, watching right there. I press further, and my fingers slide in. A light gasp leaves my mouth, and he pushes my fingers in deeper.

"Fuck, Lily, fuck yourself for me, beautiful." His eyes have taken on a shade so dark that I can't see where his irises start and end.

"Oh, Jace." I do as he asks, massaging myself for him. My hips jolt, and he groans loudly.

"Come on, baby." He plucks at my nipple, and I gasp loudly. My hips move, and I work my fingers in and out. Heat rolls over my skin and my head lolls back. Oh, god, I'm close. "You look so hot, Lily. Give me those fingers." He growls. I'm too close to give up now, so I rub faster on a whimper. "Now!" He snatches my hand away and shoves my fingers in his mouth.

"Please?"

"Please what—what do you want?"

"Your fingers. I want to ride your fingers." I take his hand and wait for him to position them before I wriggle and lower myself down. I feel electric, needy, and alive. His thumb joins the assault, and I splinter, crying out and dropping forwards. My mouth collides with his. "Fuck me," I beg.

Jace manoeuvres us and pulls me down harshly. I latch my mouth to his as he sinks deeper.

"Oh, yes." I'm panting and moving my hips slamming down with every chance I get. "Harder, god, fuck me hard."

"I can't. This fucking bath isn't big enough." He growls and swings us both up and out. Most of the water

Betrayal

has disappeared down the small drain in the floor, and Jace propels us to the bedroom. We don't get far before he spins us and presses me into the wall, lining himself up and thrusting deep. I bite his shoulder hard as each pound shakes me to my core.

"My god, you're dripping," he growls as he kisses me roughly. I whimper and moan as he slips out and walks us to the armchair in the corner. "Turn around!" he barks.

My shaky limbs just about hold me up as I'm thrust forward so I can grip the arms of the chair, then he is there, yanking my hips and roughly pushing in. He stalls, and I knock my arse backwards to gain friction.

"Jace!"

"What do you need?"

"Hard. God, so hard. Make me come." I quiver. Jace hammers away until I'm screaming out and doesn't stop until he roars out his own climax. I'm shaken and lax, and Jace is sprawled over my back—my face pressed into the seat of the chair.

"You're incredible." He presses a kiss to my shoulder, his big chest moving quickly against our sticky skin. "Come on." He lifts me gently, and we slip into bed. I wrap myself around him and sigh. I couldn't be any happier right now.

After a long day's work, I'm ready to get out of here. Carl sends me a text letting me know he is outside. With my car in the garage, it's the perfect solution. I'm in sensible hands, and I have a lift home. In fact, I'm thoroughly looking forward to our little dinner date.

I've made an appointment at the police station to

follow up Adam's restraining order, and that I think he's been following me, and any anxiety I had over it, Grant helped disperse when he put me through a gruelling workout last night.

Despite all this looming in the background, I focus on the good—on Jace and moving this forward. I have evaded further questions to move in and tried to keep things with us ticking along. He needs to open up more if he wants me to even consider talking about sharing a home because each little snippet he offers just reminds me I don't know him much at all. It serves as another reminder that I, too, need to share my troubled past with him.

My phone pings again, another message from Carl telling me to hurry up. I roll my eyes and toss the paperwork I have to hand in the filing cabinet, locking it and dropping the key in my desk. My phone starts ringing as I'm scooping my bags up and dragging my coat on.

"You are so impatient." I laugh, clutching my phone to my ear with my shoulder.

"Yes, well, I need some fizz. Get your tiny heinie out here!" he huffs, childlike, down the line.

"I'm coming," I coax, turning the lights off and pulling the door shut. I'm juggling my keys, phone, and bag, all while listening to Carl whine about the disadvantages being presented to his liver. I don't see his car but notice a set of headlights just up the road, flaring up the darkened street.

"You up on the left?" I say with my hand stuck on the key in the door—damn thing won't lock.

"*You selfish bitch!*" The animalistic roar has me snapping around. Adam is powering towards me, his footsteps echoing as he runs full pelt at me. "*You don't get to be happy!*" The hate in his voice manages to spike through

Betrayal

my petrified state. "*You ruined everything!*" he snarls before his fist slams straight into my jaw. The power knocks me back, slamming me into the window as pain shoots across my face. I cry out, and my phone flies out of my grasp and smashes against the concrete.

I stumble back, desperate to get away. Somehow, through the soul-shaking fear, instinct takes over, and I bring my fist up and crack him in the face, my small knuckles retracting against his hard cheek. Something snaps in my finger, and I yelp. Adam looks momentarily shocked, but his face contorts into an icy rage, and my cry for help gets tangled up in Adam's angry shout.

It's deafening and has me cowering away.

"YOU BITCH!" His face shakes—his gaunt skin blots red. He looks utterly terrifying.

I catch a blurred movement, then something heavy hits my head. The sound echoes through my skull in a sickening crunch. Pain splinters outwards in a sharp, furious wave, and I'm falling back.

―――

The pained whisper seeps into my mind.

"No, I've never seen him before." It's followed by a deep sigh and a sniff. "I thought he was going to kill her."

Someone growls, and it's oddly comforting.

"You said he told her she doesn't get to be happy?"

"Yes, that she is selfish, and she ruined something." A weak sob echoes through my tender head. "Jace, I'm sorry. I could hear *everything* through my in-car speaker. I don't think I will ever forget that sound—" Every word sounds like I am listening to a recording on playback, through tiny earbuds with no speaker attached.

"Why isn't Cass answering?" The mention of my friend's name starts to kick my brain into first gear. Jace, I recognise his voice. It's full of anger. Worry. "Where is the nurse; why isn't she awake?"

"They said it's okay for her to sleep." That sounds like Carl.

"I need to see her," he snaps. "Fuck." I lay for a minute in my surreal state, and for some reason, Adam's face flashes in my mind!

I wince, and someone takes my hand.

"Baby? Look at me, are you okay?" His rushed whisper, so full of concern, makes me worry.

"She's sleeping. Let her rest," someone soothes.

"I need to see her eyes!" His voice is full of such panic, and he sighs, irritated and defeated. "You don't get it," he grates out, and pressure wraps around my palm.

"Jace, I get it. Calm down. She is okay." They aim to placate, but it's no use.

"Is she fuck!" The deep growl has me twisting away in pain, my head feeling every vibration of each deep syllable. "Lily, baby. It's Jace." Gentle hands take my chin with such delicacy that gingerly, I open my eyes. The lights feel like shards of glass, and I snatch my eyes shut. "Lily, let me see you. Come on, baby, look at me," he whispers, soft lips dancing over my hairline. I do as commanded, blinking against the bright lights.

Everything seems blurry around the edges for a minute, but I lock on to the intense ambers roaming over my face in worry. His face is pulled into a deep frown. When I finally focus on him, he sighs—his lips brush my mouth, and I wince.

"Sorry," he murmurs and moves his kisses a little further right. My whole face aches, and my head is pounding as though all the blood has rushed there and the pressure is about to make it pop!

"My head," I croak. I lift my hand, but I feel weak, so I drop it back down, wincing once more.

"Baby, you're in the hospital." My eyes whip to his. Hospital—but? I blink away, trying to catch up with my racing brain. Another image of Adam flashes in my mind, and my lip wobbles. "Shush . . . " I can't. A sob burns up my throat, chased by a stomach full of vomit.

"Shit! Carl, quick pass me that bowl." Jace thrusts it under my face as he pushes me up so I'm sitting. I heave until I'm dry retching—until Adam's hateful, soulless eyes eat at any strength I have, and everything rushes back on a torturous wave of painful memories—distorted but lucid.

I sob gently as all my fears and worries break to the surface.

Only it isn't just vivid images of him outside the gallery. It's also him at my flat. I scrunch my eyes tightly, trying to deflect the image, but it stalks towards me like Adam did.

My lip bloody—my shoulder hunched over, protecting already-broken ribs and my stomach.

'Please, stop,' I beg, holding a hand up. My finger is at an odd angle, but all I can think is I need to protect my stomach. 'Stop,' I cry softly, sucking back another sob as I shake, my shoulders jerking with each painful inhale.

He bashes into the doorframe, and his eyes manage to latch onto me through the haze of alcohol.

'Fucking bitch,' he spits, but it's mangled with grief. He truly believes I have betrayed him. Guilt at my lack of love for him reduces me to silent sobs.

'Adam, please.' His eyes soften, and I back into the corner of the kitchen, watching him warily. 'I'm sorry,' I whisper, 'stop now . . .' I request softly on a broken plea. His dark eyes roam over me, and his head drops, but he keeps walking towards me, and I brace myself against whatever else is to come. He wraps an arm around my neck, pulling me in for a kiss, and I let him, praying this is the end.

A heavy fist slams up into my stomach, my lungs exhaling in sharp pain.

'No!' I wheeze, dropping to the floor. My breath is no longer in my body, and a heavy boot slams into my stomach, again and again until I'm writhing in pain.

Tears rush down my face, blinding me as they mix with my makeup.

"Jesus, Lily, breathe. Just breathe." Jace pulls back, and I look around in shock, realising I'm not at home. I jolt back and scramble away as I look around for Adam, but he's not here. Carl is staring at me in complete disbelief.

"I'm getting a nurse," he says hurriedly, rushing out the room. I'm gasping for air, wheezing as it comes in and out too quickly, too much. My chest burns and my eyes blot a little. I'm still crying, and the mascara-laced tears irritate my eyes so much that I blink rapidly. My breathing hits a level that I can't control.

"Baby, calm down, shush, you're safe. I'm here." I push back against the bed, gasping for air as a nurse rushes in with another at her heel.

"Get back, please." She ushers Jace out of the way.

"You must be kidding!" He laughs, pulling me closer. I claw at the bed as a machine begins to beep wildly.

"Miss, you need to calm your breathing . . ."

Betrayal

Multiple hands take mine but only feel like an added restraint. "Miss, I need you to relax." I can't. I can't breathe.

"Jace!" Carl snaps, and I gasp, my mouth opening and shutting like a stranded fish.

I can't breathe. *I can't.*

"Do something!" Jace roars. They ignore him, and one begins pulling liquid from a vial into a syringe. My visions blots and I go to scream, but any oxygen is drowning in my lungs, and my legs kick out in panic.

"I'm going to give you a sedative, Miss Spencer." I shake my head, moving away from them all. The sheets are moved back, and I look on in sheer panic. Carl has his hand plastered to his mouth, eyes wet with tears. It's as if my mind is holding on to every last detail, sucking it in, remembering it all, just in case it's my last image.

I gasp, short, painful pants, trying to breathe. Jace enters my blurring vision and cups my face; his mouth pulled down in heartache.

"Baby, I'm here. I love you—take little breaths," he says gently. I fix my stare on his face and sob a little. I love him too. But I feel like I'm going to die.

A sharp sting hits my hip. Wincing, I latch onto Jace, trying to tell him I love him. My eyes are wide with fear.

"I know, baby, I know," he says, dotting kisses over my face.

Chapter Eight

"She could have died!" I mentally flinch at the harsh words, my mind aching to get back to consciousness to defend myself and leave this nightmare, but I don't know how because I feel like I'm swimming in a slumberous void.

"I'm angry too. Jesus, had I known she hadn't gone to the police, I would have!" Cass's equally fierce voice breaks through my coma-like state.

"So he's broken the order, now what?"

"I don't know. I mean, she should have reported him being at the club. He knew it was her birthday, so he actively sought her out." Cass's voice feels like a sharp nail to my tender mind.

"Any other times?" Flashes of Adam float back and forth across my mind. My subconscious skips forward and offers up the information, even though I can't speak myself.

"She hasn't said so," Cass murmurs.

"But you think so?" Jace's question is uttered through what I imagine are gritted teeth.

"It seems likely, given he just attacked her." Her voice is scathing, and I will her to go easy on him. I don't know why because I'm dreading facing Jace's wrath when I'm less vacant.

A deep sigh halts their conversation.

"Fuck, I actually asked if she was pregnant the other week."

"Is she?" Cass seems both hopeful and concerned,

"No," he grumbles.

"You sound sad about that," Cass remarks. The bed dips, and my hand is taken. I attempt to grip back but can tell I haven't moved.

"Not now, Cass. I just want my girl back." There is a reprieve of silence, and the constant heavy thud in my brain lulls to a deep ache. "Did she suffer from nightmares at all?" His voice is gruff, tired, and I want to curl into him.

"Yes, why?" I mentally scream at Cass for opening her big mouth to him, but I can't do anything in this forced state of slumber.

A long, drawn-out sigh pulls at my guilt.

"She had one the other night; wouldn't talk about it, and I didn't want to push her." He curses. "Fuck, I should have. I knew something wasn't right."

"Jace, this isn't your fault. After everything he has done to her, do you really believe you talking to her would have stopped him from getting to her?"

"Yes. No. I don't know. She needs to wake up," he grumbles sadly.

I wake slowly, my eyes peeling back to find a row of worried faces. All four people rush towards me at once, but Jace makes it to me first, and soft lips brush my dry ones.

"Hey, beautiful," he croaks.

I open my mouth to reply, but a sharp sting attacks my lips. Lifting my fingers to my lips, I tentatively touch the sore area.

"You and I have got a lot of talking to do." It's a warning, spoken gently, but he is as serious as a disease. I eye him cautiously. Cass moves around the bed, and her face crumbles.

"I'm so mad at you," she sobs, wrapping her arms around me. Sean, Cass's boyfriend, winks at me, and I see Carl looking completely shattered at the end of the bed. Come to think of it, Jace looks exhausted too. I roll my eyes over him, seeing dark shadows under his eyes and a pale tinge under his usually drool-worthy tan. His ambers have lost that sparkle I love, and instead, they look murky and flat.

I sit still and take a mental inventory of the damage to my own body. I've felt pain before, bone-cracking, heart-breaking pain. This isn't like that.

I'm in pain. But it's mainly to my face—a dull, nauseating headache, throbbing to my mouth, and achy body. I do feel okay. Physically, I'm going to be okay.

"Water," I whisper before clearing my throat and avoiding the questioning glances. Carl whips off to find me a drink and Cass steps back to lean into Sean.

I could do with some painkillers, but I don't say that. The concerned and accusing looks have me holding my tongue. Carl follows a nurse, who comes over, clucking at me. She is a busty woman, and Sean's eyes widen when she walks in tits first, the rest of her eventually following. Cass slaps his arm, and I somehow manage a smile.

"How are you feeling, dear?" I eye the people around me and drop my gaze. "Never mind them, do you want something for the pain?" Her years of training have weighed me up in seconds.

"Please," I whisper. Jace growls, and I look at my fingers, knotted in my lap. I only then notice the tubing sticking out the back of my hand and the neat splint on my finger.

"The doctor will come round to speak with you shortly." She moves the drip aside and begins injecting an intravenous. My relief is almost instant. The drug soars through my bloodstream, and I relax back in the bed, nodding at her. She gives me a soft smile and eyes the big man bristling next to my bed.

Carl pours me a small glass of water, and I lift it shakily to my dry mouth. Cursing, Jace takes the glass and holds my chin, lifting the water and easing sips into my mouth. My eyes find his and he doesn't hold back the hurt swirling in the whiskey depths. I mentally shrink away and pull my head back when I've had enough. Jace plants his thick thigh on the bed and looks at me as though he has the world on his shoulder.

"Can you give us a few minutes?" he says over his shoulder, not making eye contact with them or me. Cass opens her mouth, but Sean pulls her back, and Carl gives me a sympathetic wince.

I'm in big, shitty trouble. I frown down at my hands and wait for him to speak.

"So your ex is a psycho—" he states, as his fingers move and tangle with mine. I stare at them but can't bring myself to raise my gaze. I feel an accusation ring in his voice and know from seeing the look of anger and sympathy that he is judging me for my lousy choice in men. His own pain is flickering there too. He is hurt that I never confided in him.

"He is sick," I say unevenly. I try to tug my hand away so I can twist it in my other. I know what Adam is, but there is a tinge of shame in me, and it's wormed its way so deep, riddling my mind with humiliation at having dated someone like that.

Jace's laugh is short.

"Don't defend the bastard." I drag my eyes up from my down-turned head and see the look of utter disbelief on his face. I want to tell him I'm not protecting Adam—I'm defending myself, but he has furious ambers pointed at me. "He," – he struggles over the words – "you miscarried," he stutters. "How can you defend him?"

"I'm not. I was there," I murmur, doesn't he understand I don't want to talk about Adam.

"Don't push me away, Lily." He moves up the bed and lifts me to him, kissing me gently. I wince at the sting on my lip, and he sighs. "I hate that I can't kiss you." His thumb glides with such softness over the sore part that I barely feel it. "I fucking hate that sick bastard," he spits. The mention of Adam has me stiffening.

"I just want to forget it happened." My sigh holds months' worth of inner exhaustion over the whole situation.

Jace shakes his head.

"I can't." He runs a hand over his face and clenches his fist so tightly all the colour drains. "Why didn't you report him to the police?" The look on his face says everything, but he holds back what he truly wants to say.

That I could have avoided this.

What can I say? He is right. I have been so caught up with work, and him, that I let it slide. It's feeble and irresponsible. I put myself at risk and others in danger; my lip wobbles, but I manage to make my tears subside.

He clears his throat.

"Has he contacted you at all?" His voice is tight, and I can see by the set of his face he already knows the answer, but it doesn't make it any easier to deliver.

"Yes. I have an appointment booked at the station to report him," I admit feebly.

His head snaps back like I've slapped him.

"Fucking hell, Lily," he chokes out, and I flinch in the bed, my head ringing like a church bell and guilt racking me into momentary silence. "When?" he demands.

"My birthday and the day you picked me up for lunch," I say hesitantly, my voice a scratchy whisper.

"Which lunch?" he huffs.

"Does it matter?" I wobble over the words, looking at him with sad eyes.

"What, he rang The Loft?" He is impatient for information.

"No, he beeped his horn when we went to the car," I whisper, remembering the look on Adam's face when he saw me with another man. Jace's eyes flare with recognition, then they narrow in concentration as he puts two and two together: my pale complexion that day, the sudden quietness. He nods, accepting the information.

"And that's it?" he clarifies. My eyes widen, and instantly he stands from the bed. "Are you fucking kidding me? How could you keep all this from me?" He rubs a hand over his neck, and I pull my legs up, watching him try to hold himself together. His self-control is slipping, and I feel helpless in the hospital bed.

"When?" he chokes.

"He came to the gallery the day I visited Paco. I

Betrayal

wasn't there. Harriet spoke to him. Also, I had a prank type call—no one spoke, but I could hear someone." His jaw works, but I quietly go on, "I . . . I had an email in my junk mail. I haven't opened it. I think both were him."

"When?"

"I . . . it was . . . erm," I stutter, unsure what day it is. I know uttering those words is going to have Jace tipping over the edge. "What day is it?"

"Early hours of Thursday," he enlightens me in a deep growl. I've kept him in the dark. Refused him access to the most vulnerable part of me. I should have shared, opened up—that's what relationships are about, right?

"Yesterday, no Tuesday," I admit. "I think he was outside the gallery the other day. I can't be sure of that though." He drops down into the chair, and his head falls into his hands. Cass walks back in and looks at us both.

"Everything okay?" she asks carefully. My lip jitters and I drop my gaze away.

"Has Carl managed to get her phone working yet?" My man wants to know.

"Yes, it's pretty banged up though," Cass informs us both. I nod and look up through watery lashes as Jace stands. I'm surprised he hasn't hunted it down before now.

Cass slides in and walks to me, looking back as Jace storms out.

"He's pretty cut up," she says, stating the obvious. I'm trying to hold back the onset of heavy tears. "I had to tell him. I'm sorry." I just shrug and drop back into my pillow and close my eyes.

"I want this to end," I say tiredly. I yawn, and Cass

climbs on the bed and snuggles into my side. I can't help it then, the tears leak through my lashes, hot, wet paths running down my face.

"Oh, hun, it's okay." Cass presses a kiss to my cheek.

"I feel exhausted," I sniff.

"You had a panic attack," she tells me. I frown into her hair, not recalling it but vaguely registering the lingering threat of sheer panic. I drop my tender head on her shoulder. "You need lots of rest," she tells me, her usually chirpy voice full of concern.

"What time is it?" I whisper, wishing it were Jace who was offering this level of concern.

"Coming up to eight." She yawns, and I wrap myself into her side and close my eyes. "I'll stay until you have gone to sleep." Her own voice is soft and sleepy.

"I'm sorry." My whisper is weak and full of hurt. After half an hour or so, a shaft of light pulls at the door, and a doctor strolls in, Jace right on his heel. The doctor gives Cass a warning look, and she slips off the bed, walking backward and giving me a dramatic eye roll. My lips twitch until pain radiates. I don't even want to ask what I look like.

"I'm Doctor Matterson," he introduces himself, collecting up my paperwork as he makes his way up the bed to me.

"Hello." My voice is far more assertive than I feel. I want to go home. I sit up, trying to seem alert and put together, but I struggle.

"How are you feeling?" he asks, looking at the paper and not me.

"My head still hurts, but the pain relief is helping." He nods and starts checking my vitals.

"Looks good," he says to himself, "any pain elsewhere?" My ribs hurt a bit, but I keep quiet.

Betrayal

I hold up the finger that is strapped securely. I know it's broken.

"I feel like I got hit in the face with a bat." I laugh it off, but Jace swings a set of disbelieving eyes at me, and I shrink into the bed. Apparently it's too soon for jokes.

"Yes, there is a fair bit of bruising coming out now. Your cut is minor, but the mouth is a sensitive area, so it probably feels worse than it is," he states, looking into my eyes and inspecting my head. His fingers graze over the achy area, the touch making it feel twice as sore. "These stitches are dissolvable," he informs me.

Stitches?

"Oh, will I have a scar?" I throw concerned eyes to Cass, lifting my hand to feel the area, but the doctor kindly knocks my hand away.

"It's in the hairline, easily disguised." His smile is genuine, fatherly. "Everything is looking good. I'm happy with your progress, and there is no reason why you can't be discharged within the next forty-eight hours. Should you experience a setback—" I frown at him, his hands are crossed at his stomach, paperwork held fast as he pivots on his heels a little, "—anxiety," he reminds me, making me flush, "your doctor can prescribe something to help."

He eyes me, waiting for a response. I nod, and he smiles happily.

"You have a good bump to your head, and I would like you to stay another night just for observation." I try to mentally calculate what he is saying, given that Jace said it's Thursday. So, home on Saturday? I'm frowning. "It is normal to have side effects with a mild concussion," he tells me. His pager beeps, and he checks his watch and pockets his pen in his chest. "I'll get the nurse to come and speak with you."

"What sort of side effects?" Jace asks, worry back in his tone.

"The nurse will be in to talk to you before Miss Spencer is discharged." He smiles. "If you're happy to take pain relief orally, I will ask someone to come and remove your cannula," he says, placing my paperwork at the end of the bed.

I nod.

"Thank you," I whisper.

As predicted by the consultant, I'm discharged on Saturday. Jace is almost carrying me out to his car.

"I can walk, you know," I mutter as he hurries me along, seeing his face set in a scowl and his eyes focused forwards.

"Don't test me, Lily," he warns, "besides, I like holding you." I look away, flushing when people walk past, eyeing us as I'm being escorted like a member of the royal family to the car park.

He deposits me by his sleek car and helps me in.

"I called the police," he informs me from above the car door, "they will be coming by sometime in the next few days to take a statement." His amber eyes drill holes into me, daring me to argue.

I give him an accommodating smile, and he shuts the door, closing me safely inside the car. I watch him stomp around the bonnet, and when he gets in, his lips are held in a straight line, and his face is pinched tightly.

He starts the car up and grips the wheel, his hands flexing as he stares ahead. He opens his mouth but then clamps it shut. He is struggling with this, and I feel terrible. Wordlessly, I climb over, moving his arm away to

Betrayal

straddle his lap. Sad eyes lift to mine, and my heart aches for him.

"I'm sorry," I whisper. Jace drops his head away on a sigh, caught between wanting to love me and murder me all at once. I lift his prickly chin and press my mouth to his, careful not to hurt myself. I peck at his mouth, and he lets me, but to my annoyance, he stays still. His lips remain unresponsive and cause a deep ache in my chest. Softly, I dip my tongue out and try to chip away his anger. "Kiss me," I plead, dotting another kiss to his mouth, and when bottomless amber pools find my eyes, I swallow a ball of painful tears.

He frowns at me, his usually relaxed and beautiful face fixed into a scowl.

"Why didn't you tell me?" he spits on a dry whisper. "I don't understand how you could hide something like this—you knew you were in danger."

I sit frozen still on his lap as this big, confident man cracks in front of me.

I go to move, but Jace grips my hips, holding me still. He looks at me, really looks at me, and my heart breaks a little seeing how much I have truly hurt him. By withholding the truth, he doesn't think I trust him.

When he speaks, his voice holds so much emotion, and it's all rolled into one pained whisper.

"Don't ever, and I mean ever," – he sucks in a breath and stares at me, really punching home his meaning "keep anything from me again. I thought he'd killed you."

I nod shakily, my sniffs of emotion not lost on him, but ignored all the same.

"I'm sorry," I croak. He cups my neck and pulls me down to his mouth.

I can't help but cry. I feel a wreck. His kiss is gentle

but deep. It hurts my mouth, but I ignore the sting and fold into him on a sob.

"I love you, Lily, but we're supposed to be in this together. A couple." He breathes against my mouth. Those words—the ones I have been so desperate to hear, slip by, and I don't feel I deserve them. Jace's tongue rolls over mine in a deep groan, and I squirm in his lap. He laughs scathingly. "And that's a no," he grunts, lifting me back into my seat, "sex is off the cards for a while."

"What!" I whine. "Why?"

He throws me a pointed and irritated look.

"I'm not touching you when you're this fragile," he scoffs at me, implying I'm stupid for thinking otherwise.

"I can still have sex!" I tell him, finding his thought process abhorrent.

"I'm sure as shit not giving it to you, and you can get fucked if you think I'll let another man touch you," he laughs shortly.

"How can I get fucked, if you and other men are—"

"Lily!" he snaps quietly, his hands gripping so tightly I fear the steering wheel will snap. Okay, no more joke attempts.

"Sorry." I clip my belt in and keep my mouth shut. Jace sighs and rubs a hand down his exhausted face. He pulls out of the parking space, and we are quickly driving through the city and towards the outskirts. Despite how tired we are and the convenience of my place, he still favours his house.

"Cass is going to bring you some things round." I have no personal items with me, my phone has been confiscated, well, at least, I assume so, and my handbag is gone. I don't ask where any of it is.

We fall into silence, and I watch the world drift away

Betrayal

as we head out of the city. It's at least forty minutes before we arrive at Jace's, and when we do, I'm nodding off.

He reaches over the console and coaxes me awake, gently brushing hair from my face.

"Lily? Wake up."

I blink across at him, sitting up slowly.

"Let me get your door," he says, exiting the car and walking around to me. When he closes the door and swings me up in his arms, I wordlessly allow him, although the quick motion makes my head swim, but I say nothing and rest my head on his shoulder, letting it pass. The doctor sent us home with pain relief and some information that Jace has folded neatly into his pocket.

Once inside, Jace walks us to his bedroom and rests me on the end of the bed. He leans over and pulls the quilt back, then drops down to take my ankle boots off, which get discarded to one side quickly. Leaning in, he takes the hem of my top, pulling it free from where I tucked it into my skirt. I lift my arms so he can pull it over my body, and deft fingers move round to my back so he can unclip my bra; easing it free, he drops it on the floor before he deals with the rest of my clothes. He rests a hand on my shoulder and gently pushes me back so I'm lying down. Air rushes out of my mouth, and I stare up at the intricate ceiling. He taps my hip, and I lift so he can pull my skirt down, then my knickers disappear.

"In you get," he instructs, holding the corner of the quilt up so I can slip underneath. I eye him suspiciously, but he looks back at me blankly. The cool sheets cause goosebumps to tidal wave along my skin. I rest back and watch as he tucks me in, but when he makes no demonstration to join me, I sit up.

"Aren't you joining me?" I ask, fearing I already know the answer.

"I have work to catch up on," he delivers, already walking away. I want to call him back, but don't. I know he is still struggling to process the last few days.

I swallow the 'I love you' rushing up my throat.

Chapter Nine

I've been awake for the last few minutes, but the comfort of Jace's bed has me staying put—that and the steady ache working its way through my skull. I can hear voices but can't make out any owners, other than Jace's anyway. The deep rumble is an auditory comfort.

Gingerly, I sit up, aware that the remnants of another nightmare are still plaguing my heart rate, and slowly, I push the quilt away. The cool air reminds me I'm naked, so using the throw to wrap myself up in, I tiptoe to the bathroom. Multiple sets of eyes swing my way from the sofas in the sprawling lounge—a lounge that now feels less inviting by each passing second. Why is she here?

"Lily." Jace is up and walking towards me with purpose. I dip my gaze and quietly go into the bathroom, dropping the throw and plopping down on the toilet. My mouth feels tight, and my fingers throb. He waltzes in. "Do you want a drink?" he says, leaning against the sink. I nod, and he turns away as soon as our eyes meet.

"Jace," I croak. My fingers naturally lift to rub at my mouth, and I watch as he slowly looks back at me. "I love you too." My lip wobbles over the whisper, and he swallows what I assume is a ball of emotion.

"I know. I just wish you had told me about Adam. I'm going to get you some water." He sighs. Is that it? No kiss, not even a hug?

I've really upset him. Busying myself by washing my hands, I wipe the tears away and try to lock my emotions up. I didn't know how to tell him. I still don't. I had only just felt able to breathe fully again from the constant knife-deep ache of loss when Jace ploughed into my life, dragging me to his bed and churning up all kinds of emotions I had never wanted to feel. I stare at my hands in the sink, coming to the painful realisation that I have felt so guilty for being happy—happy without the life that was ruthlessly taken from me. Adam doesn't just represent fear. He is the reason for my biggest loss: my baby.

I do want to be happy with Jace. When he returns, he silently hands me a pair of my pyjama shorts and a camisole. I smile softly at him, but his mouth is turned down.

I hate it. Hate the physical and emotional distance between us.

"How are you feeling?"

"Sore."

Jace lifts the camisole, and I weakly raise my arms to allow him to cover my top half. He points to the water, saying, "You need to keep hydrated." He looks so forlorn.

For the first time, I inspect my reflection. My face looks gaunt and pale, dark circles ring my eyes, and the neat but sore cut running along my hairline is longer than I thought. Precise stitches hook their way in and out of my skin, pulling the wound tight. My lip is swollen and bruised, and dark blood knots the skin in place. Slowly, I lift my fingers to test how painful it is, jumping when I hear him tut behind me.

Dropping my hand, I begin to slip my clothes on. I have to sit back down to pull the bottoms up. My body aches from the fall, but I ignore the stiffness of my limbs and force myself into the clothes.

"You're in pain," he states. I flick a look his way and respond with a simple shrug. My hair is a bloody mess, but I can't do much with it, so I twist it and let it drop down one side. "Your painkillers are by the bed," he tells me. Why is he being so distant?

Jace has laid out a jumper, so I slip it on and zip it up. I pick up the painkillers and swallow them quickly. The water hits my empty stomach, and I force a swallow to keep it from coming back up. I need something to eat. For the first time in a long time, I feel like I need my mum.

Closing my eyes, I lift my head and force my tears at bay.

The voices are louder now as I head towards them. Viktor, and a lady, I'm assuming is his wife, are sitting on the sofa, Neve opposite them. My eyes flash to Jace's, but he looks away with awkwardness pinching at his dark expression. There is no reason for her to be here, and he knows that.

Viktor stands and gives me a soft smile.

"Hello, lovey." He comes straight to me and wraps a loving arm around me. I have the sudden urge to sink into his embrace and sob. The need for a parent's love is too raw, and with both mine being absent, I'm emotionally clinging for anything, especially since Jace isn't offering. Viktor must sense that because he squeezes me gently. My breath leaves in a shudder, and I wipe my tears away. "Come on, love," he murmurs, "nasty bit of trouble you got yourself into." I step back, wrapping my arm around my waist, pulling at every last shred of energy I have to get through this, as my eyes meet Jace's, and he looks guiltily at me. Shame engulfs me. They must all know, and I can't bear the details of my relationship with Adam filtering through their minds. Do they know what he did to me before—how he robbed me of my child all those months ago?

My baby. Gone. Beaten from my body. She was mine. I don't want to share her. I'm not ready to give her up for other people's judgement. And despite knowing Jace is struggling and needs the comfort of his family, I can't help feeling angry that he's divulged my private life to them—to Neve.

Clearing my throat, I focus on him.

"How are you?" I ask brightly. He barks out a laugh, and I hold mine in to save me feeling the sting of pain—the irony of the situation is not lost on me.

"Surely I should ask you that?"

I waft him away, studiously keeping my gaze from seeking out my angry partner and his needy friend.

"Bruises heal." I keep my voice flat, but my face flinches at the rush of disjointed memories Adam has left me with.

"Hmmm, but the mind is a little more difficult," he says softly. My eyes lift to his, and I manage a shrug of indifference. I look at the woman sat rubbing Jace's knee. She is petite and polished, at complete odds with Viktor's rough and big exterior.

"Lily, this is my wife, Marie, and you've met Neve." My eyes betray me and slip to hers. She is avoiding looking at me at all costs. I'd prefer it if she avoided me even more, and left.

Betrayal

"Yes. Hello, Marie." I give her a little wave, my hand barely lifting, and the other, secure in the pocket of Jace's hoody, protecting my broken fingers.

Marie's eyes soften, and she has no hesitation in standing and covering the distance, gentle arms enveloping me.

"It's lovely to meet you," she soothes, rubbing at my back.

"Even under these circumstances?" I offer a weary smirk, fighting for the Lily I know best to come back.

"Well," she hums, "it would be awfully boring if we had just met for a coffee."

I laugh lightly, feeling at ease with her already. Both Viktor and herself have calming presences, and I feel no judgement from them, so maybe Jace didn't tell them everything after all?

"Are you hungry, love?" She rubs my arms lightly.

"Starving," I admit, slotting my other hand into the pocket.

Neve, never one to miss an opportunity, is holding Jace's hand and rubbing his back supportively. I feel my eyes glue to their entwined fingers, and my gut rolls with anxiety. When I look up, Jace stares at me. I lift my brow, and he slips his hand free. With any luck, he will ask her to leave.

I avert my gaze and look to the lineup of cars. I want to go home. I feel so out of sorts here. And with Jace's constant lack of affection, I feel hugely unwelcome. I know he is hurt, but I was the one who was attacked. I need the support from him. Why can't he give me that?

I rub my neck, easing the ache in my throat, and follow Marie towards the kitchen. I slow as dizziness taunts me, keeping my gaze forward and on the stools until I reach my destination.

"Let's see what the boy has got in here for you."

I hold the side, steadying myself.

"An abundance of bacon and eggs," I joke. Marie clucks, but it's motherly and a little nostalgic, I realise when I see the small pull of a smile on her face.

She opens up the fridge and begins rummaging through the contents.

"I can do that," I tell her, taking some cheese out of her hands. "I need to keep busy." I swallow, mentally recognising I feel jittery and exhausted. I stifle a yawn, and she rubs my arm.

"Let me, pet. You look ready to fall." My reply gets caught on my tongue when Marie gives me a stern look. I take a space on the stool and watch her because it's the only thing holding me back from looking at Jace.

I feel his presence at my back before I see him. He steps into my eye-line, and I can't help but think how stunning he looks. Wordlessly, he lifts my face and checks my lip and head.

"Do you know what time it is?" His voice is soft, but accusation burns in his eyes. I shake my head and pull my chin free. I can understand his sense of betrayal at my desire to keep him in the dark about my past, but he is really starting to piss me off. "Nearly three in the afternoon, Lily." My eyes widen. I had no idea it was that late. I search for a clock to clarify—I have slept for hours. His sigh is full of frustration once more.

"Oh, leave her be," Marie scolds, "poor girl has been through enough without you weighing in on her." She gives him a pointed look—the look of a mother. I would laugh if I didn't think it would hurt.

"I thought two o'clock was your favourite time of the day?" My voice is quiet, soft, and I look up hopefully, offering him a smile, but he chews his lip and stares at the tight cut on my forehead. "I'm sorry I didn't tell you," I whisper. Is that why he is being distant?

"Yeah, I know."

Marie fusses over me, and places a sandwich by my side with a steaming brew.

"Here you go love," Her hand rubs along my back.

"Thank you." I tuck my hair behind my ear and start to nibble at my sandwich when the distinctive sound of my phone blares through the room. Jace steps back from me then pulls it from his trousers, answering it.

"Hi, yeah, she's awake, just eating something." I can hear Cass on the other end. "Let her eat. She will call you later." There is a huff as long as the Nile before he cuts the call.

I eye him and hold my hand out.

"Can I have my phone back, please?" I could have spoken to her. She's my bloody friend, and I'm well enough to converse and be subject to his family's involvement. I raise my brow, becoming increasingly pissed off with his attitude. He returns my phone to his jeans and walks to his office—a decision that draws a scoff from me. What the hell is his problem?

Silence falls, and I roll my eyes, shoving a bigger bite in my mouth now my stomach feels more settled. I stare ahead for a moment before I slide down from the chair and follow him.

"Maybe give him a minute," Neve bites and looks me up and down. I'm glad when Marie sees the hostility burning across at me. I want to tell her to shove her opinion up her skinny arse, but I choose to keep my face neutral and walk off, ignoring the wave of dizziness.

I find Jace braced against the window, his head hung, and my phone gripped in his hand. He must sense me or see my reflection because he speaks.

"He hit you when you were down." He shakes his head, and I watch as his shoulders rise on an unsteady breath. "Did you know that?"

"No, and I'd rather not know." My hands slip to cover my stomach. I feel strangely exposed, knowing this information, hearing his pain. The stark fact that he can convey it so deeply through the window knocks me off-kilter that much more.

"Carl recorded the call. I heard him beating you. He would have killed you, Lily, if Carl hadn't driven at him." The vivid image he puts in my mind is as unwanted as the ones I already have stored there.

"Why are you telling me this? I've been through enough." He looks back over his shoulder, looking remorseful. "Why are you being so distant?"

"Why would you keep this all to yourself? Why put yourself and everyone at risk?" he asks, his voice rising.

I shrug because I don't know why I did. I just wanted to close the door on Adam, and I honestly didn't think he was capable of something like this. Obviously, now I know different.

I manage to keep my emotions from overflowing.

"I didn't want to bring him into our relationship." It's a feeble excuse, even if it's true.

"But he brought himself in, anyway. Lily, you should have gone to the police. He was in violation of his order. This whole thing could have been prevented," he vents—his tone quiet but harsh. My phone is gripped, knuckle-white-tightly in his palm.

I blink at the severity of his tone.

"I know that. I told you I was going to see the police. I had closed the door on it. I didn't want to have to be swept into it again. He hurt me." My voice wavers over a lump of burning tears.

I just wanted to immerse myself in the paradise that is Jace.

"You're just passing the hurt along." He quietly seethes, still struggling with my dismal decisions.

"You're being unfair. I haven't intentionally set out to hurt anyone. I made a mistake. Why are you making this harder for me?" I urge him to see this from my point of view.

"I nearly lost you, Lily."

"But I'm fine."

"YOU ARE NOT FINE!" he cries. My head snaps back, rattling with pain, and my tired, grey eyes spring open in shock. I suddenly feel conscious of the guests we have just metres away, all very much in listening distance. I draw breath to say something, but it sticks in my throat because anything I say in response will only fuel this further. We're both too emotional to deal with it properly. "You nearly died. I nearly lost you. I could have lost you," he croaks out.

"But you didn't. I appreciate you need your family here, but I'd like to call Cass back," I say softly, hoping to steer us down a calmer path. I want the comfort of my friend's voice. I'm feeling pretty outnumbered with his family here.

"Not happening, Lily." His grunt is one of both irritation and tiredness.

"That's not your decision to make." I sound far less confident than I hoped. I'll be damned if he thinks I will just roll over and let him dictate everything.

"Did you finish your sandwich?" he counteracts. I tut and walk to him with the intention of retrieving my phone from his pocket. As soon as I'm at his feet, my small hands ram into his narrow pocket, but he grips my fist, fast seizing all control. My phone isn't the only hard object I can feel against my palm. My surprised eyes lift to his, but he bats me away, hissing lightly. "That would just complicate things further." It would, but the constant buzz of electric heat we stir up in each other is dining out on all this tension. My hand is slowly retracted and empty. No phone.

"You're being ridiculous," I mutter. Is he scared I will leave if I speak to Cass?

"Can we save the domestic for later?" He sighs, holding me fully accountable.

"I hadn't realised me being attacked warranted *you* to spark a domestic, but thanks for being so supportive." I hiss and snatch my phone back. "You're angry at me for not telling you about Adam. I get it. You've made yourself *very* clear, Jace." I give a sardonic laugh and his cheeks flush. "You're treating me like shit, and quite frankly, I'm exhausted, so we can either be the couple you profess we are, or I'm going home." I raise my brow, and he sucks in a deep breath. "I need your support, not this." I begin to well up.

"Lily," he sighs apologetically.

"Why is Neve here?" I ask quietly.

"She came to see if you were okay?"

"Really?" I tilt my head. "Funny. She hasn't once asked me," I point out, and with that, I leave him in the office. I would rather not have our little spat dissected by his family. Everyone has made themselves busy, but I know they have all been hanging off every word. Marie looks slightly uncomfortable as I return to the kitchen and finish up my meal. I'm not hungry, but out of politeness, I polish it off. I expect it to give me a burst of energy, but instead, I yawn as another wave of sleepiness hangs over me. Jace, who is watching my every move like a hawk, stands and heads my way.

Betrayal

I stiffen, assuming he is ready to get into further discussion, so when he pushes between my thighs, I'm surprised. I let him because it's been so long since I felt the security of him. My hands get placed on his shoulders, and he lifts me. I go without complaint because any physical contact until now has been scarce.

Deep down, I want to push him away for his callousness earlier, but my exhaustion wins, and I drop my head on his shoulder and twist my body around his, keeping me secure. I don't know what I expect, but when he walks us to his bedroom, I stiffen.

"What are you doing?" I go to lift my head, but it feels heavier than all my other limbs.

"You need to rest," he grumbles.

"But I just woke up." I laugh and flush when it turns to another yawn. He shrugs, and my small hands grip tight to his shoulders.

"Your body needs to heal." That amber gaze scans over my face with only one intention, getting to the other side without maintaining prolonged eye contact.

"I won't sleep later."

"That's fine." I sigh and huff as I'm put down.

"It's not. I have loads to catch up on at the gallery." He pulls the quilt up and levels me with a hard stare.

"If you are even considering going into work, I will drag you straight back to the hospital," he growls.

"But I'm fine." I flop back in a huge grump, knowing deep down my attempt at negotiating with him is futile.

"Fine, is going for a run and coming back *unharmed*, Lily. Seventy-two hours ago, you were wired up on a drip, so you can take your tablets and go to fucking sleep, you stubborn pain in my arse." It's said hotly, but the beginning of a twinkle in his eyes tells me he is happy to finally have me where he wants me, with him, in his home—even if it is under sufferance.

———

I sleep for a few more hours and wake late in the evening. The house is quiet, dark, and it takes me a few moments to finally find the strength to push off the mattress. Sitting on the edge for a minute or two, I take a moment to just gather myself. I feel woozy and a bit sick. Putting it down to my lethargy, I go to stand, but my shaky legs mock me, and I slump back down. The familiar sound of the pivoting door sounds and Jace is rushing in.

"What's wrong?" His face is etched in worry, a deep frown line cutting into his forehead. I'm gripping the quilt to steady myself.

"I just feel really lightheaded." My lip wobbles and I damn it to hell for making me seem weak.

"That's it, we're going back to the hospital," he declares, quickly dragging some of my things together.

Whoa! I don't want to go back.

"Jace, just relax. It's probably a symptom of the concussion." I frown lightly at his panicked state.

"The registrar gave me a slip—you can go back in," he declares with a sharp point of his hand. The motion firmly telling me in one harsh swipe that we are going back.

If my head didn't hurt so much, I would roll my eyes.

"I don't think I nee—"

"You've got a concussion. You don't know what you want!" he snaps. I turn my head away and rest back on the bed, my eyes widening mockingly at his abrupt manner.

Betrayal

"Maybe call them and ask for some advice?" I say wisely.

"No. Don't move," he grumbles, storming off. Jeez, what a stress head!

Jace adds his charger to the small holdall and, with a determined look, sweeps me up, making my already wishy-washy head spin more.

"Urgh," I groan.

"Shit, sorry."

I wrap myself into him and press my face into his neck, feeling shakier and more out of sorts by the second. I feel as though if he placed me on my feet, my body would teeter off to the left. It's a horrible sensation and one that has my lip trembling.

An hour later, I'm propped up and drowsy in a hospital bed, with Jace firmly planted in the chair, his feet wide, elbows on knees, and a jumpy leg showcasing his impatience and worry. My hand is caught up in his and locked against his lips, the constant rock of his leg nursing me off to sleep.

"It'll be fine," I mumble.

He scoffs in complete disagreement with me. The nurse who had taken my vitals and escorted me into bed after Jace had carried me in, causing far more worry than necessary, has made a quick escape, and Jace is on the warpath, demanding, snapping, and looking ready to explode. Now it's a waiting game.

Chapter Ten

I'm coaxed awake by worried hands and find both Jace and the same consultant from the other night, each by one side of the bed.

"Hello, Lily."

"Hi," I rasp, my sleepiness making me seem far worse than I probably am. Jace has begun a short pace, keeping him close but also busy enough that he doesn't react to the doctor's obvious calmness that is at total odds with his tornado worry.

He picks up my paperwork and rifles through, scanning the notes and making some of his own, before replacing the clipboard and walking back to me, bringing a small light out from his pocket. I brace myself for the blinding shaft of light in my pupil and blink fuzzily afterward.

"All looks okay. Vitals are normal. Can you tell me how you have been feeling?"

"Achy, I feel stiff and sore, headache, really tired." He nods and smiles down at me.

"All extremely normal side effects of a head trauma."

Just as I thought.

"She's dizzy," Jace throws in.

"Only a little," I add, ignoring the dark glare being shot my way. I see the warning there. "Very dizzy," I admit softly. Jace nods, and I smile over at him, hoping it will calm him down.

"How is your balance?" the doctor inquires. I shrug, Jace has carried me everywhere, so I don't actually know, and I say as much.

"Right, let's get you up." The doctor smiles, pulling the sheet back to help me out, and Jace draws a breath to say something but slaps his lips shut. Gingerly, I stand, but my achy bones won't allow for much else. With my system full of painkillers, I hadn't really acknowledged the level of soreness in my side, and when I draw breath, it pulls, and a dull pain waves along my ribs. I grip the bed and lift my top, finding the edges of a black and purple bruise. My eyes shoot open in horror and rush to find Jace's pained ones burning back at me. He drags his face away, unable to look at my marred skin any longer, grinding his teeth loudly to stop the torrent of anger bursting free.

It hits me then like a bolt of lightning that all of his anger isn't directed at me but Adam. He's only angry that I didn't confide in him. This man wants it all with me. My heart and soul, and I have made sure to lock him out.

Dropping my top, I look back to find the consultant waiting for me to leave the safety of the bed.

"Just to the other side of the ward—" He points with the light down to the nurse's station, and I suck in a breath, wincing at the ache in my side, and begin small steps away from him. The first half-metre is uneventful, so I widen my stride and pick up speed. Dizziness washes over me, and I wobble, feeling that invisible force pulling me to the left. I grip the nearest side to steady myself, but as quick as it came, the dizziness is gone. Jace is already halfway to me, cursing to high heaven, but the doctor asks that he leave me to make the journey back alone. I do it without any further problem and perch on the bed, searching out the consultant with my eyes, and not Jace.

"It's over as quick as it comes," I mumble. He nods and taps my paperwork with the pen tip.

"How regularly?" His pen is poised, ready to write my reply down.

"So far, it's after I have woken up."

"All the symptoms you are suffering are associated with the injury you have, but it may take a little longer to recover from some more than others. Plenty of rest, eat little and often if the wooziness is making you feel nauseous, and a stress-free environment." He angles his head Jace's way.

I nod, feeling silly for having wasted his time.

"So, another day in bed, then back to work?" I ask, hopefully. He shakes his head, laughing lightly.

"You have a stubborn one." He softens his earlier blow to Jace with a pointed remark about me, and Jace grunts and drops back into his seat.

"Doesn't she need a scan or anything?" He really isn't happy with this. I blanch at the thought and look back to the consultant, silently pleading with him to give me the all clear.

"No, we have ruled out a serious head injury, all vitals are good, and symptoms are to be expected." If he is irritated by Jace's constant argument, he doesn't show it.

"So, I can go home?" I question, rubbing at my sleepy eyes.

"Yes, remember, lots of rest. I would suggest sitting up for a short time before you try to walk after napping. What is it you do for a living?" he asks, scribbling something down quickly.

"I own a gallery," I say, picking at the fluff on my top—a gallery that needs my attention. I have no Harriet, and now I'm down. It couldn't get any worse!

"I suspect the dizziness will last a few days, but it could stick around for a week or two. As soon as you feel better, then you can resume working. Just take it slowly and let your body heal." I nod absently; my mind caught up on a different matter. No work?

It's late when we finally make it back to Jace's, and he demands I stay put until he has unloaded the car, but I'm slipping free before he makes it back to me. When he grips my waist, I wince.

"Ouch!"

"Sorry." His hands slip away and take mine. I grip tightly and let him lead me inside.

I catch sight of my reflection, and my nose scrunches in disgust. "I feel grubby," I whine. My hair is glistening, and not because it is glossy—my face is pale and bruised. I look a bloody mess.

"You can't wash your hair," Jace mutters, taking the opportunity to slide my hair aside so he can inspect my cut.

"I'm going to run a bath," I tell him. His wide fingers cup my cheek, and he regards me thoughtfully. Honey-thick ambers slowly roll across my face, lingering on both bruises and dropping fully to my lips. His dense lashes are really noteworthy from this angle, and his chest expands on a deep draw of breath. I expect him to say something, but instead, he lifts his gaze, and goddammit, my heart, and stomach jump and crash together in excitement. He's going to kiss me.

I do a little mental wave of joy and wait silently for him to close the distance. With every second that he doesn't, the tension swirls and knots until it's almost unbreakable. I suck in a shuddery breath and close my eyes because the thick swallow I just witnessed is a sure sign that Jace is finally weakening and will drop his mouth to mine.

"Look at me, Lily," he whispers. My dazed lids slip open, and it takes all of my energy to force my foggy brain to comply. "You want me to kiss you," he states softly.

Yes!

I nod, and my neck jerks a little against the brace of his hands.

"Yes, please." My breathing is all choppy and short. I want that kiss more than I need my next breath.

"Promise me; the truth, always." A shaky thumb drags over my lip, careful as it skims my healing cut.

"Always," I vow softly.

"Always." His lips do that little smug twitch thing that I have come to love so much, and my eyes shine into his, and I know, given some time, we are going to be okay.

―――

I'm neck-deep in silky bubbles and swathed by a very aroused Jace. His thick arms circle my waist and keep me secure at his chest—my head is resting on his shoulder, and his full lips do a happy little jaunt down my jawline.

"Hmmm." I'm all slippery and content.

"We don't do this enough." His big chest vibrates beneath me. He's trying, but I can feel the tension locked in his chest.

"We did it last week." I laugh.

"See, not enough. There has been lots of sleep and naughtiness since then." His hands run down my arms, and he threads one through my uninjured hand. The other, fairly swollen still, is rested on the bath's edge, safe from the water.

"I'm not seeing much naughtiness as of late." I pout and make a cheeky roll of my hips. He grunts and grips my hip, stilling me.

"You're black and blue, plus if you pass out on me or throw up, I will be scarred for life." He tweaks my nipple, and I jerk under him with a little yelp.

"Your lack of desire is emotionally scarring me," I grumble, jabbing him with my elbow.

His hips thrust.

"Does that feel lacking to you?"

"Are you asking me or my vagina?" I thrust my nose in the air, and his deep laugh is as sexy as hell. I flip, sending water splashing over the edge in a mini tidal wave. My eyes widen, and my lips form a smile. He attacks my mouth, and I grin up at him, happy that he seems more relaxed and like his usual self again. I try to secure myself to him, but when I'm as slippery as I am, it's bloody difficult. He draws me up, and I take the opportunity to straddle him, rubbing myself shamelessly against him with a soft little purr. "Please," I whisper, nipping his ear and then his jaw. Stubble grazes my lip, and I purposely thrust my boobs in his face.

He curses me to next week and back, his erection knocking the back of my arse.

"Lily," he warns deeply. His palm glides up my chest

until it splays over my heart, a sweet gesture but a calculated one. I'm being kept at arm's length. I pout but let it fall away into a smile, trying a manipulation of my own.

"Is that a yes?" I roll my hips on a feminine moan and angle myself,

Jace halts my movements and readjusts himself.

"That's a no," he grumbles and tucks away a lock of hair that has managed to get wet. I slump into his body and mumble my disquiet. "Just this once, don't fight me, beautiful. Let me look after you." He pecks my nose.

"I think you're secretly happy I'm here, in your home," I say, not quite meeting his eyes. My fingers are tracing a wet pattern over his wide chest.

"It's no secret, despite the circumstances, I'm fucking ecstatic I have you here." He lets out a short laugh, and I look up from my pattern drawing and see he is battling with smugness. "I might just manage to make you move in with me, after all." He adjusts himself as a shit-eating grin breaks out over his face.

"I suppose that depends," I murmur, enjoying the feel of him tense under me.

"On what?" His head rolls to the side a little as he looks at me down his nose. His lips are quirked, and his eyes shine back at me.

"Whether this drought will continue," I whine, jabbing him in the pec with my nail. He laughs and slowly pulls me back around so my butt is pressed into his groin.

"It's painful, isn't it?" He grunts, adjusting his hard frame behind me. His body ripples and nudges me in all the right places. But he is right; my need for him is all-consuming. It's an itch that can't be scratched, a pain that can't be eased, not unless he takes me to the special high that only he can deliver.

"More than my bruises," I quip. His fingers lift and splay, silently asking me to join. I press my delicate fingers in his, and he locks in.

"Move in with me, Lily," his broken plea is uttered into my ear softly, wide fingers splay against my stomach, and I encounter an unknown, weightless sensation of feeling perfectly safe.

"Okay." I stare at the window where I find our reflections latched together. Jace's eyes glitter with self-satisfied pleasure, and his chest does a big heave of relief.

"You have no idea how happy you just made me." His fingers run back and forth over my stomach.

I wiggle with happiness.

"I can guess." I shiver as the open air glides over my skin. We've been in here a while, and I'm starting to get a little cold.

He huffs.

"That's only a fraction of my happiness." His hand fists when it gets too close to my breasts, and I inwardly scream.

"A big fraction." I snigger. Slowly, I twist and crawl up his frame once more. Jace cups himself and keeps us separate. I laugh at this big man sprawled naked in the bath, cupping his family jewels from me.

"And to think I pegged Carl as the dramatic one," I mock, as his face bunches in annoyance.

"Kiss me, you damn tease." He drops his head back to look up at me, a slow smile on his face.

"As you wish." I grin and drop my mouth. His tongue is already protruding in anticipation. I dive right in. I've missed kissing him.

We soak for a little while longer; the water is becoming cooler by the second, but neither one of us complains. There is a calm silence between us, and all I

Betrayal

sense is his low, comforting breaths and the reassuring swell of his chest against my back. My mind is serene; my posture completely relaxed. The pain in my body ebbs away with the knowledge that I'm safe, and there is nothing left unsaid between us. He knows my darkest secret, my worst, the ugly scab in my life, and he is still here, still ready to hurtle us to his world of happy.

His lips drop to my ear, and he presses his nose deep, inhaling on a rough grumble and sighing softly.

"Let's get dried off." He nudges me up and helps me out—the water sluices down my frame, and I see him turn away from the thick spattering of bruises.

"Thanks," I murmur. I move to get our towels and wrap myself up before handing another to him.

"I'm going to pop the oven on. Marie left us a lasagna on the side." I leave him to it, frowning, grouchy, and all together distracted. He is still trying to piece things together, evaluate and conquer it alone. He doesn't want to ask me the gory details because he thinks I don't want to talk about it, and he's right. I don't. But I will for him and only him. I refuse to revisit that place for myself alone, nor am I ready to broach it and initiate the conversation—Jace needs to come to me. He needs to be ready to hear it, and so far, neither one of us has wanted to taint our happy with my grim past.

By the time I've managed to dry off and get dressed, Jace is already dishing up our dinner. He nods towards the sofa as he walks towards me with my plate. I ease down and pull a face when he places it on my lap.

"What happened to it?" I frown, perplexed at the mushed up mess on my knee. Whatever it is, it certainly does not resemble lasagna.

"Nothing." His face is serious, and he ignores me further when I prod the remains of my dinner with a fork. I look at his meal. His is presented perfectly, a precise slab of meat, pasta, and sauce—it looks delicious, but mine, oh no, mine looks horrendous.

"Did the oven commit a hate crime?" Jace's head comes up, and he deadpans me.

"No, smart arse. I cut it up because of your hand," he tells me with a shake of his head. With what—a chainsaw? Jesus Christ, a toddler could have chopped this up neater.

"Thanks." I prod it about. "I guess." Choosing to ignore the scrambled state of my lasagna, I tuck in, finding that my mouth is still tight, but most of the pain has gone.

"You're welcome, I guess," Jace is smirking around his fork—his downcast eyes twinkling. "Here, let's watch this." He nods to the TV.

For a night, we do boring, normal, perfect-couple stuff. It's exactly what I need after the last few days.

"I didn't like that," I tell him a few hours later, lying in bed. I screamed through every jumpy part, shouted at the TV when anything bad transpired, and almost cried at the beginning. I hate real-life programs. I'd much rather watch something over the top and unbelievable.

"I'm never going to the cinema with you," he chuckles, pulling me closer. I'm slotted in, nice and warm, and his lips are lazily dragging across my temple. "If documentaries make you cry that much, I dread to think what a horror would do."

I grin into the darkness and sigh happily. We seem to be getting there—slow, steady steps, but we're making progress—moving toward that time when we were deliri-

Betrayal

ously happy. I want that back—him back. Tonight has been what I needed. Calm normality.

"Lily?"

"Hmm?" I pull his hand up and rest my chin on it, closing my eyes.

"I need to know the truth. I can't cope with the possibilities running through my head." The rough and whispered statement makes me stiffen in his hold. He means Adam. He wants all the gory details.

Can I do that? Am I ready? I want to be for him. However, now that the moment is here, my heart shrivels into a tight ball, and acid builds in my throat.

I scrunch my eyes tightly, trying to recall all those horrible moments while detaching myself completely to give this man what he needs to move us both back to our happy place.

"Erm . . . okay." I swallow, my voice is shaky, unsure, but when his hands tighten, I relax. They are just words, I tell myself. Adam is gone. He can't get to me, and Jace is here—beautiful Jace Bennett, who I don't deserve, is here holding tightly onto me, onto us, and keeping us both afloat. I can do this. For him, I can do it. "What do you need to know?" I know I can't just get into it. I need some kind of platform to kick me off—a starting point. Anything but the usual horrid visual I conjure up whenever I think of that sick man.

"How did you meet?" Light circles are drawn on my stomach, a constant roll of reassurance and physical grounding. Is he just as worried I'm going to fall victim to another anxiety attack when I bring these memories forward?

"A bar." My throat catches as I recall the moment Adam Burrows approached me. It's there in my mind, just as vivid as the moment it happened. I recall my clothes, his, how everything smelt, and the song that was playing. My hatred for this man has hand picked every moment with him in it and turned it into a HD-ready, graphically perfected movie when really I should blur him out and make the ones I love and care about the main focus of my life and mind. "He came right up to me and professed his undying love. I just laughed." Hands tighten around me, and I frown at how ridiculous Adam was. "He'd had a drink, and I thought he was messing about." My eyes are slowly adjusting to the darkness now, and I can see Jace's outline in the big glass window. I feel his chin fall on my shoulder.

"But he wasn't?" His lips run back and forth, the light bristle of his beard breaking the surface of his skin.

"Looking back, he seemed to know a lot about me before we'd even got to know each other. He never admitted it, but I did wonder if he had been . . . you know—" I don't want to say it out loud because the thought is too creepy to comprehend.

"Do you think he'd been watching you?" Jace speaks the words so I don't have to.

"I guess. I have no proof of that," I admit, and I don't, just that gut-deep sickening churn that something wasn't quite right.

"But you started dating him?" The accusation I hear in Jace's voice stings, but I forgive him because I'm not really doing a good job of explaining all this.

"No." I laugh harshly, giving him a little jab. "It wasn't like that. We bumped into each other again before I agreed to go out for drinks with him. It wasn't until later that I started to wonder all about that, and by then, it was too late." I shrug.

"No alarm bells, then?"

"Not really. Just the odd comment about things I

liked or did that I couldn't recall telling him. We'd go drinking, and I put it down to me being too drunk to remember." Does he really need to know more? The rest is fairly obvious. I shrug into the darkness, conveying there isn't much more to say, but he isn't sated.

"Was he physical a lot?" His voice is deep, low, and so quiet. He knows how hard this is. I shake my head.

"He never hit me, just grabbed me and would get really territorial, but we were only seeing each other. We weren't exclusive, and I thought it was a bit of fun. He started getting really needy, and demanding to know where I was, what I was doing, who I was with. A bit too obsessive, and I decided to call it quits. After I realised I was pregnant, he was over the moon. He wanted us to be a family, and I couldn't *not* give my child both parents, so we tried to make it work, but he knew it was just because of the baby. He became jealous. He would accuse me of cheating if I was late from work, commenting on my attire, asking who I had seen or spoke to in the day, and checking my phone. He just started to accuse me of anything, so I decided it was best to split, and he snapped."

We'd had a huge row. He'd accused me of everything possible, and I'd almost welcomed the accusations because anyone would have been better than him. Adam was blind with jealousy, sick with rage. The night he had beaten me had felt like hours. I'd been too scared to leave, afraid to stay. Our flat had become a prison, and every wall a cage to keep me in. I tried so hard not to think back to that night.

"He'd dragged me around the flat using my hair as a lead, and my knees were burnt from the carpet."

My eyes clamp tightly shut as thick tears pour over and coat my lashes. I shake my head.

"I just wanted him to stop, stop hurting me. He was drunk, sickly drunk. You know when you can smell it on their breath from a mile off?" I shudder, remembering that smell. It still turns my stomach now. "I thought I'd finally got through to him. I let my guard down," I say in a whisper. "He just kept punching my stomach, kicking me there when I was down."

"I'm so sorry, beautiful."

I'm crying softly now, little gentle hiccups into the night.

"A neighbour had called the cops, and they broke their way into the flat I was living in at the time. If they hadn't come, I don't think he would have stopped. By the time the police showed up, Adam had run off."

"Jesus, Lily. I'm so sorry, baby." He kisses my brow. "I'm so proud of you—of what you've achieved despite what he did to you."

"I really wanted to be a mum. I had accepted it by then. When I think about all he has done, there is this tiny part of me that is relieved my child would never know that their father was like that, and then I feel guilty for even thinking it," I admit with a pained croak.

"It's okay. There is nothing to feel guilty about. Anyone in their right mind would think the same."

"I feel guilty about you," I confess, sobbing softly.

"Why?" Jace turns me and pulls me into his chest. He smooths my hair back and looks down at me. "Don't say that, Lily—we're perfect."

"Because you make me happy, and I feel like I should have tried harder with Adam, for the baby. Maybe it would never have happened, and my baby wouldn't have died, but now I'm with you and so deliriously happy, and I don't know if I deserve to be." I bury my face in his chest. All these dormant feelings are rushing to the surface and hit me like a tidal wave. I sob and sob.

This evening feels like it is the quiet after the storm. My meltdown is cathartic. An emotional weight feels as if it's been lifted from my life. Jace holds me long into the night until I finally drift off.

Chapter Eleven

One week later . . .

Nothing and everything has changed. Jace is still keeping his distance physically, and Harriet is finally back. The Loft has been closed all week, bar the two occasions Cass managed to fit me in her diary so I could pick things up and let the cleaner in. The swelling in my face has all but gone, and I have managed to work my hair to cover the stitches. To any passer-by, I look normal, but I don't feel normal. I feel disjointed. Everyone is walking on eggshells around me, clearly worried I'm going to snap any second. It's enough to send the sanest of people crazy. What's worse is Jace hasn't touched me all week, he barely kisses me, and when he does, he prises me away to stop it from heating up. I want heat.

"So, how you doing, I mean really?" Cass says, sipping a coke up through a straw. We are at a small café, not one of our regulars, thankfully.

Shrugging, I lift my tea. I seem to have built a taste for it since Marie made me one—it's not as bitter.

"Honestly, I just want to move forward. I'm okay," I assure her. I just need things with Jace to be good, and I will feel heaps better. "Now, I know Adam is in custody, I can finally close that door and begin again with Jace." I meet her eye to cement how I feel.

"How is he?" She winces, knowing how hard it has been this past week between us. He's played the dutiful partner, but I can see the tension in him.

"Same," I murmur. "Do you think me staying with him is a bad idea?" I haven't admitted to Cass that I have moved in—I'm not sure why.

"No, it will all work out, Lily, trust in that." She rests her chin on her hand and winks at me over the table.

"But the timing," – shaking my head, I place my tea down and sigh – "it just doesn't feel like we are making progress." Maybe what we really need is space, not being thrust under each other's noses.

"Lily, Jace listened to the recording. You screamed for him, and he feels terrible for not being there." Her eyes soften but are equally tinged with sadness. I seem to be the only one happy to shut the door on the attack and move on. "Adam could have killed you, Lily," she points out slowly, cautiously.

"But he didn't." I grate with frustration. "I'm so desperate to forget it all and move on. I know you all care, but I need our," – I motion between us – "normal back." I stand, suddenly eager to get away. "I need to forget," I tell her. She nods and looks at me with concern, and I roll my eyes. "Cass, I'm fine." I sound anything but fine, and she holds my frustrated stare with a pointed one of her own. "Or at least I will be when Jace stops holding out on me." I laugh, forcing the conversation along. She cracks a smile, and I lean down and give her a hug. "Stop treating me like china. I'm really okay."

"Okay." She hugs me back and stays seated when my Uber pulls up. I wave to her as I hop in and send Carl a quick text. We have formed a tight bond since the attack. It's the only good thing to have come out of it because moving in with Jace isn't proving to be how I imagined it would be.

We seemed to have rocket-launched right over the honeymoon period and settled into our fiftieth anniversary within a week. It's dire, but I'm determined to change that. I made a quick but cautious dash to the shops before I met Cass, and my purchases are all wrapped elegantly in one of my bags. Happy with myself, I enjoy the ride back before I begin preparing dinner, my shopping hidden discreetly in our bedroom. I'm still suffering from the odd dizzy spell, so I've been mindful to take my time and rest when I can.

It's a little after eight when Jace pulls in. It's later than I thought he would be, but he has spent so much time with me this past week, he probably has a lot to catch up on.

"Hey!" I call, pouring myself a well-earned wine. It's the first one I have had since the attack.

"What are you drinking?" Jace grumbles, casting inspecting eyes over me.

I ignore his question.

"Hello to you, too," I quip. He smirks and walks straight over, looking immaculate in his suit. He left for work before I woke, so it's only now that I can fully appreciate it. "You look nice," I say.

"I know." He grins and pulls me to him. I'm doused in his perfect smell.

"Smell good too." I huff, pressing to kiss him, but he lifts his chin, ensuring he is just out of reach.

"What's in the glass?" He doesn't wait for my answer, just lifts it and sniffs before pouring it down the sink, all the while watching me with mischievous but serious ambers.

"Jace! I wanted that." I shoot annoyed eyes at him.

"Lily, you suffered a mild concussion a week ago." Just to hammer that home, he fingers my hair away from my face and inspects my cut. I tug my head away.

"Precisely. Mild. I feel fine." A little wobbly at times and my ribs are still sore, but all in all, I think I have recovered exceptionally well. My fingers are still strapped up, but any pain has gone. They're just an inconvenience now.

"You still look pale," he offers up. I roll my eyes and lift quickly to kiss him. It's unexpected, but he lets me, so I keep my lips on his and cup his face. "I have to go out of town for a night," he informs between kisses.

"Okay, when?" I drop back to my feet and stir the pan.

"Tomorrow." I nod and check the pasta. "Smells good." His chin drops on my shoulder briefly so he can inspect the contents.

"I know." I throw a smirk over my shoulder. Jace is grinning too. "It'll be ready in a few, so you have time to change if you want?" I don't want him floating around while I'm cooking.

"Miss Spencer, are you trying to get me naked?" He backs away, his head tilted just so, and a playful grin on his full mouth.

"You have no idea." I laugh. He winks and wanders off—maybe I don't need my little plan after all. I feel deflated, but I'm too excited to throw it under the bus. I'll be damned if he seduces me first.

I plate our dinner up and take it to the table. "Looks great," Jace says, planting a kiss on my hairline. I set the table earlier, and even lit a few candles, but the constant twitch of his lips tells me he knows my game. I choose not to mention it and tuck in.

"I might see if Carl and Rupert fancy dinner tomorrow?" I know he won't like me being on my own, and I'm pulling at all the strings to soften him up.

"I'm sure they will." He clears his throat, and I drop a look at him.

"You already asked them, didn't you?" Unbelievable. I mentally shake my head at him.

He keeps his face averted and twists some spaghetti onto his fork.

"Well, Carl mentioned he was free . . . " He shrugs. He rests his hands on the table edges, giving off an air of importance and daring me to disagree. It's a constant push and pull between us.

"I'm not made of glass," I grumble as my fork prods unenthusiastically at my dinner.

He is grinning at me when he says, "Don't get all pissy." His fork lifts in my direction slightly before finding its way to his mouth, just as he says, "You suggested it too." He chews slowly, then pulls my hand up and dances a line of kisses along my wrist. "Rupert said he would cook so you can rest up."

I laugh.

"I've don't nothing but rest up—this is the first time I've cooked all week!"

"It's surprisingly good." He frowns. I'd be offended if I was in denial at my lack of culinary skills, but he is right—it is good.

"Marie taught me." That woman has been a saving grace this week; she has kept me occupied and been a constant support.

"What have you been up to today?" Jace has polished his meal off already, and I'm only halfway through. "Is there anymore?" he asks, already standing and taking his empty bowl to pile more in. I drop a smile and pick at my own dinner.

"Not much. Took some photos, met Cass, cleaned up, and used the gym," I say, not paying much attention to him because I know the last part will annoy him.

"The gym?" His bowl crashes down louder than expected. "Lily!" he sighs, "look at me." I throw a casual smile his way. "I don't think you should be doing anything too physical," he huffs.

"Evidently," I mutter, pushing a forkful of food in my mouth, stalling any further conversation for a few minutes. I hear his muted laughter, but I take little enjoyment out of it. I would never admit it to him, but I need sex. It's purely his fault. I never much cared for it, and now he is denying me. I feel like a loose cannon, and as far as working out goes, it's not like I put myself through a gruelling workout. I just did a quick walk, and I tell him as much when I finally swallow the mouthful. I don't tell him I tried to jog but found it too painful, not to mention how dizzy it made me feel.

"Maybe give it a little while longer, okay?" he tells me, doing that ultra-sweet thing and kissing my hair again. I have come to realise that it's his way of trying to be patient with me, buttering me up.

"I don't know. I felt great after it—" It's not exactly a lie. I did feel more energetic, but I did have a few dizzy spells, which had me holding the rails for constant

Betrayal

support. I'm pushing myself to get better. I need to go back to work. I will go stir crazy otherwise.

Jace isn't fully convinced, and he side-eyes me and stands, taking both our bowls.

"Why don't you go and relax in the bath?" he suggests, rinsing the pots and filling the dishwasher. I grin inwardly and slip off my chair, heading for the bathroom on a quick walk. Running the bath is a perfect way to disguise the sound of tissue paper as I frantically tear it open and pull the nude waspie set on. The bruising to my ribs is still evident, but the once dark bluish stain looks yellower now. I cover the dark rings under my eyes and bronze my face to dispel the paleness that Jace mentioned. I gloss my lips and touch up the minimal mascara I put on earlier, rushing to do my right eye when I hear the distinctive sound of footsteps.

I quickly drop back to perch on the edge of the bath and cross my legs, supporting myself by stretching my arms wide. Jace strides through the bedroom and halts, his eyes widening at me.

"Hi." I allow my gaze to lift from his toes to his burning gaze, and when I stand, I take my time, knowing it will give maximum effect and silently hope any dizziness stays at bay.

"Where did you get that?" he swallows.

Lifting a hand, I trail it down the dainty bra strap and across my breast. My fingertips glide over the full mound, then hit the flat plain of my stomach. The waspie set stood out to me the moment I walked into the boutique earlier—the oyster shade and black lace complimenting my pale tone. Jace clears his throat, and I do a mini mental celebration.

"I picked it up earlier today, you like?" Of course he

likes. The look on his face and the open adjusting of his groin tells me so.

"You know I do." He walks towards me but stops and leans against the open door frame. I tiptoe towards him, biting my lip to stop my self-satisfied grin from overpowering the seductive glance I'm trying to master.

"What are you going to do about it?" I whisper and lift to brush my mouth against his. His hands land softly on my hips, and he lets me pet his mouth.

"Nothing," he replies. I stop and pull back. He is joking, surely? My eyes search his and find nothing but resolution.

"You're not funny," I quip, rubbing up against him, reaching to cup him as I do. "That doesn't feel like nothing." I moan. He's hard as rock. I want him feverishly.

"Lily." His sigh is tense, frustrated, and he pushes my hand away, and then me, slowly. I blink in shock. *He's serious*. I don't expect the short, shocked laugh, but it flies out of my mouth, anyway.

"Okay." I step away and twist my back to him. Looking at him will only show the hurt. I scoff to myself and reach to unclip the bra before turning the taps off. I remove the rest of it and let it drop to the floor, and I have my leg halfway in the water when his hands slip around to my stomach.

His breath hits my cheek, then my ear.

"Lily, you look stunning, but it's only been a week. I need you to get better." His lips drop to my shoulder, and my eyes slam shut. I shrug him off. "Don't be mad. Let's soak in the ba—"

"I think I'll just have a quick wash," I murmur. I prise his hands free and keep hold of one as I step fully in, lowering myself into the thick bubbly water. Jace is crouched at the side in seconds.

"Lily, don't be like that."

I snap to look at him.

"Like what, hurt, frustrated? It's *sex*. I'm not asking you to perform surgery!" I spit before looking away. I cup some water and watch it drain through my fingers until it forms droplets. "Leave me alone, Jace." My sigh is weary.

"Don't be ridiculous," he mutters indignantly. "I'm not leaving, Lily. It's not a question of whether I'm attracted to you."

I scoff, shrugging him away.

"Could have fooled me!" What the hell is his problem?

"Seeing you unconscious in that bed." He sighs and cups the back of my neck, coaxing me to his face. "I can't get it out of my head," he whispers. My expression is sad, and I cup his face and push to my knees, pressing my mouth to his.

"I'm fine. I feel good," I plead for him to see that.

"But?" His hoarse voice sends a happy shiver down my spine.

"But, when I said yes to moving in, I thought it would be different." Jace pulls away, affronted, but I keep my hands tight, holding him close.

"Different how?" His eyes search mine with worry. His hair is ruffled and in need of a cut. His syrupy eyes are glinting under the light, and I can't help but stare at them—his colouring is beautiful.

"Honestly?" I frown, gnawing my lip.

"Always," he murmurs. His thumb glides over my lower lip, and I take a small leap of satisfaction that his eyes follow the trail.

"I was expecting us to celebrate," – my voice is low,

teasing – "*a lot*." I stare up at him and sigh. "I want the old you back. I miss you touching me." I pout.

Jace wraps his hands around me so they dip below the surface.

"I don't want to hurt you," his admission is low—he means physically. I am a little sore, but we can be gentle. I want gentle.

"But you are." My mouth turns down, and I swallow the ache in my throat. I press his wet palm to my chest. "In here. I need you back, Jace." I drop my forehead to his and close my eyes. "We can be careful." I lean in and press my mouth to his. "Be gentle with me," I coax. I take his other hand and move them to my front so he can cup my wet breasts. His eyes drop to the bruise marring my skin. "Eyes up here, and don't stop touching me," I tell him. He smirks at me but looks hesitant. "Jace, please." I sound frustrated and dejected. "You say you want me better. This is what I need—this connection—us." I stare sincerely into his burning bronzes, and he regards me thoughtfully, his mouth pinching tightly.

In one quick move, he pulls me from the bath and walks me to the bedroom.

"I can give you gentle." His lips hover over mine before he softly sweeps his tongue in on a deep groan. I wrap my arms around his neck, keeping him as close as possible, and even when he lowers me, I take him with me, wrapping myself like a rope around his wide frame.

My body floods with heat, and every touch feels like the most static of electricity. Even when he grinds, then moves away, the buzz is still there. Jace's kiss is deep and slow. I'm so content with just that I don't realise his hand has moved until I feel his fingers *there*.

"You're soaking wet." His voice is all gravel.

"Yes." My thighs ache with the pressure I'm putting

on them to keep them wide. "I need to feel you." I pant, lifting my hips to encourage his thick fingers inside.

"Fucking hell, Lily." Dark lust roams down my body.

"Now." I clasp his wrist, pushing his fingers in. They go deep, and my body goes lax. "Oh, god!" My eyes are fixed on his; the flare of his nostrils and the tense set of his shoulders tells me he is still unsure how much he should give—how much I can take. I don't allow him the chance to worry. I keep control of his wrist and work him in and out, and his deft fingers curl until I fly over the edge. "Oh, shit!"

"Lily, slow down," he breathes, averting his eyes from the slight jerking of my hips. When he slips his fingers free, I bring them to my mouth slowly, and when I open my mouth and slip them inside, his eyes widen, and he groans loudly. He moves to kneel on the bed and starts undoing his jeans, un-popping the buttons until he can reach and pull his thick cock free. "Put your legs on my left," he instructs softly, dropping a quick kiss on my thigh. I bend and pull my legs together on his left, and Jace leans against them, keeping me from moving. He takes my wrists and plants them on either side of my head. I expect him to kiss me, but he dips his head lower and pulls a nipple into his mouth, swirling his mouth around the stiff peak and sucking gently. "God, Lily, you're drenched."

"Should have fucked me sooner." I laugh lightly, jolting when he bites my nipple. His tongue does another swirl, then his wide head is pushing into my slick heat. My eyes widen, and any breath, ready to exhale, stalls, leaving on a long sigh when he sinks home.

"Oh, hell, you feel amazing, Lily," Jace pants gruffly. He lowers to take my mouth, and I let him, rolling my tongue against his as he slowly fucks me, driving in on long, slow, deep, deep thrusts. My arms remain strapped down by his hands, and my legs are trapped under his weight. I can't move, but I don't complain. I'm already tipping over the edge. "Fuck," he chokes around my tongue.

"Oh, don't stop." I'm pulsing around him.

"Jesus, Lily," Jace moans, quickening his pace. I'm sobbing quietly when he spills himself into me. "I love you, beautiful." He cups my head, thrusts in, and then stills.

I'm crying. I don't know why, but I'm thankful that Jace holds me tight and lets me hide my face in the crook of his neck.

"I'm sorry," he whispers, "you look so fragile. I couldn't bring myself to touch you. I thought I had lost you. I was just happy to be able to look at you." He pecks my neck as wide palms rub methodically over my bare back.

I nod stiffly into his shoulder.

"I love you too."

He winks.

"I know." He smiles. "I loved the lingerie," he tells me, prising me away so he can look at me properly. I lift my head, and he wipes a thumb under my eye. "Wear it for me when I get home?" he asks quietly.

My smile is soft and followed by a sniff.

"I don't know why I'm crying," I huff.

"Lily, you have been through a lot. I've probably not helped, and your emotions are all up in the air—plus you're coming, left, right, and centre." He smirks smugly. I nudge his shoulder and hide my face. "Hey, I'm not complaining." He laughs, dropping his head into my hair and nipping my ear. "I love you, beautiful."

"Even after I hurt you?" I ask him. We haven't really dealt with his disquiet head on.

"Even then. I was angry with him, and you took the brunt of that, forgive me?" He pouts playfully—his whiskey glaze full of sparkle and mischief.

"After those orgasms, it'd be rude of me not to." I grin, fiddling with his hair. He chuckles and kicks his trousers off. He is pulling his top over his head as I slip under the covers.

"It would be criminal." He snorts and pulls me back so I'm flush to his bare body. "Get some sleep, baby. You look exhausted."

Hearing him say those words unlocks something in me. I yawn on cue and let my eyes droop shut. The blanket of darkness and his arms are all I need to lure me under.

———

I wake to gentle Jace and have spent most of the day being indulged. Jace, who couldn't bring himself to touch me, is back to finding it hard not to. I don't complain as he is due to fly out this evening, so I make the most of being with him.

"Lily," he breathes hotly. His hands cup my cheek. "Beautiful, slow down." I'm straddling him on the sofa, my small hands holding fiercely to his shoulders as I ride him. I ignore his grunt and slam back down. My body shudders, and I drop my head back as I come.

"Ohhhh!" I cry. Jace takes my hips and rocks me slowly until I feel his cock thicken and pulse inside me. His groan is deep and sexy. Dropping forward, I cup his face, kissing him as he jerks beneath me. His forehead is damp with sweat, but I drop my own to it, panting quietly. "Oh god," I hum. He holds me still and dives his tongue in.

"I'm going to be late for my flight," he chastises. His hands do a quick sweep of my body, concentrating on my breasts, and he cups them so they spill out his hands. "Goddammit, Lily." I give my hips a little roll, laughing when he moans deeply.

"Shower with me?" I plead. His eyes burn up at me, and he shakes his head a little.

"You, Lily Spencer, are a damn witch." He grabs my arse, so I yelp.

"So you keep telling me." I pout, dropping to peck his mouth. "You have half an hour before you need to leave," I tell him. He was planning on a shower anyway until I waylaid him.

"What time are the guys getting here?" He shifts so he can stand and takes me with him.

"An hour or so," I huff. I'm looking forward to our night in, but I know I will miss Jace too. The water gets turned on, and Jace steps us under the spray. "I don't think I have ever been to Edinburgh," I tell him.

"It's pretty," he hums, pulling me for a quick but deep kiss. "I won't see much of it, just the hotel where the conference is held. I have a meeting afterward but will be back around two a.m." His voice takes on a lazy drawl.

"Oh, how convenient. Your favourite time." I bite his lip, and he twitches beneath me.

"Our," he corrects, "our favourite time." He gives me that trademark wink. "Right, get down." He lowers me and swats my arse. "I've got to get ready, baby." Jace washes himself, and I am mindful not to get my stitches too wet. They are dissolving already and leaving a red scar that is neat and fine. I exit before Jace and carefully wrap my head in a towel. His phone rings, so I yell through to him.

"Can you answer it!" he hollers. I check the caller ID and falter when I see it's Neve. I click connect.

"Hi, it's Lily. Jace is in the shower," I say as I answer, and she tsks.

"Can you ask him to just meet me at the airport? Something came up, and I don't need a lift," she utters the words quickly.

"Oh, oka—" The phone abruptly cuts out and leaves me open-mouthed and staring at the now blank screen. She's so damn rude! And she is going too? I don't have time for that to fully sink in because Jace saunters out naked and looking ready to model a calendar shoot. "Neve is going?" I whisper, annoyed.

"What's that?" He rubs his hair with a towel and walks to me. "Who was on the phone?"

"Neve," I say shortly, "you never said she was going with you." I give him accusing eyes, but he is oblivious—either that or he is really good at acting.

"I didn't?" He frowns. "I'm sure I did?" Jace inclines his head and pats his wet chest.

"No," I scoff lightly, "not a word." I punctuate the last part for effect, illustrating my annoyance.

"Well, it's for work." He casts his gaze my way quickly and belatedly realises my reservations before walking to me. His hands cup my face, and he drops his mouth to mine. "I love you. She is a friend and colleague. *It's work.*" My heart is pounding way too quickly, but I nod and force a smile because I don't want to cause an argument and him leave on a fight. But I really do not like the woman.

"Okay." He pecks my mouth before pulling some

clothes on and checking he has his passport. I relay Neve's message.

"Oh, she say why?" He runs his lips across mine, not showing much interest in her call.

"No, that was it." I hold his gaze, suspecting that he avoided mentioning Neve because he knew I wouldn't be comfortable with it. I'm not.

"I've got to go. I'll call you later, okay?" My smile is fake, and he must see it because he pulls me back for a deep kiss. "I love you," he murmurs between sweeps of his tongue.

"Have a great trip," I murmur sullenly. He tilts his head, a light frown marring his otherwise perfect face. "Love you too." My voice is rougher than I expect, and his eyes flash with unease. He knows I'm not okay with this. Why would I be? It's so very obvious she is in love with him.

Chapter Twelve

Carl and Rupert arrive later than expected. They muscle in with bags of food, and Carl shakes a bottle of wine at me. I pull a face. Jace won't be happy about that.

"Oh, pfft, he's not here, and you look heaps better, a little pale, but that's lack of sun," he drawls, walking straight to kiss each of my cheeks. Rupert dumps the bags on the side and pecks my cheek.

"So, how's our favourite patient?" He rubs at my back and ignores my eye roll. "Carl is right. You do look pale. When did you last holiday?" Rupert hand-combs his beard and gives me a once over as he wanders back to the abandoned food.

"I don't even want to answer that." I think it was about three years ago, Cass and I booked a girls' break. There has been the odd spa day in between and days out, but I haven't touched sand or sea in what feels like forever.

"That bad?" he laughs.

"Jace did mention a holiday, but," – I point at my head – "this happened."

"Surely that's the perfect excuse to get away," Carl mentions. I think it over. It is, but I have been away from work for ages. I can't take more time off.

"I know what you're thinking." Rupert looks down his nose at me, a pointed gleam in his eye. "You are allowed to take time off. Besides, I think it would do your assistant some good." He winks. I know I've never mentioned Hat, but I can imagine Carl has. She is very timid at times, and my absence at the gallery has made her stand on her own two feet a bit more.

"Jace being away has been good for me. I have seen an aspect of the business I was never much involved in. It's been a good experience," Carl adds encouragingly.

"What my husband is saying is, if you could injure yourself more often, he'd appreciate it." Rupert half-laughs. Carl gawps, and I cough out a laugh.

"I'll keep that in mind." I'm grateful he is comfortable enough to make light of it; it's a refreshing change from all the concerned glances and hesitant comments.

"Rupert, that was awful!" Carl reprimands.

"A little bit funny," I defend, my cheeks heating. Carl tuts and wafts me away with an elegant flap of his hand.

"Look, if you want to sun it up, we can help out if need be," Carl says over his shoulder.

"I appreciate that." I leave it at that. I don't want to make plans just yet. Rupert is pulling items from the bags, so I walk over. "Need a hand?"

"Definitely not, go, put your feet up, have a look at what's on that monstrosity of a TV." I laugh at that because it is huge, like windowpane-huge. I do as I'm told and flick through until I find something neutral for us all and settle on a thriller. "I'm doing a stir-fry, so it won't take long," Rupert explains, and Carl saunters over with two glasses of white wine.

Betrayal

"He will never know." Carl winks, and I take the glass.

"Thanks." I sit back so I'm swallowed up by the array of cushions. Jace and I have spent most evenings strewn over this sofa, either watching some new series or listening to music. Most of our conversations involved Adam and my disaster of a relationship with him. It was never meant to be serious, more of a casual fling, just a little fun, but I fell pregnant, and my carefree life suddenly tipped on its arse, and before I knew it, Adam had moved in, and we were planning to buy a house for the sake of our child. I didn't love him, and he knew it, which only made it more difficult for him because he was utterly besotted with me. That soon turned to obsession, then aggression. Then loss.

I blamed myself for so long for causing his sickness—blamed myself because of my selfishness. If the attack gave me anything, it was closure.

I stare at the coffee table where a letter is tucked neatly in the concealed drawer. A letter Adam's parents wrote to me at The Loft, educating me on their son and his illness. Jace had curled himself around me as we snuggled on the sofa where he read it out to me, detailing how Adam was medicated before he met me, that he was impulsive and erratic in his behaviour, and informing me another girl had a restraining order against him. They had no idea that he'd beaten me and had expressed at length how truly sorry they were for the hurt he caused me and for my loss. I felt sorry for them.

I couldn't imagine the hardship of loving someone who was sick—how that must challenge them mentally and emotionally, and how exhausting and difficult it must be for them. Adam isn't just sick; he isn't a good person either—I knew that now. I no longer blamed myself.

Jace and I are in a good place, and the door to my past is firmly shut. I'm finally anticipating a future.

———

Carl holds out a pack of Maltesers, and I take a handful, popping one in my mouth.

"Mmm." Rupert is making the house smell like a Michelin-star restaurant. We eat on our knees watching the movie—Carl and Rupert either side of me. We don't talk much, and I like that. It's relaxed and easy.

My phone breaks the silence, and I just know it's him. Carl takes my bowl so I can stand and get my phone off the coffee table.

"Hey." I drop back down, and Carl deposits the bowl in my lap.

"Hey." Jace sounds harassed, distracted.

"Everything okay?" I pick at the food and pop a piece of marinated chicken into my mouth, chewing quietly.

"Yeah, you okay?" he grumbles. I frown, and Carl does too.

Neve's voice filters over the line. "What about single rooms?"

"You sure everything is alright?" I ask, forking the last bit of food into my mouth.

"There has been a mixup at the hotel, and they have overbooked," he tells me. I suppose it's due to the conference being held there. I've been subjected to similar situations, mainly with overseas travel.

"Oh, okay, can you not stay in another hotel?" I know it's costly, but surely that makes sense, and they can be refunded.

"Logistically, no. Neve is trying to sort it now." I press

Betrayal

my lips together and keep any thoughts to myself. Unease settles like a lead weight in my gut.

"Okay, well, hopefully they can arrange something?" I say diplomatically.

"I'm sure they will. Everything okay then?" He tactfully changes the subject. I shoot Carl a tight smile but drop my eyes when he gives me a reserved look.

"Yes, just watching a movie," I reply, eyeing Carl again, who is eavesdropping openly. His ear is almost pressed to the back of my phone.

"You're not drinking, are you?" His voice is low and authoritative.

"Just a small glass," I wince, and Carl rolls his eyes.

"She is fine!" he calls, and I give him a grateful smile. Jace grunts down the phone, and I hear him snap at the receptionist about having separate rooms.

"I paid for two double rooms, not a twin!" he mutters crossly.

"It's says he—"

"Lily, I've got to go. I'll speak to you sometime tomorrow." My heart constricts at what is transpiring at the end of the line.

"Sure, okay." He cuts the call. I drop the phone on the sofa, and it disappears between Carl and me.

"You okay?" He heard everything, but I appreciate his politeness. Rupert collects up our bowls and wanders back over to the kitchen. If they are sharing a look at my expense, I don't notice. I'm too riddled with worry.

I shrug.

"Problem with the hotel. They overbooked," I tell him.

"Bullshit, I called yesterday to double-check: two double rooms." He looks confused and annoyed. "Let me call him." He is up and off. I leave him to it because my bruised brain can't cope with the thought of Neve and Jace sharing. Surely he wouldn't do that?

Five minutes later, Carl returns, looking peeved, and I can guess why.

"Ring to help and get told off." He drops down on the sofa like a child.

"The wine—" I grimace, and he rolls his head my way. I can see the annoyance there, but he doesn't express it fully: Jace should have more faith in him.

"Try living with him," I mutter, sipping on my wine.

"Rather not." He sniggers. "Working with him during this whole thing has been bad enough," he admits brazenly. I watch him over my glass, a little sorry for causing all this trouble. "He has been vile," he utters snootily.

"God, really?" Now I'm intrigued.

Carl twists so we are facing each other.

"He nearly fired someone yesterday, annnnd," he adds dramatically, stalling the gasp leaving my mouth, "he told Neve to fuck off." Carl throws his head back and laughs. I do too. That little snippet of information just made my night.

"So did they sort the hotel out?" I wonder, trying not to sound whiny when I ask.

"I believe so. I just don't understand it. It was all confirmed. Jace said there were two reservations, so it's weird." I nod slowly in agreement. It is strange, but I can imagine with the conference being so big that a few wires have got crossed. As long as it's sorted, it's none of my business. I trust him, and that's enough for me.

We watch the remainder of the film in silence, and with the wine chasing its way through my system, I'm super sleepy. After I yawn for the tenth time, Rupert stands up.

Betrayal

"Right, bed!" he tells me. Carl and I burst out laughing—he sounds like a matron.

"Yes, Dad." I give him a poorly attempted salute.

"That was appalling," he drawls, picking a throw up to fold.

"Touchy," I mock. Carl is smothering a laugh—he has ingested a full bottle of wine and the majority of the first we opened.

"We'll lock up on our way out. You call us if you need anything," he says, giving me a sharp look as another yawn wracks my body.

"I feel like I'm being punished." I peek a look up at him and see his small smile.

"Just following the doctor's orders," he gloats, "ten on the dot." He taps his watch, and my eyes widen as Rupert fights a gloating smile. I come to the stinking realisation that my controlling boyfriend has actually given me a curfew. I open my mouth to say as much but slap it shut, far too embarrassed to utter the words. Mentally, I'm calling him every name under the sun!

Instead, I peck Rupert's cheek, and then Carls when he joins us.

"Thanks for coming over, guys, and for dinner. It was delicious." The anger growing in my body is causing me to shake inside.

"He cares," Rupert mouths. I nod and smile my way through them leaving, before heading to the bathroom on wooden legs.

The absolute bloody cheek of him—I'm not twelve!

When he gets back, things are bloody changing. What a control freak!

I hear the suction and click of the main door, and the engine starts up slowly a few moments later. I finish up in the bathroom and pick up my phone, sending him one short and annoyed message.

A fucking curfew!! I'm starting to think moving in was a very BAD idea!

I end it with an angry face and turn my phone off completely. Let him sweat, I think, pulling my clothes off and dragging the quilt back to get in. The bed smells dominantly of him, and it angers me further. It takes me an age to get to sleep. I'm too tightly wound.

I wake early after a broken night's sleep and groggily head straight for a shower. I'm going into work, even if it's just for the morning. Harriet has been a gem at holding the fort. I may have worked from Jace's and been in constant contact with her, but I need to be there. I miss it, and after last night's fiasco, I'm not sitting here any longer.

I pick a shirt and skirt combo and wash and dry my hair before moisturising and grabbing some breakfast. I spend the next hour picking at my breakfast, doing my makeup, and then my hair before I leave. It's bright but cold, so I whip back in for my coat, remembering to turn my phone on. It takes a minute or two to boot up, and when it does, I have over a dozen missed calls and messages. I ignore them all and lock up, setting the alarm before heading to my car.

I text Harriet to let her know I'm on my way in and that I will grab us both breakfast. I pit-stop to pick up some flowers and a card, writing a small message of thanks, and continue the rest of the journey listening to

Betrayal

the radio. When my in-car speaker rings, and I check the caller ID, *it's him*. My heart does that quirky little jig.

I don't feel quite ready to speak to him. Only because I miss him, and I know I will give in too quickly. Silence is my best defence right now, and it's also my weapon. I cut the call, happy with my willpower.

Harriet arrives five minutes after me, and everything is ready and set up. She walks straight to me and gives me a hug. She never visited me at Jace's, but from what she explains, Jace was adamant I had my rest and assured her I was fine.

"He's a tough cookie." She giggles. I nod in agreement around my mouthful.

So fine that I can't drink, use the gym, or stay up past fucking ten p.m.!

I hide my irritation with a half-smile, and we take our seats out back and munch our way through our breakfast. "God, I missed the deli-brekkie." I groan in appreciation.

"I know. I couldn't get one without you—didn't feel right," Harriet tells me shyly. She is the cutest! The look I give her tells her as much.

"I got you some flowers to say thanks," I tell her. "I popped them in water in the kitchen." Harriet's surprised face pops up from behind the wide mug she is holding.

"You didn't have to do that." She gapes.

"I wanted to. I really appreciate all your help. It means a lot." I smile wildly, starting to feel more at ease now I'm back in the gallery.

"I'm just glad you're okay. I was so worried." Her

eyes hold mine for a minute, that bit too long, and I know she wants me to open up to her, but I'm done talking about Adam. I'm done giving him space in my mind—in my life. He's had more of me than he deserves.

"Honestly, I'm fine," I say chirpily, "happy to be back at work." I casually change the direction of our conversation. If she suspects I'm skirting around the issue, she doesn't say so. I'm certain by the concern in her gaze that she still sees me as a victim.

"Oh, you said you were just in for this morning—are you back in full time?" she wonders.

I shrug.

"Well, I feel fine, so I don't see why not?" I look away when I catch her uneasy smile. It's enough to put me off my food. I finish up my coffee and head back inside. "Did those new pieces arrive? I might need your help to place them," I say. Harriet takes that as her cue to get up, but I stop her. "When you've finished and please don't feel you have to watch me. I'm not going to fall." She nods, but I can see the terror behind her bright eyes —anyone would think I'd undergone strenuous surgery or had a life-threatening illness.

I check the storage room out the back and find the new additions carefully wrapped. I bend to look through them and check the paperwork, but when I stand, dizziness washes over me, throwing me off-centre. I grip for the wall to steady myself, softly shouting out as I stagger to the side. Harriet rushes to me, my eyes slant shut, and I mentally berate her for choosing now to walk in, but I know it's not her I'm mad at. It's me.

I'm not accepting that I'm struggling. I've always prided myself on my independence, thrived on it. Now, I just feel like a hindrance. Weak.

"Oh, my god. Are you okay?" I blink slowly as my vision blots, and anxiety leaves a cold sweat over me.

My laugh is brittle.

"Stood up too quickly," I croak, but inside I'm feeling off-kilter, worried. Surely this isn't normal? I let out a few steadying breaths and close my eyes, only opening them when Hat rubs my arm gently.

"Maybe you should go home?" she suggests softly. "I know you want to be here, but I'd feel terrible if you passed out. You're really pale." She pulls a chair out for me to sit on, and I drop into it gingerly, very aware I still feel a little wobbly. My sigh is full of anger at myself.

"Do you want me to drive you home?" I lift to meet her sympathetic eyes and nod as I look away. I could strangle Adam. I feel myself becoming emotional and clear my throat as Harriet pulls me to her. "Hey, don't get upset. I know you feel fine, but your body probably still needs to heal." Her small hands glide up my back, and I stutter out a sigh.

"It's just so frustrating, and Jace is constantly hanging over me," I mutter, very much fed up. I shouldn't be discussing this with her.

"I can imagine, but everything is okay here, and it's not like you have left me in the lurch. I'm constantly calling you. I'm surprised I haven't pissed you off yet." She laughs, and I do too. Any other time, those calls would send me crazy, but I'm desperate to receive them at the moment.

"Sorry." I shake myself out of my mood and stand slowly. Harriet gathers my things, and I lock up as she goes to pull her car around the front. I give her Jace's address, and we spend the journey talking about her holiday—her checking on me every so often. Her small fists are knuckle-white with anxiety on the steering wheel. When we get to the main road, I instruct her to turn right down the gravel drive, and we crunch our way up the tree-made tunnel. When the house finally comes into view, she exclaims loudly and stalls her car.

"Bloody hell!" We both lurch forward in our seats, and I burst out laughing. Harriet's face is a picture of horrified embarrassment, "Oh my god. I'm so sorry." She covers her face, her shoulders shaking with silent laughter. I'm howling, tears pouring down my cheeks as I struggle to unclip the belt. I haven't laughed this hard in ages, and I sorely needed it.

"I can't believe you stalled," I wheeze. We're both shaking silently as laughter overtakes us, an invisible possession playing with our emotions. When I manage to calm myself and bring my breathing back to normal, I push free from the car. "If Jace had security cameras, I would watch that back." I chuckle loudly. Harriet scoffs and looks away, trying to disguise her smirk.

"I wasn't expecting," – her hands spread as widely as they can, with her still belted up in the car – "well this, I . . . it's—" She looks beyond, to the gleaming glass and smooth wooden house.

"I know." I bend to look through the open door at her. "It's pretty spectacular, isn't it?" My uncertain gaze looks at the structure with confusion. It's every girl's dream. I'm just not sure I can deal with the male owner's controlling manner.

"And then some," she states enthusiastically, as she checks her watch, "best get back." Her eyes find themselves taking in the house once more.

"Thanks, Hat," I say, tightening my coat.

"Anytime. I'll call you later to give you an update." I nod and close the door. I need to give her a raise. It's a crime not to. I've just been so wrapped up in, well,

Betrayal

myself—an ugly trait that I can't shake. I've become selfish in my older years, over-cautious and caged, but I'm really trying to move my life forward with Jace. I just don't like being held back because it's what he thinks I need.

My phone is blaring at me from my tote. I know it's Jace, and despite my annoyance at him, I feel bad for causing him stress while he is at work. I key the code in for his door and push my way in as I answer.

"Hello," I sound miserable.

"There better be a good excuse for why you have ignored my calls, Lily!" he seethes. I follow suit, imagining him yanking at his tie in anger. His nostrils always flare, and a vein in his neck protrudes as though trying to break the surface to shout at me too.

"I didn't want to talk to you." My reply is forced through gritted teeth. I really thought I could go back to work, and that would be it. That once I crossed that final line, this whole ordeal would be over. Instead, it seems one thing follows another.

His short laugh is sarcastic.

"Forgive me for caring about you," he spits incredulously.

"Controlling me," I counteract. He growls, and I roll my eyes. "You made me look stupid!" I spit.

"I'm trying to look out for you," he snaps. His sigh floats off into another argument, but this time it's not at me, and I sit quietly as he snaps at Neve too. The fact that she is managing to grab his attention, despite him being on the phone to me during a spat, infuriates me further.

"You sound busy. I'll see you tomorrow," I say and cut the call before he can reply. When he rings back, I ignore it and send a message.

We'll talk when you get back.

I'm really not okay with all of this. It's beyond ridiculous. He calls twice more but soon realises I'm not entertaining his behaviour or being subjected to Neve; even if it is electronically. I hate the thought of her enjoying our little fight.

Instead of letting my mind churn up all my hurt and run with my negative thoughts, I find a chick flick, curl up on the sofa and spend the rest of the day emailing Harriet, texting Cass, and mooching through social media. By the time evening comes around, I'm bored to my bones and decide to run a bath. I give myself a full spa treatment and pamper myself until I'm in a natural, relaxed coma. I need little encouragement to get into bed, and as soon as my head hits the pillow, I'm gone.

I'm woken by the shrill sound of my phone ringing, but within moments of it starting and me coming around, it stops. I recognise the sound of the main door whooshing open, and Jace strides towards me with a look of worry on his face. With little regard to my sleepy state, he switches the light on, and I shrink under the intense blare.

"What the hell!" I croak, "Jace, turn it off!" The room goes black, and I hear his heavy footfall, feel the bed dip, and then he is there, hands nestled either side of my head.

"I thought you had gone home," he grumbles. Of course he did. I'm glad he can't see me roll my eyes. If he weren't weighing the quilt down, I'd kick him.

"I'm tired." It's hard for me to twist with his weight

Betrayal

on the quilt, but I manage it *just* and turn away from him.

"Where's your car?" He rolls, so he is facing me and no longer trapping me. I blink through the darkness until slowly, my eyes adjust, and I see the outline of his remarkable face.

"At the gallery." My voice trails off in my yawn. "Go away. I'm angry with you." I pout, closing my eyes on him. He is still in his suit, smelling heavenly and looking sharp, with his hair styled and jaw trimmed to a shadow.

"Why is it at the gallery?" His whisper is a simple question, any accusation is completely gone, and he sounds cautious. He knows I'm seriously pissed off. I sigh into the blackness.

"I went to work but felt dizzy, so Harriet drove me home. You're right. I'm not fine. Happy now?" I sound like a spoilt brat, and a small part of me cringes at how melodramatic I'm being.

"No." Deft fingers brush into my hair. "Why didn't you call me?" He presses forward and finds my mouth. I tug away, fighting off the need to cement my mouth to his and let him make me feel better.

I give him my best, are you kidding me look.

"Because I'm mad at you, and you were miles away." I accentuate each word slowly, wanting to add, *with her!*

"Lily, look—"

"You gave me a fucking curfew, Jacc, like a child!" I pull away and sit up. "Even if you were right about me not being one hundred percent, dictating my bedtime is embarrassing." I feel the sting of that now, and my eyes prick with tears. Sniffing, I push the pillows back so I'm more comfortable. But the fact that I'm still not okay is pulling at my emotions. Why aren't I better yet?

"Hey." He is sitting up too. The bedside lamp clicks

on, and he is watching me carefully. He looks tired, his eyes heavy, and his jaw unshaved. "Lily, shit, I'm sorry. I didn't want them overstaying their welcome, or you staying up out of politeness, and you've been crashing before ten most days, anyway." I refuse to accept his valid point—I have been sleeping more.

"I want to go to sleep." I move to the other side. It's cold, but I close my eyes and will him to turn the light off. I'm too angry to have this conversation, and my reaction will be emotional and not rational.

"Did you mean what you said about moving in being a bad decision?" His hand slips around my waist, the light stays on, and I open my eyes to find him staring at me through the bank of windows. The glow makes his eyes look honey-thick, hypnotic, and his hair is flopping forward.

"You're trying to control me," I tell him slowly. "I don't like it." I punctuate the words. "I don't stop you from doing your own thing or tell you what you should be doing. I like you for you, not for how I could make you." I tilt my head to make my point, then close my eyes. I really am boiling mad.

"That's not what I'm doing." He is quiet, thoughtful. He may believe that now, but I know he is thinking it over. Good.

"Feels that way, and if it is that way, then yes, it's bad that I moved in. Good night." I wait for the light to dim, but it doesn't happen. Instead, his hand moves down and pushes between my legs. "Sex isn't going to fix this." I sound bored, petulant.

"You don't know that." His voice has dropped an octave, and his hands rotate in little circles. I feel sorry for him because he honestly believes this is the answer. Instead, I swing the quilt up and get out of bed with the

Betrayal

intention of moving to a Jace-free zone. "I'm sleeping on the sofa," I grumble, but my head goes all wishy-washy, and I stumble into the glass with a short yelp. Jace jumps toward me and grabs me as I slide down the pane. The look on his face causes me to sob in a gurgle of fear.

"Fucking hell." He pulls me to his chest, and I stay for a minute, with him crouched down by me. "Come here." He pulls me up, and I go on a gulp of worried air. Jace walks us until he is sitting on the chair in the corner; my legs bent, either side of his. I drop onto his shoulder and lay my head there. "If you say you're fine, I will tan your arse." He grabs my arse for effect. My heart is thrumming crazily against my breastbone.

"But I do actually feel okay," I mumble into his shoulder. Jace's sigh is loud enough to wake our non-neighbours. I sit up slowly. "It's just if I stand too quickly." I cup his face and plead with him to hear what I am saying—plead with myself to believe it.

"And the tiredness?" he points out. I shrug. I guess my body is just healing. We aren't going to agree; that much is obvious. We eye each other for a minute, and I can see the genuine worry laced in his gaze. I can't do this now. I'm so confused about how I feel around him. I'm angry and scared, and I want him to hold me until I feel that undeniably serene wave of safety that I experience when he is close by.

"Take me to bed," I whisper, my thumb glides over his plush mouth.

"Bed-bed or the sofa?" He laughs, nipping my thumb.

"Piss off." I smirk reluctantly, still feeling the sting of his ridiculous curfew. I should tell him to get on the sofa where he can stick his curfew up his arse, and I make a similar comment as he takes us to bed.

Chapter Thirteen

Jace's alarm drags me out of my heavy sleep. He curses and turns it off, twisting to look at me. I blink groggily at him and pull the quilt over my head.

"Too early," I whine, stretching lazily.

"I know, sorry. I forgot to turn it off." His voice is riddled with tiredness too. He manoeuvres himself so he is under the quilt, and through the morning light, I can see his face well. "You're still mad at me." It's a statement, softly spoken and full of reluctant remorse.

"That all depends on how you choose to treat me, Jace." I don't want to nag him, but surely he must be able to see it from my point of view.

"Like a queen." His smile is small but sure.

"We'll see," I muse, wriggling into him for added warmth. I yawn into his chest and close my eyes. I know he planned to go into work later today due to his flight getting in so late, so he is happy to grab a few more hours and thrusts his leg between mine and hooks an arm over my waist.

"Let's have a lazy morning, and then later, if you're

feeling up to it, we can go out for the afternoon," he suggests. His hand rolls up my bare back, and he pulls me tightly to him. I want to stay mad at him and tell him we are a team, but I know I haven't made things easy for him.

"What about work?" I nuzzle into him.

"I caught up on emails on the plane—we can grab dinner out?" It sounds perfect, but my eyes are too heavy, and my breathing is low and lazy, so I hum in agreement.

"I'm taking that as a yes," he muses. I manage a nod, and I'm fazing back out into a light but blissful sleep.

The wind whips at my hair, the air is bitter and cold, but Jace has his arm wrapped around my lower back, and I'm leaning into him. He arranged for us to go on a Thames night cruise. In all my years of living in London, I have never once stepped foot on a boat. Everywhere is lit up, threatening the oppressive darkness above. Below, the water laps and splashes at the boat as it chugs along. I expected there to be more people, but we are one of three couples. Jace pecks my hair.

"I'm stuffed," he complains for the third time. I grin and pull his other hand around my front. I'm sporting a food baby of my own.

"I love Gustav's. I've been with Hat," I tell him. I then proceed to enlighten him about my awful date with Mitch. "I honestly wanted to slap Cass." My laugh is throaty.

"Ah, so that's the man I was up against?" Jace has my hips and pulls them back into his hard groin, reminding me of how much male is enveloping me.

"Never," I scoff. "I cancelled, and he just showed up

at The Loft," I tell him over my shoulder, "which meant he tracked me down. It was creepy." I shudder. Jace is silently laughing behind me. "What?" I snuggle into him and look out at the twinkle of city nightlife.

"You must think I'm a creep, then, because if you recall, I followed you too." His smile is audible, even if I can't see his face.

"That's different." I grin, remembering how he just kept popping up in my life and dragging me off for wild sex. "I was attracted to you, too. Mitch looked like my old math teacher." I waft his silly remark away.

"Well, if he held any resemblance to mine, you have my deepest sympathy," Jace drawls, pulling a laugh from me. "Seriously, the man looked like a serial killer in a gilet," he informs me, and his chest vibrates with each laugh.

"Mitch had this nervous nod thing going on." I'm laughing hard now too. "He looked like one of those toys people stick in the back of their car. I couldn't help but compare him to you." I go a little breathless, making that admission. Jace grips my chin and tips my face to peck my lips, as his eyes stare into mine.

"You got off lucky then, I'd say." Jace brushes my hair back again to keep the wind from picking it up.

"You would. You won." I jab him lightly with my arm, smiling happily up at him.

"Yes, I did." He is painfully smug. "Besides, look at me," he drawls. "I'm definitely a Nobel prize." He surprises me further and flexes his free arm.

"God, you are so full of yourself," I scoff, but yes, he certainly is a prize. My prize. I never expected to be this happy. It wasn't on my agenda.

"Here." Jace hands me my camera again, and I take a few more pictures as we cruise up the river. A shadow falls over us, so we both look up to see one of the men sitting behind us smile in greeting. He points at my camera.

"Do you want me to take a photo of you both?" I grin widely.

"Yes, please." I give him a quick rundown of my camera, and he moves to the other side of the boat. The camera clicks away, and Jace and I smile broadly. Or at least I do. Jace bites at my neck and then pulls me in for a deep kiss. I laugh shyly. "Get off." I blush furiously, and our photographer smirks, handing it back over.

"Did you want a photo?" I offer, finding his partner smiling at him.

"Oh, no, thanks. We come on this regularly," he tells us and winks back at her, "we have dozens of pictures."

"Well, thank you." He leaves us, and we thumb through the photos. When we get to the one of Jace mauling me, he begins to grin widely.

"I like this," he breathes. His thumb dances over the screen, and he shoots me a hot look from below thick lashes. "I like me, when I'm with you." He swallows, slipping his hand below my coat to rest on my stomach.

"Ditto, minus curfews and wine control," I mutter around a cheeky laugh. I tuck myself back in, and Jace snorts out a gruff reply that gets lost in my hair when he sucks on my neck.

"Stop it!" I slap my hand over my neck, grinning. We sit in silence, enjoying the scenery. It's not much longer before we are back in the comfort of his flash car and flying back to his.

———

We share a shower, and Jace takes it upon himself to massage my shoulders. In fact, he is so painfully gentle and slow in his ministrations that I'm left in a state of delirious relaxation. He carries me back to his bed and lays me down, pecking my nose.

"You look drugged," he chokes out on a light laugh.

"I feel it." I grin, staring up at his slumberous eyes.

"Well, don't go to sleep. I have something to show you. Get some clothes on, or else we will never get anything done." He slaps my arse playfully and finds himself some clothes. When I make no intention to move, he pulls me out a t-shirt of his and flings it at me. I sit up and pull it on, forgoing underwear, and follow him to the lounge. I drop down on the sofa and flick the TV on, finding something uninteresting to have on as background noise. Jace collects his laptop and plonks himself ungracefully next to me. "These are in my top ten," he tells me, once his laptop has fired up, and he has logged into a site. He spins the computer, where a list of holiday villas stare back at me.

"Oh, wow." My finger moves on its own accord, and I open up the most viewed one, his favourite. I need my glasses for this, really. I lean over and pull open the small drawer under the coffee table and slip them on.

"Those fucking glasses are like Viagra." He pushes at his cock when it springs to life behind his work out trousers. I grin but lean to check the details of the villa, and he takes full advantage and hooks a finger in the neck of my shirt and pulls it to look down my top.

"Now, look up at me slowly," his instruction is soft, needy. I can't hide my smile, but I do it anyway, and he shakes his head.

"Fucking perfect." A wolfish smile splashes over his

face before he attempts to tug the laptop free, but I hold it tightly.

"Not happening, Bennett. I want to look at these holidays," I tell him forcefully, and swat his hand away when it slides up my thigh. We'd already discussed that waiting until next year to go away was better, as the winter work rush was already upon us.

"Well, you could at least cross your legs. It's like being taunted with Pandora's box." He takes my ankles and yanks me to him. I squeak and grip the laptop to save it from falling, and his t-shirt rides up, leaving me exposed.

"Jace! Stop it." It's a false plea. I love his playful side.

Lifting my foot, he kisses my ankle.

"Never," he declares. I twist and lay my back against his chest. The laptop is covering my lap, and as I tug the t-shirt back into place, he mutters something about me being a spoilsport, but I ignore his childish jibe.

"This is your favourite?" I confirm. It is a little more than I expected to pay, but I can see the appeal. It is situated in a small fishing village on a hillside in Croatia.

"Yes." He points over my shoulder at the screen, instructing me to select the next photo. I do, and a stunning sea view covers the screen.

"Oh wow, this looks incredible," I gush, moving the cursor over the image to enlarge it. The coastal view is impossibly attractive, secluded, and dreamy.

"Let's go. They have availability throughout March." Jace hooks his feet over mine, so I'm trapped.

Biting my lip, I scan the price.

"I don't know. It's more than I thought," I tell him honestly.

"Lily, I've got it covered. I want to do this for you. It's a little way off yet, anyway." I suck in a deep breath, but

Betrayal

he stops any words from coming out. "I know it's not going to be baking hot or a long time away, but it will be ours. Don't you just want to be tucked away with me on a little island?" Well, when he puts it like that. I mumble a reluctant yes. I feel his grin against my neck as he reaches to shut the top of the laptop down. "Good, because I already booked it." His chest vibrates with laughter when I snap around, almost jarring my neck in the process.

"Why am I not surprised?" I purse my lips, and he licks across the pouted seam. My lips relax into a smile.

"Lily Spencer, why didn't I find you sooner?" He poses the question for us both and goes quiet as he contemplates this himself. I shrug. I have no idea, but I'm glad we found each other, eventually.

He tugs the laptop away and flips me, crushing me to the sofa.

"You ready to be thoroughly loved?" His hips do a slow, hard roll, and my gasp gets lost around his tongue. "I think that was a yes." He grins.

I have felt the absence of the gallery. When I arrive on Tuesday morning after a weekend of relaxation with Jace, I'm feeling thoroughly refreshed. Harriet is waiting for me with a steaming mug. I've decided to take it slowly this week—every other day for half a day. Carl and Cass have both been popping in to help out when needed.

All the bruising has gone down, and I have managed to cover any yellowness with cosmetics. In fact, everything is perfect, as though all of my stars have aligned, and I'm now reaping the benefits. They do say things get worse before they get better, and with such a commanding man by my side, any discontent has abated.

"Morning!" I smile, laying my things down on the desk and taking the cup held out for me. "Thank you." Her eyes linger on the expertly disguised scar in my hairline, and she looks away when she knows I have caught her out. I know she still has questions, but I don't intend to discuss it. It's done. It's over, and everything in my life is perfect.

"I feel like I haven't seen you in months," I joke, blowing on my drink.

"I know. Are you sure you're okay?" The hesitant tone suggests she believes otherwise. "You worried me last time." Harriet moves a little closer, anticipating another wave of dizziness.

"Me too, but I'm feeling okay. I've just got to take it slowly. Let's get me up to speed. I'm sure there is something I have missed." I steer the conversation on to more neutral ground, trying to slip around her anxiety.

Harriet cups her drink and leans on the desk.

"Sure." She takes a quick sip and smiles with a heavy groan. "Is there anything better than coffee in the morning?" she states. My mind's eye flashes back to this morning and the amazing oral sex I was woken with.

I laugh and try some coffee, lifting my cup in fake agreement and swallowing the bitterness swirling around my mouth. Yes, there are better things than coffee, and they involve Jace Bennett, but I'm not about to share that with her. I swallow the dark liquid unwillingly.

"Any bills that need my immediate attention?" I question, slowly dropping down in the chair and looking out of the window at the steady traffic moving along the street.

"Oh, no. Jace sorted all that out." She frowns at me as though my accident left me with a dickey brain.

"Jace?" My cup stalls halfway.

"Yes, he was here all Wednesday—" Her voice trails off when she realises I am none the wiser. "I think he just wanted to ensure you had little to worry about." She grimaces at the tightness pressing in on my face. He never mentioned a thing to me.

"What else did he do?" I'm gobsmacked and angry. Should I be angry? I know he is only trying to help, but this is my business!

She blanches.

"He was just checking the finances and stuff like that," she whispers, her light eyes widen with guilt.

What!

"Harriet, why didn't you call me?" Her lip wobbles and I sigh inwardly. "It's not your fault," I smooth over, "but this isn't his business, and although you may find it highly romantic, I find it intrusive." She clears her throat with a nod. Shit, I feel like a massive bitch.

"I'm sorry." She bites her lip and looks away, causing guilt to shift through me.

"Don't be. I know how persuasive he can be," I mutter. "It's really not your fault," I assure her.

"I promise that will never happen again," she vows. "I really am sorry." Her fingers twist, reminding me of her age.

My smile is forced.

"I know. It's fine. Honestly." With that, I stand and head back to my office, simmering with anger.

As soon as I close the door, I pull my phone free and bring his name up, calling him.

"Hey, baby, missing me already?" He laughs. I wish I could respond with what he wants to hear,

"Why did you look through my finances?" It comes out sharper than intended, but I can't bear the thought of him snooping through the diabolical state of my finances when he has a booming business that rakes in god knows how much money. It's fair to say I am barely scraping the surface of even being in a stable situation. I merely keep my head afloat, and although the events and marketing pay off, I'm still not making much money.

"I was just managing the bills," he deflects.

"But you looked through my finances," I repeat, picking up a bill that is still sealed on my desk. No doubt a new one that will be another noose to my finances.

"What's yours is mine." His response makes me stiffen.

"Well, as you will have found, there isn't a lot for you to have," I spit, painfully embarrassed and thoroughly annoyed that he has been snooping through my life.

His laugh is light.

"I'm not after your money. A problem halved is a problem shared, beautiful. I thought we were in this together?" His voice drops in a question, reassuring and teasing me, all at once. I can hear the smile in his voice. I sigh and try to box away my misplaced feelings. "You're doing great with the gallery—on a steady roll. That's good. I'm really proud of you, baby." His genuine praise softens my hurt.

"Sorry," I'm remorseful and pliant.

"Good, you can show me just how much later," he quips. I can hear the steady tap of him on his computer.

"You're filthy," I mutter, hiding my reluctant grin.

"Just how you like me." He laughs heartily.

"Thank you for taking care of The Loft." I finally push past my pouting lips.

"Always. My appointment is here. I'll grab dinner on

the way home. Love you, even when you're a grumpy, stubborn woman." He chuckles.

"Oh, you have a nerve! You need a word with your inner control freak," I splutter around an incredulous laugh.

"You like my inner control freak," he drawls. "And before you deny it, I think you should cast your mind back to Sunday night," he throws in.

"Sorry, can't, I have more important things to do. Like work," I quip, holding back a laugh, but my mind is already running back to re-encounter the loving but demanding session he bestowed on me.

"You're *there*. I made you cry," he gloats.

"Oh, look. I have another call coming in," I huff, happily irritated he can read me so well.

"That's my ego reminding you we're both right," he scoffs out on a deep chuckle. I burst out laughing. "I've got to go, gorgeous. See you tonight."

"See you later." I'm grinning wildly.

I give myself a moment to think before I throw myself into work. The coffee Harriet made is finally cool enough, so I sip it. I pull back and look at the cup before trying it again, and screw up my mouth in disgust. I have to force it down my throat because I refuse to spit it back in my cup.

"Hat!" I yell. I can hear her footsteps but continue shouting, anyway. "Did you get new coffee?" She enters with a perplexed look on her face, and she shakes her head, sniffing the cup as I push it away. "Perhaps it's gone off? It tastes weird." I frown at her, asking silently if she thinks so too.

"Oh, sorry, I can make you a new one?" She offers, picking it up and sniffing it.

"Oh no, thanks. I didn't mean for you to make a

fresh one," I say. "Probably should stick to water. I still feel a bit groggy," I admit, and concern pulls at her mouth.

"Do you think you came back too early?" She looks ready to pass out herself.

"No." I laugh. "I was going crazy. I feel fine physically. It's just this tiredness and the on and off nausea, but that's mainly if I feel a little dizzy." Her eyes widen a fraction, and I regret opening up to her, especially when I know how anxious she is, anyway. "When I get up too quickly," I explain, in the hope that she will relax.

"Is that normal?" She makes herself comfy in the chair opposite mine.

"Apparently," I grunt out. I think I have been through enough without the consistent side effects. Surely it has to end soon?

"Well, just keep taking it slowly." She shrugs at me and takes my cup, sniffing it as she goes. It really did taste vile.

Chapter Fourteen

The next week follows a similar pattern. I have been taking it slowly at work and feel much better after seeing the doctor and being given the all clear. As far as my life goes, everything is how I want it to be. Things are good with Jace, and I'm enjoying how things have progressed between us. The dynamic has changed, and we have so much to look forward to.

It's early, but I'm up with Jace and ready for work. It's hard to fall back to sleep when being woken up by such a brute. I have ignored his playful jibes all morning and spent the last ten minutes searching for my phone.

I finally find my phone in his office. I unplug it and quickly swipe on the notification on the lock screen until my eyes are pulled away by the paper strewn over the surface: planning permission, extension drawings, building contracts, and finalised plans all spring out at me. I shift through them, seeing an elaborate design. It takes me all of two seconds to realise it's The Hub. The roof is elevated and slanted out over one end—a huge bedroom consisting of an en-suite, walk-in wardrobe, and a balcony over the lake. A family bathroom, three spare bedrooms, and an open, higher lounge surround a galley landing and two-story windows, which bask in the stunning view. It looks like an exclusive mountain resort!

"Hey, beautiful, have you seen my keys?" Jace's rough morning voice pulls me around, the papers still in my hand.

"You're extending The Hub. Are you planning to sell after completion?" My eyes look back to the plans that have taken a lot of thought. I hope he isn't going to sell, but I see no reason to extend when it's only us two? The place is big as it is. I'm not sure I want to move to the city. I like the remoteness of this place. He wanders in, looking sharp in his suit.

"What's The Hub?" he asks, expertly tying his tie. My cheeks flush lightly because it has always been a silent endearment of mine.

I tuck my hair back.

"Here, this," I tell him, quickly hoping to skate over it, "why would you sell it? Is that why you're extending; to sell?" I whisper. I love this place. He's only just asked me to move in, so why would he move us out?

"The Hub," he whispers, his tone thoughtful. He smiles at me, his nostrils flaring with poorly disguised satisfaction. "I like that." He wanders to me slowly and takes my butt in his hands, tugging me close. I have to tilt my head to look up at him, and his bright eyes take in my face with a knowing but personal grin, a smile used only for me.

"Why are you extending?" I lift the papers, willing him to answer.

"For us. Why did you think I was selling?" He laughs at me with a shake of his head and pecks my cheek quickly before picking up a few more files. I lift the papers and stare at them, perplexed. In all honesty, I don't understand much of what I'm reading, but looking over it with my newfound knowledge, I don't know why I came to the conclusion I did. I suppose the extension seems too big for the two of us. It is too big. Selling is the next viable option.

"I don't know," I admit. "I guess I worried you were and then ran with it," I huff stupidly, placing them back on the desk.

"Well, worry no more: The Hub," he says slowly, smiling softly at me, "is ours." His lips do a happy dance along my jawline.

"I like The Hub." I lift my nose in the air and raise my arms so they hook around his neck. I want him back on my neck.

"I like it too, baby." That voice, the low one he uses, makes me shiver, and his eyes smile knowingly at me.

"That never gets old," he tells me, rubbing his hand lightly up my side, the files pressed into my back.

"I will, and then you won't find me attractive," I grumble playfully. He pulls back, affronted, but his eyes, those endless sap-coloured orbs, are gleaming.

"I'm older than you," he points out, thrusting his hips for good measure. "If anyone is at risk of being found less attractive first, it's me." He runs his nose along my cheek and inhales my perfume. His groin swells and hardens, and his throat rumbles with a deep groan as his teeth nip and dance along my jawline.

"I could never *not* find you attractive," I confess shyly, staring at his remarkable face.

"Same applies to you, woman. Now kiss me and tell me where my keys are." I press a soft one to his full lips as he sweeps his tongue in, and I sigh loudly, running my nails into his hair and holding him close.

On a defeated groan, he pulls away.

"You'll put me out of business soon." He chuckles, unhooking my arms. "Keys?" he reminds me, stepping away.

"Maybe in the book hive?" I suggest, not remembering where he placed them last night.

"Okay, I've got to shoot, have a big meeting with the construction company, and another with some hotel guy." He steps back and checks the files are all in one piece.

"So big, you can't recall his name." I laugh.

"Carl will update me." He winks, sending me an air kiss.

"Was that how it was with me?" I say sweetly. I even bat my lashes at him. Jace is already out of the office door, but he comes back and leans against the frame, arms spread wide so his chest expands through the space.

"It wouldn't have mattered how it was with you: one look and I was a goner." He grins through a lip-bitten stare.

I can't help but heckle him.

"Even with Megan?" I pout my lips, and he shudders.

His arms drop from the framework.

"God don't. I drank way too much and just thought" – he wafts his hand out – "fuck it," he spits, still unhappy with his poor decision.

"Literally," I drawl, shooting a flirtatious look up through my lashes, and battling the urge to laugh.

"Don't plague my mind. I'm happy thinking only of you." He comes back to me and reaches down to squeeze the full globes of my arse. I press into him, feeling and absorbing that natural sensation of safeness.

"Me too." I press up and kiss him. "Have a great

day," I say, and running my fingers over his collar, I let him pull me on for a quick, deep toe-curling kiss.

"And you, baby. I'll grab Thai on the way home." His lips peck at my mouth between each word, and he hums his approval and powers me back, so I thud against the glass. His tongue dives in and sweeps through my mouth on an earthy groan.

"You'll be late!" I pant, not at all bothered if he actually is. I could stay locked in this lakeside hideaway forever.

"I'll miss you," he grumbles, unlocking our lips and dropping his eyes so his lashes shield them.

"I'll miss you too."

"Love you."

"Ditto." I grin, and he awards me with a wink before going to find his keys.

I'm beginning to depend on him and that physical connection only he can offer. He has lured me into a soul-deep lust and hazy, loved-up bubble. I'm swimming in relationship heaven. We're possibly cringe-worthy, but I'm too happy to give a shit.

Jace leaves me, and I study the extensive drawings. There is enough room for ten people to live here. I stare at the master bedroom plan for a long time. The walk-in sits adjacent to the bathroom and bedroom, but is open to both. I like that it is still its own room. It puts his already drool-worthy ensemble to shame. His current bedroom is being converted into a utility. The office and gym are staying, but the layout is changing slightly, and another room is labelled 'Lily'. I frown and look over more pictures, plans, and paper where he has jotted notes, but there is nothing to suggest what the room is for. I realise the time and grab my phone and bag, reluctantly cutting my snooping short.

My drive to work is eventful. It seems everyone is in a rush and lacking patience, and when I finally pull up outside The Loft, Harriet is walking up the street.

"Hey!" she calls.

"Traffic was a nightmare again. I can't get used to this commuting." I laugh tiredly. "I'm going to have to start leaving earlier," I grumble dramatically.

"I'm glad I can tube it some days," she tells me, meeting me at the door.

"So, how was the date?" I ask, pushing the key into the door. I still get an inner shudder from when Adam attacked me here. Harriet is on edge too, it seems. She checks over her shoulder, and we both push inside. Silly really, as Adam is paying the price of his actions.

"I really like him," she sighs, "he's funny and kind." She unzips her coat and fiddles with her hair.

"He seems to be rather taken with you, too," I respond. We both head out the back, and while I put my bags away, she is flicking the coffee machine on.

"He asked to take me out again," she calls through to me. I'm really happy for her. Simon seems such a good guy, the kind your parents want for you. Harriet had told me that he works in design for a large marketing firm.

"That's good. Have you arranged anything yet, or is it another surprise? Where did you go last night, by the way?" She never did mention where he took her.

"We went to a show at the theatre." Her face is full of excited disbelief. I slide my lunch into the fridge and make a cup of tea, all the while observing her girlish excitement.

"Anything good?" I mentally file it away to suggest to Jace.

Her face pulls at the side.

"Some artsy show. I didn't really understand what

was going on half the time," she admits sheepishly. I laugh at her honesty. "It was captivating though." My lips pull a little. "A broken love story." She frowns, no doubt thinking back over the show. "It was very romantic," she muses thoughtfully.

"He definitely scored brownie points then?" I squeeze the tea bag out and dispose of it.

"Yes," she breathes. "And he kissed me," she blurts out, her cheeks flushing wildly. I pull back at the highness of her voice. "Is that bad?"

"It's a kiss," I reassure her, and she brushes her dress down. "And?" I coax more out of her. She sighs, and I grin, nudging her out of the way with my hip so I can make the coffee she has forgotten about. "I'm really happy for you, Hat."

"Me too," she squeaks, "just don't want to get my hopes up too much." She scrunches her nose up.

I nod: it's realistic and safe.

"Just take it slowly and enjoy," I tell her, not at all sure where my sudden wisdom has come from, as it left me high and dry where Jace was concerned.

Her phone pings, and she busies herself with that for a moment. "Your eleven has cancelled and wants to rebook next Thursday." I mentally run through my calendar.

"I have lunch booked with Alfredo. He is in London for a few days. Can she do three-thirty?" I ask around my cup.

"I'll check and let you know. Also, we are running out of coffee beans," she says, half distracted with her first task.

I wrinkle my nose.

"Well, that won't do." I laugh. "I can grab some tomorrow on my way in. Right, I need to call the bank," I excuse myself, heading back down to my office.

My day is slow, so Harriet and I decide to grab lunch together and head to the park, my camera in tow. I perch cross-legged on the bench, and between sips of my herbal tea, I lift my camera to take a few pictures. The lens opens up, and the object of my admiration tunnels in my vision. A tree is dipping down into the water, the branches reaching for the inky liquid. The leaves have admitted defeat and abandoned the bark, dropping free and floating like tiny boats. I catch a fish breaking the surface and smile as I pull the camera away and thumb through the images.

"You always photograph water," Harriet observes. I skip through my images until I find a similar one I captured when I was at Jace's.

"I know. I like it. It's calming, serene. I'm definitely a water baby." I laugh. I know Harriet is more drawn to sketching portraits, defining and toning with charcoal. She's good, and I have no shame in admitting she is better than me. But she isn't ready to share her talents just yet, and I won't push her. I know Alfredo would buy her work in a second. She is somehow able to capture the inner pain of her subject. Her creative eye brings it to the surface of the paper, in its most raw form. She has a real talent.

"Jace's house sits on a lake, as in literally sits over it." I laugh. "His bedroom drops away into it, and past the tree line are more lakes. It's stunning." I point to the image confirming the lakes.

"Wow, it's so vast," she gapes and holds up a muffin

Betrayal

for me. I take it and pick at the fruit submerged in the fluffy sponge, murmuring my thanks to her. "I bet it's so peaceful at night when you're that far out." Where I pick at my muffin, she dives right in and takes a big bite.

"It is. I feel hundreds of miles away." I pop more cake in my mouth and pack my camera away before picking my tea back up.

"We should head back."

———

Work is just as slow in the afternoon. Harriet makes a sale, but I find myself stuck on the phone to the bank for the second time and then have to take a further call from the police following up on the attack. Cass calls to inform me she is coming round later, which I'm looking forward to.

By the time closing comes round, both Harriet and I are racing to get out of the door and home.

"You look shattered," she says, waiting with me while I lock up. She is constantly checking over her shoulder.

"He's not coming back," I tell her. She shifts nervously, and I feel bad. For my own selfish reasons, I have kept her in the dark, and left her to run the place alone, worried some psycho might turn up and do the same to her.

I swallow my pride and suck in a breath.

"The guy that attacked me was my ex, who I had a restraining order on. He broke that order, and he is now serving time. He isn't coming back, Harriet." She gapes at me and nods stiffly. She hasn't a clue what to say to me, and I don't blame her. It's a mess.

"I've put you through a lot, and I'm sorry," I apologise to her and clear my throat.

"No, I am. I didn't expect you to divulge such personal information, but I'm glad you did." I smile sympathetically at her. Anyone would think it was her who has the crazy ex. "I feel a lot more at ease," she says awkwardly. "I'll see you Monday?" she asks, deliberating over her mental calendar. We agreed I'd give tomorrow and Saturday a miss. I feel exhausted.

"Yep, have a great weekend. Any problems, call me." I watch her walk down the street before I head to my car.

Cass is already there when I pull up. She follows me in, we both kick our shoes off, and she grabs some wine. I collect two glasses and ice before holding them out for her to fill, and we move to the sofas. I pull a fluffy blanket over my feet, ignoring the niggling dizziness hanging over me.

"So, you're living here then?" Cass side-eyes me as she sips on some wine. I stare at the glass and offer her a shrug.

"Not officially." That's a lie. I don't know why I feel so awkward telling her.

"So unofficially," she scoffs, "are you living here?" Her tone is verging on boredom.

"Jace wants me to," I whisper, filling my mouth with wine to avoid further questioning.

"And?" she urges me, shaking her wine midair as she tries to coax more information out of me.

"And what?" I mutter, not happy with this conversation.

She rolls her eyes.

"You're hard work." She kicks my foot. "Do you want to move in?"

"I've not been given much choice." That's not entirely true, but I honestly think he would have bullied me into living here.

Betrayal

"Lily, stop being so evasive," Cass groans at me, her patience gone. "*Do you* or do you *not* want to live here," she accentuates, giving me her best Cassandra Faraday glare—the once she reserves for when her patience has worn thin.

"Yes." I swallow the nerves that word brings to me. The rational side of me screams that it's too soon, but every other part of me is basking like a pampered cat at being so lavished on by Jace. Everything has slotted together so nicely. It's early days, but being under the same roof is nice, really nice. We are totally content.

"So where is he?" She looks around as though she's missed him somehow, which would be hard, given that we are sitting in a giant glass box.

"Gone to my flat to pick up more stuff. Also, he is working on an extension." I lift my glass and use my free hand to work the TV.

"This late? Hasn't he got minions for that?" I roll my eyes at her.

"For here. Says he wants to build up and put a balcony out over the lake." I'd spoken earlier with him about it. I managed to grab a few minutes after my lunch and between his meetings.

"Wow, he is certainly very serious about you being here."

"Is it a mistake?" I pick at my trousers.

Cass shakes her head.

"No. I think it would have happened eventually, and by eventually, I mean in the next three months." She laughs. "The man likes to move quickly. He knows you're a flight risk!" She gives me a pointed look.

"I am not!" I cough around my glass.

"Oh, hun, you so are, and now he gets it." She

shrugs her dainty shoulders. "We should arrange a date night, all four of us." I rest back and grin at her.

"Sure, sounds good." My eyes glitter with excitement. I could use a night out.

"We can go to that Italian place you like," she suggests, kicking her feet up and sighing happily. It's the first time in a good few weeks that we have had some girl time together.

"Okay, I will mention it later." I can't see Jace disagreeing.

"How are you feeling?" Cass wonders, her eyes fixed on the screen.

"Good. I should be back to work full time on Monday. Jace is still watching me like a hawk," I confess.

"You don't still mean" – her eyes flip to my crotch – "I bet you're sealed up!" She visibly shudders.

My mouth drops open with a shocked laugh. I grab a pillow and clip her with it. "Cassandra Jane Faraday!" She is just awful.

"Don't hit me. Blame the hunk who won't hit the trunk!" She is a mess of snorting giggles.

"*The trunk*." My mouth pulls down at the side, but then I roll my eyes at her and smirk. It's hard not to when she is laughing all over the sofa. "And everything in that area is fine. Honestly, things are going so well."

"Well, I'm glad," she tells me, shifting, so she sinks low into the sofa and is perched on a huge cushion. "You deserve to be happy." I knock her foot with mine in thanks, and we snuggle in to watch an episode of her latest TV obsession.

Chapter Fifteen

It's been our busiest Saturday to date, and Harriet and I have been run ragged.

"I cannot wait to get home and sink some wine," I tell her with a short laugh. She is smirking and drops down into the chair up front.

"Tell me about it. Where did all those people come from?" She closes her eyes and massages her temples. "Thank god it's the weekend."

"Got any plans?" I say, loading up my handbag.

"Sleep and more sleep. I'm still recovering from my holiday," she grumbles. "I think Faye was trying to kill me."

"Joke's on her then." I wink as I head down to my office to grab my phone. I'm tidying my desk and checking that I locked the back door when Harriet calls down to me.

"You have a guest!" On cue, the bell dings, and I poke my head round to have a look. It's Jace.

I hear his deep rumble as he says hello to Harriet, then he is on his way down to me.

"Hey, gorgeous."

"Hey, yourself. I thought you were seeing Viktor this afternoon?" Not that I mind that he is here.

"Change of plan. You ready? I have a surprise for you." He reaches me on the other side of the desk and pecks my lips. "You smell nice," he comments.

"Ditto." I grin and cup his face, giving him the kind of kiss I need after this morning.

"Don't start what you can't finish." He chuckles against my lips.

"You know I'm not a big fan of surprises," I admit, his face still in my hands.

"You will like this. Come on." He takes my hand, and Harriet waves us goodbye as she tightens her coat.

"See you Monday!"

"Bye, Hat." Jace watches while I set the alarm and lock up. I turn to look at him. "Is this why you demanded you drop me off today?"

"Pretty much."

"Well, Cass agreed to drop me home," I remind him.

"No, Cass agreed to go along with it. She knew I was coming for you."

"Ah, so you're in cahoots?"

"Cahoots?" He grins, then nods to the car. "No, Cass knew this surprise is what you need, so she did as she was told. You should probably take a leaf out of her book." The cheeky devil. I lift my brows and see his raise too. He is challenging me.

"Well, with the Cass I know, it's the kind of leaf you wouldn't want me to have."

"Why is it a marijuana leaf?" he asks, deadpan. I burst out laughing as I get in the car.

"So, are you going to tell me what this surprise is?"

"Nope."

"Not even a hint?"

"Nope." He starts the engine, and I buckle up.

"A clue?"

"Lily, it's not a surprise if I tell you anything."

"Can you not jus—"

"No." He laughs. "You're the worst at this." I smirk and relax as we head through the streets and out of London. Initially, I assume we are heading home, but it becomes apparent we aren't. I'm itching to ask, but I keep my lips firmly shut and settle in for the journey, however long that may be.

After an hour of steady driving, we roll into a sleepy village. It's picturesque with a cute stream and thatch-roofed homes. It's a million miles from any bustling city and exactly the kind of atmosphere I need after today and the last few weeks. The only information I was able to prise out of Jace was that we are staying somewhere overnight. We wind our way through the village until we are almost passing through, but then Jace takes the next turning, and I see a cottage tucked away between a few fields.

"Is this where we are staying?" I grin. It's perfect, cute sash windows and not a person in sight.

"Yes. The owner prepared lunch so we can snoop, eat, then I want you on your back." He gives me a devious wink, and I can't help but laugh at him.

"What if I want those things in a different order?"

"Back, eat, snoop?" he queries as we hit the drive and cruise under a huge willow tree. "Snoop, back, eat? Eat, back, snoop?" His voice is laced with amusement, and I roll my eyes as he comes to a stop out the front. I hop straight out. I definitely need to eat.

"Can we eat first?" I say as Jace pulls two cases out the back.

"Sure, the code for the key box is 1857: Eat, back, snoop it is," he says, loud enough for me to hear. I shake my head and get the key before letting us in. Jace gives my arse a squeeze as I hang my coat up. His hands wrap around my waist, and he sighs, dropping his chin to my shoulder.

"Surprise, beautiful."

"Thank you." He is so thoughtful that I could bloody cry. Emotion clogs my throat, but I keep it at bay.

"You deserve it, and, quite frankly, I needed it too." His lips brush my temple, then he is off carrying the cases with him. He does need this—we both do. It will be good for us both.

"Did you pack for me?" I ask as his wide frame disappears up a narrow flight of stairs.

"No, I value my life, and you don't seem the type to want to wear an all-in-one puffer coat." I laugh and look up at him, bunched up on the small staircase. "Cass came over this morning," he says, adjusting his stance to allow more room for his head. I swallow a smile.

"I'm going to check what lunch we have," I tell him. The hall is narrow like the stairs, but the rooms are spacious and cosy, typically farmhouse and quaint. It's really sweet and spotless. My man did well.

I open the fridge and find it stockpiled with fresh fruit and vegetables, some ready-made sandwiches, and a jug of cloudy apple juice. Perfect!

I hunt around for a few more bits and set us some places at the chunky table as Jace comes back downstairs. He grabs a handful of crisps and slings them into his mouth before pulling a face.

"Vegetable chips," I say, enjoying watching him chew them unhappily.

I pick one up and nibble it. I like them, but evidently, he would rather eat my burnt eggs again.

"Please tell me that sandwich isn't full of just salad?" He scoops me up, plopping me on the countertop, as he pushes his way between my thighs and cups my face, not allowing me any time to answer because his mouth is on mine: hot and hungry. We kiss, his hands massaging my arse and keeping me flush to his rigid length.

"Lunch," I pant.

"You ate a crisp," he whines. I burst out laughing, and he gives me a cheeky smile. "Are you really going to refuse me—refuse yourself?" Amber eyes blink up at me—glittering and full of fire. "I want to hurtle for a little while—hurtle right between these gorgeous legs and wake this sleepy village up." He grins, biting my lip. I groan and tilt my head, giving him access to my neck. "Is that a yes? Besides, it's nearly 2 p.m.. It'd be sinful not to fuck now."

I run my fingers through his hair.

"Why do I get the feeling you will say about anything to get me on my back right now?"

"This feeling?" He thrusts forwards, and I chuckle. "Lily, I have thought of nothing all morning except tasting in between your creamy thighs and sinking deep until I can't bloody think."

"Take me to bed," I demand. His eyes sparkle, and he sweeps me up, manoeuvring until we reach the bottom of the stairs.

"Fuck." He laughs. There is no way in hell we are getting up those stairs with me in his arms. I wriggle free and begin jogging up the stairs, eager to find the bedroom, but I'm hauled back and kissed roughly up the wall. I have a little height on Jace as I'm on the top step. His hands are frantic on my clothes, tugging me free until each item is flung haphazardly up or down the stairs, then his own are coming away, and his wide chest comes into view before he dips to drag a nipple into his mouth.

"I love these gorgeous breasts," he affirms, his gaze fixed to each pebbled breast. "So fucking sexy, Lily." He lifts me then, encouraging me to wrap my legs around his waist only so he can move us up a few more steps and bring me down on the top one. His lips find mine in a hard, crushing kiss. My hands are gliding into his hair to hold him at my mouth—he is an expert. No one kisses like Jace. His lips are full enough to cushion his assault—his tongue hot enough to have my limbs liquefying. When he pins my arms above my head and grinds into me, I'm a whimpering wreck.

"Jace, now, I want you in me now," I pant.

His chuckle has my eyes fluttering open, and as soon as they do, I'm lost in his ambers, where passion swirls like thick honey, pours into me, and sweetens my soul. God, this man.

"You want me, do you?" His head is tilted, and I know that look—he's teasing me. I jolt my hips. Yes! His hand slides down my arm, along the side of my body, then he is shifting to give himself access. I'm ready for him, and my legs open, welcoming him in.

"Yes, touch me, dammit!" I lift my mouth because I am craving our connection, but his fingers beat my mouth. His eyes watch mine vividly as he sinks his fingers deep inside me, and I choke out a sweet moan.

"Ah, Lily. God. If only you could see how beautiful you look, all blushed and sexy." His lips graze mine, then are gone again as his fingers begin pulsing in and out. I'm lost to the sensation, my arms still thrown above me as I rock my hips to his pace.

Betrayal

My limbs are shaking.

"You're too good at this. I'm going to come."

"So soon?" He grins, his hand tilts, and I jolt off the top step. Jace plants a hand on my stomach to keep me grounded. "Here's your sweet spot." He presses against my inner walls, and I cry out loudly. His fingers don't stop, and I'm choking out a plea as he works me to an orgasm. I always just felt he was super lucky in the sex department as his good looks were enough to get anyone off, but he really has learned my body. My orgasm comes soon after until I'm sobbing.

"Fuck me," I plead. He does, but with his mouth. Then he's dragging us both off to the bedroom.

A short while later, I lay with my arm slung over his chest, which is still beating furiously, as my own is. We don't move. Don't speak. That was delicious. My toes curl as my body still hums and pulses. Moaning happily, I rub against him and sigh as the after-effects roll over my skin. Jace rolls and cups me.

"You're throbbing," he growls sleepily.

"And starving." I laugh. I've really worked up an appetite. Grinning, he bites my neck and drags me into his chest, slinging his leg over mine.

"I can't move," he grumbles. "Let's stay here all afternoon."

"I need to eat. I need energy."

"You don't need energy. I have enough. Just lie there and let me take advantage."

"I'll be back in a minute with the food." I roll out from under him and give his butt an ogle before I wander downstairs and begin loading up a tray with our lunch.

Jace has barely moved an inch when I get back upstairs. I rest the tray on the ottoman at the end of the bed and peer around to find him snoozing lightly. I'm quiet so not to wake him. I pull on his discarded t-shirt and, taking a sandwich, I sit in the window seat. There are fields for miles and miles. A blanket of natural beauty as far as the eye can see. It's another thirty minutes before Jace begins to stir, and I have already eaten my way through my lunch and some of his. He rolls over and blinks at me, tucked up on the ledge.

"Morning." I grin and pop a bit of cheese in my mouth. Jace is still coming round. He looks about the room and then blinks forcefully, urging his brain to catch up with his eyes.

"Fuck. I fell asleep."

"You did."

"What's the time?"

"Nearly half three." I try to stifle the laugh rushing up my throat, but I can't help it. "You don't need energy. I've got enough," I mimic, and he laughs.

"I did. It's all been zapped out of my dick and into you. That's why you're still up," he tells me, patting the bed next to him.

"You're full of shit." I giggle.

"And you're full of sperm." He grins dirtily.

"Jace!" I choke out. "Gross." My nose wrinkles and I climb up the bed until I'm sprawled over him. He sighs, and I lay listening to his heart pump against my ear. My fingers are running circles over his taut flesh as his own become lost in my hair. On a gentle lift, he pulls my mouth to his and gives me another toe-curling kiss.

"I've booked us a table for dinner at seven." His lips peck my mouth one last time, then he's rolling us. He drags the quilt up and over our heads, our feet poking out of the bottom. "But what I really want is to stay in bed all day, making love to you."

"Then let's stay in bed," I reply, running my hands up his arms and hooking them around his neck. "There is plenty of food here."

He scoffs.

"Looks like you ate most of the lunch."

"I really was starving," I admit. I wrap my legs around his waist and fuse us together.

"No shit. I'm going to lose half a stone if we stay in!" I slap his arm, and he grins and drops, squashing me to the bed. Huffing out a groan, I adjust to his weight and sigh. I really can't believe how happy and content I am with this man. It feels good to have someone to enjoy my life with. I've been so focused on my own life for so long that it's good to share that focus and direct it on someone else. "I love you like I love two o'clock," I tell him, running my thumbs back and forth over his stubble. His lips find my thumb pad, and he kisses it.

"I love you too, gorgeous." I smile up at him. I never thought I would be sharing those words with another person. At first, I was too scared to, then after Adam, I didn't think I deserved to, but hearing them, saying them, has lifted the biggest weight off my shoulders.

"What are you thinking?"

"Just that I'm really lucky that you found me."

"Yes, you are." He grins and pecks my mouth before heaving us out of bed.

"Oh, the cheek, and are you not lucky?"

"I feel like I've got a horseshoe hooked around my cock." His grin is so devious, so playful that even though I want to be annoyed at his backhanded compliment, I just hold him tighter instead.

"Super lucky then."

"Go and start the shower. I'm going to eat my lunch, then I'll join you."

Jace has chosen a seafood restaurant not too far from the village we are staying in. We've finished our meal and opted to share a dessert, which looks like it would take a small army to defeat. Layer upon layer of chocolate cake and sauce sat between us both. I've stared at it for over a minute, and I know the moment it passes my lips, my appetite will be back, but I'm stuffed.

"Maybe we should ask for it to go?"

"I still can't believe this is for one person," Jace says dryly, "it's nearly a quarter of a cake." He shakes his head and grabs a waiter as they pass, asking them to box it up for us. We pay the bill, and Jace suggests we head to one of the local pubs.

"I did see a pub on the way here. It was just off the main road."

"Okay, we'll take a look. That cake may have to wait until tomorrow, gorgeous," Jace says, helping me into my coat. I throw a grin over my shoulder and slip my hand into his as we head out of the restaurant.

The air is cool, and the temperature has dropped. I shiver and welcome the warmth of the car as we set off to find the pub I noticed earlier. It's busier than we expect, but looks inviting nonetheless. It's very old-English and has low ceilings, so much so that Jace has to duck his way in and lean on the bar just to save his head from being squished.

"I think this place is for hobbit's only." I giggle at how ridiculous he looks bent over in his parka.

"I'm going to need a massage after all this." He winks. A woman comes over, frantically wiping the bar down. Her eyes flare when they register Jace fully, and she leans on the bar too, so they are inches apart.

"You are definitely not from around here," she hums thoughtfully. "I would remember if I had seen you before. What can I get you?" Jace twists, bringing me into view, and her pale cheeks heat. She is very pretty and very forward.

"Babe, do you just want a glass of wine or a bottle?"

"Just a glass?" I respond, allowing him to tug me into his chest. The woman looks a little put out that I'm there.

"Let's have a glass here." His head swings back to the bartender. "Can we get a bottle to take out when we leave?" he asks, surprising me.

She tucks her hair behind her ears and distances herself from him.

"Of course, what wine will it be?"

"Pinot, please?"

"Medium?" Her tone is clipped and short, as though she really doesn't want to be conversing with me. Well, tough.

"Sure, thanks?" I side-eye Jace, who has also picked up on her tone. Jeez, what a psycho. I wonder if it's embarrassment, but she looks annoyed as hell with me.

"I'll have a lager. Any," Jace says, cutting over her when she starts to ask which lager he would prefer. We wait for our drinks before manoeuvring between the crowded pub to find a seat. We are lucky to get a place at the window seat, not too far from the open fire. We're sitting side by side, and Jace tugs me so my legs are crossed and into him, his hand on my thigh.

"You feeling relaxed yet beautiful?" Jace asks, sipping on his beer.

"Yes, relaxed and very full."

"Good."

"I'm just going to pop to the ladies," I tell him. The

crowd is thick, so it takes me a little while to get through the throng. When I do, the bathroom is empty, so I'm in and out within minutes. Without the din of music, I'm able to just think for a second, and by the time I'm heading back to Jace, I'm suppressing a very mischievous smile.

Jace must sense it too, because he gives me a quizzical look.

"You okay?"

"Hi," I breathe softly. He smiles inquisitively as he watches me take a seat next to him. "You don't mind, do you?" I ask him. He's confused, and rightly so. I'm not acting myself at all. He shakes his head, and I smile seductively at him. "You are definitely not from around here. I would remember if I had seen you before." His eyes flare with understanding, and his mouth twists into a dark smile.

"Just passing through," he plays along.

"Lucky me." I bite my lip and give him a look from below my lashes.

"Jace." He holds his hand out, and my breath shudders out. Shit, we're doing this. I feel giddy and hot with excitement, and by the flare of his nostrils and the glint in those perfect damn eyes, he is enjoying this as much as me.

"Lily."

"Well, Lily, it's a pleasure to meet you."

"Likewise." I start to tuck my hair behind my ear but stop, realising that's a little too like myself. I shake my hair out and stare at him head on. "I hope you don't mind me being this forward?"

"Not at all."

"I saw you across the room and thought, that man is

gorgeous." My eyes drop to his lips, and his tongue dips out, taunting me.

"Unfortunately, due to the overwhelming amount of OAPs in here, I wasn't lucky enough to catch sight of you until now. I'm glad you came over."

"You are. Why?" I ask, crossing my legs and picking up my wine from earlier. I swill the glass and look at him, conveying how much this is arousing me.

"Well, you are beautiful, obviously," he tells me, looking over me with interested eyes. "You smell delectable and," – he pauses and looks around the room before leaning in to brush his lips to my ear – "since you sat down, I have thought of nothing else but how you will feel under my tongue."

My breath stops, stutters, and then leaves in a long rush of air.

"Jace."

"Lily."

"I want you."

"I'm not that kind of guy," he tells me quickly.

My blush is bright, and I can't help but smirk. Oh, he so is.

"I think you are," I remark, resting back and sipping on my drink. Jace follows suit, and for a moment, we have a staring contest. The tension is palpable, heavy, and I'm enjoying this more than I thought.

"What gives you that impression?"

"Well, the fact that you told me you want to taste me," I say, deadpan. Jace laughs loudly.

"Touché. Minor slip-up."

"Nothing minor about that," I say, looking towards his groin area.

Jace frowns at me.

"Get back in character," he tells me, and I straighten

my back. "Well then, Lily, my new drinking buddy, let me finish my drink, and we can get to know each other a little more," – he tilts his head and drops his eyes to my crotch – "intimately," he hums.

I lift my drink.

"Bottoms up." I wink and take a healthy gulp.

Chapter Sixteen

I wake with a start and roll slowly to find Jace flat out beside me. I smile and stare at his profile. The slight curl at the tip of his hair is becoming more prominent. His lips are slightly parted, and I take a moment to enjoy every cell of him, from the bristles around his jaw to the smooth expanse of his chest as it inflates on each inhale. I'm sure I'm very much biased, but he is stupidly handsome.

I lay still, just watching him, happy in the silence and early morning sun breaking through the flimsy curtains. My fingers reach out and rub along his collarbone as he exhales roughly, and his eyes press tightly together.

"Lily," he mumbles incoherently I grin and hum, but he is still asleep. My fingers roam, tracing around his nipple and his pec.

Quickly, his hand snaps out and grabs me. I gasp and laugh as ambers burst with happiness into mine. He rolls us both and nuzzles into my neck.

"Morning." His voice has that sexy, deep, sleep-induced husk to it.

"Morning." I wrap myself around him, and we lay like that for a while, not really saying anything but just happy in our own company. When he finally rolls us again, it's out of the bed. I get scooped up with a huff, and Jace is stalking us both to the shower.

It's nothing like the shower at The Hub, but I huddle in and enjoy being pressed up against Jace.

"So, what's planned for the day? Do we need to head back soon?"

"Only if you want to?" He turns me around, and I reach up to hoop his neck.

"I'm happy to stay in here for a while."

"You couldn't get a sheet of paper between us, let alone an erection," he states grumpily.

"I don't want it between us. I want it in me. Stop making excuses, Bennett."

"I like bossy you. She's horny a lot."

"Regular me is horny too. You just don't give me a chance to show you." I grin because he always beats me to it.

Jace cracks a devious smile.

"Show me now." With a quick peck to his lips, I hoist myself up and reach to position him at my slick entrance. His eyes are rapt, his lips parted, and the second he pushes in, I drop my mouth to his for a drugging kiss.

God, this man is like nothing I have ever known.

———

It's late when Jace and I finally get back to The Hub. We stopped off at an upmarket restaurant on the way back for dinner. It was the perfect way to finish our romantic weekend away. The cottage was everything we both needed, a secluded spot, unreachable, and nothing but each other for company. Jace has been his constantly attentive self, and I feel thoroughly spoilt and loved by the time we pull up in the darkened gravel driveway.

"I'll get the bags. You go and open up," he tells me, unclipping my seat before he gets out. I smirk at that. It's the little things that he does that slip their way under my skin and make my heart swell. That and when he makes love to me like he has done the past twenty-four hours. He has made sure I feel utterly adored.

I make it to the door as Jace's boot clunks shut, and I push my way in and disarm the alarm before flicking some lights on. Jace follows me in and takes our things straight into the bedroom. We are back only minutes when car lights head down the driveway.

"Jace, someone is here," I shout through to him. I know I have agreed to live here, but I still feel it's really his house. It's nearing 9 p.m. who is visiting this late? The car parks up, and as soon as the lights dip, I see it's Neve. She hops out, slams the door, and comes up to the house with determined strides. She doesn't knock or wait to be invited in but storms inside with a face like thunder and drags her eyes down the length of me disdainfully.

"Where is he? Jace!" she shouts. He comes quickly, looking panicked, his eyes shooting to me, then her.

"Hey, Neve. What's up?" He looks on edge, and his welcome is forced. He shifts and leans against the doorframe, but he looks stiff, and I frown at him, unsure what is going on with him.

"Where the hell have you been? Why haven't you answered your phone?" she shouts, and my brows rise. Jeez, warpath much! Surely work can wait until tomorrow?

"I took Lily away for the weekend, and we didn't

want to be disturbed," he mutters, dragging his hands through his hair.

She scoffs and looks back at me as though I'm dirt. She's not accusing him—she is accusing me, but of what, I have no idea.

"Of course, as long as Lily gets what she needs," she snipes, flicking her hair dramatically over her shoulder. God, she is such a damn drama queen.

My mouth drops, and Jace's brows snap together. He looks pissed at her, but before he can rebuff her, she holds her hand up.

"Well, while you were ensuring Lily wasn't disturbed, Viktor was having a stroke!" she snaps.

"What?" Jace and I are both in shock, and he has paled.

"Why the hell didn't you say that as soon as you came in?" Jace shouts.

"Because you never had any issues being disturbed before, and as of late, you've been putting others on the back burner. You needed a fucking wake-up call."

I ignore her comments and grab my bag. She is so wrong about me. I'm not making Jace put other priorities on the back burner. Am I?

"Is he okay?" I ask. Jace looks heartbroken.

"Hmm. He is still in hospital, under observation." She is looking at Jace the whole time, and he looks guilt-ridden and in shock. I walk to him and rub his arm.

"Jace, come on. Let's go to the hospital," I say, and he blinks and nods, stiff and confused. I pick up his keys from the side and look at Neve when he slips his hand in mine and mutters that he doesn't think he can drive. "That's fine. I'll get us there. Which hospital, Neve?" My heart is breaking for him.

"You can follow me. We've been trying to contact

Betrayal

you since last night," she adds, making Jace drop his head in shame. I twist into him and take his head in my hands and lift up to press a kiss to his cheek. He shakes his head, and my heart twists painfully for him further. I've never seen him like this: so utterly crushed, bewildered, and lost.

"We didn't know. It wasn't malicious. He will understand that—they both will," I reassure.

He nods, but I can tell he doesn't quite believe me. Neve has planted a nasty seed, and she has done it with the blame firmly on me. I get in the car and quickly adjust the seat and mirrors. It's me who clips Jace in as he is in a complete daze. This has affected him deeply, and it hurts to see him in pain. I don't know how to fix it, but I will ensure I do, just like he has done for me so many times. I need to be the strength for us both now. If anyone has taught me how to support someone, it is this man with his steel backbone and attentiveness.

It's another forty-five minutes before we are at the hospital and on our way to Viktor's room. The hospital is a burrow of white sterile corridors and sick people. It has such a distinctive smell, both clean and dirty, like every tear of sadness and drop of blood has been swept away with sanitiser but yet still stains the place. It's the oddest combination.

I keep Jace's hand in mine, showing my support. I rub his arm every now and again as we move through the never ending corridors. Jace hasn't said a word—his whole demeanour is of a wounded animal. It's worrying me that he has retracted within himself so much. I bite my lip and keep his hand in mine, squeezing it every now and then. As soon as we hit the lift, despite our hands being attached, Neve pulls him in for a hug. Her eyes are powering into me as his fingers slip from mine, and his head drops to her shoulder. Pain lances through me. I try to act unaffected, but the truth is my partner is seeking comfort from another woman—a woman who is very much in love with him, and I can't even vocalise my hurt because he is really struggling with Viktor's stroke.

I keep my gaze averted and watch the number on the lift change as it sweeps past one floor, then another. Jace has moved back, and part of me wants to snatch his hand back into mine, and the other half wants to slap him away. She speaks to him like shit, purposely stamps on his feelings, and manipulates his emotions, yet he turns to her as though she will make it all better. He wouldn't even hug me. My thoughts are spiralling. I mentally scream at myself that it's not about me, but I feel winded seeing him in her arms. She's gloating, a light but cruel smile pulling at her painted lips. It's only just dawned on me, but she looks impeccable as always: her blonde hair down her back in faultless waves, skin-tight jeans, and a cute little jumper.

We step out of the lift, and I see it then, the silent commotion they cause together. Men break necks looking at her, and women melt for him; and all the while, I'm quietly following behind like a starved teenager, desperate for his affections. I can't quit my thoughts, and I feel riddled with guilt for even letting it get to me when there is a man I respect and care for sick somewhere in this place.

We finally reach Viktor's room, and despite the hour, we are briefly allowed in to see him. The time of day hadn't crossed my mind at first, but luckily, the head nurse on his ward reluctantly lets us through when she sees how forlorn Jace is. Marie catches sight of us, and she comes up to Jace with a little hiccup. He wraps her in a bear hug and begins apologising profusely for going

Betrayal

away for the weekend, and it makes me feel a ton worse for having taken all his time up this weekend. Am I really taking all his focus and allowing him to shun others?

I don't know who he was before we met, or who was important to him, who he spent time with, and when. I barely see his friends, and when I do, it's with him. I just thought this was his normal.

"Oh, come on, don't be silly, you deserved some time away. You work too much as it is. I can't remember the last time you took a holiday." Marie pats his back and then rubs his arm when he shoves his hands into his jean pockets.

"What's the latest?" Neve asks, leaning into Jace and keeping me back. Marie hasn't noticed me yet, and I don't speak up. I feel very much like an interloper at the moment, and Neve's brassy attitude always leaves me feeling a little brittle.

"No changes. He's overcome the worst. I think we will know more in the morning when he wakes up," she says. "His stats are good. I think he is just exhausted."

"Why don't you go home and get some rest. I can stay with him tonight," Jace offers.

"I do need to freshen up. I suppose he is stable. I haven't got a car," she mumbles, unsure what to do.

"Lily can drop you back," Neve says. Marie turns, and I smile from behind Jace.

"Oh, love. It's so good to see you."

"I'm so sorry, Marie. We feel awful for not checking our phones," I say. My voice catches briefly, and Marie gives me a hug.

"Enough. You two are as bad as each other," she chides, "but I will take that offer of a lift?" She looks at Jace, then me. I nod and smile, unsure where that leaves Neve in all of this.

"Sure, I can take you back."

"Great, let me just check in with Nurse Williams, then we can head off. I really appreciate this," she says. She looks tired, fraught, and pale. With that decided, Jace moves over to Viktor, who is fast asleep with an IV in his hand. I watch as he leans, drops his head to Viktor's, and mumbles something softly to him.

"He's got his boy here, so I know he is going to be alright," Marie whispers emotionally. I give her a quick squeeze before she goes to find Nurse Williams.

Neve, who seems all too happy to be here with Jace, takes a seat in the chair beside Viktor's bed, and I keep my face averted because I know it will show my hurt.

It's only moments before Marie is back, with Nurse Williams in tow. Nurse Williams makes it known only one person per patient is to stay on the ward, and I hide my smirk when Neve looks pissed.

"Of course, we're leaving shortly. Can I take your direct number?" I ask her.

"Why do you need that?" Neve asks, pulling her hair to one side before crossing her arms. Jeez, why is she always so snarky?

"Well, I'm assuming Marie hasn't got it either, so if Jace's phone dies, at least we can all keep in contact and up to date this way," I say slowly. Surely I'm not the only one who thought that? I look at Marie, who smiles in agreement.

"Oh." Why does it matter to her, anyway?

"Let me know if you need me to bring anything in for you tomorrow?" I say to Jace, pecking his cheek quickly and grabbing Marie's bag. I wonder if he has just realised we are going to be apart for the night. He takes my wrist and pulls me to him quickly.

Betrayal

"You don't mind?" he asks. Neve scoffs, and I go red, feeling like he is making true to her words.

"Of course I don't mind. It's usually you that has an issue with us being apart." I laugh gently, trying to clear the air and put Neve in her place, but his fragile mind takes the hit instead. His face falls, and he nods.

"I'll chat to you tomorrow then," he says.

I give him a soft smile and drop a kiss to his lips.

"I'll miss you—keep me updated," I say and step away, studiously avoiding looking at Neve and rubbing Marie's back as I follow her out.

Nurse Williams clears the room after us, ensuring Neve is exiting the ward too. I feel a little lighter, knowing he isn't with her, and I really shouldn't because this is about Viktor and his recovery.

"I feel terrible that we weren't there for you, Marie. Jace feels awful. He has hardly spoken since we found out." We all enter the lift together, and silence fills the small square metal tin of a car. I hate these things with a vengeance. I say as much, and Neve rolls her eyes, but Marie is happy for the distraction.

"I got trapped in one while I was on a school trip to France. We were between floors nine and ten. The air-con went out, and it took two hours for them to get the lifts working again. It was horrible," I say, laughing lightly.

"You kids must have been so scared."

I nod, thinking back to that time.

"And hot. A few of them stripped to their underwear. You should have seen the teacher's faces when the doors opened."

"I can imagine." Marie chuckles.

We come to a stop, and Neve smiles at Marie.

"I told Jace I would be back first thing, so if you need a hand with anything, let me know."

"Okay, thank you, Neve." Marie takes her bag from me and begins looking for a tissue as her eyes fill.

"Night, Neve," I say.

"Yeah, night." She waves over her shoulder dismissively. I refrain from running after her and yanking her stupidly long, perfect hair. I swallow my anger and give Marie a supportive smile. Both Marie and I are silent on the walk back to Jace's car. It's cold, and it only adds to the sadness lingering in us both. As soon as we are in and belted up, she sniffles, and her tears come thick and fast. I reach over and pull her into a hug, holding her as she weeps.

"Oh, I am being so silly. Sorry, love." She sighs thickly, straightening up to wipe her tears again.

"No, don't be. We're sorry we didn't get here sooner. We would have come home first thing."

"Well, how could you? I only told Neve an hour or so ago because I couldn't get hold of either Jace or you," she says, pulling another tissue free, unaware of the bomb she has just dropped.

"Right, of course. Sorry. I just thought you had been trying us all weekend."

"Oh, no. I didn't want to worry anyone. When I knew Vik was stable, I decided to call Jace, but that was only at six this evening. Jace had mentioned taking you away. I didn't want to ruin your holiday."

"Marie. Don't feel like you can't ever call us. Please do, no matter what. We'd prefer to know."

"Yes, love." She sniffles and settles in for the ride. I watch her closely as my mind is whirring. So Neve only just found out. I have to give it to her: I admire how quick she is, turning something so serious to her own advantage at the drop of a hat. This whole situation has made me realise how callous she is. I wonder if she knew we were away, and that's why she has made a scene. A tumble of random thoughts all cross my mind, but I don't think I will ever be able to align my mind with hers. There is a wickedness about Neve that has never sat well with me. I should be thankful I'm not capable of thinking like her.

It's another twenty minutes before we arrive at Marie and Viktor's house. Viktor's success in business shines through from the three-story townhouse in central London. The street lamp glows a spotlight on the cute and well-cared-for garden.

I see Marie up to the door. Her hand is shaking, so I help her in and find that their house is a stunning array of famous artwork and antique statues.

"Here, let me make you a drink. You take one sugar, right?" I ask, taking her bag and placing it on a gold studded armchair in the entryway.

"Please. I'm just going to grab a fleece. I'm a little cold." It is cold in here, but I think it's more that her adrenaline is wearing off, and she is a little in shock.

"Maybe pop the heating on too," I suggest and begin sorting her drink. I go about flicking the odd lamp on, drawing warmth from them before she comes down, makeup-free, and looking completely shattered. I follow her into the living room, which is just as tasteful as the rest of the house. "I didn't realise you were both art lovers?" I say, happy that we have that in common: that and our love for Jace.

"Oh, yes, we have a fair few pieces dotted around the place. Viktor and I would love to come to the gallery sometime."

"Well, you're both more than welcome. I do

currently have a piece in at the moment that I think you would both like," I say. It would be perfect in their home. It's a landscape of Paris, and the colours are everything this house is: gold's, beiges, and a slight flare of red. Their home is truly beautiful, and probably the kind of home I would have aspired to have for myself had I not fallen for Jace and The Hub.

"We have been looking for a new piece in the hallway. We auctioned the previous one to a charity for domestic abuse," she murmurs, lost in thought.

"He will be okay, Marie. He is a formidable man."

"That he is."

"Would you like me to stay? I don't mind. I don't really feel comfortable leaving you alone?" I ask, sipping on my drink.

"Would you mind? I do feel a little shaky." Her admission is followed by more tears. Placing my cup down, I go to her and sit beside her as she weeps.

"Of course I don't mind. He will be okay. I have no doubt. Jace won't let anything happen to him." My voice is full of soft conviction. Jace would move heaven and earth for that man. I still don't know their story, and now is not the time to pry, but he loves Viktor and Marie.

"His health is declining, and this time he looked scared. I feel like his time is running out."

Oh, god, poor Marie, I can't imagine how worried she must feel, and I'm scared I'm not going to say the right thing. This brings back memories of how distraught Jace was when Adam attacked me.

"He won't leave you, Marie. I feel like your story still has plenty of pages to fill."

"What a lovely thing to say." She sniffs, and her delicate fingers dab her eyes.

"I know Jace has been worried about his health after

Betrayal

the last scare. We will all have to be extra strict with him." I smile.

"He will hate that. He thinks he is indestructible."

"Hopefully, this is the wake-up call he needs." My reply is cut off when my phone rings. "That's probably Jace." I get up and fish my phone out as Marie tells me she is going to sort the spare room for me.

"Hey."

"Are you home yet?" His deep voice is quiet. I know he will be sitting beside Viktor in that dimly lit room, with all those machines beeping and assessing his vitals.

"No, I'm going to stay with Marie for the night. She broke down in the car and just now."

"I feel sick that she has been dealing with this alone," he confesses shakily. I know his head will be in his hands as he punishes himself.

"I did want to talk to you about that. I felt so bad seeing her cry like that, and I apologised again, saying we would have been there this morning, but she said she hadn't even contacted anyone until this evening, as she hadn't wanted to worry us." I deliver the news on a soft murmur, knowing he will either get angry at me for constantly putting up a wall with Neve, or he will direct it where it should be. At her.

"Is that so?" he scoffs. Oh, he is mad.

"I shouldn't have said anything, but I was just as shocked. She tried us at six this evening, then called Neve. I know she is your friend, Jace, but she purposely made you feel bad. She really doesn't like me, and I think this just goes to sh—"

"Lily." He sounds impatient. "I really don't want to get into a Neve hate-fest right now." Wow. I bite my lip and swallow the argument rushing up my throat. I know I don't like her, but I have always tried my hardest to be polite to her. Be welcoming. She is outright rude to me, and Jace never backs me up. My frustration at the undercurrent she is causing in our relationship is stewing, and I wish he would acknowledge her for what she is rather than making me put up with it. Is it because he thinks I'm weaker than her, give in quicker, or am easier to handle?

"Sorry. I shouldn't have said anything." I know Viktor is our priority, but surely he can see how twisted Neve is—why on earth would she do that?

"You should, but not now." He sounds so tired. I wish I could be there with him. He is hurting, and I can't help from here.

"Okay. How are you doing? Any news?" I ask, trying to change the subject.

"No changes. He is still asleep. The nurse is happy with how he is. They caught it just in time, and she doesn't think it will have affected his mobility or speech."

"That's good then."

"As soon as he wakes, we will know for sure."

"Do you need me to bring anything tomorrow? I know Neve is heading in, but I can grab you a change of clothes."

"No, don't worry. Neve is grabbing some bits I have at the office and bringing my laptop."

"Oh, okay." Why is she doing it? Surely that's my place as his girlfriend, or am I being possessive? I rub at my head, trying to dispel the on-coming headache. I feel like, no matter how long I am with Jace, she will always find a way to squeeze into a spot just between us.

He must hear or sense my withdrawal.

"It makes sense. You have the gallery, so Neve can drop my things off."

I clear my throat and close my eyes. It sounds reasonable, so why does my heart feel like it's being gnawed at?

"Yeah, sure." Marie comes back down and looks at me expectantly. "No changes," I tell her. "Marie is here. I will pass her over. Night, Jace." I give her the phone and stand quickly, taking out cups and washing them up.

I really don't want to be sharing him with Neve in any capacity. It's bad enough that she works with him, and I know how she feels about him: I see it in the ways he looks at him, how she speaks of him, and the misplaced anger at me for just being there. What hurts most is that he does still turn to her. I know relationships are new to him, but he would hate me to turn to another man for things. I know that much about Jace, so why can't he reciprocate and keep her at a distance?

Chapter Seventeen

I'm on my way to the gallery, feeling as though my heart is in a vice. Despite Jace's assurances, I feel guilty for carrying on as normal. A member of his family is unwell, and I need to be there for him. I make a decision and call Hat and tell her to take the morning off and that we will open up this afternoon.

"Are you sure you don't want me to open this morning? It's no bother."

"I feel bad if I ask that," I say. I don't want her thinking I am just dumping everything on her.

"Lily, honestly, it's for a few hours. I will be fine, and if I'm not, I can give you a call. Go and check on Viktor, and I will see you in a bit."

"Have I told you that you're a star?"

"Always. I'm happy to do it. See you later."

"Sure. See you." I make a quick dash to the shop to grab some lunch for everyone and head straight to the hospital. Being here, in this whitewashed place, gives me a sense of dread. I don't know whether it's because it reminds me of my attack or my mother's death, but the general sense of dread hoops around my neck and lies there, making me feel unsettled. I hurry to Viktor's room only to find it empty.

What the hell? Has he been discharged? No one said anything. I quickly head back to the ward reception and find Viktor has been moved to a private room. Of course he has. I take the lift up to the third floor and make my way along the corridors until I come to a private ward. There, a smiling nurse guides me to the room.

"Mr Klein is just through the doors on your right." I give her a nod of thanks and push inside. I stop short when I find Neve standing between Jace's knees, his head resting on her stomach. They jump apart, and I blink in shock. I open my mouth to say something, anything, when Marie comes in behind me.

"Hello, love, it's nice to see you here," she says, giving me a quick hug. I smile and drop my gaze to the floor. I really want to be imagining things, for my mind to be overactive, but none of this feels okay to me. I know they are friends, and I repeat that mantra over and over again as Marie gives me a little squeeze of thanks. Through it all, I somehow find my voice.

"I picked you all some lunch up for later. I know what hospital food is like." I keep my gaze fixed on the bag as I begin pulling things out. "Jace, I got you a BLT. Marie, I wasn't sure what you liked." I clear my throat, trying to disguise the emotion there. "Or you, Neve, so I just grabbed a few to choose from." I can feel the hot press of tears behind my eyes. I hate that he is seeking comfort from her. He hasn't even spoken to me this morning. I feel like I'm being made a mockery of.

"Lily, thank you. That's so kind." I lift my head and plaster a bright smile on my face. Marie takes over, looking in the bag. "This is great, thank you, love."

Betrayal

"Any update?" I ask, keeping my gaze averted from Jace. Neve is no longer between his legs but leaning against the wall. I feel like I caught them in a moment, and despite him being my partner, once again, it feels as if I'm the interloper—like I shouldn't be here. I don't actually feel as though I am wanted here. Jace hasn't said a word to me.

I decide to leave.

"No, he woke briefly, but not enough to gauge how he is." I nod when Marie speaks up.

"That's a good sign, though, that he is responsive. Well, I have to get to the gallery, so I'll probably call later." I throw a quick smile around the room, my eyes briefly landing on Jace's guilt-ridden ones.

"I'll walk you down." His voice rumbles roughly.

"No need." My smile is brittle, and he knows without a shadow of a doubt that I am not okay with this, and his guilty face only proves I'm right to feel off about it all. I know he will accuse me of being dramatic and selfish, and a part of me knows I am. This isn't about me, but I'm feeling really unhinged with her around, and I know deep in my gut that she isn't to be trusted. I step out of the room and begin walking quickly through the ward and out into the main corridor. I hear the door swing open behind me, and I know it's him. I head for the lifts and press the down button, my eyes stinging with pent-up emotion.

The lift pings, and I rush in as I hear my name being called. I'm alone in the lift, and I'm grateful no one witnesses me pressing the button furiously to close the doors. Jace's arm and body slides through the closing gap, and I stare at him, trying so hard not to show my hurt and confusion or my anger because I am feeling all that and then some. What is the damn deal with her?

"Hey, it's not what it looks like." He pulls me to him, and I go stiff and twist free.

"I'm not doing this," I tell him, "like you said, now is not the time." I remind him of his own words, and he gives a short laugh.

"Jesus, Lily. It's not the time. You're right. Yet you are still getting pissed any time she comes near me!" he snaps. "She is my friend."

"Okay."

"My . . . Viktor is laying in that bed, and you are getting pissed because I gave one of my longest friends a hug."

"No, Jace. I don't like it because she straight out lied to you yesterday to make you feel shit. It worked, and yet you're still seeking comfort from her and not me. You tell me to come to you always, yet you never turn to me. Ever. You go straight to her."

"It's a force of habit." He chews his lips, seeing I'm on the verge of tears.

"Well, enjoy your habit. I've got work to do."

"You are being so selfish!" he snaps, and I know he is right. Viktor is unwell, and I'm having a bad case of insecurity.

"I know!" I snap back. The lift pings to a stop, and a few people step in. Jace and I stand in silence all the way down until we are out and walking through the car park.

"So you admit you're selfish," he says to my back as I weave through the cars. I whirl on him so that we both come to a halt between vehicles.

"No, I admit at this moment, I am being selfish. Because even though I know there is a sick man in one of those beds, I still can't stand the sight of you in her arms. She's so damn rude to me, no matter how nice I am, yet it's me who is told to be patient, accept her, and try for you." I point at him.

"I know you try with her," he says quietly.

"She doesn't reciprocate. I endure her little digs, and I don't bite. I keep up appearances for you. But, yes, seeing you turn to her twice for comfort, when I am right there, is like being kicked in the heart with a hammer because she isn't just your friend. She is in love with you, Jace!"

"It's not like that," he grates out. His face twists in frustration.

"You're that blind to it. Jesus, Jace, wake up." I grind my teeth because he is either in denial or acting dumb, but neither makes me feel better.

"We have known each other since we were kids. Of course she loves me. We're as good as family. You're bein—"

"Do not say unreasonable or over the top because whether you claim friendship or not, a woman knows when someone else is trying to make a move."

"It was just a hug. It doesn't mean anything."

"It does to me, Jace. I will never expect you to walk away from her, even though the truth is screaming in your face, but I can't watch you give into her all of the time and placate her because it's easier to ask it of me than her."

Jace frowns.

"What? I don't give in to her."

"No? You ask me to try with her, to put up with her, but I don't see her trying. You have no idea how underhanded she can be when you're not there. You turn to her, and it's what she wants, and it hurts. It hurts me," I whisper. I feel stupidly emotional and completely ridiculous because even though I am hurting, Viktor is sick, and I have made this about me, and I hate that I have. "I'm going to work."

"Lily, can we talk, please? You know how I feel about you. She really is just a friend. I'm sorry." He tugs me, but I don't want to go to him. I just want to leave and call Cass.

"I need to go," I say.

"Lily, wait. I don't want you to go when you are upset."

"Answer me one thing. Why did you both jump apart when I walked in?"

"Because I knew you would be upset." He swallows. His eyes are tennis balling between mine, vividly watching for any reaction.

"Knew it, but still did it anyway. Nice. I'll speak to you later. I just want to get to work." My murmur is low and full of unease.

"Lily, if I caught you hugging Sean, I wouldn't act this way," he says as I back up.

"Sean isn't in love with me. You couldn't bear Travis coming near me, and that's because although I have only ever viewed him as a friend, you, as a man, could sense he was interested—to you, he was a threat." His jaw works. "It works like that for women too."

"I'm with you," he says resolutely.

"Well then, maybe stick that home to her a bit more. I know it probably hurts her that I'm suddenly around, and I'm sorry, but it doesn't sit well with me. I'm not okay with it. I try with her. I try so damn hard, Jace, and she barely looks at me—maybe she should learn to try," I say quietly.

A couple walks past us and looks at our little standoff. Heat rushes to my cheeks as they get in their car. I turn and begin to walk away to my car, which is a short

Betrayal

distance away. I never wanted to have this conversation like this, or at all, and I feel so childish arguing about something that is so evident. This feeling has been there in the back of my mind ever since I met her, more so when I had to listen to her go on about all his conquests —and he let her. He never reins her in or tells her to be respectful. I blow out a deep breath and unlock my car as thick arms come round my waist.

"I'm sorry. I can see why you're upset, and I'm guilty. She is hard to handle, so it's easier to ask you to be accommodating. It's a shitty thing for me to do, and I'm sorry." He breathes roughly into my ear.

I could cry with relief. Finally.

I sag into his wide chest, chewing my lip before I twist into his arms.

"I don't want us to fight, Jace. I don't want to come between you and your friends, but even *they* have warned me about her." He frowns, and his cheeks heat. Yes, it's not just me being irrational. "You're hurting her because she is in love with you, Jace," I tell him softly. He blinks, unsure, and sighs, seemingly lost in thought. He really doesn't see it. I feel for him. How can he not notice?

"Give me a kiss," he murmurs, looking down at me. I search his eyes and find tiredness there. I feel awful for bringing this all up now. I lift and peck his mouth, but he has other ideas. He cups my face and sweeps his tongue in on a moan. "Last night was long. I missed you," he confesses between kisses.

"I missed you too. Are you staying again? If so, I think I'll stay at my apartment." I'm pressed into my car, but he soon shifts and looks down at me, annoyed.

"Why? The Hub is our home. Why go to the apartment?"

"It's closer if you need me." He smiles, and my heart

does that stupid flip. Hot ambers burn down at me, and I bite my lip. It's that look—the one where I know all that is in his head is sex. He leans into me, and I feel it, the hot hard press of his arousal. His phone buzzes in his pocket, and Jace snaps back, pulling it free.

"He's awake!" he says, elation and fear rolling over his features and relief filling his glazed eyes.

"Go," I tell him, pushing him back to the hospital. "I'll call you when I get to work so you can update me," I say quietly.

"You're not coming back?" he asks on a frown, his tone baffled.

"I want to, but I'm not sure. I'm not family, so . . . " I know how strict hospital rules are, and rightly so.

"You're coming, Lily." He takes my hand, and we make quick work of the car park and hospital, rushing back to Viktor's room.

I find it odd that Neve is sitting outside in the corridor on a chair and wonder if I will be allowed in.

She stands as she sees us, and her eyes narrow at our clasped hands.

"Only fami—"

"We are family," Jace says brusquely. He pushes open the door and pulls me in. Jace's face crumples, but he doesn't shed a tear. He walks straight to Viktor, who looks beyond ecstatic that Jace is here, and gets pulled into a bear hug. "You're going to make me grey," Jace states. His tone is thick with emotion. I blink at Marie, who is already crying, and my own tears slip over.

"You silly bunch." Viktor laughs deeply. "I'm fine, look." He holds his arms out, showing just how okay he is. No sign of a slur or issues with mobility. He is so lucky. "My Marie acted so fast that this stroke practically ran away!" He laughs. He is overjoyed, maybe it's the dance with death that's making him so excited, but I'm surprised he is in such good spirits and so energetic.

"You had us all worried," I say. Jace grasps Viktor's hand, and Victor throws him a loving smile, pats his hand, and ruffles his hair.

"You not going to cry too?" His brow lifts as he directs his question to Jace.

"No, nice try." They both laugh, and I roll my eyes at Marie, who is trying to look busy, moving things about and neatening the bag at the end of Viktor's bed.

"Have they said much to you?" Jace asks.

"Stats are good. I'm in for observations tonight, but probably out tomorrow. It'll take more than that to ruin my retirement."

"You retired because of the first scare."

"Never, I just made you all think that. Right, who has some chocolate? I'm bloody starving!" he announces as the nurse walks back in.

"Chocolate will have to wait. Lunch is being served now, and we have ordered you the lentil casserole." Viktor's face sours, and Jace coughs on a laugh he is holding back.

"Now, do I look like a man that eats lentils?" He addresses the nurse, his voice playful.

"No, Mr Klein, but you also are out of other options as we ordered the lunches earlier, and that is all that is left."

"This damn stroke is becoming an inconvenience."

"Oh, only now it is?" I laugh, and the others laugh too.

"Now, I know they only let family in. Does this mean you have some news for me—good news?" He leans to check my ring finger, and I go bright red and garble.

"Not quite yet. I'm still getting her used to the idea

of living with me," Jace admits with a wink. My whole chest fires with butterflies at his open response. I give Viktor and Marie a small smile and allow Jace to tuck my hand in his.

For the next hour, we chat about work and Viktor's discharge. Jace is collecting him so Marie can get things in order at home. Viktor starts to look sleepy, and Jace stands.

"Right, old man, you get some rest. I will be here tomorrow to take you home," he says, leaning to give him a quick cuddle. "No dying on me. I like you," Jace mutters, and Viktor chuckles.

"Shame, you're starting to piss me off; far too bossy."

Jace seems far lighter as we leave. Neve isn't waiting outside. I would have thought she would have wanted to know how he was since she has been here all morning.

The next few days follow the same pattern. Jace spends his days working from Viktor and Marie's, and I then join them for dinner. On the fourth day, I suggest they come to us for dinner.

"We'd love to have you over." I chance a look at Jace and see his eyes burning back at me. It's the first time I have openly acknowledged we are living together. "Of course, only if Viktor is feeling up to it. It will give Marie a break. It won't be strenuous—just here to ours," I say on a swallow after Marie declines.

"I will definitely have to help, or else we'll all be eating charred food." Jace winks at me, causing Viktor to laugh. I shrug on a chuckle.

"Look, I never said it would be a nice meal." My joke brings laughter all around.

"Let's do it. A change of scenery will do us some good, Marie, and like Lily says, it's not strenuous. I'm just going from one house to another." Marie is so frightened to let Viktor out of her sight, and I thought this would be a good way to lower her guard.

"I suppose so."

"I'll drive you both over and back again," Jace says, leaning back in his seat. His arms slings along the back of mine, where his fingertips trail up and down my back.

"Great, I will grab some bits for dinner tomorrow." I know for a fact that Viktor loves seafood, so I thought I could make a big risotto. I'm already planning my day tomorrow, so I can whip and grab all the bits.

"I'm looking forward to it." Viktor sighs. He still looks worn out, but he is so much better. I've become so attached to them both since being in Jace's life. They are both so selfless. I want to make sure I'm here for them as much as they were for me after Adam's attack. The one thing I have found odd, but I'm keeping studiously quiet about, is that Neve hasn't been on the scene. I recall Marie seeming shocked she was even at the hospital, and now Viktor is home, she hasn't even popped in one evening to check on him. I don't believe she was or is remotely concerned for Viktor. It was all about Jace—a way in. I really hope she isn't going to be a problem for us.

"Are you ready to head home?" Home. Those four letters make my chest flutter. It's silly to think how fast I ran from this man, and yet now we are living together. I don't think I have ever experienced this level of love for another person. My love for Jace isn't just face value. It goes so deep, deep to the bone, further still, to the furthest recesses of my mind and soul. He seems to be able to read me so well, to anticipate my needs, and always be a step ahead of me, and in return, I am determined to love him like he's never been loved before. I have no doubt in my mind that Jace hasn't had it easy. He never talks about his parents, and although I am desperate to ask, I can see he views both Viktor and Marie as that. I don't wish to offend him by suggesting otherwise.

"Yeah, sure. Are you sure you don't want help with the washing up?" I ask Marie, who is already picking up the odd pot.

"God, no, we'll see you tomorrow." We say our goodbyes, and Jace and I drive home in our own cars. He, of course, gets there far quicker than me—I've never known someone to drive so fast!

By the time I finally pull up, the house is lit up like a Christmas tree, and I know it will be a hell of a lot warmer than my car. I lock the door and head up the steps, surprised I can't see Jace with it being so bright. As soon as I push through, the lights all shut off with a loud whir. All the power is out. What the hell!

"Jace?" I shut the door and wait for his response, but nothing, not a single sound. Unease spreads over me, and although I will it not to, my heart begins to palpate with fear. "Jace, please don't mess with me. I never admitted it before, but I'm not a fan of the dark!" I say with an awkward laugh. I pull my phone out of my jacket and use the torch to look around the house. "Jace, this isn't funny! Where are you?" I sound annoyed, and I don't want to be, but after Adam, I feel so skittish in these situations.

"I'm right here," he breathes from behind me. What the hell? I jump and fall back into him.

"That's not funny," I whine.

"I know it's not. The power was out when I got back.

I got it working for a few minutes, then nothing." He kisses my cheek. "I'd never let any harm come to you, anyway."

"Sorry. I got a little freaked out. So do you think it's a power cut then?"

"Yeah," he mutters as the lights flicker on. Jace grins. "Hopefully, it will stay on now. He's not coming back, you know." He means Adam, and I nod, biting my lip. "You're safe, Lily."

"Why would it go out? It's not stormy." I look around the house, looking for anything out of place.

"Hey, relax. Honestly, it's happened before. I think I share electric with the village over the fields. It's a few miles away, but if they are having work done, it will affect us too. It's probably been like it all day."

"Oh well, I hope it sorts itself out. Otherwise we won't be able to have Viktor and Marie round," I say, taking my coat off and kicking my shoes under the sideboard. "I hate these shoes. They kill my feet."

"Why wear them then?"

"They look nice," I retort as the lights shut off again, and I squeak in a panic. Jace's laughter carries. I feel his fingers, and then he is pulling me to him. "How am I supposed to get ready for Stanley's event?" I've been looking forward to this evening for weeks.

"Pack a bag, and we'll get ready at The Loft, and in the meantime, I'll get my electrician out." I grin happily at him in the dark. Perfect!

Chapter Eighteen

With Jace wanting to accompany me to Stanley Ebon's annual gallery event, I gave Harriet the night off so we have The Loft to ourselves. I've chosen a black wrap dress and nude heels, and I'm dithering about with what jewellery to wear when two hands move past my head, and a cold object trickles around my neck. My eyes fly to Jace, then to my neck in the mirror where he is holding a delicate necklace with a simple teardrop diamond in the centre. My fingers run the length on my neck, feeling the chain, before circling the diamond.

"I . . . Jace this is—"

"Does that mean you love it?" He clips it into place and drops his chins to my shoulder as his hands find my waist. "You look stunning."

"Yes, I love it, but why?" I don't understand why he has gifted me this.

"Because I love you, gorgeous, and I know I hurt you for turning to Neve." I chew my lip at his words. I don't want to say much more about it, as we've been over it all, and since then, I feel like he truly knows how out of place I feel when he allows her to barge her way between us. "I didn't want you to see me that way. I feel all these emotions with you that I can't contain, and honestly, I've never been like this. It makes me sound like a huge wuss." He laughs. I turn and kiss him.

"You're not a wuss."

"I know, but I'm always saying all these things that I would never have even thought of before, like how damn innocent your grey eyes are now. It brings me to my knees. See, wuss," he jokes.

"Well, you bring me to my knees too."

"I wish I did. I'd be feeling pretty damn happy right now."

I quip my brow and ignore his comment.

"Maybe later." I wink. Okay, so I didn't ignore him completely. "I like that you say those things to me."

"I know you do; that's why I say them. Is this dress new? It's a little revealing." He runs his finger down the low V created by the wrapped material.

"It's not. It just seems it now as the necklace is making you look there." He frowns and goes to remove the necklace. "Nope! I'm keeping it on. I love it. Honestly, Jace, it's beautiful." I kiss him again, and his smile turns lopsided. Cupping my face, he leans right in and gives me the kind of kiss that would win an award— the slow, tongue-curlingly-deep kind that sets me on fire. I come up panting, and he winks.

"No wandering off. I need every man to know that the sex on legs in the naughty black dress is mine." He pecks my lips and checks his own collar in the mirror over my head.

"I think I can do that."

———

Betrayal

Ebony Art is nothing like my sweet little Loft. It was originally an old swimming pool. I have been once or twice, and both times, I have been in awe of the space. Some of the original pool remains, running a narrow strip through the centre of the main gallery to make a tranquil water feature. Beyond this, walls of art and more rooms showcase some of the most renowned artists. It is easily one of the most exclusive galleries in London. Stanley Ebon is not what I would call a friend, but we call on each other from time to time to borrow art, so receiving his invite was a big surprise and the perfect time to network.

Jace and I arrive just before opening. He helps me out and threads his fingers with mine, giving them a possessive squeeze.

"I'm taking further precautions," he says on the last squeeze.

"Precautions. What do you mean?" We walk hand in hand across the road. The exterior is lit up like a beacon; soft purple lights make the black window sills seem both extravagant and mysterious. It's cleverly done. I know Stanley won't just make this about art; he will throw one of the biggest parties. I'm a few steps ahead of Jace, eager to get in and see the art, but Jace gently tugs me back, holds our hands up, and squeezes tighter for effect.

"Precautions. I knew at the first sign of art you'd be blinkered and wandering off. I'm keeping you locked in, witch. Our hands are not parting."

"What if I need the toilet?" I pout. He seems playful, so I enjoy this for what it is.

"Then I will stand outside until you are done. But our hands are one tonight." Conviction rolls from his mouth. He is being deadly serious; as much as his eyes are sparkling like crazy, he really is keeping me close by.

"What are you so bothered about?" I ask. He pulls back on a frown and looks around. Is there something he isn't telling me?

"Nothing, I just want to make sure I keep my gorgeous lady by my side all night. Is that too much to ask?" It's him who is pouting now. His amber eyes are like honey-coated diamonds, and I shake my head in a grin and lift to peck his mouth.

"Great, now I have lipstick face."

"This stuff was expensive. There is no way it is coming off," I tell him, encouraging us along the path, as he drops his mouth to my ear.

"Shame, I was looking forward to seeing that smudged on my cock later."

I gape at him, then bite my lip.

"I have a cheaper one," I tell him and giggle when he growls into my neck.

"Witch."

"Brute." Jace grins devilishly at me, and we head towards the entrance, where I slip the tickets from Jace's inner jacket pocket to hand them over. We are given champagne on entry. It's still early, but the inside is a hive of activity. Soft lighting throws an alluring glow over the artist's work. The photographs show pain, shame, hurt, angst, love, and happiness, all caught within a second but telling years of pain, and speaking days of hurt. The work is sensational. I head straight over to a piece that is shrouded in amber light—amber like Jace's eyes. The photograph is black and white and solely of the side of someone's face. They are crying, but also smiling. It's a beautiful picture.

"Look at how they have caught the light. Can you see how defined that tear is? It's genius," I turn to say and find Jace smiling down at me. "What?" I ask, sipping quickly on my flute of champagne.

"You go all glassy-eyed. It's nice to see."

"I love art," I say simply.

"I know. Do you like this?" He nods at the photograph.

"I do," I say quietly, turning back and staring at it. I'm looking at someone's deepest emotions on a big glossy print. Whoever captured this image caught this person's soul-deep happiness. Their love. It's shining from their eyes, reflected in their tears, and it's truly beautiful. Their smile isn't perfect, but it makes it all the more pure. "They don't even know they've been captured. They have no idea, but it's there for us all to see."

"I hope they know. Otherwise I think they'd find it intrusive," Jace says. An older man steps up beside us, wearing a suit and sporting an impressive goatee.

"My fiancée—she knew about the photo," he winks. "I asked her to marry me." He throws a gloating look at us. "As you can tell, she said yes."

"It's so beautiful; the light; what you've don—"

"Yes, that took some setting up. I needed the right light for this. I wanted to ensure I caught enough of her face that it would hold on to each curve, see here," he points, and Jace manoeuvres us to the side to allow him room, "she actually has a scar along her cheek, but the light disguises it. She thanked me for that, but I wanted the scar." As I look along the wall, I see they are all of his fiancé.

"She is my muse," he says, following my gaze.

"Berin Rhodes." He holds out his hand. I recognise the name instantly. I had tried to borrow a piece of his from Alfredo for my event, but it had been sold. He is big in the states.

"Lily Spencer." Jace briefly frees my hand so I can shake Berin's, then it's back in his.

"You own The Loft. You're a friend of Alfredo's," he says. Wow, I'm shocked. I didn't think this man would have come across my name.

"Yes, and this is Jace Bennett, my partner." Berin and Jace shake hands, and when Berin's fiancée appears, we fall into a steady conversation. I'm yet to see Stanley, but for the time being, I'm going to network and get my name out there too.

———

As the evening wears on, Jace and I walk around the room. Seeing Berin and Olivia from afar, they seem a really nice couple. I'm looking about the room for Stanley when a stocky man with white hair and a protruding belly comes straight to Jace, beaming.

"Ah, thank god. Another non-artsy male." He grins toothily at Jace, who seems to know this man.

"Sort of. This is Lily, my partner. She is a gallery owner, so it comes in the fine print that I'm quite partial to art these days. Roger, how are you?" Jace asks. Roger pats at his wide belly, sucking in short breaths. Jesus, he looks like he is going to keel over. I give Jace a worried glance.

"Good, good," he huffs. "Gwen is about somewhere. She will be happy to see you," he says breathlessly. I feel sorry for him. It's not that hot in here, but with his three-piece and weight, he must be stifling.

"I didn't realise you were both here," Jace says and frowns, looking around the room. I'm assuming Gwen is this man's wife, or maybe a friend? Jace must know them both. A decorative set of nails comes over Jace's shoulder as a stunning blonde woman circles him, all lowered lashes and a soft smile.

"Hello, Jace," she breathes, and I just know with every fibre of my being that they have slept together,

"Here she is. Lily, this is my wife, Gwen." Wife? So Jace slept with Roger's wife—his much younger wife? I hope it was before she decided to set her sights on Roger's failing figure. The man is at least twenty years her senior. I'm not one to judge anyone for their age gap, but when the man looks like he is close to a string of heart attacks and the woman is a stunning model of a female, I judge. I'm judging now, judging her for ogling Jace right in front of my face.

"I knew you would remember Jace." Roger looks at me. "Jace designed our new build," he says, I nod out of politeness, but Jace has gone stiff by my side.

"How could I forget?" Gwen replies on a purr, her eyes searching Jace's face heatedly. Roger can't be that dumb, surely?

"Nice to see you again." Jace's strained voice is anything but nice; he is not comfortable with this at all. "We're actually off to find Stanley. He is a friend of Lily's. Excuse us," he says, adjusting his clammy hand in mine and giving them a curt nod. He tugs me along, and I stare at the back of his head. I knew he had a past, and that it was probably colourful—but married women! It makes my throat sore, and my chest ache. I didn't expect that of him, and I'm judging *him* now too. I'm quiet as he pulls us along until we circle a big statue, and he can nudge me back behind a white gauze curtain.

"I know you are thinking the worst, and I deserve it. I was a stupid, selfish guy, and I hate that part of me. I'm not like that anymore. That was me before you, Lily." His eyes go from the floor to me, and he is pleading with me. "That was before, and it sickens me that I was so callous with women. Then you come along, and it's the biggest wake-up call. Like every curse I'd had to listen to before, every insult I had received from being such a . . . a dick came crashing down, and all I could think was no one had better have ever done that to her. How will she even like me if she knows?"

I can't formulate any words or take in what he is saying, so I blink away and pull in a soft breath.

"She's married, Jace," I whisper. Does he not care?

"I know, and it was wrong. It was over a year ago. She wouldn't leave me alone, and after a while, I just gave in because I didn't owe it to anyone not to. I didn't care for her or Roger. I still don't."

"I think I need to nip to the toilets," I say in a quiet croak. My murmur is met by a short hiss of pleas, but I gently tug free, place my champagne flute on the nearest tray, and walk quickly to the ladies. As soon as I'm inside and locked in a cubicle, I fire a quick message to Cass.

Can't talk but just had the pleasure of meeting one of Jace's conquests, and her husband! Oh, god, Cass, I feel sick ☹

Her response is almost immediate.

Well, shit!!! Was she a dog? Kidding. We all have a past. Sean cheated, and you still accept him. Jace loves you. Don't let this get too you, hun x

I chew over her response. She is right, of course, but it still stings. I suck in a breath and just let it all sink in.

Betrayal

I'm really no good with conflict of any kind. I feel, and I run. It's like my body won't allow me to acknowledge it there and then. I need a little time to swallow it all and process.

I still don't like what Jace did, but the fact of the matter is I can't change it. It's done. I can't let it affect us. I have to move on from it.

Thanks x

I tap back quickly, hearing the outer door swing shut as Cass messages me to call her if I need to. I flush the loo so it doesn't seem odd that I was in the cubicle and push free, heading straight for the sinks, when someone leaning at the end of the vanity draws my gaze. Gwen. I count to three in my head, waiting for her little comment. Surely that's why she followed me in here.

―――――

"Trouble in paradise?" she asks with a smirk. Her blonde hair is twisted into an elegant knot on her twig neck, and her collarbone could scratch her own eyes out, let alone mine. She is willowy and top-heavy, but I refuse to react yet. She must have seen Jace pull me aside. I wash my hands and turn my head to see her sizing me up. Size away, love, it's me he wants. How pathetic. My mind screams 'gold digger'.

"Not at all. Personally, if I were you, I'd be more concerned with my own love life than that of others, unless, of course, you can't actually bring yourself to sleep with that unassuming man." I dry my hands, ignore her gaping mouth, and walk past, throwing her a wink. I don't know who is more stupid for even entering into that relationship, him or her. "Try and enjoy your evening, Gwen. I know I will." I leave with a gloating smile on my face and swoop up another glass of champagne as Stanley comes over.

"Finally! I didn't think I was ever going to get the chance to speak to you. You look fantastic," he says, leaning to peck my cheeks. He is donning a three-piece suit and a ridiculous amount of aftershave, but Stanley always does go over the top.

"The gallery looks incredible. I forget how beautiful it is. The turnout has been brilliant. I hope one day I get this kind of interest," I tell him honestly.

"Half of them just want to say they have been here. You know what people are like; they want to indulge enough to gloat," he huffs. I wonder if he isn't doing as great as this event suggests. I give him a sympathetic smile as I rest my flute on my arm, cupping my waist. It can be a sting to your pride. I felt that after my first event.

"Well, you'll be sure to get some sales tonight."

"Oh, yes. I just wish the nosey riffraff would bugger off." He gives a wave to someone across the room and points to a painting above my shoulder as Jace walks over. His eyes narrow when he sees Gwen leaving the 'Ladies' with a scowl on her face. "This one, I love. It's very loud, but it softens each time I see it," he says.

Jace nods at him and pecks my brow, and leaning, he says, "Jace Bennett. I'm Lily's partner."

"Stanley Ebon. I recognise your name. Why do I recognise your name?" He pouts, then steals my champagne. "You don't mind, do you? I have an awfully dry throat from talking the ears off of everyone." He passes it back while looking at Jace.

"Maybe through Bennett and Klein."

"Yes, of course. You did some work over the road, the new roof for the museum."

"That's right. Viktor, my business partner, is a huge art fan. We came over here once or twice," Jace recalls. He adjusts his stance, and I do a double-take for the third time this evening. He looks incredible in a suit. He never told me he had been here before.

Stanley taps his tooth.

"Yes, I remember him not being well when you brought him out. I'm sure I read that somewhere." Stanley is like the social centre of Earth and knows all the gossip, and Jace gives an awkward laugh.

"Yes, pretty much. He is doing well, thanks, enjoying retirement." He doesn't mention his recent health scare, so I keep my lips firmly shut.

Stanley looks at me.

"This one is a little diamond—nice to look at and tough as hell. She drives a hard bargain." I blush profusely at Stanley's observation of me and find Jace giving me a pointed smirk.

"Only when the need arises," I say in defence with a wide smile on my face.

"Of course." Stanley winks. "You look gorgeous in that dress. Oh, there's Edward Humphreys. Excuse me." He pecks my cheeks again and smiles at Jace before striding off with a wave on his way to someone else.

"I feel like if I put him and Carl in the same room, there would be one hell of a cat-fight." I laugh lightly and wiggle my foot in my heel. My toes are aching, and I'm done for the night. I've met one or two new people and swapped business cards. I think most are on their way to being drunk, so there is no need for me to stay.

Jace clears his throat and twists me so I'm facing him. His hands are placed on the outer globes of my bum.

"I noticed Gwen leave the toilets after you." He frowns down at me, furiously chewing his lip. I run my finger along it, halting him.

"I don't think she will be bothering us again," I say. He grins. His eyes sparkle, and his nostrils flare with a smile.

"You put her in her place?" he says lightly.

"I did." I press onto my toes and peck his lips.

"Indulge me. What did you say?" His eyes are dancing wildly. This is turning him on. My cheeks flush, so I lean into his ear and repeat my short encounter with Gwen to Jace.

"Fuck me, Lily." He moves his head enough to slant his mouth over mine.

I'm breathless.

"I know. I felt so good afterward." I giggle, embarrassed that I staked my claim on him like that. I'm as red as my lipstick, and the champagne is going to my head. "Take me home."

"Gladly."

Chapter Nineteen

With Jace running late, I figure Thai is off the menu, so I decide to make a stir-fry. It's quick, and the most talentless of people could make it, so I should find it a breeze.

Flicking the radio on and pouring myself a glass of wine, I go about making dinner and flit about, tidying things away. We left it in a mess this morning, so I fold the throws and plump the cushions. When the sound of tyres on gravel brings my head up, I notice it's not Jace's car; it's Neve's.

I groan loudly and move back to the kitchen, checking my reflection as I do. I hate to admit that she makes me feel unkempt and awkward.

She doesn't knock and walks straight in. "He's not here," I say and hold a glass up in the way of an offer. She takes it from me with a tight smile and proceeds to find herself a different wine, as though I may have contaminated the freshly opened one. I'm being dramatic, but the woman makes me so mad.

"He might be awhile," I tell her. She has her back to me, her concentration fixed on pouring the wine.

"I can wait," she states in a manner that means; *I'm waiting.*

"I didn't realise he was expecting you. I only put enough on for the two of us." I don't want her to stay, but I say what I know: Jace would want me to be welcoming. Neve sips her wine and moves around the kitchen slowly. She eyes me and takes a seat on the stool at the island. Her long blonde hair is curled with an art I can't perfect, her face is contoured, and she looks like a model in her leather jeans, lace trim top, and sky-high heels.

"I heard cooking wasn't your forte," she muses. Her lips twitch, and I feel the jibe right down to my toes because it means Jace has been discussing me with her, and I don't like it.

"Oh, it's not. Thank god, it's not my culinary skills he's after," I quip. It's quite possibly the most juvenile thing I have said in a long while, but god, she pulls this unwanted nasty side of me right out. I want to claw her eyes out. I catch the tail end of an eye roll and force myself to grit my teeth.

"I'll give him a call if you like?" I pick up my phone with the very thought of doing that.

"Don't bother. He'll be here shortly," she says with utter conviction. Her finger runs the rim of her glass, and she gives me a forced smile. Oh, he will? He rang not long ago to tell me he was running late. I raise my brows a little at her pointed remark. She's probably tracking him on GPS, I think bitchily.

I turn away, refusing to show interest.

Sensing my dismissal, she lifts her glass and says as she places it back down, "It's Friday, and we usually had dinner before you moved yourself in. He leaves around six forty and will be here for quarter to eight." I stare ahead at the wall, wanting to tell her I was asked to move in, but it's very obvious she has made her mind up about me and vice versa. Nor do I tell her he is running late.

"How observant of you," I mutter. What is this girl trying to prove? "So, you do want dinner then?" I try for kind, but it comes out in a bored huff.

Her laugh is sarcastic—the thought of eating my food repugnant, no doubt.

"No!" She scowls bitchily.

"Okay." I frown at her but turn to stir the vegetables. Fed up of her company already, I turn the radio up a notch more, happy to drown her out.

"You don't like me." It's not a question, but a callous statement aimed at causing more tension.

"I could say the same to you." I keep my face averted and flick a look up the drive, eager to see the headlights of Jace's car, but darkness mocks me by allowing me to see her spiteful gaze.

"I suppose I don't blame you," she hums. I feel my shoulders stiffen but force myself to relax. Is she goading me?

"Okay." I don't allow her room to elaborate, but her brashness knows no bounds.

"Especially for a girl like you." Her choice of words niggles me more. As though she sees me as some naïve twit.

"Meaning?" This time I do bite. But I don't satisfy her with an eager look. Instead, I begin mixing ingredients to make a sauce. I'm putting no love into it and considering my cooking skills are nil-to-none, Jace has little luck of it tasting better than the underside of a shoe.

"You seem the jealous type. Maybe a little insecure." She makes no apology for highlighting her personal observations of me. I'm not that person, but with her, those attributes have reared their ugly head. I turn then and swig my wine, using it to point to her. For the first time since Jace asked me to move in with him, I really feel this is my home, and she is making me feel uncomfortable in it. It's another tally on the hate board for me.

"Yet, here *you* are, trying to make a point. Surely that says more about you than me?" Dipping my head, I regard her pointedly and let my words sink in. I refuse to be intimidated by her and figure enough is enough. "You want Jac—"

"I've had Jace," she cuts me off, her glass slamming down as she stares at me pointedly across the island. I don't mean to flinch, but her words hurt me.

I knew it! Deep down. God, I knew it, but having it clarified stings. I blink my pain aside and swallow. I want my voice to be confident when I reply. Sighing, I neck the rest of my wine.

"We all do things in our teens. It's just life." I shrug her off and decide to take it up with Jace himself. Now Neve has confirmed it, he better be ready to fight to win my trust back. He lied to me. It's not until I lift the spoon to stir the simmering sauce that I realise I'm shaking.

"I'd hardly call the conference our teens, or your exhibition, but who I am to argue. You clearly think you have won the unobtainable." She laughs, and I drop the spoon.

My exhibition? The conference? That was barely a week ago!

"You're lying," I whisper. Anger and shock collide in my stomach and attack my heart. I can't hide how much I'm shaking or the lack of colour in my face.

"Why would I?" She shrugs confidently. "I have nothing to gain from lying, and I figured you suspected, so all I have done is cement the truth. I don't have to like you to know you don't deserve to be lied to." She flicks her hair back over her shoulder and watches me. Her harsh but beautiful face is locked on mine.

God, while I was regimented to a curfew, he was with her! Sleeping with her!

I swallow dryly, still in shock that he could be so callous. My mind sinks further back to the night of the exhibition as I recall the events that unfolded: her obvious irritation at being there, and her sly words.

"Thanks for coming," I had said.

That was the idea. She was mocking me even then, knowing she would be trussed up in bed with him. I feel sick to the stomach. We weren't even a couple, not really, but the conference? I'd moved in then. I was asleep in his bed while he used work as an excuse to fuck her. Was the mess up with the rooms another taunt from them both?

I don't understand. Why would he chase me if he has been continuing an affair with her? My stomach flips in an aggressive roll. I look up through the fog of pain to find Neve battling a smug smile.

"I have to hand it to you, Lily, you really caught his attention for a while, but he always comes back." She bites her lip and swirls her wine as Jace's car ambles down the drive.

She is so utterly sure of herself that his presence doesn't cause her concern, and that in itself makes my stomach drop like a lead weight. She shows no fear or worry for herself because she knows she won't lose him. *He always comes back.*

I watch as he gets out of the car, and sickness spirals in my stomach. I leave the pan and walk quickly to the bedroom to collect my handbag. I search for my charger, but I can't see it through the build-up of hot tears. In a rush, I grab the small pile of makeup and forgo the rest of my stuff.

I can feel my heart running a mile in my chest. I can't think about what she has just told me. Not fully. I'm not ready to comprehend it. Every cell is repelling it. The overwhelming need to flee is the driving force in my choppy actions. I hear the deep rumble of his voice, and it makes my chest squeeze. As quick as I take my next breath, I tell myself I hate him.

Jace walks straight to me with a look of worry etched on his face, and that is all the confirmation I need. His lie is out.

"Lily, wait. I don't know what she has said—" I bash past him. "Lily, what's wrong?" When he grabs my wrist, I swing and slap him hard. I have the sudden urge to pummel my fists into his face, but I use his shock to snap my arm free.

What's wrong? He knows. His face told me that already.

"What the fuck did you say?" he yells at Neve, who is unaffected by his outburst. She lifts her wine and rolls her eyes at him.

"The truth. She would have found out sooner or later." She is looking at him with an abundance of irritation. She raises her glass to me like she has done me a favour. In some ways, she has.

I rush to the door, but he captures me around the waist.

"Lily, please. Let me explain. Fucking hell, don't run." I twist and slam my hands into his chest, giving myself a little distance when he staggers back in horror.

I'm clutching my things to my chest to stop me from hitting him again.

"I asked you!" I shout. "I gave you the opportunity to

Betrayal

be honest." I hiccup as the first rush of sob-fuelled tears hit.

"Baby, don't cry. I'm sorry." He moves but sees me flinch, and it's enough to momentarily stall him.

"You lied to me!" I shout. "You were fucking her!" My lip gives way, and it all comes out in a broken sob. When my hand comes up a second time, he grabs it and pulls me to him. I've always abhorred violence, but my god, I want to hurt him.

"Lily, please. Don't leave. Talk to me." His usually heavy, syrupy eyes are wide with panic, and his face has lost some colour.

"Get the fuck off me!" My wrist is held tight, and I can't get free.

Neve looks utterly bored but watches us, nonetheless. I want to care that she is here witnessing it all, but I'm too damn hurt. Pride leaves me with one foul, brutal sweep of pain.

Jace swings a look at her.

"Why?" he snaps. "It wasn't your place." He's seething, and he looks to me with remorse, worry, and guilt plastered over every inch of his face, but I don't care for any of it. In fact, it's the first time I have looked at him and found him unattractive.

"Or yours apparently," she mutters, necking the last of the wine in her glass.

"Lily, it's not what you think," he says in a rush.

"No?" I laugh sarcastically, "So you haven't been fucking your *friend*." My tone is scolding, and my lip curls in disgust. "She's like family. Nothing happened," I mimic. "Fuck you!"

"It's not like that." He keeps me at his front and rubs a hand over his face. "It's . . . she's—" He's looking everywhere, even to her for help, and his mouth opens and closes, but he can't draw the words together to explain. It wouldn't matter. I'm done.

"What?" I scream. He made me feel as though I was irrational, but I knew it. Deep down, I knew something was off!

"Yes, Jace, what am I?" Neve laughs.

"Shut up, Neve. In fact, please leave." He motions to the door. God, he actually thinks I'm going to stay. After this! He is deluded.

"Don't bother," I tell her. "I'm going. Don't fucking chase me this time." When I look at Neve, she's smirking at me. "He can come back to you as much as he wants now!" She shakes her hair out and locks my stare.

Deep down, I know this is what she wants, but I can't see past that he cheated and lied to me. Lied and allowed me to second-guess myself about feeling uncomfortable and uneasy around her, even when I gave him the opportunity to come clean so we could deal with it and put it to rest, he chose to lie.

"The truth always," I spit, and his face falls again. "Just not for me though, right?" I don't even want him to answer that.

"Lily, please."

"Do you love her?" I ask, my voice breaking. It shouldn't matter. It's inconsequential now. It's over, and I can't trust him, or her for that matter.

"It's not the same." He sighs. "Stay, talk to me?" he pleads softly.

"You can't have us both," I croak. I hate myself for uttering those words with her so close to enjoy them because she knows she has won.

"Don't make me choose," he whispers, and his hand goes lax.

Betrayal

"So you do love her then." My arm drops away. Who is this man?

"Yes, but it's not—" I flee, pushing open the door.

"Lily!" he roars, and I rush down the steps and to my car, yanking the door free and locking myself in. The tears come thick and fast. Jace is banging on the window, but he twists momentarily and shouts back at her, standing on the porch. I can't hear what is being said, not through the drum of my heart in my ears and the loud sobs wracking me.

I choke out a sob and turn as he repeatedly pulls at the door handle.

"You bastard!" I scream, "You fucking bastard!"

His eyes are wide with worry.

"Don't drive. Not like this. Fucking hell, Lily." He is still trying at the handle, the force creaking the door, and panic is etched all over his face. A face I don't ever wish to set eyes on again. I turn the engine over and begin to move, but he moves with me, keeping hold of the car. I speed off, and Jace swears loudly before I'm flying down the drive, sobbing uncontrollably.

I'm well above the speed limit, and on my empty stomach, the alcohol is dancing a chaotic race through my veins. I don't call Cass or head home. I avoid the obvious and take the route to the gallery. I park haphazardly around the back and enter through the rear entrance. Despite my blurry lashes, I force my way into The Loft, lock myself in, head in the dark to my office and open the safe, flicking through the contents until I find the business credit card. It's an impulse that crashed into my mind on the drive and one I won't back down from.

I don't want to be anywhere he can get to me, and I know with every bone in my body that he will chase me.

He doesn't know how to let me go. Some twisted part of him won't let this be. Everything I just learned about him, I hate—how could he do this?

The sound of my name being called from the entrance of the gallery, accompanied by the rattle of the door, makes me jump. My heart is splintering wildly once again, and his pained voice snatches my heart and pumps a whole new level of anger around my shaken body.

I stand shielded behind my office door, sheltering me from the owner of a voice I have loved from the very moment it graced my ears, and eyes that hypnotise me into the most euphoric states—just a piece of wood hiding me from the cause of such deep-rooted pain. My hand lifts onto the handle, but I drop it and take a few shaky steps backward, my eyes blinking another wave of fresh tears loose.

I rush out of the back, thankful the door automatically locks, and weave through the small alleyway that backs on to the little courtyard. I check the car park before I step out under the streetlamp and rush to my car, a wobbly mess.

I waste no time in zipping out and taking the turning that pushes me further from him. I think back to all the times he has been late or not answered his phone, times I never paid much mind to, times that seem likely opportunities to continue his playboy lifestyle.

My naivety mocks me, and I feel a complete fool for thinking I could ever handle or keep a man like him—a man who has never committed to anyone but himself.

I brush my wrist along my tear-coated cheek and pick up speed. I drive right into the heart of the city so I'm swallowed up by traffic, and my car becomes nondescript and my location a mystery. My heart feels heavy, and the painful ache and dread bouncing around in my stomach aren't helping.

I hate that I so easily acknowledge that these feelings will walk with me for a very long time, feelings that will attack me in the dark of the night when I'm alone and at my most vulnerable. These feelings will latch themselves to earlier heartbreaks, coupling up and standing in force against me. My lip quivers and a low wail exits my dry lips.

I don't understand any of it. Not how he could even do it to me, let alone why. My wicked thoughts ride with me until I come upon a hotel with underground parking. My heart does another painful, sickening swoop when I think of how available she is to him at work or if it even stops with her. I beg the plaguing thoughts to leave me alone.

They don't. Not when I mumble my way through my booking or when I mindlessly trudge to my room. I push in and barely acknowledge the small interior. I'm tormented by too much emotion and so many rancid and sickening thoughts that I yank up a pillow and scream into it. The thick material I have pressed to my lips muffles the high wail. I scream until my voice cracks, and my chest is heaving. I scream until I'm rushing into the bathroom and vomiting. I scream until I'm sobbing, and sleep is the only temporary reprieve from my troubled mind.

I wake in the early hours and pace in the tiny room. It's too small, too unfamiliar, and the lure of my own place is too great to ignore. My phone is chocker with messages and missed calls from Jace and Cass. I turn it off, not willing or ready to deal with anyone—even the thought of having to converse with the hotel clerk when I check out gnaws at me. I just want to slip away unseen.

I grab the little I have and step out into the corridor. The hotel is silent and empty—a physical representation of how I'm feeling. I'm happy to find the main reception desk unoccupied, so I slide my key on the top and leave.

———

I walk quickly to my apartment after I edge my way down the street, looking for any sign of Jace. I push the door open. It's dark and peaceful, but my head is a jumble of chaotic thoughts. I click the door shut, and it comes then, in a bone-curling, painful ache, and I discard my bag on the sideboard with a loud crash as I lean into the wall.

The first sob is quiet, low, but once it's out, it unfurls into a shudder of long, muted sobs. I want to hit something. I want this pain to end.

"Lily?"

I jump, choking on a scream. Jace stands, making himself visible, as the moonlight pulls him into view. My throat swells with pain, and I drop my head.

"Leave," I whisper as I realise I'm shaking like crazy. "*Get out*," I repeat more forcefully, desperately. I can't bear to look at him, so I don't. I keep my head averted.

"Please. I need to explain." His voice cracks.

"GET OUT!" I grab the nearest thing and launch it at him. It smashes, and whatever it was echoes off the walls in a sharp crack, and my gaze turns narrow and cold.

He walks towards me, hands out,

"Hey, hey. Calm down." His hands are shaking. "Listen to me. I can explain. I need to explain," he croaks weakly.

Betrayal

"I don't want you to. Get out." I pull the door open wide and stare at him hard as tears run thick and fast down my cheek. "Thanks for coming." I push through gritted teeth. It takes a moment for my words to register, and when they do, his eyes widen, then sadden. He drops his head and takes a few steps toward the door, as he drags in a deep breath and runs a hand up the back of his neck.

"I never meant to hurt you." He stands in the doorway, and I see the key in his grasp. He is looking hopefully at me, obviously feeling that he has my attention, and he refuses to let the chance slip by. "Never," he says as he swallows thickly, his own lips shaking. "You need to know that." I can't keep my eyes on his, not when I feel this distressed and enraged.

"My key, please." I don't know where this strength is coming from because every molecule is screaming at me to run into his chest, yet my fingernails want to sink into his cheek. I hold my shaky hand out, and reluctantly he passes it over.

"Lily wai—"

"Goodbye, Jace." His mouth is flaying like a fish—his healthy tan now a pale sheen on his remarkable face: the face of a liar. He talks quickly, every word spoken with torment.

"I'm not going anywhere. I'm going to make this right." His hand is flat on the door, my chest heaves uncontrollably, and a mechanical laughs barks from my chest. He blinks, unsure of what to do or say next. "However long it takes, I'm not going without a fight. You need to listen to me. I don't know what Neve told y —" The very sound of her name makes me flinch, and I slam the door shut. It rattles on its hinges, and the brutal force makes even me jump.

The silence afterward is deafening. I just wish I could quiet my feelings too.

I stare at the door, every cell of anger running just under the top layer of my skin, crackling and spitting until it reaches my hands. My fingers curl, and I pound on the door with a sharp scream.

"I hate you!" I roar brokenly.

Chapter Twenty

Four Weeks Later . . .

Four long, painful weeks of sheer, gut-wrenching heartache. I feel it even in my skin. The pain is lingering in my veins and is being pumped around my system quicker than my own blood is.

It hurts. *God, it bloody hurts.* I know my eyes are reflecting the depth of my angst because no matter how widely I smile or upbeat I make my voice sound, everyone looks at me as though I'm about to break, but I think I already have.

Being in this much pain is exhausting. I can't sleep, and when I do, I'm attacked by vivid dreams of him. I wake in a sweat, and nothing seems to shift the crushing sensation in my gut. It's making me sick.

Another wave of nausea rolls through me, and I tense in bed, ready to fly to the toilet. I drag in a deep breath through my nose and slowly breathe it out. I blame it on the dreams—they're so real. As soon as I succumb to the exhaustion and finally allow sleep to win,

I'm waking in a pool of sweat, shivering, and feeling sick to my stomach. The burn of whiskey eyes lingers in my mind, and in a groan of emotional pain, I twist, closing my eyes to rid the thought of him.

There has been no contact.

After the first week of him constantly turning up at The Loft, and Harriet politely telling him she would call the police—he stopped.

Stopped emailing. Stopped calling The Loft and me. Stopped contacting Cass. Nothing. He physically vanished from my life.

I don't know what that means, but I can't even think outside my own grief. The severing was so quick and final.

It's eating away at me—the lack of contact. I can feel the thick ball of hurt lodged in my throat. This time, when the nausea comes, it doesn't stop at my stomach; it races up my throat in a bitter, acidic roll, and coughing, I rush into the loo and drop to my knees as the poor amount of food I had managed to keep down disappears into the toilet.

I wipe at my mouth, but soon enough, I begin to heave once more and vomit until my stomach burns and aches. Nothing but my own organs remain, and I feel a sweaty, pathetic mess.

Resting my face against the wall, I close my eyes and sit for a minute. Slowly breathing in and out to rid the after-effects of the nausea.

I wish I were a fly on the wall: his wall. I want to take a small cell of satisfaction from knowing he is hurting as I am, but I don't believe someone who lacks morals like he does will have a hard time letting me go. If anything is hurting, it will be his pride. I can't imagine a woman has ever willingly chosen to leave him. Not that it matters. Neve will no doubt be occupying his time fully now.

I'm constantly at war with my gut instinct and the painful memories of him. I should have listened to my gut all along; something niggled the whole time, right from the first moment we laid eyes on each other.

My mind flies back to that first day when the deep, penetrating, syrupy gaze locked on me with a smirk of crude satisfaction. He knew how attractive women found him, and I was no different.

Or maybe I was.

Because I *was* stupid enough to let a man like Jace Bennett lull me into believing I was something to him. Stupid enough to move in with him, even though that same niggle weighed on me still.

Megan should have been enough of a deterrent. I tell myself I should be thankful the breakup happened so early on. It's my only hope of trying to build myself back up.

I tell myself it is for the best. I couldn't bear to think how hideous this would have all been if it had happened years down the line, or worse, if I had children with him. I know that pain too. I could never choose that pain for my child.

My stomach does another swirl of sickly unhappiness, and my eyes pop open as my hand lands on my sensitive belly—the sudden thought cruel yet undeniable.

No!

I heave again at the hideous and possible predicament, but throwing up doesn't make the fear of the indisputable any easier. Shakily, I stand and stare at my pale, tired expression. My mind flies over the torrent of painful memories and stops at my attack. I was sick after I was attacked, Jace had said. We'd had sex. A lot.

I shake my head as the unfair conclusion lands in my life, mocking me in silent laughter. No. This can't be happening. I think of anything to repel the unwelcome thought, but the seed has been planted, quite literally, I fear.

I brush my teeth and spit furiously into the sink, feeling sick with a different kind of dread. I move to my room and out into the living room, where my phone is charging. I know the local chemist is twenty-four hours, but I check the time regardless, pulling on a pair of jeans and an oversized jumper. I shove my feet in my shoes and grab my keys and purse. I have no makeup on, and I know for a fact, my hair looks matted on the left because I've sweated so much. By the time I get to the street, I have managed to drag it up into a scraggly bun, but I don't torture myself with checking my reflection. I must look as panicked as I feel desolate.

Chapter Twenty-One

I barely recall the drive, but at this early hour, I beat the rush. I head straight to the counter. If the assistant thinks I look dreadful, she doesn't show it. I ignore the ding of the bell sounding behind me and chew my lip. I just want to grab a test and get home. I'm fidgety and unsure when I meet her head on.

She looks fresh and clinical in her white pharmacist attire.

"Good morning. How can I help?" Her voice is bright and perky, at total odds with my own wobbly vocals.

"Oh, hello, a test, please." I shake my head, my thoughts a jumble. "A pregnancy test." I clear my throat and pray my eyes don't reflect my sheer terror at the prospect.

"Lily?" The deep whisper has me gasping, spinning, and tensing all at once, and I come face to face with Jace. I can't comprehend anything more, other than he is here, and I am purchasing a pregnancy test. My mouth drops open, and any colour that had refused to leave me during this hideous ordeal disintegrates on the spot. He followed me here. Does that mean he's been sitting and waiting outside my flat?

"We offer a free testing service if you like, Miss?" Jace's intense eyes go from me to the woman grasping a kit in her hand like a neon sign.

"It's not for me," I spit. "A friend," I explain. My poor heart is pumping wildly in my chest, and my stomach plummets and twists in a tight knot.

"Lily, can we talk?" he murmurs behind me.

"I have nothing to say to you," I whisper, my wide eyes holding the lady's as I spur her on. She must sense the tension because she is thrusting it in my hand as soon as I pay, and before I say thank you, I'm rushing to the door.

"Lily, please—"

His broken plea does nothing to me. I whirl on him in the street. It's quiet out, and the foggy sky represents my mood. I see him then. He looks worn out. Good.

"No!" I shout in his face, taking a step forward, and my hand swipes out and catches his shocked face. The sound is sharp and loud. The pleasant burn up my hand is oddly comforting, but it's quickly followed by the harsh sense of guilt at being so violent with him. "Stay the hell away from me," I screech, horrified by my actions.

"I can't." My handprint is pink and vivid on his cheek, and my palm tingles, reminding me I have sunk to a new low: Adam low.

"You can and you will," I scathe. I hate myself for hitting him, and I don't like who I'm becoming. I blame him for that too.

"Is that really for a friend? Cass?" His amber irises seem hopeful for anything to keep the connection between us. I'm silently praying there is no connection

Betrayal

left, but dammit if my body isn't singing a happy song at his proximity.

"Yes." I hold his stare. The lie comes easily, and I even sound believable.

"Give me a chance." He swallows. Oh, he knows he is asking for the world right now.

"I did when I stupidly agreed to entertain this attraction." He reaches for me, and I slap his hand away.

"You still feel it," he shamelessly points out, even if his confident voice is husky with emotion.

"Yes, because it makes my skin crawl." He pulls back as though I've slapped him again.

"You don't mean that." His hand does that annoying thing I once found attractive, as it delves into his hair, and then he looks up through inky lashes, his head bent in defeat.

"I do. I hate that I even met you." I take a step back because I need the distance. My lip quivers, and my eyes fill. I can't look at him and not feel the crippling lust I have always been bombarded with.

"I love you. Don't cry." He is quick to close the distance, too quick, and as his hand takes my arm, and he pulls me to him, I jump and push free.

"Lily, please let me explain. I will do anything."

"Great, leave," I snap, "leave me alone." I sound hysterical. I look homeless. I haven't washed this morning, and makeup has become a chore I have chosen to forgo. "It's over," I spit.

I jump in my car and speed off. My eyes—like the magnet to him that they are—fly to the mirror where I watch him swear profusely, and punch his car, causing the alarm to flare up in a shrill scream.

I barely register the drive home. I just know that I can't do this alone. I'm sitting waiting impatiently for

Cass to come over—the last ten minutes have been the longest of my life so far. My leg is jiggling about, my lip a worn chewed-up mess, and I have even bitten into my nails while I wait. My apartment door flies open, and Cass's face widens in shock. I'm guessing I look worse than I originally thought.

"No matter what, it will be okay," she tells me. Cass pulls me into a hug, and I go, but I'm a jittery mess. "Come on." She pushes me toward the bathroom.

I know my voice is going to break because I can feel the emotion hanging in there, "What if . . . " I can't bring myself to say it out loud. "Cass, I don't think I can have him in my life and never *have* him. I'll never be rid of her," I choke out.

"Let's do the test. You could be worrying over nothing," she coaxes diplomatically. She looks slightly unkempt, and I know I have got her out of bed.

"What if I'm not?" I swallow, the knot of anxiety getting bigger.

"Then I'm here, and Sean is here. We will always support you." I nod at the severe expression on her face. "You are stronger than you think," she tells me with a stern look.

Cass finds the tests on the side and begins unwrapping it all, and the crinkle of the cellophane makes it all seem so real suddenly.

"Oh, god." I'm shaking. This isn't what I want. Not now. Not after everything. Life can't be that cruel.

"Calm down." She nods to the empty seat. "Go on." I blink through wet lashes.

"Do you think he believed me?" I whisper, chewing my nail once more. Cass slaps my hand away from my mouth.

"I envy those nails. Don't ruin them." She huffs, then

Betrayal

shrugs. "I don't know. He must have followed you there," she offers up. I'm too anxious to hear what she is saying. I take a deep breath and pull my jeans down, but just as my bum hits the seat, I stand.

"I don't want her in my child's life," I choke out. "She's crazy. What if they get together? My child will be subjected to that, *her?*" Cass pulls me in for a hug and holds me tight. I should feel some sort of awkwardness at my jeans being caught around my knees, but I don't.

"Then we fight." She brushes my hair and kisses my cheek. "Stop tormenting yourself. Let's find out; then we can deal." I nod and lower once more.

"Okay."

Cass passes me the stick, and I pee on it.

"How long does it take?" I say in a rush.

"Did you not read the back?" She rolls her eyes, already anticipating my answer.

"No," I mumble. Cass begins reading out loud.

"Can take a minute or two, plus for positive an—" I hold it up to her. She smiles at me softly, her eyes filling with happy yet sympathetic tears.

"Congratulations," she chokes, her face full of emotion.

Everything south of my eyebrows collapses. I drop the stick, bury my head in my hands, and sniff loudly.

"This isn't supposed to happen!" I sob angrily as gentle arms cup my body.

"I'm here every step of the way," she breathes. I hiccup and cry quietly

It seems an age before I stand, and when Cass helps me up, my legs feel stiff from sitting in the same position for an extended period of time. Her voice has been a comfort, but I don't hear a word she says, not until she pulls my head up to hers and looks at me.

"Let me run you a bath." She swipes under my eye, removing the wetness coating my skin. I sniff and drag in a lungful of air.

―――

I'm numb. Cass is sponging my back. My face is twisted away, pressed to my knee so all I can hear is the heavy thump of my own heartbeat. I've wrapped my ankles over each other and my arms around my knees. It's utterly pathetic.

"I hate seeing you like this." She is struggling to keep her own emotions in check, and her voice is thick with tears. My emotions are now at a standstill, in a permanent state of shock. There would have been a time when I would have been eager to see the mini Jaces running around with their whiskey eyes and dark hair. After losing my first pregnancy, I should be screaming with happiness, but I feel nothing. No elation. No sadness. I've opened up a void, and I'm stuck here. I no longer feel the crippling grief, but that's a relief I shouldn't celebrate. However, I am relieved to have the respite of being suffocated by such pain. I feel cold. Angry. Yes. That's the only thing I can feel: anger.

Anger at some higher power for laughing down on my misery and tossing more on the pile. I never wanted to become someone who pities themselves, but I do now.

"I want to be alone," I whisper. Her hand stills on my back, and I scrunch my eyes shut tightly. I love this woman infinitely but, right now, I want to scream into my pillow and hide, and I can't do that with her here.

"Let me call Harriet," she interjects thoughtfully.

I shake my head.

"No, I need to go in. I can't have more time off." I

twist my face and look at her. Her pretty eyes are rimmed with tears, a sob creeps up my throat, and her comforting arms slip around my naked frame.

"Lily, I love you. You're so strong. I know this feels a cruel twist of fate—" Her hands tighten around my shoulders.

"Isn't it?" I sniff.

"Maybe this is what is supposed to happen. Maybe it's the slap in the face he needs?" she replies quietly. I shift, and the sound of water laps around us.

"I don't want her in my life. I can't," I croak.

"It wasn't all bad. I truly think he cares deeply for you. It doesn't add up, an—" She has the look of someone who knows they are going to hurt you by saying something, but believe you need to hear it anyway,

"Please don't say we weren't actually together. He lied repeatedly. Made me sit through dinner with her. He is a liar," I vent, "and the conference—explain that," I spit cruelly, knowing it's not her fault or place to bear the brunt of my anger.

"I know he lied. I just think he was scared of losing you. Have you actually heard him out? He's pretty torn up about it." She rubs my arm, urging me to see it from his side.

I scoff in disbelief.

"I can't believe you're defending him. They slept together at the conference." I sound bitter, incredulous.

She shushes me when my eyes widen.

"I'm not, not at all, but maybe this little bean is here to give you that strength. Maybe talking to him will help you move on." Cass adds, "Or—"

I shoot disbelieving eyes at her. I know that tone, and I am not getting back with him. Hell, no!

"You're hurting so much, though." She sniffs, holding me tighter again.

"I miss him." The one person who would have made me feel indestructible has reduced me to ashes. "But I can't forgive him." I shudder.

"I know. He isn't perfect, but I forgave Sean. You know about Neve now. The truth is out now," she tells me. I turn away, not ready to hear her words. "Don't be so quick to judge; you know better than anyone we all make mistakes, but they don't define us, Lily. I wouldn't trust her as far as I could throw her, but talk to him, hear his side. I don't think he would cheat on you. Did he admit to sleeping with her at the conference?"

"I want to be alone!" She doesn't deserve my curt reply, and I hear her sigh and flinch at the sound. I'm acting out of character, destructive and angry. The sensible and lost part of me is screaming for me to get it together. I don't.

"I love you, Lily Spencer, with all my heart, and if you can't pull it together for you or me, then do it for your baby." She leaves without a response from me.

I sit in silence, feeling the sting of her words after she has gone, and begrudgingly admit she is right. I have plonked my scrawny arse in a pit and wallowed for far too long.

I sit in the bath until I'm wrinkled and cold, and work forces me to get out and get ready. Any enjoyment at dressing has long left. I pull on a black dress and grab some underwear and stockings. I dry, straighten, and pull my hair into a severe ponytail and keep my makeup simple. I look pale and tired, but with the anger, I feel a sense of resilience wash over me.

I grab some fruit and crackers as I leave and head straight to work. As soon as I turn the corner, I see Jace's car, and with a deep groan, I pull up in a free space and head straight to the door.

"Hi, Lily," he breathes softly.

"Leave me alone, Jace." I push through the door and silence the alarm, and he takes the opportunity to slip in.

"You look how I feel," he mumbles. I aim at him with unimpressed eyes. "I'm sorry." He scratches at his jaw.

"Thanks," I mutter, pulling the door wide open and gesturing for him to leave as I stare at him—actually, I stare through him. This anger is my strength; it's a shield, and I'm utilising it happily.

"I need to explain," he tells me adamantly. His golden gaze is sure and determined.

"No, you want to. It won't change my mind." I stare up at him and see the pain in his eyes, and it sparks more fire in my gut. "You want to know why?" I spit out.

His hand slips to the crown of his head, and he sighs softly at me, seeing none of the woman he knew.

"My father cheated on my mother. He lied to her, and he lied to me. She died in my teens, and her body was barely cold when he married his bit on the side." I speak the information emotionlessly, as though I'm reciting it from a book.

His back tenses, and he casts a worried look out to the street. Good.

"I'm sorry to hear that," he tells me.

"No more than I am, but do you want to hear the best bit?" I give a short laugh.

He holds my stare with uncertainty.

"I haven't spoken to him since." I step up so I am right in his face. "I cut him out. You are no different to him." I roll my angry gaze over him and disgust hangs off every word.

"I am," he whispers. Oh, I beg to differ.

"You came to my exhibition and professed your feelings for me, even though you were still shagging your mate, and then you left with her, to shag her some more, correct me if I'm wrong?" I lift my brow at him as I walk away, needing some distance.

"I can't." He shrugs, looking so miserable my heart lurches.

"I can't believe you were still sleeping with her. Why bother with me?" I hold my hand up when his lips move to reply. "Don't answer that. I can't forgive you. I don't want her in my life. I don't trust her, and if that means losing you, so be it. Now get out." I march to the door and swing it open again.

"Lily, please."

"You once told me she is family. That you can't cut her out." His eyes widen with worry. "I won't ever ask you to choose again. But *I* can make that choice, and I want out."

"Please—"

"What happened at the conference?" I search his gaze and see his eyes drop. He is on the doorstep, and I give him the filthiest look I possibly can. "Goodbye, Jace," I swing the door shut as he begins to tell me nothing happened.

I don't believe him. I lock myself in and walk away, ignoring the rattle of the door.

I'm shaking by the time he leaves. I rush to the back, but the tears I fear don't come. This anger has become my friend. I nibble at a cracker, flick on the coffee machine for Harriet and choose a fruit tea for myself, taking it to my office with me as my phone pings with an email.

It's Jace.

Betrayal

You will never know how truly sorry I am. I can't change the past, but I would wipe it clean if I'd known I would meet you. I love you always.
2 a.m. is lonely. I miss you. I miss who I was with you. I hope one day you can forgive me enough to allow me back in your life.
Yours always
Jace x

For some reason, my eyes lift to the window down the hall and out into the open gallery, to where he is staring at me through the window of his car. Slowly I stand and slam the door to my office shut on his hopeful whiskey eyes.

The next week drags. If Harriet is finding my despondent mood difficult, she hasn't said so. She also hasn't pried for information. There is no mistaking how utterly heartbroken I am, as sadness has left my face in a perpetual frown.

I have thrown myself into work. It's my solace. In fact, my need to block everything out is doing wonders for my business. I have landed multiple sales, began arranging another exhibition, and most evenings, to save me the pain of being home alone, I have made every effort to attend functions, building my rapport with other owners and artists. I'm burning myself into exhaustion, but my mind is busy, and that's what I need right now.

Harriet has put my lack of appetite in the mornings down to me being miserable. It's easier than admitting I got myself pregnant by my cheating ex.

Only Cass and Sean know my unsettling news. I still

haven't quite come to terms with it. There is no doubt that I love this child. None whatsoever. I have felt glimmers of happiness at the news, but it is easily shadowed by the despair at what that means long term for me and my baby. Where will Jace and Neve come into it all?

I try my hardest to avoid those thoughts because the feelings that accompany them are hideously heart-wrenching. The level of hatred I feel towards Neve shocks me. I hate her for so many reasons that I no longer know where that hate starts and ends. It's so tangible that I can almost taste it, and with her being so close to Jace, those same feelings are factoring into my thoughts whenever I think of not just them, but him.

With my friends' unwavering support, I'm keeping as positive as possible and finding the odd time to do a little baby browsing. After my miscarriage, I'm doubtful about buying anything. I'm not usually so superstitious, but I can't bring myself to click buy.

I still can't get my head around everything that has happened these last few months, and the level of anger I feel inside is shockingly out of control. I know I won't ever get closure, not when there is a child involved, nor will I ever begin to understand Jace or Neve's mindset. Their depravity and callousness astounds and sickens me. I can't believe I dated someone like him.

Him and Adam. My taste in men is questionable, that's for sure. This whole ordeal has really knocked me sideways. I've questioned everything about myself. Who I am and what I want—those are things I can no longer answer, but the one thing I do know is that I want to be a mum. It's a less than comfortable situation, but it's my situation, and I get something good out of this.

Harriet knocks on my office door, and I jolt out of

Betrayal

my thoughts. She's gone over her makeup and pinned her hair, so I know she is seeing Simon again tonight.

"I'm off now." She gives me a shy smile, and I grin at her from over my desk, being sure to throw my depressed frown off my pale face.

"Have a nice night. You look lovely," I say, shutting down my computer then stacking some files together to put in the cabinet. Her chiffon blouse and tight jeans make her look really willowy.

"Thanks. Need me to do anything before I go?" I shake my head and push back, collecting my bag up as I do.

"No, go and enjoy yourself. There is a piece of art in Lorton & Bouffe that I want to view. Did I send you the link?" I murmur while I place the files away.

"Yes, it will definitely fit in with the Capulet piece." I nod in agreement, stuffing my phone and glasses in my oversized tan bag. "I think it's really great that a percentage of sales will go to charity. I looked them up. It's such a good cause," Hat breathes passionately.

"Yes, it's a small company too, so I thought it'd be really beneficial." I swallow a lump of emotion. "I've contacted Maye, the founder, and she is thrilled. She is definitely coming to our exhibition," I say, moving through my office. I want my next exhibition to be about more than just me or art, I want it to make a difference, and Maye's charity is the perfect cause to plan an event for. No one needs to know it's personal to me. Cloud For You is a non-profit charity that offers support and counselling for parents who have suffered the loss of a child. Harriet falls into step beside me, and she smiles.

"That would be brilliant, really intimate."

"Also, I did want to ask you something. I know you're a little hesitant about putting your work out there, but maybe you could draw something in support of Cloud For You?" I stop and look back at her to see her working her lip into an absolute frenzy. "You're super talented, Hat, I'd love to showcase your work, and this is such an amazing charity. You have such an authentic and unique style. Just think about it, okay?" I rush to speak after seeing her anxiety spike. "No rush. Well, obviously the show is in a couple of weeks." I laugh lightly, and her shoulders relax a little. "It can be anonymous if you'd prefer; that in itself would pull everyone in. Don't stress yourself tonight. Go and enjoy yourself." I rub her arm.

"I'll do it," she blurts, and her quick rush of words shock me. I thought she'd be a little harder to win over.

"Really!" I grin widely and give her a hard squeeze. "Hat, this is great. I can't wait to see what you do." She is grinning like a fool too, and I know what the true cause of that smile and her newfound confidence is.

Simon.

Dating him has changed her. She has begun to see herself in a new light. One she likes. I remember the sentiment well. I felt indestructible when Jace came into my life. The unwavering attention heads straight to your core, and you begin to glow from the inside out, blossoming into a fresher, brighter version of yourself.

Only now I'm wilted and slowly drawing back in on myself.

"Lily? Are you okay?" My eyes snap up to find Harriet crouched with a frown.

I shake my head, knocking my thoughts back into line.

"Yeah, sorry." Rubbing my forehead, I blink away the hurt on my face. "Just got lost a little there."

She hugs me close, and I let her pull me in.

Betrayal

"I can cancel, and we can go to a movie or something?"

"God, no, don't be silly. I'll be fine. I'll get there. Sorry, I know I've been a miserable sod. You've been great," I mumble, faffing with my hair to hide my discomfort.

"You haven't been miserable, not really, just quiet, and it's okay," she adds quickly when my eyes find hers, "but I just want to say that I'm here if you need me." She blinks innocently at me,

"I know, thanks, Hat, but honestly, I'm okay." I lift her coat for her to put on, and she gives me a quick hug before she leaves. Once she has gone, I click the lights off and sit at the small desk up front, staring into the darkness. It's moments like this when I can't quite believe this is my life—all this hurt and pain I'm experiencing, and then other times, I feel a burst of optimism, a sense of hope, and it urges me to move on, look forward and appreciate the things I do have in life and what I have to look forward to. Pressing a hand to my stomach, I let out a long, deep sigh.

"I promise, I'm a fighter really," I say into the dark. "I won't let you down."

———

I've spent the last week or so keeping Cass at arm's length, and any contact has been purely through text. It's the coward's way, but I just need to come to terms with all this before her usually bossy self starts nit-picking at me again.

I have filled my time with sourcing other artwork, and I even go as far as to think about redesigning the gallery interior. Harriet is trying to keep up with my constant moods and changes in direction. She knows very little but has been a complete diamond.

I had an appointment with the doctor who confirmed my pregnancy. I'm due next summer, and I'm slowly coming round to the idea, but have ignored Cass's suggestion that I come clean with Jace. I can't bear to face him or allow myself to have anything to do with Neve either—I suspect she has got her clutches in him already.

She can have him, but she can fuck off if she thinks I will ever let her have anything to do with my child. For the first time, I feel a burst of happiness.

My stomach is slightly rounded. It's not visibly noticeable, but I can tell the changes when I get dressed: my favourite pair of grey work trousers won't zip up, so I find a cute dress that flares out and manage to disguise the small bump. I just look a little bloated.

I sit and do my makeup, picturing me perched here with a little girl or boy on my lap, their curious fingers reaching for all my brushes. I smile into the mirror, but my mouth turns down when I imagine what that would feel like if Jace were also here—how he would stroll in and lean to peck us both on the heads, telling us how perfect we are. I know I can do this on my own. I just never suspected I would have to.

I am holding on to him more than I should be, and after everything he has done, my heart is still pining for him. I make the quick decision to go to The Hub this weekend and collect the remainder of my things; that way, I can cut all ties completely.

I can meet him somewhere neutral like Bobo's and tell him about the baby after I've collected my belongings. Happy with myself, I rush through my morning routine and head to work.

Harriet has got the day off, and Cass mentioned she has a conference in York, so I do every little inconvenient job around The Loft I can think of to keep my mind busy.

Most of my morning is spent re-jigging the artwork and planning a solo exhibition for Paco, whose work has completely taken off. The harrowing and complexity of his vision is like canvas gold.

He could choose to exhibit his work with a more renowned gallery, but his loyalty is faultless, and even though he has been approached repeatedly, he has stuck with me, and I can't thank him enough.

I take a minute to make myself a tea and sit up front when my phone rings. It's Cass.

"Hey," I answer, blowing on the steaming mug. I check the paperwork in front of me and push my glasses back up when they slip down my nose.

"Hey, how you feeling?" Her tone suggests I will be feeling like crap.

"Really good." I'm breezy and chirpy because I do feel good. The hurt of losing Jace is still there, but it's more manageable now. It hasn't gone. I've just become accustomed to it.

"Oh." Her reply signifies her shock. "Okay, well, I'm glad. Any sickness?"

"Yes, but stocked up on ginger biscuits as they seem to help, and I moved the kettle into my room so I can make tea and not move." I laugh.

"God, are you that bad, still?" She vocally winces.

"It'll pass soon," I say hopefully.

"I've thought of another name," she squeaks out with

excitement. Rolling my eyes, I sip on my tea—she has a new name every day. I enjoy hearing them, even if most of them are odd, and some most definitely have been made up.

"Morgan for a girl. Bryce for a boy." I wrinkle my nose, not happy with either. I have secretly fallen in love with the name Mila if I have a girl, but boy's names are still lost on me.

"Sean suggested you come round for dinner on Sunday?" she adds.

"Names, no. Sunday is good." I laugh.

"Oh, I love Bryce," she whines playfully.

"Well, call your child it then," I scoff.

"Maybe I will," she hums.

"Is this the part where you tell me you're pregnant?" I ask, knowing full well she will happily live her motherhood through me before she even considers having her own child.

"Oh, ha, ha. You are on form today!" She sounds sarcastic as hell, and I love that we are slowly getting back to our normal. It feels good.

"New me and all that," I quip.

"You're really feeling positive? Not just saying it?" she asks softly. "Because if you are, that's great, and if not, that's also okay," she slips in kindly.

"I'm getting there, just need a little more time, then I will, you know, tell him."

"Okay, good. He should know," she replies.

"I know." My sigh is long.

"We'll see you Sunday then?" I can hear someone in the background, so it's no surprise that she cuts our conversation short. "Got to go," she says.

"Okay. See ya!" I disconnect before she does and continue looking over my paperwork.

Chapter Twenty-Two

Driving here has cost me. I feel shaken and emotional, but what cuts me more is that when I amble down the driveway, mentally telling myself I can do this, and I need this to break that invisible chain linking me to this man, is that I find not just his car there but Neve's too. The house isn't lit up, but the flicker of low lights illuminates small fractions of the long building.

"Bastard." I'm shaking. My whole body is uncontrollably jittering. My legs feel useless, and my mind is now running frantically every which way as I contemplate having to not only face him but her too. He'd told me he would go out! When I messaged earlier to arrange a time to clear out my things, he promised he wouldn't be here.

Hot anger slams into my fragile mind, and I truly believe it is the only thing making me push forward. I refuse to allow them to intimidate me to this degree. It's the mouldy cherry on top of a very shit cake that gives me the fight to gain closure on this whole shit storm of a ride.

As I round the cars, the house opens up, and it comes into full view, but I don't care for that. All I can see is Jace, reclined on the sofa, his head back, and Neve straddling him in her underwear. My steps falter, and a sob flies from my throat in an agonised, low wail.

How could he, after everything?

I don't truly believe our passionate fling was all one-sided, but I don't recognise the man relaxing with this scrawny slut in his lap. This is the Jace I hate. The one I was scared to meet and give myself to. I should have listened to my gut.

I dash the tears away angrily and storm up to the house, pushing the door open. The cool night air whips and rolls through the toasty house and both sets of eyes pull to me. Neve's smug eyes twinkle in a hard glare, but Jace looks mortified. He lifts his head, but it drops back down.

"Li . . . Lily," he slurs, "what are you . . . " He is frowning in confusion at me, his voice thick and broken. I smell it then, the stench of alcohol. Bottles litter the table and lay on the floor, and the place stinks of smoke too. His head rolls my way, and his lip wobbles. "Lil."

I laugh sardonically.

"Don't bother. I'm not interested. I'm so glad I'm not caught up in this fucking disaster anymore," I spit. My stare drops to the spiteful little girl sitting on his knee because that's what she is—a child. No grown adult would be so purposefully juvenile and malicious!

My stare holds, and she doesn't like it. Good. Her back stiffens.

"What?" she snaps, flipping her hair and dropping into his crotch, making him grunt. Her lips quirk, but my attention is pulled to the man so intoxicated that he can barely lift his head or string a sentence together. Yet

Betrayal

Neve is as sober as a nun. I narrow my eyes at her and smirk.

"You won." I shrug on a light, disbelieving laugh. "You won," I admit, looking no less broken than the man slumped in the chair. He really does look like shit. He hasn't shaved, for, well . . . I have no idea, but by the thick blanket of hair plastered on his face, I would say a good three weeks. I hadn't noticed before now, but each time I have seen him, he has had a chin full of hair, and his face has looked sharper, more angular—has he lost weight?

Neve smiles slowly. I reciprocate it.

"You won because I walked. Not because he chose you." I point to Jace, who is trying to lift her fragile weight off his clumsy frame, my name a difficult groan on his lips. "This is what you won." Neve drops her stare back to Jace, heaving to push her off.

"You won a man in love with another woman. Congratulations." I cough on a scathing laugh. I say what only he has said to me—it's not an assumption, maybe a lie from his lips, but I'm willing to use it to have the last word with Little Miss Barbie. Jace's face comes into view, and through the fog surrounding him, he blinks determination into his face.

"Fuc . . . get . . . of . . . f . . . " His slurring is a cause for concern. How much has he had to drink?

I shake my head, forcing my apprehension away; it's not my problem. But I can't help noticing how dreadful he looks: worn out, older, sallow.

I leave them both and feel the bloom of a tiny bud of satisfaction pressing through the fire of anger. They can have each other because karma is cruel, and they deserve nothing more than their own bitterness.

I begin pulling things from his drawers and fill a bag.

There is a resounding crash that shakes the house, followed by his husky tone moaning in pain. I can't ignore it. I rush back to find Jace, staggering to his knees, his feet uncoordinated and weak, the coffee table on its side, and all the contents with it.

"Li . . . Lily!" he roars. I blink and rush back, trying to find my belongings, as heavy, clumsy footsteps thud and slide over the floor, followed by thick, drawn-out curses. He thuds into the doorframe, and my eyes flash up to find his. He chokes out a sob, and I truly glimpse a look at the effects of our breakup in his worn, red-rimmed, bristly face. "Li . . . Lily. I'm . . . sorr . . . fuck—" He shakes his head as if he can't find the words or even formulate them.

"You're absolutely wankered!" I spit and throw a t-shirt as a form of defence at him when he reaches for me. I see that he is fully clothed, unlike Neve, who is wearing a tiny scrap of material worthy of the bin.

"Not . . . wha . . . t . . . You . . . thin . . . k—" He shakes his head again, and I dare myself to meet his eyes. His pupils are painfully dilated. He makes to move but slides down the wooden arch, his hand reaching for me.

"Get away from me!" I mean to shout, but it comes out in a croaked whisper. What is wrong with him? He blinks sluggishly, and I watch his detached movements and the slow and almost alien way he moves to look at me. Jace lifts his hands, blinking at them, and swallows thickly—his head rolling as he fights a war against sleep.

He drags in a choppy and short breath.

"Don't . . . lea . . . Lily . . . Shi . . . it. I don't feel . . . good—" He looks like he is on drugs, and I pull back in disgust. His weary confusion and shortness of breath send a sinister thought crashing through my mind.

Betrayal

She wouldn't have. Surely?
He told me he wouldn't be here.

I sidestep him, flinching when his thick hand loosely and weakly cups my ankle. I move out of his hold, and he makes a murmured plea. The only form of comfort I offer him is my hand on his shoulder. I give it a little squeeze, and he chokes out a shuddery breath.

"Cra . . . zy bou . . . you—" he slurs thickly, and my eyes prick with hot tears.

Neve is bent, picking up the bottles, and I storm over, finding everything I hoped I wouldn't. I snatch the pillbox up off the floor and see the evidence of a powdery substance stuck to the rim of Jace's whiskey glass. I take that too, as she flies around. "Hey!" She moves to take it back.

"Those are mine!" she shouts, her blonde hair whipping around her like a sword.

"Then why the fuck are they in his system?" I scream, taking two steps forward so I'm in her face. She flinches, and on their own accord, my full hands come up, and I slam them into her chest. She cries out as she falls and lands with a thud on her skinny arse. "You sick bitch!" She blinks worriedly at me and looks around, possibly for something to help her or maybe hurt me.

"Don't bother." I knock an empty bottle towards her. "You just lost him. Anything else will just strengthen that decision. You need help, Neve. What the fuck is wrong with you?" I snap, staring at her with bewildered disgust. I cannot fathom any reason why someone could do or even think to do the harm she has.

"I love him!" she cries, her body jerking with loud sobs.

I grip the packet and thrust it at her face.

"This is not love!" I roar, and my throat constricts painfully. My chest is heaving, and my arms are shaking, and she sobs, but I couldn't care less for her pain, or her in general. I rush back and drop what's in my hands in the bag. I fall to Jace and lift his face. His head rolls, his eyes are closed, and his breath is hot with alcohol.

"Jace, can you hear me?" I gently shake his head. "Jace?"

"Mmm." His brow twitches, but his eyes remain closed. How much did he have to drink? How many tablets did she give him?

I start screaming for those answers, but Neve doesn't reply, and by the time I return to the living room, she is pulling on clothes. "How much has he had to drink? How many tablets did you give him?" She looks up but ignores me, unfazed about Jace's current state.

I stop and look at her as another thought leaps into my already shocked brain.

"Have you done this before?" She blanches, and I laugh in disbelief. "You're disgusting!" She is barbaric!

She actually has the audacity to scoff.

"No, I haven't. I thought it would help him sleep," she mutters, tying a little string behind her neck to cover her breasts.

"Surely the alcohol would have sufficed!" I snap.

She shrugs, making me see red.

"Those kinds of drugs shouldn't be mixed with alcohol. That can be fatal!" I cry. I should know, I was prescribed something similar after Adam and the baby. How stupid is she?

Her whole face drops.

"It was only two tablets, a small dose."

"But how much has he had to drink?" I scream. Talking to her is useless, and I'm in full panic mode now.

Betrayal

I know I shouldn't lift him in my condition, but I coax him awake as much as I can. "I need you to stand," I huff, pushing my shoulder under his armpit and heaving him up. His face swims in confusion before he clocks me and gives me a toothy grin.

"Fuc . . . kin . . . bea . . . tiful—" Jace leans into the wall for support, and I manage to get him a few steps through the house when he drops down and crashes into the side. His arm waves out and takes the table's contents off with an ear-splitting crash. I jump, and Neve, for once, looks uncomfortable.

"Look what you've done!" I cry at her. Jace slumps into a chair, and when she comes over to him, my hand comes up like a stop sign. "Stay the fuck away from him. He'll never forgive you for this!" I'm shaking, lost in volatile seas. I know I could seriously hurt her, so I step back, my shoulders heaving uncontrollably in anger, and my breathing unsynchronised when I think of what I want to do to this woman.

"Now get the fuck out of this house!" I seethe. I stay rooted on the spot as she grabs her bag and runs out of the house.

It's a few minutes before I feel the light touch of his fingertips on my arm. I shrug him away, my fingers delving into my hair with agitation and worry. I look at him for a second. Do I call an ambulance? His breathing isn't normal. I pace, but my legs feel weak, and my body stiff. I'm still hiccupping through heavy tears that I hadn't known I was crying until I heard the light sob.

Jace is mumbling, so grabbing my phone, I call Cass, who answers on the first ring.

"Hey, girl, everything o—"

"I need you to come to Jace's," I sniff and sob.

"Oh, hell. What's happened?"

"Can you come?" His eyes are rolling in his heavy head.

"Yes. Shit. We'll be there soon." She shouts for Sean, and her breathing seems heavy with concern. "Lily, what's happened?"

"I . . . I . . . Neve. She's done something to him," I garble as I really take stock of that.

"We're leaving any second, okay?"

I nod and sniff loudly.

"Jace is in a mess," I warn.

"Okay, look, make yourself a tea, pop a sugar in it, and wait for us, okay?"

"Neve gave him a sedative," I say around choppy tears. "And he's been drinking."

"We're in the car. Maybe call 911 for advice?" It's logical. I should have called immediately—I feel a burst of nauseating guilt. I can't think straight.

"Okay," I stutter.

Everything after that seems to happen fast and in slow motion. Cass and Sean arrive at the same time as the ambulance. Cass runs to me as the paramedic follows Sean through, with another who hops out of the passenger side.

"I think he is unconscious," I sob, quickly walking back in to check on him again, lying lifeless on the floor.

"Do you know what he has taken?" The first asks. I barely look at their faces. I'm in such a wreck. I dither for a minute, then rush to the bag, pulling out the squashed box.

"Here." I drop it in their hand while the other is checking over Jace. "She said he had two," I whisper.

Jace looks so vulnerable. I look away as they peel open his limp eyelids.

"Who did, Miss?" The paramedic kneels over him, attaching equipment quickly and calmly.

"Err, his friend," Cass scoffs, and Sean throws her a look, silently conveying she should keep her anger in check.

"He's been drinking, and he was staggering about, struggling to raise his head and slurring. He looked confused but tried to walk to me," I say in a rush, tucking my hair behind my ear. Cass encourages me to sit on the bed and murmurs to me something about a tea. I watch with blank worry as the paramedics start checking Jace over, each one stating vitals and noting them down. They talk directly to Sean, as I'm a nail-biting, pacing mess. I hear mentions of: 'stale alcohol smell, bottles aren't newly opened, small dosage sedative', everything sounds as though it is relevant, but my mind is still tinged with anger, and now guilt.

I can't believe Neve has done this. That stilts me into shock. Cass rushes to me with a drink. I take it, but any feeling has gone. I barely recall the sensation of it in my fingers.

"Why?" I say to my friend. "How could she?" I shake my head and blink a tear away. "She could have killed him," I sniff.

"He's going to be okay, Lily. They are taking him in."

To the hospital? The only thing that draws her attention to me crying is the shake of my shoulders, and she hushes me and pulls me in for a hug.

I watch through blurry eyes as Jace is moved to a stretcher and carried to the ambulance.

A few months ago, this man walked down slate steps into my life with a sexy smile. He chased me relentlessly, drove me crazy with pleasure, made me fall in love, and now I'm sitting, watching him be carried away on a stretcher, through an unkempt house, looking the most vulnerable I have ever witnessed. His unconscious head bobs lightly as he is carried with care through the wide living space and away from me.

I want my whiskey-eyed man back.

―――――

I wake to the light flutter of warm air on my skin. My lashes take the brunt as my eyes fight to open. On a groan, I drag a hand across my face to sate the tickle. Another stream of air attacks my lashes, and I squint my eyes open.

Deep, remorseful golden irises watch me thoughtfully, and for a minute, I lay completely still, the last few days filtering back with a sharp and painful stab to my brain. I blink, and Jace tilts his head, watching me closely. Our eyes meet, and I search his for more than emotion. He had me worried sick.

I rode with him in the ambulance; Cass and Sean followed behind as he was blue-lighted. He'd remained unconscious through triage, and afterward, when he was placed on a ward to recover, still victim to the drugs, unconscious and very un-Jace like, all suspected effects of the substance interaction, the paramedics and nurses had advised me.

It had been a long and tense twenty-four hours while he slept the sedatives off. His heart rate had been worryingly low, his blood pressure a state. Neve had been a pill short of overdosing him.

I'd been so wrapped up in my panic of losing him that I hadn't considered calling Viktor or Carl, and by the time I thought about it, Jace was coming round. He was groggy, hoarse, his face pale, and his eyes wore a sadness I knew all too well. But I couldn't sit with him. He hadn't wanted me to contact Viktor or Marie, so I didn't. I slunk away and contacted Carl—too raw to be in such close confines with him.

Yet here I am, giving his PA some respite and making sure he is okay. Deep down, I couldn't leave the hospital. I had stayed outside the ward, checking in with Carl, and watching him through the small pane of glass that allowed me a slight glimpse at Jace's bed. I couldn't leave then, and I can't leave now.

I'd like to say it's put it all into perspective for me, and in some ways, it has, but I can't forget what he did. I can't lose him either.

Slowly, I shuffle so I'm sitting up, and Jace props himself up on the coffee table, his legs spread either side of mine. He gives me a resounding sigh and leans back to regard me thoroughly. I fidget under his heavy gaze, but I can't look away.

"How are you, Lily?" His voice catches, and I bite my lip to hold in my emotion, shrugging as I tuck my hair away.

"I've been better," I admit. He nods and dips his head.

"I am sorry." His voice is low, deep, and scratchy, and his lips are dry. His eyes are dull, and his skin looks tired and dehydrated.

"Me too." My wobbly lip betrays me, and Jace scoots closer, pulling me into a hug. I resist at first, but he holds me gently but firmly to his chest, and as those thick arms engulf me, I relent. I scrunch my eyes tightly and press my face hard into his neck.

"I'm sorry for everything." His voice details a map of

emotions. I can't speak, so I simply nod. He leans back, giving me room, and I'm glad. His touch makes my breath falter.

"I didn't know you had texted me," he whispers softly, holding his phone up in explanation.

I know that now. Neve must have planned the whole fucked up mess when I contacted him.

"I know." It all has painfully come to a head. She has manipulated everyone and put Jace in danger.

"I had no idea she . . . " He sighs and covers his face on a slow headshake. "I've known her my whole life. I'd never physically hurt her—I didn't think she was capable—" He looks away, lost in a sea of hurt.

"I understand," I tell him quietly. I may not have known Adam for years, but his capabilities were a painful slap to my sensibilities. "Some people are just wired differently," I murmur, rubbing my bare toes into the thick rug. "You see snippets, and you doubt them, but what really is the hardest part is accepting your own doubt. Because you know yourself better than you know them, and that's supposed to count for something, and when it doesn't," – I shrug out a deep sigh – "it's a real head fuck." I scoff harshly.

"I'm sorry." I reach my gaze up and find his remorse about the way he acted after Adam's attack filtering back at me. He thought the worst of me, but he didn't truly understand the situation.

"How are you feeling?" I stay where I am because standing would put me at closer quarters to him, and I'm not quite ready for that.

"Rough." His smile is soft and a little sad, and I'm not surprised—his body has been put through the mill. I dread to think how his liver is coping with all the alcohol he has consumed.

"I didn't tell Viktor, but he called this morning. He knows something has gone on. He sounded worried. I think you should call him back," I suggest. Jace eyes me for a moment before he takes my knees and tugs me closer.

"Don't!" I pull back, but he holds me tightly. "Jace," I plead for him to let me go. Instead, he leans in and drops his hands on either side of my face. When his eyes drop to my lips, I look away. He cups my chin slowly but purposefully, making me look at him.

"I fell in love with you that first night," he breathes. I shift, and his voice sounds desperate. "I couldn't believe I had finally got you back. I watched you sleep, and I knew you were different. I didn't know what to do about it. I was so scared I would fuck it up. I thought I finally had you, and then you ran anyway." His smile is nostalgic. "Always running," he murmurs, as his reminiscent smile turns into a sad smirk.

"You didn't do anything wrong," I finally admit. "I was as scared as you. I still am." I look at him with all my hurt swirling in my dark grey eyes. "I hate that you slept with her. But I hate it more that you lied." My damn lip trembles.

His eyes flare with guilt, his full lips flatten, and his hand runs over the back of his neck before finding my knee again.

"Lily, please?"

"I gave you a chance. I asked for you to confess. I knew in my gut, but I trusted you, and I fought with that self-doubt constantly. You made me doubt myself." My voice thickens. "I felt so unhinged with suspicion, then guilt over thinking that of you, and the whole time, you allowed me to believe it." He must have known. I stare at him, wordlessly letting my hurt slam him full force in the face.

"I'm sorry." He swallows. "I knew it would cost me you." He rattles my knee, physically urging me to see it from his side.

"You hurt me." I sniff.

"I know." He gives a despairing shrug of his big shoulders. "I'm sorry. If I could take it all back and change it, I would." Jace drops his lips to my ear. "I love you. Please forgive me?"

Surely, stepping back on this path would be stupid. Ludicrous. I remember Cass's words when she and Sean brought us back to Jace's from the hospital.

If you truly couldn't forgive him, you wouldn't be here. Deep down, you knew about her. You're angry that he lied, and that's fair enough, but you would have run if he'd confessed. He just didn't want to lose you. Let him make it right, Lily—no couple can surely go through any more drama than you two already have. Rebuild and let him love you.

"I give you my word, nothing happened at the conference. She messed with the bookings, and we shared a twin room," he says with utter conviction. "I was scared you wouldn't believe me after what she had told you."

"And that's it?" I whisper, finding his eyes and searching them for any signs of a lie.

He sighs.

"She tried to make something happen, but I told her whatever had happened in the past was done, that I was sorry, but I finally found someone I wanted to build a life with." He swallows thickly, his endless amber eyes pleading with me to forgive him.

"I can't ever forgive her," I say quietly. It's not an

admission of forgiveness of him, but I see hope in his beautiful eyes. "This is so hard." I sniff.

"Lily . . . Stay here this weekend." I stiffen in his hold, but he keeps me in the cage of his arms. "Hear me out, please," he begs gently. "Twenty-four hours, give me that, and I will never ever let you down again," he promises. Holding my hands in his, he rubs little gentle circles across my skin.

I struggle to get free.

"I don't think it's a good idea." I know it's not. I'll sleep with him if I stay. I know my own weaknesses where this man is concerned.

"Perhaps not, but it's the only one I have, and I can't bear to watch you walk away again," he whispers.

"Jace," I sigh, sounding regretful. It's too much again, too quickly!

"Please, Lily. Just as friends." He drags his hand over his scrunched-up face as though us being friends is a foreign concept. "I'll sleep on the sofa, but I need to explain. I need to put this right. And if I can't, I need to know I tried my hardest." He swallows, his eyes big and hopeful. "This is still your home," he mumbles.

"It just hurts so much," I whisper. That tight, heavy ball in my stomach won't budge, and I know it won't for a good six months, as the guilt of my secret pregnancy is weighing on me too.

"Let me try to fix it. The truth." He swallows, and I look up through wet lashes. "You can ask me anything!" Full disclosure? I examine his eyes thoroughly. "I can't lose you again," he vows desperately.

"I'm not sure I'm ready to trust you," I tell him. He is asking for the world right now.

"Let me work on that," he states, "all I'm asking for is

twenty-four hours." Shaky hands take mine and squeeze them softly, reassuringly.

"What, to change my mind?" I scoff and look away, giving my brain the small reprieve it needs from his intensely lost eyes. I'm at war with myself—am I being naïve again?

"I don't expect it to be that easy, but you still love me." There is no arrogance, just the simple, painful truth. I could spend forever denying that fact, but it's written on every cell in my body. "I just need you to know why." He sighs. "To remember why this is worth fighting for." I search his gaze and feel a twinge of fear at the prospect of him being out of my life.

"Is there anything else I should be worried about? Any more secrets?" I ask hesitantly.

"No, and I never wanted there to be Lily, but I realised how bad a mistake it was when I met you. I'm not proud." He admits gruffly, and his cheeks even flush a little. "Before you decide, I need you to know Neve no longer works for me. I contacted my lawyers first thing—she's gone." There is no remorse, just hard confirmation, and hope.

"Completely?"

"For good," he affirms with a light sigh and a sad smile on his face. In the space of a month, his entire life, like mine, has been tipped on its head!

"How do you feel about that?" I question quietly, knowing this can't be easy on him either.

He huffs out a tired laugh and tugs me closer by slipping his hands under my knees.

"Good and relieved. It's hard to admit how unhealthy someone is for you, even if they are just your friend, let alone someone who you have spent most of your life trying to protect," he mumbles regretfully.

Betrayal

"I'm sorry." I rub his hand supportively.

"Don't lie." He smirks, a tinge of sadness in his rough voice. "I don't blame you for being relieved too. I know you tried to accept her." He frowns with a shake of his head. I disliked her from the outset. I eye him sceptically because I think deep down, he knows that too.

"I do feel bad. She has had a tough time." I frown. "Losing her parents, that must have been hard on a child," I murmur, confused at her vile actions but trying to be supportive for him.

"Yes, but she can't use it to manipulate people like she has. Both you and I have lost our parents. That's how I met Neve—we were both in the system. My parents were addicts, and I was removed from their care when I was five." My eyes flash to his in shock.

"Oh, god, Jace. I had no idea!" My own loss seems so minimal compared to his. If he was in care, he was young, too young to lose his parents. My heart bleeds at the horrible thought.

"I know." He pulls me in for a hug, and this time I go willingly. He just opened his heart up to me, and the only way I can say thank you is to hug him back. "Come, walk with me. I'm not sure I can sit here, face to face, and discuss it." He swallows, and nodding, I slowly rise. He takes my hand with a soft smile. "Does this mean I get twenty-four hours?"

I nod slowly, still unsure.

"I'm not staying here though." My voice trips over the words, but I need him to know I can't just sweep everything under the carpet.

He sucks in a deep breath. I've met him halfway. He can't possibly ask for more.

"That means more than you will ever know, Lily." Jace stops at the door and looks down at me, and his hand runs along my jaw. "I love you, beautiful lady." I drop my gaze because it hurts too much to accept that right now. I open my mouth to tell him I'm not ready to go there yet with him, but he drops a finger to my lips. "Let me fix this."

Chapter Twenty-Three

We set off down the path on to the back lakes. The wind has dropped, so I'm grateful for the scarf Jace gave me.

"I can feel your mind whirring from here," he muses.

"I'm just a little stunned. I assumed, I mean, I knew Viktor wasn't your biological father, but—" I can't find the right words, and I feel a bit stupid for being so oblivious to what was right under my nose. "I don't know what I thought. He acts like you're family, and I just thought that maybe you and your parents had fallen out. I didn't want to push it because I never want to discuss my own family." I shrug, recalling Jace and Viktor's loving relationship—so at ease with one another—it was obvious they held a lot of pride and respect for each other.

"He is. Well, as good as. That's why I don't dwell on the past." Jace thrusts his hands into his pockets, and I follow suit because it's bloody freezing.

"If you're not ready to discuss it, I understand." I look up from around my scarf. It's heavy, but a warm weight around my neck.

"Sharing isn't my problem, Lily. I don't want you to think differently about me," he says ruefully.

"I won't. I think perhaps it will help me understand you and what went on with Neve." I glance his way as I utter her name. I hope it will help me lay it to rest.

"Even I don't understand that," he grunts. "I was already in the system when I met her, twelve, and in and out of foster homes. I couldn't settle. I didn't want what I'd had growing up—being around all those foster families didn't feel right. They weren't mine, not really, but nothing else felt right either. If I'm honest, it never has." His voice goes gravelly with emotion, and he drops a quick look at me before staring out across the murky lake. "Not until you. Meeting you, I felt suckerpunched." I bite my lip but refrain from interrupting him. "I still do, Lily."

"Me too," I croak. I clear my throat and follow him slowly down an incline. When we reach level ground, he continues. "Neve was six when she came to the care home, and for some reason, she latched onto me. At first, I didn't want to know, and I kept pushing her away and avoiding her, but she always found a way to keep close. I gave up and took her under my wing. It gave me purpose." He clears his throat, recalling darker days, days that I imagine are far worse than I can even comprehend.

"Do you think she will be okay?" I ask gently. As much as I believe in karma, I feel a sliver of sympathy for her. Living a life in the system can't be easy, and the one thing she ever loved, I took away from her.

"I don't know, but I did everything I could to keep her on the straight and narrow." He sighs, and we head towards the larger lake. Jace lifts a branch, and I duck under, waiting for him to meet me on the bramble-free side. His eyes hold mine when he stands tall. "I made mistakes too." He means her.

"None of us are perfect," I buffer his decisions.

"I know it won't make it easier to accept, but it never meant anything to me. I suppose that may be worse because it did to her, and I think I knew that deep down." He clears his throat. "I . . . " His face looks beaten with guilt. "I've never had to explain myself to Neve—it just was. As a matter of fact, I've never had to consider anyone else. It's allowed me to be selfish, and I was—very selfish." He clears his throat in discomfort. "I've no real family, so I guess she was my constant; family who wasn't actually family. There was no line to cross, and a lot of confused and hurt feelings that we both were trying to get through." Jace drops his head, frowning at his feet, still perplexed by his actions.

"You cared a lot for each other. I can imagine those lines can get muddied when there is no actual definitive restriction. You're not blood related," I offer my own excuses.

"It only really felt like a mistake when I met you. Before, I never cared because she was just always there, and we never spoke about it. It just was—" He shrugs with a loud sigh. "I've always felt beholden to her. She knows about my life, my past. Hell, she has lived it with me, but she has been this huge anchor around my neck that I could never shake. I couldn't move on fully, and at the same time, I couldn't just walk away and leave her in the deep end. I've seen the life she lived; *know it*. But I think her going is for the best." His head tilts back, and his gaze fixes up high as he comes to terms with everything that is changing in his life.

"Will you tell Viktor?" Or will he continue to protect her? He drops a look at me and pulls his hand free, taking mine in his after giving me a questioning look. I let him take it.

"Probably." He squeezes my hand. "I think he tolerated her for me; they were never very close." I nod and look away. We stand in silence, staring out over the sprawling view and countryside. So vast and raw. Even in our turmoil, we find a moment's peace to enjoy it.

"He and Marie can't wait to see you again," he muses softly. I recall both of their loving, worried glances. "Since meeting you, I have some serious competition." He smirks. "Marie is ready to whisk you off on a spa weekend!"

I never had that with my own mother. It would be nice, and I do miss her and Viktor.

Jace and I have our own demons to battle; with Neve thrown in the mix, it was like watching a volcano erupt from afar. But without her—maybe we stand a chance?

"I don't think this will be easy." I frown at our hands. His touch isn't the instant comfort it was, I feel a little awkward, and I hate that. I want the fire back. "But I do love you," I whisper. Jace turns me to him, his gaze sad, hopeful, and desperate. "Don't make me regret this, Jace Bennett," I warn him.

"Never," he vows. I tug my hand free and see his gaze drop at the loss of contact. I need this distance. I can't think clearly when he doesn't give me that little luxury of space.

"Let me hold you, just your hand. I won't ask for anything else, but I need to touch you, Lily. Let me have that." He takes my hand regardless.

"And what about what I want?" My brow lifts itself, and I watch him fail to hold a smirk back.

"It's standing right in front of you. I just need to make you remember, and to help you forget everything else." His mouth turns down a margin, and he tucks my hair when it gets caught up in the wind and wraps across my face. "Our love is fierce. I trust in that, and my instinct tells me this is what you need. No one loves you like I do. I know that love caused you pain, but you hurt me too, beautiful." I gasp lightly, wanting to defend myself, but something inside of me shuts me up. "You cut me off and assumed the worst of me."

I swallow the ache of pain in my throat. Yes, I did, and he is still here, trying to keep us connected, still fighting for me. Us.

"We heal together, and then we can carry on hurtling." He pecks my hand and tugs me along the lakeside. I don't answer because I'm still fighting the compulsion to flee. My heart is here, but my head is stuck between wanting to love him and wanting to run. And my stomach is a cage of butterflies. I know I need to confess to him. I look away before he sees my inner worry.

"Tell me about Viktor." I'm keeping the focus on him, for now.

"Well, he told you how we met. I used to break into the construction site, and after throwing me out multiple times, he took me on. I was still a kid, and he would walk me around and explain everything to me. I shared his passion. He told me to go to college, and he would hire me afterward. I couldn't afford it, but I refused to open up to them. Against all odds, college happened. I was determined to make something of myself, to get out of the hell I was living, but I knew even with all the effort I had put in, it wasn't enough. I was offered a place through a funded programme, and I wasn't about to let the opportunity go to waste. It wasn't until years later that Viktor admitted he had covered my schooling. I owe him everything." I listen further, without saying much. My mind is taking all this information in, but I'm also aware that I'm hiding a secret that could change everything.

I don't want it to push us further apart than we already are.

We are walking back up the incline when I stop, and Jace halts with me. I feel a rush of nervousness.

"I have something I need to tell you," I croak. My hands entwine together, and I puff out a breath, blowing the nausea away. My stomach is a rave of butterflies.

Worried eyes dance over me, and I rush on.

"I know you're going to be mad, and I want to say I'm sorry first and that I had every intention of telling you. I just wanted to get all my belongings first. I wanted to cut ties before I told you." I stumble over the words. We've never discussed children, and hearing the level of depravity of his own childhood, I worry he won't want his own children. What if this is what breaks us? I blanch at that thought.

"Lily, you're worrying me." Jace tugs me to him and rubs my arm, his own eyes looking fearful, desperate. I open my mouth once, twice, and then it just comes out, quickly and panicked.

"I lied to you. I'm . . . I'm pregnant," I whisper. My heart is galloping away in my chest, but the look of annoyance I expect, the anger, betrayal, doesn't come.

Jace's face breaks out into a huge grin. He looks a little shocked but thrilled.

"You're sure?" he chokes out. His dazzling eyes search my face, and I nod with a hesitant smile. The elation that has been my own is finally ours. He pulls me to him and holds me close before I'm pushed back just as quickly. "How far gone?" His eyes drop to my stomach as though he can see through my skin at the little blip growing there.

I'm startled. I really was expecting him to be cross. After all, I withheld this information from him, lied at the chemist, and have kept him out of the loop since I found out. I search his gaze, looking to find anything other than deep amber joy burning back at me, but that's all I see, happiness.

"A few weeks. My due date is mid-June, the eighteenth," I confirm. Jace tugs at my coat and unzips it. The cold seeps in, but his warm eyes counteract any shivers. His hand presses to my stomach, and I laugh.

"I'm hardly showing." I brush him off, but his hand remains.

"I know this body," he announces, "and you do have a little added podge."

"Podge?" I scoff. "Thanks!" Typical male. I roll my eyes, but I can't lose the dopey grin I have.

Jace's is megawatt and contagious as his hand presses to the slight curve, a smile dancing over his lip.

"It's not a bump yet." He looks up at me, and I can't help but lift my hand into his tousled hair. "I won't let you down, Lily, I promise." His eyes drag up from my stomach.

I look away because I can't quite allow myself to believe him. We are quiet the rest of the way, and I leave him with his thoughts as we head inside. Jace offers me a coffee. He looks exhausted—his eyes dark and ringed. I ask for a tea and move to sit on the sofa, folding the blanket I left stranded and flipping it over the armrest as I tug my legs up, trying to keep warm. Jace lights the fire, and it creates a nice ambiance.

Once he makes the drinks, he comes over and sits next to me.

"How are you feeling?" I ask.

"Groggy, hungover." His cheeks flame, and he looks out of the window. "I don't usually hit the bottle so hard." His brows bunch together, a small sign of self-criticism.

"I know." I guess I don't, not really, just what I have seen, but he doesn't strike me as the binge-drinking type.

"I used to drink a fair bit, hit the bars—" he offers up hesitantly as his eyes latch to mine, watching for a reaction.

"Pick up women—" I slip in. I knew when we met that he was a serial player. His eyes held that mischievous light, and the way he carried himself was too cocksure. Not so much anymore.

"I had nothing much to live for and no one to disappoint. You can't disappoint yourself if you don't care." He swallows, and he looks at me. I offer him a sad little smile. I really had no idea this vulnerable man was hidden beneath all that arrogance.

"Not even Viktor or Marie; your business?" I sip my tea and wait for his reply. Jace takes his time answering. I imagine that laying out all his regrets is a bit like pressing salt into an open wound.

"They were keeping me afloat," he replies gruffly. It's obvious he's not okay with this line of conversation, but for me, he is putting himself through the discomfort.

"I see." There are far more demons in his closet than I ever allowed myself to believe.

"And now I'm scared that if I lose you, I'll become the person I was the other night." I shake my head. He isn't Neve.

"Jace, you won't," I tell him confidently. I may not know his back-story or who he was before me, but I know who he is when we are together. I owe him a big apology for being so quick to believe Neve's cruel words, even when I knew I couldn't trust her.

"How do you know?" He angles his head. His hand slips over my thigh, and he squeezes the slight muscle.

"Because you have a child to think of. That's what should be important to you now." My eyes hold his, and I try to convey what we need from him without actually speaking. I need to know that even if things between us don't work out, he is going to be the best dad he can be to our child. His head drops, and his lips get lost in the grip of his teeth, as big shoulders lift and drop with a deep sigh.

"But I don't have you," I feel a sliver of guilt at being so hard on him—all I see now is a lost boy, not a big, commanding man. I see a boy lost in a sea of hurt and more abandonment. I try to alleviate that worry for him.

"I never said no to us, but I can't just jump back into a relationship with you." His heavy head lifts, and I see that he is trying not to let his emotions take over his fragile composure. I finish my drink and stand.

"What are you doing?" He stands too, looking grief stricken. His eyes drop to my stomach, and his big palm rubs around his neck, a clear indication he is anxious and agitated.

"Going home. I need a shower and some time to think," I tell him softly.

"Lily, please." He takes my wrist, and his eyes slam shut. His fist is shaking, and it kills me to see him so torn up and vulnerable.

"If you're feeling up to it, we can grab breakfast tomorrow?" I suggest, hating how forlorn he looks. His eyes prise open, and I can see it is taking every smear of self-control to let me go. I put him at ease by saying, "I can't trust myself around you. I need to know we are doing the right thing for all of us." My hand instinctively goes to my stomach. I want the best for my baby, and I need to know he does too, and not just because it means he gets me back. Plus, I've been in this situation before, and it's bringing memories to the surface.

"Breakfast." He nods. "I can pick you up at nine-thirty?" he compromises, slowly letting my wrist go. He looks battered and tired.

"Only if you're feeling well. If not, we can grab lunch or dinner, either or?"

"All." He laughs faintly, and I share a smile with him.

"Don't force yourself. We need you better," I tell him, giving him a hard stare and reminding him of how difficult he was after my attack.

"I will be. I won't let you down," he states passionately on a low breath. I nod and step away.

"See you tomorrow." I give him an awkward smile. It's almost like we don't know each other anymore.

"Call me if you need anything," he blurts as I push through the heavy door. I look at him over my shoulder, finding him with his legs firmly apart and a determined gleam in his eye.

There is the man I know.

———

Betrayal

I wake to a message from Jace telling me he will be at mine for nine-thirty. I've slept later than expected and wait for the nausea to rattle my body. As usual it stays back, allowing me to believe I may have finally beaten it, but then it hits me with a violence I can't control. I push free of the quilt and dash to the toilet as everything pours out of me until my eyes sting, and I'm dragging in air through my nose noisily. Resting back, I close my eyes and sigh.

"You're going to make me rake thin." I smirk tiredly, rubbing my tender tummy. I'm pushing to my feet to brush my teeth when my phone begins dancing across my bedside table. I pad to my tiny bedroom and find Jace's name flashing up at me. He is probably in a panic because I didn't respond; he'll be going out of his mind.

"Hi." I aim for bright and airy, but my throat is still tickling from the burn of acid. I clear it and inwardly sigh when I hear him let out a long breath. Tucking my phone between my ear and shoulder, I recline on the bed as the nausea hangs around in my stomach.

"Hey, everything okay?" He goes for casual and indifferent, but I know him well enough to know he is fighting against the thoughts racing around his tense mind.

"Yes, sorry, I didn't respond. Morning sickness." I make light of it by laughing. I'm so used to it being a part of my daily routine, I don't account for his trepidation over it.

"Oh, shit, do you need me? I didn't even think—" he trails off and mutters lightly under his breath.

"No, but thanks." I sit on the edge of my bed and try to just breathe in and out at a pace that focuses my mind on that and not the turmoil my gut is in. "It will pass," I tell him.

"Have you suffered much?" he hums. The rush of wind at his end muddies the line, but I still hear his soft words. It's such a doubled-edged sword of a question, but I know that he is referring to my pregnancy.

"I'm sick most mornings," I admit, my stomach loosening up when my sickness finally disperses and allowing me the luxury of walking through to the kitchen to put the kettle on. "I think a lot of my dizziness was because of this little . . . " My words drift off.

I don't want to complain, but I feel pretty lousy most mornings. The sickness and dizziness are a small price to pay to eventually feel the weight of our baby in my arms, see the colour of their eyes, and kiss their soft skin.

"Brute." His voice slides down the line in a husky murmur. My eyes close, and a sad smile rolls over my face.

I laugh lightly, a soft tickle down the phone.

"Yes." Just like him.

"I don't know anything about babies," he admits. His thick voice sounds tired, and I imagine he has been up most of the night with my admission playing on a loop in that tragically beautiful head of his.

"That makes two of us," I add. With Adam, I had started to prepare for a child, recalling earlier memories of my mother and reading a few baby blogs, books, and surfing the net for little snippets of information, but it had all been locked up away with the devastation of losing my first pregnancy. "But I know not what to do." I mean my father, and I hope he can hear that in my tone and relate with his own loss and the rollercoaster that is Neve—all things that have taught us not what to do. "I just know I love this child more than I love myself, and I will do everything to keep him or her safe and healthy," I say with quiet conviction.

"I know you will. You're such a strong woman, Lily. I know you're in pain, and yet you've always kept one foot forward." His thick swallow drowns out my hum. "Your love outweighs your worry. It's one thing I adore about you." His guttural confession makes my eyes sting.

I frown against the phone pressed to my ear as the kettle hits a climax and whistles like a banshee. I step away and bite my lip.

"I don't know." I shrug like he is here and can see me. "I kept running," I muse, trying to lighten the deep conversation.

"To protect yourself, which given the last few weeks, would prove you were right to do so," he mutters regretfully.

"Jace, I don't want to keep going over the past. It won't do us any good." The mere thought of talking about everything again sends me mentally running for the hills. It is a little bit too raw. I've not had the chance to even come to terms with everything on my own. But it's always been like this with this man. Every time I feel I need the luxury of space and time to process everything, he just saunters in, dishes it up on an oversized plate, and before I have even finished that, he is tearing me from my underwear and muddling my brain even more.

"I know, but I don't want you to think I'm just brushing it aside, taking the easy road. You deserve more than that." He angles his voice, so it's demanding but soft —urging me to see it's all for my benefit.

"You do too," I whisper, gripping the phone tightly. I'm trying to forgive him. I won't forget, not for a while, but I can try to forgive. Seeing the level of Neve's manipulation and hearing Jace's past has given me cause to lie awake most of the night. I still haven't managed to pull myself out of the whirling emotions that have clouded me for the past few weeks. All I know for certain is that the thought of losing him for good, the fear of him leaving this world and me behind, is foremost in my mind. "I think our pasts have both been a burden, and we need to let it go. We were happy at one point. I want to get back to some semblance of that," I say, hoping I'm as genuine as I sound.

"You do?" His deep voice rushes out in a hopeful breath. "Lily, I fucking miss you so much beautiful." My heart constricts.

"Can we take it slowly?" I clear my throat and pull the phone away when I hear him clear the emotion from his own throat. "Everything has changed so much. I just need to know I'm doing the right thing, and I think you need to do that too." I'm trying to be as diplomatic as possible—he is still recovering from a pretty traumatic ordeal, yet he seems more bothered about me. Plus, I don't want to send him in an emotional tailspin by saying something that will hurt him.

"I am doing the right thing," he says with utter conviction, "my mind won't change. I'm not going anywhere." I can picture his passionate face at the end of the phone.

I open my mouth to tell him I just need to keep things on a more platonic note when there is a knock on the door. I jump and stand, as if that will help me to see who it is through the wall.

"One minute. Someone is at the door," I say distractedly.

"It's me," he breathes roughly.

"What?" I blurt, moving to the door. I quickly glance out of the window to find his car parked haphazardly outside.

"Let me in." I cut the call and open the door to find

Jace freshly shaven. His face is looking brighter and healthier, and he is in a light knit jumper and jeans, a little smirk playing at his mouth. He lifts some flowers, and his eyes run all over me: my pyjama-clad body and fuzzy hair, as I've not even had the chance to grab a shower yet. He steps forward, and I step back.

"I'm not ready," I mutter, and his face breaks out into that trademark slow smile.

"I can see that." His eyes fall to my bare breasts under the small camisole top and drop further to my bare legs and light pink toes. I rub my eyes, trying to feel a bit more awake. I've still not even finished making myself a drink. "You look exhausted." Sympathy laces his husky voice. I duck my head when he moves completely into the room, and I close the door and watch him watching me. "Do you still feel sick?" His hand lifts, but he drops it before it finds my skin.

I shake my head and grab a thin and long cardigan hanging on the small hooks near my door. His eyes flash as I cover myself up.

"Why don't you grab a shower, and I'll make you a coffee?" He cups my upper arm, and I scrunch my nose up.

"No coffee." I make a face and find laughing eyes looking down at me.

"Okay, no coffee. What does my girl want?"

'My girl'. My heart aches and lurches. Ducking my head, I reel off what I want and head straight for the shower. By the time I'm out and pulling some clothes on, Jace is knocking on my bedroom door with my tea.

I feel awkward all of a sudden, and he furrows his brow and rubs at his neck.

"I'll wait for you to get ready." He nods back to the living room.

"No, it's fine." I give him the most genuine smile I can. I don't want him to feel uncomfortable around me, or me him. He drops down on the bed behind me and waits quietly while I do my makeup. I've hardly worn any this past month, so I don't go overboard, just enough to disguise the dark circles and to put some colour back in my cheeks.

"How's work been?" I ask him. Our eyes meet in the mirror, and I find syrupy orbs shining through the sheet of glass at me.

He shrugs.

"Okay, I guess. All okay with the gallery?" I offer a smile. I haven't been in much, and when I have been there, I have been lost in my own mind. Our conversation is so stilted and clumsy that I drop my gaze and try to think of something to say. It was never like this with us before. Maybe it's us trying to muddle our way through with the lack of physical contact. It's the one thing we always got right and possibly our biggest flaw because we couldn't keep our hands off each other. It was the driving force in our relationship.

It hits me like a lightning bolt then; we need to learn to love each other without the raging lust. I'm staring straight ahead, my face locked in thought, when Jace calls my name.

"Hey, where are you?" he says, pushing to sit closer to me. I blush and turn so we are facing one another.

"Why does this feel so awkward?" I huff, shooting him a regretful look.

"Because I'm not inside you," he drawls. His neck tilts back, and the thick column rolls as he swallows his own laughter down.

"I'm being serious," I moan, trying not to bend a little to his typical banter. He always knew when to be light-hearted or gravely serious, and both had me sighing internally and falling harder in love with him.

"So was I." His voice sounds deeper, and he keeps his face averted to save him the trouble of looking at me while not being able to react to his feelings. My cheeks heat more, and when he looks back, he catches the red flare with his thumb. "You still look so sad," he murmurs.

"Jace, don't. It's all just a lot to take in and re-learn," I mumble, standing up and moving away from him. "Let's grab breakfast," I say breezily. Maybe if we move out of the small confines of my apartment, the tension won't be so thick.

Chapter Twenty-Four

With my stomach being as fragile as it is, I stick to toast and fruit. Jace, on the other hand, ploughs through a full English breakfast, but I keep my thoughts to myself, happy to see him eat. He looks pretty worn out. Once I line my stomach, I find myself reaching over to pinch some bacon.

"Oh wow," I hum, chewing thoroughly.

"Do you want me to order you some? Are you feeling better?" He lifts my chin to check my face, and his touch tingles my skin.

"I feel loads better, but I'm okay. I find little and often helps," I tell him.

He is smiling sympathetically at me over the table and seems hesitant, but before I can ask him what's wrong, his hand delves into his hair, and I know he is deliberating saying something to me.

"Jace, just say it." I laugh, nibbling at the little amount of bacon left on his plate as he forks a mouthful in. His brow rises, and he looks surprised. "I know you want to say something," I tell him, picking up my water and taking a sip. When he swallows his food, he exhales softly.

"I don't want to upset you." He frowns, pushing food around his plate.

"Saying that makes me want to know more. I'm sure you won't upset me. You're annoying me by not saying it," I scoff light-heartedly, taking the remains of his bacon and biting into it.

"Okay, well, I wondered if, in your previous pregnancy, you suffered with morning sickness?" He clears his throat after voicing his concern awkwardly over the table to me.

The usual tinge of sadness that comes whenever I think or talk about that time is there. Still, I find myself smiling, enjoying being able to discuss the baby I never had without it circling back to Adam and my miscarriage.

"Yes," I reply quietly. "I was probably this far gone," I tell Jace. Something dark flashes in his eyes, but he takes my hand and urges me to talk to him. That one small gesture of silent comfort makes me feel brave enough to talk about it with him. "But I was just as sick. I had shut it all out of my mind, but now, things keep filtering back in, and I keep thinking, oh, I remember feeling like that or, my baby will be so many millimetres." I laugh lightly, and he shares a smile with me.

"I know you didn't find out what sex the baby was . . . before, I mean," – his hand squeezes mine – "do you want to this time?" I haven't thought about it. I've been too focused on keeping healthy and ensuring I go full term to even allow myself the luxury of that,

I shrug.

"Honestly, I haven't thought about it. I'm just so happy that I'm pregnant at all, but before, I had this gut-deep feeling I was having a girl—it was too early to find out, even after—" I trail off, frowning. I clear my throat and meet his gaze head on. "Do you want to know?" I ask him.

He scoots his chair closer and pulls my hand to his mouth.

"Lily, as long as I have you both, I'm happy. If we wait, I'm okay with that, and if you want to know, then I'd love to find out." I nod and slip my hand free. I don't want to break the moment, but my body is buzzing with addictive electricity. I can't think when he is this close, touching me, and looking at me like I'm the centre of his universe and then some. I know he is my world, but my life just exploded, and I'm still trying to work it all back in; find my own place again in this mess.

"I can't think." I rub the back of my neck and blow out a deep sigh, and when I lift my gaze, Jace is fighting a grin. "Don't look so smug," I drawl. He chuckles and leans back in his chair.

"It's just good to know I've not lost you; hurtling is my favourite thing." He leans forward and clasps his hands on the table, looking over me heavily.

"I thought I was your favourite thing," I respond lightly, "oh no wait, two a.m. is your favourite thing." I begin to laugh, enjoying being able to take a jibe at him. His lips quirk and pull into a bright smile.

"Anything to do with you is my favourite thing," he declares. His compulsion wins, and he leans over to tuck my hair behind my ear. I regard him from beneath my lashes, and when I look up fully, Jace is staring at me with such open appreciation that I blush. He smiles slowly.

"Hey, beautiful." He exhales deeply, and my lips twist in a soft smile.

Hey, to you, too.

His fingers twist and play with the ends of my wavy hair.

"I've missed this, us, you—" he tells me.

"I have too."

"Really?" His frown, although light, is still visible to me. He sounds so serious and unsure.

"Of course I have. None of this has been easy for me. I missed you the second I drove away. I'm glad we're talking," I confess shakily. "We need to, with this little one on the way." I pat my stomach, dropping to take in the small but evident bump now proudly protruding from my body.

Jace clears his throat.

"Yeah, of course," he says throatily. "We need to for the baby." He sits back, casting a perplexed look across the quiet café. My smile slips, and I stare off too, unsure what just happened.

We stumble through the rest of breakfast, hardly saying anything and leaving us both feeling more and more unnerved by the time we pay and leave. Jace, for the first time ever, seems to be completely lost in thought. I'm not sure what has changed all of a sudden, but he looks pretty sombre and far away.

"Thanks for breakfast." Rather than walk to Jace's car, I pass it and thread my fingers together because he seems distant. I lose my step when he isn't driving us forward.

"Where are you going?"

I throw a look over my shoulder and frown.

"I think I should go home." I tilt my head and try to keep my face neutral because I'm really starting to learn

Betrayal

what losing my step around this man feels like. It's worse than after the attack, when I was irritated at him and his distance. It seems we are taking one step forward and two backward. This breakup has brought some serious inner turmoil to the surface, so maybe that's why we're struggling so much?

"You're running," he states, face plummeting and a small tick appearing in his jaw.

"No, stalling," I stutter. It's the truth, it's not goodbye but more good day. "Just stalling," I mumble.

"Lily, you're a terrible liar." He sighs hotly.

Yes, I am, but he seems to be finding this so much easier than me.

"You only got out of the hospital yesterday, and I'm still full of all these feelings." I press my hands to my chest. "Two days ago, I was still so angry at you, confused and lost, and then you were rushed to hospital and everything else that came after that—things I believed, that turned out to not be your fault—" I huff on a tremble of my lip. "One minute we're laughing, and the next we can barely string a sentence together." I frown at the ground, shoving my hands into my coat pocket to hide the fact that I want to knot them together, a sure sign I'm feeling anxious.

"Hey, don't get worked up, come here. We can sit and talk in the car where it's warm." Jace crosses the little space between us in two big, determined strides. He pulls me to him, and I go as stiff as a board. "You have every right to be angry at me. Hell, I was livid when all the shit with Adam went down. I get it, and I'm sorry, but I stuck by you even though I wanted to just stay hidden and get my frustration out alone. I couldn't look at you without seeing you beat up and unconscious or myself beating the living shit out of that arsehole." He kisses my hair, a small gesture, but I melt into him. "I'm not saying do it my way, but ignoring it won't work. We have too much riding on this. I won't lose you. I want us to be a family."

I look up to find him holding my heavy gaze with his own softer one.

"Let me take you home. We can talk. Work some things out."

"I just need some ti—"

"I'm not giving it to you. Time doesn't make things go away or easier to deal with. It drags it out. I may not deserve much from you, but I'm taking it, anyway. Please, get in the car." Jace takes my hand and pulls me back toward his car.

I know he's right. I run at the first sign of trouble, the tiniest slip of open confrontation or having to deal head on with my emotions. I'm a coward. I chose the easy option and not always the best one.

"We know the worst there is to know, so it can only get better from here," he tells me, settling me in the passenger seat. "You can't run, Lily, not anymore." The door clunks shut, and I stare at his retreating form, giving myself a good talking to.

The apartment is warm and cosy by the time we return. We remove our coats, and I find my boot slippers and grab us both some water. I've had enough tea to fill me up all day.

Jace is reclined on my small sofa, legs wide apart, and feet firmly placed. His arm is hooked over the edge, and his face is lost in a sea of thought as he stares out of the window. I stand and watch him for a moment, wishing I could crawl inside his head and pick through everything he has stored in there. I don't know him well enough anymore. I'm not sure I ever did. I thought shutting the door on our past would be the way forward, but an hour in his company and Jace has managed to flip it all back on its arse and demand we discuss it. He's right, of course. My way of dealing with things is to not deal with them. Not him, though. He wants to drag me down a bumpy road and is willing to hold my hand on the way.

He turns then, sensing I'm watching him, and I jump into action and cross the room, placing our waters down.

"Thanks." He scratches at his jaw and waits for me to take a seat. I opt to sit at the far end and pull my legs up, twisting so I'm facing him head on. I let out a short but deep sigh.

"Okay," I start, and his mouth kicks up at my attempt at being authoritative. I ignore him, of course. "I know I have something special with you," I start on a light mumble.

"You do," he replies, reinforcing my statement. His own body angles towards me, and he takes my ankle, cupping the slight limb in his large grasp. "Lily, I may have kept things from you, but my feelings were and are real."

I nod, pulling my sleeves over my hands and shoving them between my thighs.

"I don't like that you lied to me, but I understand why you did. I run when things get too much for me; it's a coping mechanism and not a good one." I blush. I'm very aware of my own downfalls, even if I don't like to admit them at the time.

"We can work on that, in time. I don't expect you to trust me because I ask you to. I lied to you, and I hurt you, and I let Neve hurt you. I know what she can be like, so I know it wasn't easy for you," he admits, ambers pouring heartfelt sincerity at me.

"I know you didn't cheat because we weren't even together, but—"

"We had been intimate, so it was wrong of me. I never set out that night to sleep with her," his confession is delivered with a soft plea, spoken gently to keep me grounded and not let me feel overwhelmed with jealousy and anger—to keep me from running. His thumb rubs therapeutically along my soft skin. "I was so angry with myself." His jaw ticks, giving me a small show of that anger now. "We left the gallery, and I got drunk. I just wanted you to want me back. I didn't know what I needed to do to make you feel the same way about me. I'd never felt like this before, so I didn't know how to handle it — or you. I just knew that I had never wanted to keep someone as much as I did you."

"I did want you back. I do," I correct myself when his face falls a little. "I was still dealing with stuff after Adam, and it was just a lot. You can be pretty intense." I laugh humourlessly.

"With you," he declares, "only with you, Lily." We share a tender look.

"Plus, I know that I judged you the same way as I did my dad, but I shouldn't have. You're not the same person. I'm sorry." I bite my lip, feeling shitty once again for being so callous with him.

"It's okay. I'm glad we are finally getting down to the gritty stuff." He gives me a lopsided smile, and I want to crawl in his lap and let him hold me. Instead, I snort. I don't like gritty; it gives me hives. "It's good for us to get it all out in the open. We need to if we want to make things work for us and baby Bennett." His smile is self-indulgent, and he rests his head back but keeps his face on me.

"Baby Bennett, huh?"

"It's got a nice ring to it." He grins, his eyes twinkling.

"Yeah, I guess it does," I muse.

Jace's hand grips my ankle a little harder.

"Come here." His instruction is gentle, and I watch the way his eyes burn and smoulder. I shake my head, but he tugs me anyway. "I just want to hold you, Lils, break down this wall between us." As soon as my torso is close enough, he scoops me up, turning me around, and pulls me back to his chest, and drops his chin on my shoulder. "Hey, beautiful," he sighs.

"Hello, brute." He chuckles at that, and my smile is at total odds with my rushing heartbeat.

His voice is thick when he speaks.

"I'm sorry for everything. I'm sorry I haven't been here for you with the baby."

"You didn't know."

"Because I fucked up." He squeezes me lovingly.

"We both did," I mutter, picking at the cuff of his jumper.

"You remember how it felt when you first met me?" he rumbles. Jace shifts his face and tucks my hair away before resting it back on my shoulder.

"Yes." I remember the blistering intensity of our first night together too. My breathing changes, and when Jace drops his nose into my hair, I know he is there with me too.

"Remember that, Lily, when you're feeling vulnerable or unsure, hold on to that if you can't hold on to me. I know right down to my bleak, shitty soul that I'm the right man for you. I know without a shadow of a doubt, you're my woman. It won't change for me. I know you. I know I'm good for you, and that's why I challenge you. So when you're feeling backed against a wall or ready to hightail it out of here, just remember who will be there to hold your hand on the other side," he affirms roughly, his breath a hot promise along my cheek.

My lip wobbles.

"You're going to make me cry." I shift to ease the emotional discomfort hanging out in my gut.

"I know you think you've cut yourself off from your dad, but did he ever really try to connect with you again after your mum died?"

I shake my head. I'd screamed at my father and yelled that I had never wanted to see him again, and he'd happily obliged. Over the last two years, I've started to receive cards, but the damage has been done. And my stubbornness has got her heels well and truly stuck in the ground.

"Everyone you have loved has gone. I know what that feels like. The new ones you meet along the way, you keep at a distance because if they go, you think it won't hurt so badly, but nothing can hurt more than the loss you're already carrying." I nod again, my tears spilling over my cheeks. "You're a loss I refuse to have; not until I'm grey and old and miserable." He laughs, and I do too, quickly dashing my tears away.

"I know you because I know me, and that's why we connect because you're the other half of me that was walking around lost too." Jace squeezes me and kisses my hair. "I love you, Lily. I love you with everything I have."

My voice feels thick before I even speak.

"I know," I say, "I love you, too."

"Let's take this slowly. We already know what works for us. Let's tackle what doesn't before we move forward." I'm giving Mitch a run for his money because all I can offer is a nod.

"Now, let's talk about this little surprise," – his palm lays flat on my stomach – "have you thought about names you like?"

I settle back and tell him everything, from how I found out to how much I initially struggled to come to terms with it and why I wanted to disconnect myself from him before I told him. How I love Mila for a girl but couldn't think of a boy's name because I would get lost thinking about him and how Cass has been shoving names down my throat left, right, and centre.

"But none that you like?"

I shake my head.

"What about you?" I tilt my head to try and meet his eye, and he grins and frowns, thinking it over.

"I was thinking of some last night. I like Leo for a boy and Luca and Finn. Marnie for a girl, Bella too." He clears his throat. "I actually like Bryce," he tells me, and I scrunch my nose up in disagreement. "Mila is nice," he adds around a chuckle. The distinctive vibration of his phone in his pockets has me scooting forward. He pulls it out and shakes his head tiredly. "Viktor, he keeps checking up on me," he says softly.

"He cares for you a lot,"

"I need to tell him the truth." His cheeks heat. I know he will go full bat and not hide anything, even if it means putting his own head on the chopping board to the man he respects the most.

"He loves you, Jace. I think it will mean a lot that you open up to him." I want to tell him he doesn't need to confide everything to him, but I know Jace has been carrying this around too long.

"Yeah, I know. I'm going to take this," Jace shifts me

forward, allowing him the room to get up. He doesn't go far, just to the armchair where he fields a few questions and arranges to meet with him later. I get up as he hesitantly says, "There are a few things I think I need to tell you—"

I'm privy to the one-sided conversation, and when Jace says, "Yeah, yeah. I'm okay. Things are going well," I figure he has told them we are back on talking terms. I give him some privacy and slip off to my bedroom. I'd planned a day of cleaning, so I begin to potter, folding laundry and placing it away, all the while aware of the deep rumble of his voice. It soothes me from the other side of my apartment. After a few more minutes, it goes quiet, and I hear as he heads to my bedroom. He's hooked his fingers on to the doorframe and is watching me when I finally look up.

"I've got some things to take care of . . . before I see Viktor." He frowns, his gaze dipping to the floor. It's a Sunday; surely he can't mean work. My questioning look encourages the truth from him. "Carl needs to go over some things from the lawyer. Neve is kicking up a stink," he admits.

"Oh." I frown. How she has the audacity, I do not know. It makes me angry, but I hold it in.

"Do you need me to do anything? Give a statement about that night, or—" I shake my head, shocked she is still being difficult.

"I'm trying to keep things civilised. I massively underestimated her, and although I hold most of the cards, I don't want her doing something stupid." He clears his throat. I appreciate his honesty, but it bothers me that she is still affecting him.

"You don't mean . . . like hurt herself?" I whisper. He shrugs.

"I'll speak to you tonight?" I nod, and he hesitates before he drops a quick peck on my cheek. He grins, and with a wink, he is gone. I'm grinning at the empty corridor before I close myself in my apartment, feeling a bit lighter than I have done these past few weeks.

Lighter about us, but concerned about Neve's never-ending tactics.

Chapter Twenty-Five

Cass is rifling through my wardrobe as I finish applying the last of my makeup.

"I know I left it here," she mutters, yanking and stuffing items in and out. "It's the black, shimmery one, looks like oil?"

"No, I haven't seen it. Are you sure you didn't misplace it when you moved in with Sean?" Her arse is sticking out of my wardrobe, her head a concoction of clothing.

"No," she huffs amid the piles and piles of dresses.

"Well, I haven't seen it," I tell her.

"Yes!" she squeals and drags something out, holding it high. "Knew it!" I scrunch my face. I can't ever remember seeing it in there. "You need to sort this shit out. It's a jumble sale in there," she huffs and puffs, not bothering to pick up the clothes she has dumped on the floor. I eye the clothes, then her, and she grumbles before grabbing them all and shoving it all back in.

"And yet you still found that." I clip my earrings in and stand, slipping my feet into my ankle boots.

"How are you feeling?" She drops down onto my bed, the dress bunched up in her lap.

"Nervous still," I admit, "is that silly?" I look over my face, briefly checking my makeup.

She shakes her head in the mirror.

"I was like that with Sean, but you said the last few dates have been great, and he always ties you in knots. You two have this mad chemistry," she comments openly.

"Yeah, he does. That's why I wanted to take it slowly and not complicate it so much." I spritz myself and grab my jacket.

"If you don't feel ready now, you never will." Cass gives me a reproachful look, and I don't blame her. I have kept Jace at arm's length, not just because of what happened, but I needed to work on me and my trust issues, issues that sparked when my dad just upped and left at such a painful time in my life. Jace doesn't deserve the hurt my father caused. I want to give him the best version of me. Not a cracked one.

I reapply my lipstick and look back over my shoulder as I say, "I know. I miss him, and The Hub. I want us to be a family. I miss being around him. I want to go back to what we had before everything went south."

"Are you going to ask to move back in?" Her eyes go wide with excitement.

"Yes." I grin, I had wanted Jace to be the one to raise the question, but it will mean more to him if I ask. God, I really do miss him. This past month has been long, slow, and difficult, but so worth it. I've learned so much about him, and with every date, we are slowly getting back to being us.

She pleasantly shocks me by saying, "I'm really

proud of you, Lily. You've had a shit year, but you're a different person now." She squeezes my hand.

"Thanks for always being there for me. I know I haven't been the easiest." I blush.

"I'm sure Jace will disagree." She cackles, moving away when I swat her for her underhand comment, cheeky bugger!

"Oh, ha, ha." I'm stifling a deep grin. "Can you lock up? I don't want to be late?" I lean to scoop up my bag and give her a quick kiss on the cheek.

Jace is parked out front, and his eyes widen when he sees me in wet-look jeans and a floaty top. I've paired it with leopard print boots and my leather jacket.

"I'm running out of clothes that fit." I laugh.

He exits the car and beats me to the passenger side.

"You look stunning," he compliments, pecking my cheek. I slip in a breathless thanks and check my reflection while he rounds the bonnet and gets back in. "We can go clothes shopping tomorrow. I'm free all day," he says roughly. His eyes flick up to me, and I smile.

"Sure, all my clothes are fitted, and this little bump is determined to be noticed." I rub the small swell and smile inwardly. I can't believe I'm finally going to be a mum.

Jace pulls back in surprise.

"Really, where on earth could they have got that characteristic from?" His brow is furrowed, and he is fighting a smile.

Shrugging, I pick at nothing on my trousers, a thoughtful smile playing around my mouth.

"His brute of a father?" Jace's eyes are twinkling like mad, and his chest rises on a deep contented sigh.

"That's right, baby. This little brute," – his hand splays over my small bump – "and I are going to drive you crazy. Lots of sleepless nights and late mornings." He grins.

"Got to let me move back in for that," I quip, fluffing my hair and feigning indifference. If Jace could read my body, he would see my heart clapping like a thousand hooves and my lungs expanding too fast. I'm a little breathless, so I clear my throat quietly to dislodge the ache there. When he doesn't say anything, I bring my head around to see he's smiling like an idiot.

"What?" I chuckle nervously.

"Lils, I've wanted to hear you say that for so long. I'd have moved you back in a month ago." He isn't belted up like me, so when he moves to cover the distance, I stay still. His big hand comes up, cups my face and neck, and his smiling face lowers on mine. I blink happily at him as soft lips glide over my parted mouth. "You've made my night. You know that, Miss Spencer?"

"I do," I whisper.

"Ah, two more words I want to hear very soon." I go still with shock. Is he?

He presses a deep kiss on me. Soft but firm lips attack my senses, falter my mind, and the rush of passion is so strong, I lose my train of thought. I kiss him heatedly as flashes of wedding dresses and wedding bells filter through my mind. Jace pulls back enough to allow himself to speak, and when he does, his voice is low and husky.

"I want you home. I'm missing out on all of this. I miss you," he says quickly.

"We have the scan on Monday," I remind him. I haven't kept him completely in the dark. I update him regularly, but I know he wants things to go back to how they were. I do too.

"I'll pick you up, ten-forty?" he questions, even

though I know he has memorised any information I have given him.

"Yes, ten-forty."

He nods and flicks the volume setting up a notch on the steering wheel. I don't feel like I have thoroughly appeased him, and I know why. He has been busting his balls for me since we first met, and I have always maintained a level of control and kept myself at a distance by not vocalising how I feel, certainly not like he does. I know he enjoys that aspect as much as I do. Caring for me is second nature to him, a devoted chore that he perfects with every ounce of his being, but I need to reciprocate. This man deserves more than just me. He is entitled to the world, and I'm only giving him a small portion in return.

We travel for another twenty minutes before Jace pulls into a string-lit car park. The tyres crunch over the gravel until he comes to a stop between two four-by-fours.

"It looks very romantic." I smile.

"Yes, well, I'm trying to impress this stunning woman I'm crazy about."

"Oh, I think she will approve," I say, mildly disguising my grin, "possibly even earn you brownie points."

"I'll bank those and collect at a later date," he tells me on a wink and pushes free.

I'm already pushing the door open and have my feet out, but he rounds the car and meets me at the door, anyway. We're coddled between two vehicles. Jace keeps his face bent down so we're eye-to-eye.

"Thank you for bringing me here." That earns a soft smile.

I reach for his cheek, and his eyes fall on me. I smile,

lifting to my toes and pressing a gentle kiss to his mouth. His eyes are brighter than a thousand fireflies.

"I've missed you, pretty lady," he says against my lips, his hands now resting on my hips.

I stutter out a deep breath.

"I need you to know I appreciate everything you have done for me—do for me," I add with conviction. "The way you love me never gets old. In fact, it makes me a bit selfish." I blush, but he grins and pecks my lips quickly, allowing me to carry on. "I want everything with you, a family, The Hub. I miss you more than you know. I want to ring you and tell you things all the time," I say breathlessly.

"Then why don't you?" He takes my face and keeps our eyes locked.

"Things have changed so much. It's not just about us anymore, and I needed to know us was just as important as having this baby."

"Jesus, Lily, without you or us, there wouldn't be a baby, and I can't wait to share it all with you. I need you back. I miss you." He searches my gaze before he dips and kisses me. "I want us to be a family. I'm ready when you are. I can't wait for you to come home."

I nod.

"I'm ready. I want to come home. Kiss me again," I whisper on a soft laugh when he smiles boyishly at me.

We have crossed a non-physical threshold. Jace is being more tactile, and neither of us seem as tense. I think we both were unsure when to make the next move, and more importantly, who would do it. But now that we have, I feel ecstatic. We are heading out of the city when he turns.

"I need to show you something," he says breathlessly,

his mouth pulling into a smile, "it's a surprise, but I know you will love it."

"Are we going to yours?" I ask, looking for any familiar landmarks.

"Ours." He throws me a wink. "It's ours, Lily."

"Sorry, it's just, does this feel weird to you?" I laugh nervously. "Like the first time we met?"

"Good weird though." He grins. "There has been this gaping hole between us. I'm so glad we've begun to close that gap. I don't want to wave you goodbye, Lily. I want to wake up with you." He looks my way quickly before resuming watching the road. I lean over and rub his knee.

"I want that too, Jace." His smile is wide but hesitant. "Maybe I can stay the night, then move my things back over the next few weeks?" I croak quietly. He nods but keeps his lips closed as we turn off the main road and along the single track to his. As soon as the trees open up, I gasp. The whole house looks new. It's two stories high and boasting a slanted roof and balcony. It looks more incredible than I imagined. "Oh, wow. Jace, this is amazing!" He stops, and I'm out of the car. The site is lit up, but no workmen are around.

"I asked that they keep the lights on. I wanted to show you." He takes my hand. "Come inside. It's better than I pictured it," he says, drawing me towards the house. The ground floor is covered in dust sheets. "Where have you been sleeping?" I whisper, seeing a framed photo of us placed on the book hive. Jace drops his chin to my shoulder. "Hotels or the office."

"Oh," I murmur, my gaze fixed on the wide, happy smiles in the picture. The river cruise. We move along the hive, and another picture greets me, the cruise again.

I'm laughing, and he is kissing me wildly. My cheeks are flushed, but our eyes are dazzling.

"I love that picture, Lily." Firm hands envelop my waist.

"Me too." That is the 'us' we both want back.

———

He shows me around the house. I recognise the layout from the extensive drawings I'd seen. All the wall foundations are in place with new bathroom suites, and furnishings are waiting to go in. Upstairs is still incomplete, but equipped with three spare bedrooms and a family bathroom. Jace explains that the electrics and plumbing need to be fitted. I stop at one door and find the word 'Pea' written on a sticky note and placed centrally.

"Pea?" I query, pushing in without an answer. I gawp when I find a kitted out nursery with stunning baby furnishings. The cot looks ornate, and there is a matching dresser and changing unit. Everything is covered in dust sheets, not that it's necessary as the room is spotless.

"I could hardly write 'Podge', now could I?" His chuckle falters when he sees my teary eyes.

"If you don't like anything, we can change it," he assures me, coming up behind me.

"No," I blubber, wiping my eyes, "I love it, Jace." I walk in, running my hand over the cot. It's already made up, and a blanket is hanging over one side, protected by clear packaging.

Thick arms wrap around my waist.

"The utility is just being fitted. I changed my mind about the units," he tells me, but I shake my head. I know I will love that too. He has really good taste.

"Just one thing was missing," he says regretfully, "you. I'm so glad you want to come home, Lily."

Twisting, I wrap my arms around his neck and press a quick kiss on him. My eyes pull back to the pretty room.

"I am too, but it looks like we won't be home for a little while." I laugh. Why didn't he say he was sleeping elsewhere? I feel terrible and say as much.

He shrugs.

"Does it matter? I'm not going to be anymore." He tugs me to him. "You're lucky you broached moving back because I was about ready to tan your arse." He laughs, nudging his groin into mine.

I give him a sassy smile.

"If I'd known that, I'd have kept my mouth shut." I move out of his grasp when he laughs throatily.

On a shaky sigh, Jace says, "Lily, there's something I need to ask you." His sombre tone makes me slow my movements. He sounds worryingly serious.

"What's that?" I twist to find him on one knee. I gape and slap my mouth shut. My heart is slamming away crazily but joyfully in my chest. A single, delicate, and petite ring is nestled snugly in a velvet box, with an ornate and vintage diamond glinting up at me.

"Be my wife, Lily Spencer? Be my family? Say yes so we can have everything that was taken away from us. Marry me, Lily." I'm so shocked, and he looks a little stunned too before he rushes on. I reason that he probably didn't plan on asking me tonight, and maybe his emotions got the better of him. "Fuck, this isn't how I planned it, but you want to come home, and now you're here, and I feel so fucking alive again, beautiful."

His gaze is glittering, excitement and fear swirling in

those amber orbs, as he runs an agitated hand through his hair.

"It may seem too soon, but after living a solitary life, it always feels I was cheated out of meeting you. I waited too long for you. I want to marry the woman I love and bring lots of little Bennetts into the world." He stands and takes my face—my shock, stretching into a wide smile. "Dammit, Lily, I want to see that smile every morning, and I want all of your laughter. I want to see your achievements and share mine with you. I want all my memories to be of you. Us!" He motions to my swollen stomach. "Marry me, Lily Spencer?"

I sob out a yes, and wrap my arms around his neck as he kisses me swiftly, deeply, and passionately. I hold on to him with everything I have, and he sighs out a shuddery breath.

"I wondered what it would feel like with your stomach pressed up against me," he murmurs. "I love that our little baby is cocooned inside you. I honestly never thought I'd ever have anything like this. Thank you, beautiful."

He cups my jaw and kisses me before lifting my hand and sliding the ring onto my finger.

"I planned to wait until we were settled, but I can't wait anymore, Lily. We're missing out on too much. I want to hurtle with you. I want to feel breathless and free." He sighs, kissing me deeply: slow and delicious. Jace cups the back of my head and holds me to him as he devours me at a leisurely pace. He pecks my lips slowly, pulling away before he pulls on my lower lip. "I can never thank you enough for giving me another chance. I don't deserve you."

"Jace, you deserve more than you know. I love you. Thank you for taking a chance on me and showing me what love is." I find his empathetic, loving eyes on mine. "It's more than I ever expected. It's something I never thought I could have either, and I wouldn't change our story for anything. I love you. Kiss me."

He holds me for a while, standing in the nursery before murmuring about showing me around the rest of the house. With it primarily being open plan, it doesn't take us long to move around the spacious and contemporary structure. After twenty minutes, Jace is pulling me eagerly to a door back up on the upper level. I give him a quizzical frown.

"What's in there?"

"It's yours. Have a look." I eye him, seeing his anxious smile and excited eyes. I shrug and walk past him, curious to see what is behind the heavy door. My hand is on the handle, the grip reminding me of the token of fierce love now wrapped around my finger. My gaze drops to the ring, and I smile before I glance back at him. He is grinning like a child, and shaking my head, I push in and stop short of the threshold.

I'm speechless, utterly moved by this man's continuous desire to please me on all levels.

"Jace, I . . . "

"Do you like it?" Thick hands span my waist, cupping my swollen belly, as his chin finds a home on my shoulder. He sighs when I sag back into him.

"I love it," I whisper, and my eyes take in the unfinished darkroom. I'd mentioned once how I was forever hidden in one of these at university. It's perfect. "Thank you," I whisper.

"You're welcome, baby. It won't be much longer now, another few months, and it should be completed."

"That soon?" It still looks in disarray. Jace steers me out of my mini haven, and we descend the stairs.

"Hopefully, unless we have any sudden complications, but most of the foundations were in place. I made sure to include those on my first build. We're lucky to have had a fairly dry winter. The tree coverage also helps." He's in business mode, and I laugh inwardly.

"When did this all begin?" I ask as we head back to the car.

"The day I was discharged from hospital. I knew that I had to build this for you. I wanted to win you back," he hums.

"By building me a house?" I smirk when Jace pulls me to a stop and cups my arse.

"No, beautiful, I wanted to build you a home." Leaving me no time to respond, he pecks my nose, then dips lower for my lips. "I've been pushing it forward. The contractors have been here most weekends and evenings too. That's how it's happened so fast." Weeks, that's how long it's taken. The outer shell is already showing the promise of our future.

"It's amazing. I can't believe the transformation, just from adding another floor."

"Because I pre-empted wanting to extend in the future, I have saved myself and the builders a lot of time," he comments.

"I can't wait to see it finished," I tell him, getting into the car. We drive back, chatting animatedly about plans for the garden. Jace is against a pond now we're expecting. I love all the water, and I say as much, and we argue lightly about the pros and cons with a little one in the house.

It's not long before we are pulling up outside my flat. He meets me out the front and holds my hand up to the main door. He begins to smile, and I clock it, grinning too. He looks mischievous.

Betrayal

"What?" I ask, nudging his hip with my own.

"Remember when I dropped you here that night and followed you to the door?"

"Oh, the gentleman act?" I scoff playfully.

"If you recall, I was!" I'm back in the dark doorway and pushed into the corner, barricaded by this big man and his knowing smile.

"Not for long." I laugh.

His eyes drop to my lips being chewed.

"I wanted to kiss you badly, then," he husks.

"Why didn't you?" I never understood why he pulled away.

"I felt electric. I wanted to keep that feeling, and I thought you wouldn't do the shoot," he admits ruefully.

"I wouldn't have done it," I tell him honestly, sharing in his glittering happiness. My reaction scared me too much. If he'd have kissed me, I'd have cut the contract.

"This should have been our first kiss," he murmurs, his face holding that same quizzical desire from that first night. For a moment, I'm thrown back to a time when I didn't know this man, to a time when *we* weren't written, to *that* moment. His lips are a crushed bruise on mine, and I reciprocate with intent, humming my happiness.

"Are you not going to invite me up for coffee?" He wiggles his brows, making me snort, and patting my arse cheeks, he follows me up. When we get in, Cass has cleaned the place up. I make a mental note to get some flowers to thank her. I take my jacket off, and Jace takes it from me, hanging his and mine up. He then offers to make me a drink.

"Oh, a tea please, decaf," I say as I find something uninteresting on the TV, and he joins me with two steaming cups. We sit down and chat for hours. There isn't a worry between us. Everything is out in the open, and we have only the future to look forward to. Jace lifts my hand and inspects my ring before he threads his own hand with mine. The ring is as delicate as it feels alien on my finger, a foreign weight I haven't yet become accustomed to but love already.

"Here's to hurtling," he whispers in my ear. I turn and cup his face with my free hand to cement his toast with a kiss.

I would hurtle to the end of the earth and back again with this whiskey-eyed man.

Hurtle to my forever after.

The End.

Epilogue

They say the way to a man's heart is through his belly. They must not have accounted for me in that saying; the way to mine is through my soul. The way to mine is with Lily Spencer.

I've had the honour of having her in my life for the past three years, her big grey eyes and teasing smile, framed by long thick hair—hair thick enough to wind around my wrist. My nostrils flare when I think of how damn lucky I am to have a woman like her by my side, she's a witch, all fluttering eyelashes, and passion personified, and she simply floors me.

Everything has changed for us—for the better. My life is a dream. I have my stunning wife and gorgeous little boy. I gaze at his chubby cheeks and open mouth as he snoozes in the car, and my hands tighten on the wheel, knowing he will be out for a while, and I will have my wife all to myself for a few rare quiet minutes.

Hell, if someone had told me a few years ago, I was going to be a smitten, loved-up family man, I'd have laughed in their face and possibly fucked their wife for good measure.

I can't shake the guilt of the frivolous past I have lived, but I know for a fact it's what makes me love my girl so hard.

She's that little bit of heaven I never knew existed.

A bit of heaven I'm damn addicted to.

We've fought our battles, and although we lost each other along the way, we're stronger than ever, fiercer. I'm a better version of me than I ever knew possible. I have the world at my feet and the absolute love of my life holding my hand.

Everything I hadn't even known I was working towards is within these twenty-four acres. Safe and hidden away in our little Hub. I crunch down the driveway and smirk. Not so little.

Luca murmurs in his sleep.

"We're home, little man. Where's your Mumma bear?" I muse quietly, looking up at the display of windows, trying to find my anchor. One perk of this design is I can see everything the minute I turn the bend and hit the open driveway. The house is a wide glass display of luxurious homeliness. Lily really has got good taste. I mean, she picked me, so anything after that is a given. My eyes flick to the mirror where honey-thick irises look back at me. My eyes are her undoing, and I thank whatever higher power gave them to me before I exit the car and unclip Luca from his seat. He is out for the count, looking as angelic as possible, and a movement in the house pulls my head that way, to her. She is moving quickly through the top landing with a frown that has me kicking the door shut—that and the fact she hasn't noticed me.

Something is up.

Betrayal

I'm frowning deeply as I head to the door and use my shoulder to pivot my way in. Luca sniffles and presses his face into my chest, murmuring in his sleep. I can't hold back my smile because even when he is asleep, he seeks me out. He's a daddy's boy, that's for sure.

I take the stairs two at a time, my lean legs eating up the space, and I'm quickly pushing my way into Luca's room. I grab the remote on the small shelf and press the blinds into place before I secure him in his toddler bed and slowly peel his tiny shoes off. His breath huffs out, followed by a small snore, and grinning, I drop and press a kiss to his feather-soft skin.

"Love you, brute," I whisper and walk backward, watching to make sure he stays asleep. I'm pressing his stair gate into place when I hear the toilet flush in our en-suite.

I find Lily pacing as her grey eyes stare at something in her hands.

"Hey, what's up?" I ask softly. She jumps, and her wide eyes flash to mine as her cheeks pinch red. My eyes drop to the thing in her hand, and she holds it up guiltily.

"I'm late," she says and walks straight to me, biting her lip in a giddy smile when my mouth pulls into a shit-eating grin.

"Too fucking right," I huff. We've been trying for months. Her hands are shaking, so I scoop her up, my heart swelling with satisfaction when her soft laugh floats through the room.

"Where's Luca?" she murmurs.

"Fast asleep. You should have waited for me." I pout and peck her mouth to stop her gnawing furiously on her lush lips.

"Sorry." She blinks uncertainly up at me. "I've felt

nervous all day. I really want this one to be positive," she tells me.

I take us to our enormous bed and sit with her in my lap, the pregnancy test clasped tightly in her small hand.

"Let me have it," I demand gently. As soon as I relieve her of the test, her hands knot, and I smile sympathetically at her. "Lily, we already have perfect—anything more will be a bonus," I say gently. "A perfect bonus," I tell her, and she drives her hands into my hair to save her from twisting them together. She kneels up and presses her mouth to mine.

"I know, I know," she whispers, her forehead touching mine. Her endless cloud-grey eyes shut, and I know she is trying to prepare herself for the same disappointment we've shared with each test, all the while keeping beautifully positive. Lily's constant light shines through at me always—she's the bravest person I know. "I just want to give you lots of little Bennetts," she hums, trying to keep her emotions in check. "It will be ready," she says in a rush of air. We both drop our gazes, foreheads still in contact. I twist the test over, and a sob leaves her mouth.

Happiness flourishes through me like an uncontrollable tidal wave, crashing through my heart and making it burst with pride and joy.

"Another bear cub!" I grin, seeing her eyes shine with tears. She sniffs back another sob, and I slant my mouth over hers, my own eyes stinging with unshed tears.

Delicate fingers cup my bristly face. Her vulnerability is her biggest strength, and she feels everything just as deeply as I do. Only once I won her back did I truly begin to learn who this woman was, learn who I was. We're a force. A dream. We have the kind of love that captures the attention of others—this undeniable bond that even now baffles and awes me.

I'm her safest place, and in return, she has given me the kind of life I spent my years feeling I wasn't worthy of. I'm indestructible with her at my side. I laugh into her mouth as she pushes at my suit jacket.

"Kiss me," she demands, as teeth rip at my lip and she forces me back, her tongue delving in to attack my own. I roll her and push her hands high and hold her still.

"Lily," I say on a rough husk, "beautiful. I don't want to do anything to jeopardise this. Let's get in with the specialist first." I search her eyes, and she shutters her pain. After Luca, we lost a baby, and it has been a challenge to conceive since then. Luca is a miracle.

Adam caused some damage, and birthing Luca took its toll on my girl. Until now, we have been met with repetitive disappointment.

"Me either," she breathes, her chest rising harshly below her shirt. "Just hold me." Her eyes flicker between each of mine. "I just want to feel you." Her low whisper sends a thump of love to roll through my chest, and nodding, I swaddle her face with my big hands and lower my mouth to kiss my wife in the way she deserves.

I strip us both down to our underwear and pull her to me so we are skin to skin, lips touching, her inky, damp lashes bringing a self-indulgent smile to my face.

"Don't be scared," I tell her. Lily's gaze drops away, but she brings it back, showing me how resilient she is.

"I don't want to be—" Her sigh is resigned, but her beautiful eyes shine with childish hope. "I am scared," she confesses shakily.

I dip and press my forehead to hers, breathing deeply. My life centres around this woman, and it kills me to know she is feeling such a mix of potent feelings. "I know. Let me go and give the hospital a call, then we can have a lazy afternoon. I'll make a carpet picnic, and we can slob with our little man."

Sighing, she smiles at me, and I wink and peck her mouth.

"I'm crazy about you."

"You're just crazy," she mutters and twists on a roll when I pinch her toned arse. Her yelp has me laughing.

"Damn witch,"

"Brute!" she calls when I saunter off. I lift my finger, telling her to be quiet when a little cough sounds from Luca's room. She is slipping from the big bed and walking towards me with the confidence of a woman who knows she has her man by the balls. My eyes roam freely over her body, and when she reaches my side, she looks up at me, mouthing, 'Crazy for you,' as she slips past and pushes her way into Luca's room—his baby voice calling for her.

I wake slowly. My eyes remain closed, but I can hear the soft huff of Lily beside me. It's the first night in months that she has slept solidly. Prying my lids open, I lie still and take her in. She's so fucking beautiful. Her skin has got a healthy glow to it from our recent holiday, and she looks the most relaxed she has in months. I'm ready to book another just so I can whisk my family away and have them all to myself again. I need to clear it with the specialist, but we should definitely celebrate.

Another baby. Viktor and Marie are going to be thrilled.

We're booked to go to the clinic in two days, and that

has allowed us both to relax a little. I can't bear to watch her smile through another heartbreak. I want to give this woman the moon and the stars, but the universe keeps intervening, and I feel like it's my karma for how selfish I was just a few short years ago.

I stare at her with the world on my shoulders, silently pleading to an unknown force to give my girl everything she wishes for. I reach to touch her, but stop. She needs to sleep. She's putting too much pressure on herself to give me what she deems the perfect family. I'd love more children, of course I would, but I am also ecstatic with the family I have now. I slide out of the bed and sit on the end, yawning.

"Daddy!" Luca calls. I lift my head to see his cheeky little face grinning at me from the gated doorway down the hall. I push up and walk quickly to him, kissing his head as I lift him over the gate.

"How's my favourite little man?" I ask, running my hand through his curly mop.

"Sam! Sam!" he chants.

"It's like that, is it? I only love you endlessly and give you the world, but you want Fireman Sam." I lift my brow, and his legs kick excitedly. "You got a kiss for me?" I grin at his sleepy face, as his lips pucker, and I smack a kiss on him. "Shall we make Mummy some pancakes?" I ask.

"Pa-cakes!" he squeals, gritting his teeth and shaking with excitement.

"You're crazy," I say and take us both downstairs, dragging a throw off the sofa and shaking it out on the floor. I place Luca down, who begins pulling cushions down so he can lie on them. I need to get him a bean-bag, I think, watching him struggle to gain his balance on the uneven surface.

"Sam, Daddy!"

Lily comes down half an hour later. She scoops Luca up and covers him with kisses.

"Why didn't you wake me?" She carries him over to me and drops him on the countertop, leaning into him and blowing raspberries on his rounded belly. A gurgled squeal erupts from his little mouth, and we both flinch at the sound.

"You needed it." I nip her shoulder and kiss her mouth when she turns into me.

"Luca, kiss!" His small lips pucker, and his cheeks blow out like a puffer fish, and chuckling, I give my little brute what he wants.

"Resting for two now," – I wink – "maybe we will have a little Mila after all." I sigh hopefully. Luca wriggles to get free as his favourite theme tune comes on. Lily lowers him, and I pull her to me, happy to have her to myself for a second.

"There's only one thing that makes me hornier than you do." I kiss along her jaw.

"Oh, really, should I be worried?" She laughs, her brow slanting up high. I drag my teeth along her chin and move to grab her breast through the thin material of her top.

"Pregnant you, makes me crazy horny," I admit. "It will all be fine," I add, when I see a look of trepidation pass through her clear gaze. Despite our struggles, we try to keep grounded and not let the grief swallow us up. It's out of our control, but how we act and treat each other, regardless of those trials, is what keeps us striving.

Her smile is small.

"Well, I'm not spending a lifetime pregnant so you can walk around with a stiffy," Lily blurts on a soft laugh.

"Stiffy!" Luca sings.

I snap my eyes to Lily, who looks appalled. I double over in a belly laugh.

"Oh my god, no that's not funny," she whines.

"Stiffy!" Luca giggles, seeing how the mere word has brought tears of laughter to my eyes. Luca sings the words over and over in a toddler-fuelled mumble, and I shake and roll my hips to the words, grabbing Lily and thrusting my hips into her bottom.

"Don't encourage him," she chastises, trying to pull away from the hot press of my cock burning into her arse.

"Who Luca or my very hard co-"

"No!" She laughs, slapping her hand over my mouth and stopping me from uttering that word. I nibble her ear, then sigh and drop my chin to her shoulder, and my chest expands on a deep contented sigh. "Could life get more perfect? Look at him," I muse as we watch Luca, who has his little chubby knees bent whilst he bops to his favourite program. He thrusts his little hand in the air. "Stiffy!" he chants.

Lily's head drops back on my shoulder in a groan that quickly turns into a happy laugh, and she shakes her head in agreement—it doesn't get more perfect than this.

"Hurtling with you both has been the most fun I've ever had," I tell her, turning her so I can look at my beautiful girl. I smooth her hair back and observe my wife's gorgeous face with slow appreciation. "I love you like crazy, Lily Bennett," I declare on a rush, and I do wholeheartedly and with every fibre of my being. She is exquisite. Perfection, and somehow, she is mine.

"Back at you, my brute," she murmurs, dropping forward to seal it with a kiss.

Acknowledgments

Firstly I wish to thank my friends who pushed me to chase my dream,
My book buddies who read Whiskey promises when it was a pitiful draft and told me to write more. My son, who forever tells me to never give up, you, my poodle, are an angel.
When I first started writing this series, I didn't think I'd ever finish. I also wrote it as one book, Portrayal, one humongous book, which I had to then split in two, and that's how Betrayal came about. It's an extension of my love for Jace and Lily. The story I thought would never end. I'm still gutted I had to write those two words: The End. However, I had other characters wanting my attention, and so I gave it to them.
Thank you so much for reading!

About the Author

A. R. Thomas is an indie author from England. She lives with her son, and when she's not screaming from the sidelines at his latest sporting event, she is usually lost to the thought of a book. She manages to make the most innocent of things sound dirty; it's both a gift and a curse, but thankfully her friends encourage her.

If you would like to connect with A. R Thomas she would be thrilled to hear from you.

facebook.com/ar.thomas.357
instagram.com/arthomasauthor

Printed in Great Britain
by Amazon